ORIGIN

J.T. BRANNAN

headline

First published in Great Britain in 2012 by
HEADLINE PUBLISHING GROUP

2

Cataloguing in Publication Data is available from the British Library

ISBN 978 0 7553 9684 9

Typeset in by Granjon by Palimpsest Book Production Limited,
Falkirk, Stirlingshire

Printed and bound in Great Britain by Clays Ltd, St Ives plc

HEADLINE PUBLISHING GROUP
An Hachette UK Company
338 Euston Road
London NW1 3BH

www.headline.co.uk
www.hachette.co.uk

For Jakub and Mia

Acknowledgements

I WOULD LIKE to thank the following people for their help on the road to publication: my parents, for their long-standing belief in me; my fantastic agent Luigi Bonomi, as well as Thomas Stofer and the rest of the team at LBA; my superb editor Alexander Hope and everyone at Headline Publishing; Dr Jeffrey D. Means at the University of Wyoming; Matthew B. Barr and the staff at the Institute for American Indian Studies; my friend Tom Chantler for his valuable assistance and scientific advice; and my wife Justyna, without whose constant support, drive and creative input this book would never have been written.

'Three may keep a secret, if two of them are dead.'
Benjamin Franklin
Poor Richard's Almanack

PART ONE

PART ONE

1

Lynn Edwards opened the base-camp door and stepped straight into a frozen hell.

'Where did you last see him?' she shrieked over the howling wind, panic in the eyes of the man before her.

'The ridge!' Stephen Laverty screamed back, pointing into the vast, ice-covered wilderness behind him.

Lynn looked over Laverty's shoulder. The ridge was over four hundred metres away – not far in the real world, but out here on the Antarctic Pine Island Glacier, it might as well have been four thousand. *What had he been doing there?*

As if reading her mind, Laverty shouted to her, 'He just went out to find a better site for his readings. But the ridge slipped, and he went down.'

It wasn't time for recriminations, but the missing man should have known better. Lynn was the lead investigator for the NASA team that was investigating the rapidly melting glacier, and Tommy Devane was responsible for the hot water drilling that was a major part of that mission. The sites had already been painstakingly selected, but Devane had obviously wanted to explore further. In the Antarctic, Lynn knew such foolhardiness could prove fatal.

She sensed movement behind her, and turned to see four

other members of her team join them. She nodded, and gestured at the ferocious landscape beyond Laverty. 'Over there,' she told them. 'Past the ridge.'

'What the hell was he doing over there?' Sally Johnson wanted to know, to murmurs of general agreement.

'We can argue about that later,' Lynn yelled. 'Right now, we've got to get him back.' She turned to face the brutal Antarctic wind. 'Now let's go!'

Pine Island Glacier, otherwise known as the PIG, is one of the two largest glaciers that drain the West Antarctic ice sheet into the Amundsen Sea, a large ice stream that flows down the side of the Hudson mountains into Pine Island Bay. Satellite imagery has shown that it has undergone a noticeable acceleration in recent years, making it disperse more ice into the sea than any other drainage basin on the planet.

The team led by Lynn Edwards was tasked with gaining an understanding of the interaction of the ocean and the ice by taking complex sets of measurements and then modelling the results to give an overall 'virtual' image of the action of the entire glacier.

The PIG itself was in one of the most remote areas of the vast ice-bound continent, eight hundred miles from the nearest permanently manned research station. Lynn and her team had arrived just a week ago from the large US research base known as McMurdo Station, some thousand miles south. They had flown in a small Twin Otter aircraft and landed at the old Matrix base camp, which they had reopened.

The week had gone well, and Lynn had established the

base camp quickly and efficiently with the help of her team of eight hand-picked scientists.

They had discovered the ridge on the second day. Just four hundred metres from base camp, the ridge rose over one hundred metres from the surface of the glacier in a long, pristine line across the frozen horizon. The drop-off at the other side – which Devane had apparently fallen down – was nearly three times that distance, a slightly angled cliff left by the action of the ice calving away.

The basic sameness of the bleak white scenery made navigation and assessment of distance an almost impossible task, and Lynn could only pray that Stephen Laverty would be able to lead them back to the place where he last saw Devane.

If he couldn't, Tommy would be dead within the hour.

Tommy Devane adjusted his body, testing each limb in turn, then his neck. *Nothing broken.*

He sighed in relief, looking back up to the top of the 'ridge', which appeared to be more of a mountain when seen from this angle. He counted his blessings – his thermo-electric suit had cushioned the fall to a large extent – and then cursed himself aloud for being so stupid. He was a professional! What had he been doing?

He cleared his mind. Feeling sorry for himself wouldn't help in any way, he knew that for certain. He also knew that, even though base camp was a mere four hundred metres away, if he couldn't get back over the ridge, he would soon be dead. He looked up at the towering mountain above him, its sheer sides mocking his hopes. *Fat chance.* He wasn't getting back up there without a lot of help.

J.T. BRANNAN

He knew Laverty had gone to get help, but he also knew that there was always the haunting possibility that he would never be found.

Unwilling to give in to panic, he pulled himself to his feet and started to examine the ridge. The slope was almost sheer, with nothing but ice to hold on to. Instinct told him to continue along the ridge, try and find some way of climbing it, but his head told him to stay where he was. If Laverty led the team back to the point where he had fallen and he was no longer there, he would be in a world of trouble.

And so he would wait. He would wait, and—

What on earth?

Devane's eyes went wide as he saw the ghostly image, just a little further along the base of the ridge.

Could it be?

He shook his head, his eyes transfixed. It was a body, seemingly buried in the ice.

Wise move or not, he knew he would have to go and investigate.

2

Lynn and her team had finally arrived at the ridge. They skirted the edge, careful to avoid any calving ice, not wishing to go the same way as Devane.

'Is this where you last saw him?' Lynn asked Laverty, the lowered wind allowing them the luxury of communication without having to scream at one another.

Laverty nodded his head. 'Yeah, I'm sure.' He pointed to the readout on his weather-proofed GPS. 'As sure as I can be, anyway.'

Lynn nodded her head in return. 'OK.' She turned to the rest of the group. 'Otis?'

A small, wiry man came forward. Otis Burns was the principal oceanographer on the team, and also the most accomplished climber. At a trim one hundred and forty pounds, he knew he was the obvious choice to go over the edge. He grinned at Lynn. 'Rope me up, baby,' he said with a wink.

'Steady!' Lynn called to the three team members who were belaying the rope over the edge of the ridge. 'Slowly does it!' She peered over as far as she could. 'You see anything yet?' she called to Burns, who was now at least a hundred feet down over the other side.

'Nothing!' came the voice from the frozen depths beyond.
'I can't see anything down there!'

'OK, we'll keep going,' Lynn replied. 'Keep—'

'Wait!' The cry was heard by the whole team, the tone
unmistakable. Burns had found something. 'I think I see
something over to the west! I . . . Yeah, someone moving,
right down below at the bottom!'

There was a pause, and the woman and two men holding
the rope felt it move slightly, and knew Burns must be
adjusting himself, swinging to face the person he had found.
'Hey!' they heard Burns shout. 'Over here!'

Lynn waited for news, anxious. The next words from
Burns surprised her more than she expected. 'It's him! He's
all right!' There was a pause. 'But he wants us to come
down there after him!'

Lynn frowned. *What the hell?*

Two hours later, half the team was down with Tommy
Devane, who had been secured in a new thermal suit and
been given emergency rations, although he had almost
refused them in his excitement. And when Lynn saw what
he had discovered at the bottom of the ridge, she was not
surprised in the least.

The body was only partly covered by ice, the glacial melt
having exposed one half, perfectly mummified by the frozen
conditions. It was the body of a man, modern in appearance.
He was blond, short-haired and clean-shaven. He could
almost have been one of them. Who was he? What had he
been doing there? How had he died? How long ago? The
questions tumbled through Lynn's mind in quick succession.

She knew the body could be very old indeed – in 1991,

a frozen mummified man had been discovered in the Italian Alps, and carbon dating had shown him to be well over five thousand years old. But this body was different. For a start, it was clothed in a material of a sort she had never seen before.

'What's he wearing?' she asked Devane, who had spent his time examining the body while waiting for the team to arrive.

'I'm not sure. Some sort of armoured textile, but I've never seen anything like it. It seems incredibly complex.'

'Some sort of military special ops?' Lynn asked Jeff Horssen, a data analyst who used to work for the US National Security Agency, a hotbed for secret military technology that the average citizen never saw.

Horssen examined the material, exceptionally well preserved by the ice. 'Could be. They're working on some really advanced cold-weather gear, I know that much. But this isn't like anything I've seen.'

Lynn looked back to Devane; his expression said that there was more to come. 'So what else?' she asked him.

'I don't know about *advanced*,' he said with a curious mix of surprise and delight, 'but how about *ancient*?'

The bewildered looks on the faces of his teammates delighted him even more. As the hot driller, Devane was used to taking ice core samples – thirty-centimetre wide sections of ice drilled down and recovered from up to a kilometre deep, showing ageing layers like the rings of a tree. Air pockets, perfectly preserved in the ice, could give climate information on the region stretching back tens, even hundreds of thousands of years. An expert on the subject, he merely pointed at the steep iced walls of the ridge.

Lynn followed his finger, and looked at the wall for several moments before realization dawned. 'Oh my—'

'Yes,' Devane confirmed. The ice that had sloughed off from the main glacier body had left striations on the cliff face that were akin to an open ice core sample, the lines able to be read for miles across. 'From my estimate of these readings, that man we've just found was buried here under the ice no later than forty thousand years ago.'

3

'WE'VE FOUND SOMETHING down here,' Lynn announced over the UHF radio to the teammates back at the Matrix base.

'What?' came the static-laden reply.

'It's a frozen body. Mummified. Potentially very ancient. And with some anomalous artefacts.'

'Huh?' Lynn could hear the confusion. 'Like what?'

'Things better not to discuss on an open line,' Lynn decided. 'We're coming back to base.'

The UHF transmission was picked up by the National Security Agency's Keyhole satellite, and transmitted directly to the supercomputers at the agency's headquarters at Fort Meade, fifteen miles south-west of Baltimore. Within fifteen minutes, it had passed through various levels of analysis; but on the orders of one man the message went no further, and was 'lost' for ever.

Stephen Jacobs clenched his fists in anger. They were so near completion! *So near!* He couldn't let anything stand in the way of the organization's dream. A mummified body buried in the Antarctic ice with 'anomalous artefacts'? It could, of course, be nothing. But Jacobs also knew what else it might be, and such a discovery would cause too many questions to be asked, at just the wrong time.

He sighed. He would have to speak to his superiors. He could let nothing jeopardize the dream.

'So just what the hell is it?' asked Sam Maunders, a seismologist, when all team members were reunited back at the Matrix base – home, such as it was.

'As far as we can tell,' Lynn began as Devane started distributing cans of beer from the fridge, 'it's the body of a man – apparently the same as a modern human – which seems to have been buried in the ice approximately forty thousand years ago.' She looked up as Devane slid a beer across the dining table to her, smiled in thanks and popped the lid. *What the hell*, she thought as she took a long pull from the can. *You don't make a discovery like this every day*.

'We found the body with what appears to be modern clothing,' Lynn continued.

'Like what? What do you mean?' Maunders asked, fascinated. This was much more exciting than shifts in the ice, that was for sure.

'Advanced arctic clothing, some sort of light yet highly insulating material.'

'But what does it *mean*?' asked Joy Glass, the lead computer analyst.

Lynn just shook her head. 'At this stage, we don't know.'

There followed wild speculation over what they had found, and the atmosphere was jubilant, excited, and just plain crazy. Despite their mission, a forty thousand year old mummy was simply far more exciting than gathering seismic data and carrying out oceanic modelling. It was potentially earth-shattering in its significance.

If it was true, Lynn reminded herself as a scientist. They would need a lot more examination time, and a lot more resources to get to the bottom of the matter. She was all too aware of the damage done to 'Ötzi the Ice Man', the mummy found in the Alps, when it had first been discovered. The authorities had assumed that the body, discovered by a couple hiking in the mountains, had died in a climbing accident. They therefore weren't trying to preserve and protect the body, they were simply trying to free it from the ice. As a result, they shredded his clothing, used his bow as a tool to prise him out, and even jack-hammered a hole through his hip.

Such mistakes were not going to be made with their own find; Lynn was determined to follow strict scientific procedure in the extraction and examination of the body. This attention to detail – even when the excitement of discovery threatened to overwhelm her – was what had put her at the top of her field.

Evelyn Edwards – known as Lynn to her friends – was exceptionally gifted, having graduated top of her class at Harvard and then clawing her way to the top of a still very much male-dominated field.

Her looks – although envied by many – had not made her academic life any easier. She had been a plain girl in her youth, and she sometimes wondered whether this was why she had followed such an academic path in the first place, but she had eventually blossomed into a beautiful young woman. She had smooth, olive skin that suggested something exotic in her ancestry, and thick dark hair that framed her bright, unusually green eyes. Her body was lithe and athletic, honed as the years progressed by regular early morning runs, gym work and kickboxing. But in the world of science, such looks often made people take her less than seriously; it seemed that people thought that women who looked like her couldn't possibly be *intelligent* as well. She struggled against the odds, her natural talents overcoming the bigotry and highly opinionated views of her contemporaries, until she was one of the top research scientists at NASA.

But the qualities that made her excel in her profession made her a failure in her private life. Her marriage had lasted less than two years, and she knew that she had to shoulder much of the blame for that. It wasn't Matt's fault, not really. They had been deeply in love, and had been engaged and married within a very short period of time. Too short, as it turned out. Matt Adams was an American Indian tracker, a robust man who liked to live as one with nature, in tune with the 'great spirit'. Lynn had been immediately attracted to his wild, carefree behaviour, had been enticed by his barely contained enthusiasm for anything and everything. He had truly known how to embrace life. And he had loved her with all his heart.

Lynn felt bad now when she thought of him, as she often did at the Pine Island Glacier, the name so close to his home reservation of Pine Ridge in South Dakota. She wondered if he was still there now, and what he would make of the recent discovery. No doubt he would be delighted – he had often told her about how American Indian myths suggested that the United States had been populated tens of thousands of years ago by a very advanced people.

She smiled as she thought of him, but soon cut the thoughts off and returned to the business at hand – a quality that was both a blessing and a curse.

She picked up the secure radiophone and put through the

call to NASA headquarters. A message like this could only go right to the top.

The operator came on the line, and Lynn wasted no time. 'Get me the Administrator.'

Samuel Bartholomew Atkinson was the Administrator of NASA, the 'high chief of space' as he was lovingly referred to by his staff.

His love of the cosmos stretched back to when he was just three years old, so his mother told him, and he had pursued a career in the stars with a passion that bordered on the ferocious. He was now in his dream job, and loved every minute of it. Sure, there were challenges, but what satisfaction was there in life without challenges? His position gave him a level of knowledge about the cosmos that would have scared his three-year-old self, but he valued that knowledge now above all else.

The message that had just come in from Evelyn Edwards was disturbing in the extreme, and he was going to have to play it up the line. He told Lynn that he would be back in touch within the hour.

His fingers dialled the number quickly on the secure phone on his desk, and Stephen Jacobs answered on the first ring.

Atkinson filled him in as fast as he could, but Jacobs stopped him halfway. 'I know, Samuel. And I've already spoken to our friends.'

Atkinson seemed surprised. But then again, Jacobs was a man who was full of surprises. 'And what did they say?'

Jacobs cleared his throat. 'They say that it is definitely something to be worried about. There could be a connection, although there's no real way of knowing before examination. But it is cause for concern. We need to contain the situation.'

'Yes, sir. Our next course of action?'

'OK,' Jacobs declared, 'listen carefully. This is what I want you to do.'

The radio phone rang in the metal confines of the small base's communications room. Lynn picked it up immediately.

'Hey, Lynn,' Atkinson said in his good-natured, friendly tone. 'How you doing?'

'Excited,' Lynn confirmed. 'Excited but ready to do this thing the right way. What do you recommend?'

'You're to remain on the base for the time being,' Atkinson said. 'We don't want to compromise the site. We've got a specialist team already en route to your location. You are to liaise with that team, and offer them all the assistance you can. Is that clear?'

'Yes, sir,' Lynn confirmed. 'ETA?'

'Estimated time of arrival is 0700 tomorrow morning. Connecting to McMurdo, then on to you. Be sure to give them a warm welcome.'

'We will, sir.'

'And Lynn?'

'Yes, sir?'

'This has been classified Ultra. Nobody else knows about this, and we want to keep it that way. Unless it's through me, you are to cease communication with the outside world as of right now.'

Ten thousand miles away, in his private office in Washington DC, Atkinson replaced the receiver and rubbed his eyes. It was going to be a long night.

4

THE TEAM ARRIVED as promised exactly at seven the next morning, landing in two identical Chinook AH-46 twin-rotored helicopters just fifty metres from the base, snow and ice spinning high up into the air from the powerful downdraught.

Six men from each helicopter quickly deplaned, heads down as they ran underneath the slowing rotors. Lynn had the door open for them, counting them in one by one. The pilots would come later, after securing the aircraft.

Nothing was said until the whole crew was assembled in the dining room, the largest of the rooms in the small Matrix base camp.

One of the men – Lynn noticed that they were *all* men – stepped forward. 'Dr Edwards?' he said, extending a large hand. 'Major Marcus Daley, US Army Corps of Engineers.'

Lynn took the hand, shaking it firmly. 'Army?' she asked, surprised. She took a quick look at the others, spread out behind Daley in a fan formation. Definitely military. The air about them was unmistakable.

'Hey, who else is gonna deal with an emergency operation thousands of miles from civilization? It's us or you wait another two weeks for a civilian team. If the body's uncovered already, you don't want it decomposing.'

Lynn nodded her head, understanding. 'Yes, of course. I'm sorry, I didn't mean to seem rude, I just wasn't expecting a military team. You've extracted bodies from the ice before?'

Daley nodded solemnly. 'Soldiers die in frozen parts of the world all the time. And we never leave a man behind.' He gazed into Lynn's eyes. 'Now take us to the body.'

Lynn had to admit that there was something to be said for military efficiency. By lunchtime, the army engineers had been shown the site, done a full reconnaissance of the area, and drawn up a detailed plan of action, which Lynn had quickly approved. It seemed they had indeed done this before.

Back at base, Major Daley sat with Lynn and Devane in the dining room, cups of strong hot coffee on the aluminium table between them. The two NASA scientists were taking Daley through the events of the initial discovery, and the major was asking questions and taking notes.

'So since talking to Atkinson last night, you didn't go back out to the body until this morning?'

Lynn exchanged looks with Devane, then shook her head. 'No. Samuel ordered us to return here and stay until you guys arrived.'

Daley nodded. 'Good.'

'Why?' Lynn asked, all too aware that her answer hadn't been entirely truthful. After their meeting and discussion with the team the night before, she and Devane had descended the ridge again, documenting the find with high-definition cameras and taking detailed notes. Using their own specialized tools, they had even managed to shave some skin cells from the frozen body and cut some of the hair for later DNA analysis, as well as taking a small strip of clothing for radiocarbon testing. The unpredictable weather on this freakish continent could mean that the entire site could have been covered under several feet of snow by the time a specialist team turned up. The body could well have been lost for another forty thousand years, and Lynn was damned if she was going to let that happen. She felt uncomfortable admitting this to Daley however, and so the evidence they had gathered now rested in her personal backpack, stowed in her private cabin.

'OK,' Daley announced. 'We'll go ahead with phase one of the plan at fifteen hundred – extraction of the body. We'll get it into one of the pressurized refrigeration units on board the first Chinook and then we'll all extract by twenty-two hundred tonight.'

'What?' asked Lynn, shocked. 'We're *all* extracting? What about our mission?'

Daley disregarded her concerns completely. 'You're now part of a major scientific find, Dr Edwards,' he said charmingly. 'Your mission has changed.'

True to his word, Daley ensured his team had the body out and loaded by that evening.

His men were so efficient, Lynn couldn't help but be impressed. They extracted the body with an almost loving care. Lynn and Devane watched fascinated as more and more of the ancient corpse was revealed. The strange clothing continued downwards, ending in some sort of cold-weather boots. And then there was something else, something *metal* buried next to the body.

Lynn moved forward to have a closer look but was gestured back. 'I'm sorry, Dr Edwards,' Daley said with gruff impatience. 'These extraction tools we're using are dangerous. Please remain in the safety zone.'

Disappointed but not surprised, Lynn moved back. Daley hadn't wanted her there at all but she had argued her case thoughtfully. The army guys, no matter how experienced they claimed to be at such work, were unfamiliar with the unique conditions on the Pine Island Glacier, and Lynn told him clearly that they would need expert advice if they wanted to ensure no harm was done. Seismic anomalies, sudden moves in the ice, changes in air current – any could precipitate dangerous ice falls, or worse.

Daley had capitulated but only wanted a maximum of two people to help. Lynn was happy she would be able to observe the extraction but regretted that the majority of her team would be unable to share in the excitement.

It was clear that there was no excitement of discovery for Major Daley and his team. They approached the job professionally, no more and no less. And by ten o'clock that night, the body was on board the first helicopter as promised, the army engineers along with it; whilst on the second aircraft, Lynn sat with her NASA team, watching the small Matrix base as it disappeared into the swirling mist beneath them.

5

LYNN LOOKED OUT of the window, down at the dark, near freezing waters of the Drake Passage, the small area of ocean between the Southern and Atlantic Oceans that separated Antarctica from South America.

They seemed to be flying very low, and she found herself wondering where they would be landing for refuelling. The Chinook's range couldn't be much more than a thousand miles, which would put them over Chile or Argentina. Were there any US military airfields in either of those two countries? Or perhaps, given the sensitive nature of their cargo, they were going to refuel in mid-air, negating the need to land anywhere before re-entering the United States.

Her reverie was interrupted by Harry 'Truman' Travers, the lead seismographer for the now-abandoned mission. 'At least we'll get to see our families sooner than we thought,' he said with feigned enthusiasm.

The rest of the team murmured agreement, including Lynn, although she was acutely aware that she had no real family to return to. She was an only child, her parents having died in a car crash not long after she was born. She had been raised by her grandmother but this wonderful woman had also been taken tragically, just two years ago from cancer. Without a husband or children of her own, there was no one.

She was glad when Sally Johnson changed the subject. 'So what do you think will happen to us?'

Horssen grunted, his intelligence background giving him an insight into such situations. 'Simple really,' he said. 'They're either going to put us on parade, wheel us out in front of the world media and put the spotlight on us in a big way.' He paused.

'Or?' Devane finally asked for all of them.

'Or we'll be quarantined, kept out of sight. Depends on how sensitive the government decide the finding of the body is. Because this is *exactly* the sort of thing the government would cover up.'

The man who had been posing as Major Marcus Daley looked across the dark sky at the tail lights of the second helicopter, flying low across the waves.

There were some aspects of his job he liked, and others he didn't. As it happened, this was one he liked. Many men would have baulked at what he was about to do, but he never considered any other option. It was cold-blooded, of course, but he simply didn't care. His actions would benefit and protect the organization. And the dream.

He pulled the small metal box out of his cargo pocket, checking the flashing light.

He looked once more across the ocean to the second Chinook, his finger on the button, waiting for the right time.

'It'd be nice to know where we were going at least,' Devane announced, stretching his body out in the small, cramped seat.

He had read Lynn's mind, as she stared again out to sea, wondering exactly the same thing. *Screw it.* 'I'll go and ask the pilot,' she announced, unbuckling her belt and rising from her own cramped seat. It was *something* to do on the long flight, at least.

Grabbing her backpack, she moved down the small aisle, bumping knees with her teammates. 'You can leave that here, you know,' Otis Burns joked. 'We're not going to steal it.'

Lynn blushed, knowing Burns was right. And yet she felt strangely protective of the backpack's contents, especially now that all the other evidence was with the US Army.

'What can I say?' she joked back. 'I've got trust issues.'

She turned back down the aisle and was at the cockpit door in just two more steps. She knocked once, then again. There was no answer.

'Hello?' she said, knocking louder. She shouted and knocked again, louder and louder. Still no reply.

She felt for the handle, turned it. The door opened slowly, and Lynn stepped forward into the cabin.

Her eyes went wide, and the breath caught in her throat at the sight that greeted her.

Commander Flynn Eldridge – who had given the false name of Daley to the scientists – adjusted his position, straining to see the second helicopter just five hundred metres off the starboard side, its lights tiny specks in the distance.

He checked the time on his watch, then double-checked the navigation coordinates.

He looked to the aircraft's navigator. 'Here?' he asked for confirmation.

The navigator nodded. 'Here.'

Eldridge nodded back, and pressed the button.

'There's nobody flying the helicopter!' Lynn yelled in terror.

Upon entering the cabin, Lynn had been greeted not by the sight of pilot and navigator as expected but by a completely empty space, except for a single, flashing green light on the control board.

'We're being flown by remote!'

The whole team was instantly in uproar, tearing up out of their seats, heading for the cockpit to look for themselves.

And then Lynn saw the flashing green light increase in speed, until it stopped.

And turned to red.

Five hundred metres away across the Drake Passage, Commander Flynn Eldridge and his team watched with detached professional interest as the black night sky lit up next to them in an immense fireball.

They saw the circular, expanding ball of fire hang in the air for seconds, struggling to stay up, before it plummeted down towards the icy sea below.

Eldridge nodded in satisfaction.

Job done.

PART TWO

1

MATT ADAMS POURED the tepid tap water over his cold breakfast cereal, eyes bleary. Milk was expensive, and in his current state, he could barely tell the difference between milk and water anyway.

Adams had not had a good night's sleep in more than a week. Sometimes the nightmares were like that – they would come in cycles, often two or three a night, and then there would be nothing for months.

For the past week he had managed the odd hour here and there when his body literally collapsed, but then the dreams would come, and he would be wide awake again, unwilling to close his eyes, no matter how tired he was.

He knew what caused it – there was no way in hell he would ever forget *that* – but the fact remained that he was a shadow of his former self, a washed-up wreck of a man. The news he'd received that morning wasn't doing anything to raise his spirits either.

Evelyn Edwards – previously Evelyn *Adams*, back when they had been married – was dead. Killed in some sort of helicopter crash flying back from a NASA mission to the Antarctic.

The wreck had been strewn across the Drake Passage, and it was unlikely that any bodies were ever going to be recovered. Instead of a funeral, a state memorial service for Lynn and her team was going to be held in Washington DC in just two weeks.

It was NASA that had called to tell him the tragic news, and invite him to the memorial service. There weren't many other people outside of her professional circle to invite. With no family to speak of, most of the people she knew were from within NASA.

Adams had told the lady on the other end of the phone that he would be attending. As he ate his cereal, his mind kept spinning back towards Lynn.

The thing was, he still loved her. A tear rolled down his cheek, and then he looked at the cereal bowl on the table in front of him, no longer even able to tell what it was.

An hour later, he was still there.

Pine Ridge Indian Reservation is located in the south-west corner of South Dakota on the border with Nebraska. Administered by the Oglala Sioux Tribe, it covers almost three and a half thousand square miles, and incorporates three of the poorest counties in the United States.

Marginalized at the best of times, the American Indian population of the United States has faced major problems with poverty, education, health and welfare, and this condition is nowhere so obvious as at Pine Ridge.

As Adams rode his bicycle unsteadily to work, he considered himself lucky to have a job at all. It wasn't a good job – and certainly not in the same league as his previous employment, which had come to such a tragic end – but it was a job nevertheless. The wage was low but at least he didn't have to worry about his rent.

With less than four per cent of the reservation's land suitable for farming, and very much ignored by the federal government, the result was that poverty was endemic and conditions were ripe for alcoholism, crime, and other associated problems. And so as Adams arrived at the small tourist hut at the edge of the Badlands National Park, he considered himself one of the lucky ones.

The Oglala Sioux Tribe is a proud one, part of the seven tribes that had once made up the Great Sioux Nation.

Matt 'Free Bear' Adams belonged to the tribe, which was known by its members more properly as the Oglala Lakota Oyate. Its fabled ancestors had fought the US military in Red Cloud's War and the Great Sioux War, and had been amongst those massacred at Wounded Knee.

Adams' own ancestry was less clear, however. Found outside the tribal police headquarters in Pine Ridge at an estimated age of two days old, his parentage had never been determined. He was taken under the wing of the local police chief, brought in to live with the man's own family. This had only lasted the first few years of Adams' life, however. When the kindly old man was gunned down in the city one cold November night, Adams had soon found himself being passed from pillar to post. An orphanage here, a foster home there, he had lived in more than two dozen places before he entered his teens.

But the young Adams was resilient, the spirit inculcated in him by the police chief in those early years never far from the surface. He never let the situation get him down, never gave in, and always kept fighting.

It was Adams' fighting spirit that finally brought him to

the attention of Jim 'Big Bear' Maddison, the leader of the Strong Heart Akicita warrior society and a distant relative of the great Chief Crazy Horse, best known for leading a war party against US government forces at the Battles of the Rosebud and the Little Bighorn.

Like the police chief before him, Maddison brought Adams under his wing. When he was introduced to the tribal elders, they recognized not only his fighting spirit, but also his deeper, spiritual nature, and so took their own interest in him.

The tribe's traditional war, hunting and tracking skills were treated as something of an anachronism by most Lakota, no longer considered relevant for contemporary needs. Such skills had not been passed down from generation to generation since the 1800s, and yet some of the Lakota holy men still retained knowledge of the old ways.

These men observed nature and formed a relationship with all aspects of the world – animals, plants, and the land itself. And so when it came to seemingly physical processes such as tracking, they would not rely on visible sign alone, but also listened to what the world was telling them about itself.

Not many people were capable of this connection to the earth, or attaining such spiritual alignment, but the young Adams had shown an incredible aptitude for the teaching of the Lakota elders. This had led in turn to trouble with other members of the tribe, who argued vocally that a child with no tribal lineage or ancestry should never be allowed to receive such instruction.

And so despite Big Bear's protection, Adams' life was not an easy one, never able to avoid the stigma of his orphaned status, and constantly having to fight to get what was given free to most. But his spirit shone through, until he became the most highly regarded tracker on the reservation, and had the name 'Free Bear' gifted to him by Maddison and the Lakota holy men, to illustrate how he had freed himself from the trappings of ancestry and made a name for himself through sheer ability and force of will.

What Maddison and the tribal elders would think of him now – ready to take out a group of tourists on the Badlands Native American Experience – was anyone's guess. But as he led the party of twelve tourists on horseback into the wonders of the Badlands, he wasn't thinking about disappointing Maddison.

Instead, all he could think about was Lynn.

The tour was four days long, and the group camped out overnight, gathering around the campfire to discuss the day's experiences and listen to Adams tell tales about the land's mythology.

Despite the low night-time temperatures, Adams spent his nights out beneath the stars. There were millions of them, brilliantly bright in the absence of manmade lighting, and as Adams sipped a cup of nettle tea, he felt his mind – his *spirit* – start to roam the cosmos.

But then thoughts intruded, bringing his astral journey back down to earth with a jolt. *Lynn*. They had been in love, married, then divorced – and now he would never see her again until he, too, ascended into the spirit world.

It was in the Badlands National Park where they had first met, and Adams took another swig from the cup and smiled as he remembered.

He was just twenty at the time, nearly two decades before, and had been hunting a male pronghorn across the grassy plain, a lone animal that must have become separated from its herd. He didn't intend to kill it; his aim was to get as close as he could to it without it realizing. He wanted to be able to be so close that he could touch it. *That* was skill.

And so he had lain in wait for hours, tracked the beast for miles, and stealthily moved closer, ever closer. He had been within just ten feet of the magnificent animal when he had sensed them.

Two people. Travelling on foot. Just over one mile away, to the north-east.

He listened harder, ear close to the ground, senses acutely tuned. He prayed the big pronghorn wouldn't sense them too.

He edged closer – eight feet, six feet, four, two. The sounds of the unknown pair were louder now, but Adams was sure he could reach out and touch the animal before it heard them.

'Look at that!' he heard a young female voice cry out.

'Get your camera!' he heard another, and that was enough – just as he was reaching, the animal startled, head turning to the high-pitched cries, and then it was in motion, accelerating away across the plain.

Adams sighed and looked up. There was no use getting angry. What did tourists know? Maybe they should know better but they never did, and Adams had long ago learnt that fact of life.

He knew the two girls were close now, he could hear them chattering to one another.

'Aw, you were too slow!'

'He got away!'

'Maybe we'll see him again . . .'

He decided to have some fun and try and recoup something from the day.

Perfectly invisible in the long grass, he waited until they were almost on top of him, and then sat bolt upright in front of them.

He was going to give a comical 'Boo!' but his breath caught in his throat as he saw the girl on the left.

She was the most beautiful girl Matt Adams had ever seen.

It turned out that the two girls were on spring break from Harvard, and instead of catching a flight to Florida or Cancun and spending the week in drunken debauchery, they had decided to travel the Great Plains and gain some physical insight into their country's history.

The beautiful girl was called Evelyn Edwards, and was majoring in astronomy and physics, subjects Adams didn't immediately see her being interested in. She looked more like a model than a physicist.

The other girl was her roommate, and was certainly plainer than Lynn – Adams had quickly found out what she liked to be called – and was more the type Adams would associate with astrophysics.

After apologizing for scaring them and explaining who he was and what he had been doing, Adams had then invited both ladies back to his hometown of Pine Ridge for dinner.

Lynn's friend had baulked at the idea but Lynn, clearly interested, had agreed for both of them.

What followed in the days after was a whirlwind romance,

as Adams exposed Lynn to the wonders of the American Great Plains, providing a light-hearted release from the pressure of her studies. It was a sad fact that her friend was soon forgotten, and travelled back on her own after the first two days indicated that she was something of a third wheel.

On the last day before Lynn was due to go back to Harvard, Adams had taken her out into the Badlands again, and they had sat under the very tree he was now lying under. They had talked long into the night, and then he had reached forward, touching her cheek gently with his fingers.

And when they had finally kissed, Adams had instinctively known that they were destined to be together.

The tour came to a merciful end and Adams returned to the cabin that served as base of operations for the tour. He took care of the horses, then showered and changed.

After receiving his cash payment from the tour manager, he decided to get on his bike and head straight for the nearest bar.

He wasn't a drinker, but occasionally – if the nightmares persisted – he tried to see if the alcohol would help him sleep. Sometimes it did, sometimes it didn't; and sometimes when it did, the dreams came back worse than ever. Fearful of having the nightmares in front of the tourists, he had not slept at all on the tour and was now at the stage where his body was demanding sleep of *any* kind, even the kind filled with nightmares.

After just one hour, Adams had had enough. He was already on the verge of being drunk, and feared what would happen if he had any more. He could already tell that the drink wasn't going to help him sleep this time, and so he paid his tab and left for home.

Cycling down the streets in the cool night, Adams picked the wrong road twice, which caused him to laugh out loud. *You used to be the best tracker there was! Ha! Look at you now, can't even find your damned house!*

But he eventually did find it, a dilapidated one-storey squat-house – bedroom, bathroom, lounge-diner and kitchenette, small yard outside surrounded by a chain-link fence.

It wasn't much but it was home.

Home sweet home. Adams giggled as he left the bike in the yard and staggered up towards the porch, pulling open the outside screen door.

Leaning against the door frame, he fumbled for his keys, then fumbled again as he tried to get the key in the lock. He wasn't quite drunk, but the alcohol was cetainly not aiding his co-ordination.

Finally, after much cursing, he managed, and stepped through the door into his lounge.

And then he sensed it for the first time, something he should have picked up long ago.

There were other people in his house.

He started to move but stopped in his tracks as he felt the cold steel of a large calibre handgun press hard into the back of his head.

In an instant, Adams was stone cold sober.

2

THE LIGHTS CAME on, blinding in their intensity after the pitch dark, and a sharp pain shot through Adams' eyes, directly into his brain.

He got his bearings moments later, and saw there were four men in the room with him, including the one behind him with the gun. They were all dressed in identical dark blue suits, white shirts, dark blue ties. Adams was in no doubt that the other three men also carried guns.

Two men were out to the flanks, whilst one stood straight in front of him, just two feet away. This man – short crew cut, sharp eyes hidden behind rimless spectacles, his movement fluid, relaxed – approached Adams, staring into his face with barely concealed disdain.

'Where is she?' he asked in a cold monotone.

'Who?' Adams asked, genuinely confused, and not just by the alcohol he had consumed that night.

The man opposite didn't reply but merely punched Adams straight in the face with a leather-gloved fist.

Adams' head rocked back, blood flying from his nose out across the thin carpet. He fell to one knee, momentarily dazed. The pain was sharp, causing his eyes to water reflexively, but he knew that this was the least of his worries.

'Let's not play games here, Mr Adams,' the man said calmly, the violence not affecting him in the slightest. 'You know who we mean. Where is she?'

Adams shook his head, eyes down at the floor as he spat blood from his mouth. He looked back up. 'Seriously,' he said, 'I've got no idea what you're talking about.'

The man sighed, rolled his eyes theatrically to the ceiling, and stomped viciously down with a booted foot into Adams' face.

His head rocked back again, and he saw stars. His ears popping, he looked back at the man in front of him, eyes questioning.

'Your ex-wife,' the man explained in exasperation. 'Dr Evelyn Edwards. *Where is she?*'

Adams' head rang again, but not from being hit. It was confusion. *My ex-wife? Lynn?* 'She's dead,' Adams said bluntly. *Isn't she?*

'If she's dead,' the man said ponderously, 'then how do you explain the email?'

'Email?' Adams wondered aloud. 'What email?'

The suited man came forward to hit Adams again, but he held his hands up, placating. 'Hey, hey, I don't know what you're talking about! I've been out on a tour for the past four days!'

The man paused, considering the matter. 'You mean you've not seen the email?' he asked at last. He pulled a sheet of paper from a pocket, holding it up directly in front of Adams' face.

Adams closed his eyes, re-opened them, trying to focus. It was a print-off from an email. He recognized his own email address, but not the sender.

He looked harder, clearing the pain from his head as he read the words.

Matt. It's Lynn. I need your help. Someone is trying to kill me, but I don't know who. It might be the military, the government, even NASA. I don't know who to trust, except you. Please, I know it's been a long time but I need your help. Meet me at the park. And please come. As soon as you can. Lynn.

Adams was dumbfounded. Was this message from Lynn? He looked at the date. Two days ago. That was *four days* after the helicopter crash that was supposed to have killed her.

'So what do you make of it, Mr Adams?' the man asked. 'Which "park" is she referring to?'

Adams' head was spinning but clarity hit him suddenly. Lynn was alive, in danger, and she needed his help. Why else would the men be here, unless they believed the message was genuine? And if they were trying to find her, with force and with weapons, it could only be for one reason – to finish the job, and make sure she was dead.

Adams knew he wasn't up to much at the minute, but the anger that suddenly coursed through his veins seemed to revitalize him. They wanted to kill Lynn? *Well, we'll see about that*, Adams thought silently to himself. *We'll damn well see about that!*

His mind and spirit unified as one for the first time in many years. Free Bear jerked backwards, head twisting out of the way of the gun barrel, his hand snaking round to grab the gunman's arm.

With the other three men still to draw their weapons, Adams knew he had a chance. His elbow jerked back violently, connecting with the gunman's jaw and knocking him cold. At the same time, Adams grabbed the handgun, finger slotting through the trigger guard.

The man in front had his own Sig Sauer semi-automatic halfway out of its quick-release belt holster when Adams fired. The shot hit him centre mass, propelling him backwards through the small room, a plume of blood bursting from his back as the round left the body in a gigantic exit wound.

Adams angled swiftly to his left, firing again. The alcohol was having an effect, though, and he caught the third man in the shoulder, but it was enough to incapacitate. He ignored the man as he fell to the floor, eyes wide, going into immediate shock, and instead turned instantly to fire at the last intruder.

This man, realizing that fumbling with his gun might prove fatal, was instead charging towards Adams, trying to close the distance and disarm him. It was a good strategy. By the time Adams had turned, it was too late – the man was on top of him, shoulder driving hard into Adams' gut.

The wind knocked out of him, the gun went spiralling into the air, landing near the kitchenette. And then Adams felt the weight of the man on top of him, his big meaty fingers gripping his throat, squeezing the life out of him.

The whisky, the lack of sleep, the blows to the head, the sheer confusion of everything that was going on was too much for him, and he felt himself giving in to the pressure of the fingers, his brain going light from lack of oxygen.

No! There was no giving in; there simply couldn't be.

His arm pushed out from under the big man's body, reaching for the cheap glass coffee table near the sofa. Just as his eyes were going dim, he used the last of his energy to smash through the glass.

The sharp sound of breaking glass made the man pause, relax his hold slightly, and that was all Adams needed, as he grabbed a shard of broken glass from where it had fallen on the floor, driving it into the big man's neck with a feral yowl of triumph. The carotid artery was severed and a great stream of bright crimson blood sprayed out and covered his own face.

Adams lay on the floor for several minutes afterwards, blood pooling off his body on to his cheap carpet.

Finally, he got to his knees, then to his feet, and surveyed the carnage. Three men dead, one unconscious from shock.

But Adams was OK. And he knew exactly where to go. The park.

Lynn was alive.

3

STEPHEN JACOBS SIPPED his herbal tea from a china cup as he stared at the screen on the large walnut desk in front of him.

On the screen, the eleven other members of the organization's elite leadership stared back at him. It was a secure electronic conference call, bringing together twelve of the world's most influential power brokers for an emergency discussion.

Yasuhiro Obata looked seriously into the camera. 'Have we been compromised?' he asked simply. As the head of Japan's largest *zaibatsu* business conglomerate, he was used to direct speech, a fact some of the more political members of the inner leadership found rather disconcerting.

'No,' Jacobs answered, equally directly. 'The body has been secured at our Nevada facility, and everyone outside of the organization has been neutralized.'

'Except for Dr Edwards,' interjected Sergio Molina, the Italian motorsport kingpin.

Jacobs adjusted himself in his club chair before he answered. 'It is true that we have yet to find Dr Edwards, yes. But the operation to locate her has just begun.'

On the screen, he saw Yuri Andropov, the owner of Russia's largest media concern, lean forward. 'And if she talks beforehand?'

'It will not come to that, I am sure,' Jacobs replied and took another sip of tea. 'Besides, she knows very little. If she surfaced, what would she say? Nothing that people would believe, anyway. And let us not forget that our organization controls eighty per cent of the world's media. The story would be killed in any case. But put yourselves in her place – she feels someone is trying to kill her, which is why she contacted her ex-husband rather than the authorities. It's highly unlikely she will want to bring attention to herself. No, ladies and gentlemen, I think we are safe for the time being.'

'How much longer do we need?' asked Lord Thomas Hart, the longest serving member of Britain's House of Lords.

Jacobs turned his eyes to the image of Professor Philippe Messier, the Director General of CERN, the nuclear research centre and particle physics laboratory near Geneva, Switzerland. 'Professor?' he asked, passing the ball along.

Messier cleared his throat. 'Things are progressing well. We should be ready to test the device before the end of the month.'

There were looks of great satisfaction on the faces of all the assembled leaders, even hints of excitement. The dream was close to being realized.

'We can't afford to take any chances,' said Tony Kern, special aide to the President of the United States. 'Do whatever you have to, Mr Jacobs. Just make sure Dr Edwards is taken out of the picture.'

Jacobs nodded his head. Taking out Dr Edwards wouldn't be a problem. The wheels were already in motion.

* * *

Matt Adams stretched as he got out of the searing hot taxicab, straight into the frenetic, bustling metropolis of Santiago, Chile.

The population here was predominantly Amerindian, and Adams' classically Lakota features blended in perfectly. It was like a home away from home.

Adams had his own passport but he knew it wouldn't be long before his name would be out on the wire. The agents wouldn't report back, and the powers that be – whoever they were – would immediately assume he was on the run, possibly attempting to meet Lynn at the unknown location. And while they obviously had no idea where this was, which would limit the coverage they would be able to put out, they would certainly be able to make life hard for him.

But Adams was not without his own resources. He had flown in from Mexico just an hour before, after first visiting an old friend of the Tohono O'odham Nation, a vast tribal land that bordered Mexico.

He had borrowed a passport and some cash from the man, careful of what he had told him. It wasn't that he thought his old friend would be loose-lipped, it was rather that the less he knew, the safer he would probably be – after all, his friend was still employed by the federal government. Adams had used the borrowed passport to travel from Mexico to Chile, the photograph being close enough in appearance to arouse no suspicion and as he adjusted quickly to the new environment, he set off in the direction of his rendezvous.

Once he had regained sufficient strength after the fight at his house, Adams had searched the bodies. Unsurprisingly, there was nothing to be found. No ID, no jewellery, no tattoos, not even any labels in their clothes. The only distinguishing factor was that all four men had been packing identical Sig Sauer P229 .40 calibre semi-automatic handguns, held in spring-loaded belt holsters. The guns were sold at a thousand dollars a unit, and their presence told Adams a great deal.

The team was professional, so much so that Adams had to conclude that they were government operatives. But which government? The lead interrogator had spoken with an American accent – possibly a Brooklyn base, but smoothed out over the years by travel until it had picked up something of West Virginia. He suspected the team operated out of Washington, and this had been borne out when he found their car parked four streets over. It was a metallic grey Ford sedan with civilian plates, but Adams knew the type well enough. Classic government undercover issue. Again, it was scrupulously clean, but for Adams this only confirmed his suspicions. Only an elite government agency would be so careful.

But if an agency of the *US* government, then which one? CIA, FBI, DEA, DIA, NSA, Department of Homeland Security? There was a veritable alphabet soup of organizations that could be involved. It could even be NASA, as Lynn seemed to suspect, although Adams wasn't aware that the space agency had any direct action wing. Still, nothing would surprise him any more.

He had decided to use the car as far as he could, and after packing a small bag and gathering his meagre savings from a strongbox under the kitchen table, Adams had travelled north out of the reservation. He drove as far as

Bismarck up in North Dakota, where he had abandoned the car and bought a Greyhound bus ticket to Winnipeg, Canada.

Instead of getting on the bus, though, he had trekked further into town and hitchhiked his way back down south. The subterfuge wouldn't last forever, but it might waste some of his enemy's resources and give him a window of opportunity to reach his real destination.

Within twenty-four hours he was crossing the Mexican border on foot, on one of the countless unmanned trails he had discovered when he had worked in the area years ago – before the 'incident', before the nightmares, before his life had gone to hell.

Boarding the plane at Mexico City, he had suddenly been overcome with a terrible fatigue. It was the aftermath of adrenalin, a backlash of the parasympathetic nervous system creating the powerful desire for sleep.

He recognized the gift for what it was, and as he took his seat in the cabin, he allowed himself to close his eyes and relax.

And at last, mercifully, he slept.

Adams took the bumps slowly along the desert road in his Toyota Landcruiser, taking the twists and turns at under five miles per hour; no matter how hard he pressed the accelerator, the vehicle would go no faster.

He looked through the windscreen up at the burning sun, and looked away, his head aching.

He pulled over to the side of the road. It was no use. He'd been on the truck's trail for three days now, and was no closer to catching it. He needed a rest, just half an hour

45

to shut his eyes. He'd been here before so many times, knew what the consequences would be if he fell asleep, and yet he was powerless to resist. He had to carry on, had to try and get there in time, at least once, at least this time. But he was so tired . . .

He was in the desert, on foot now, tracking the tyre marks that had gone off the road just half a kilometre from where he had been resting. The sun was lower in the sky, several hours having passed. He cursed himself, knowing what that would mean. He would find the truck like he had a thousand times in the past, open the doors, hoping that this time it would be different. But he knew it wouldn't be different, and yet still he soldiered on, tracking the tyre marks for another mile over the dusty terrain, until he found the truck lying there deserted in the dying rays of the afternoon sun.

He edged closer to the truck's rear doors, one hand on his pistol while the other reached out for the handle, the metal searing hot.

Taking a deep breath, hoping beyond hope that it *would* be different, he yanked the doors open.

And again, like every time, he stared at what lay in the back of the truck, opened his mouth, and screamed.

Adams woke with a start, the hand of the female passenger next to him resting on his shoulder, rocking him awake.

He looked at her through half-closed, confused eyes.

'Are you OK?' she asked him, a concerned look on her face.

Adams tried to smile at her. 'Sorry,' he mumbled. 'Just a bad dream.'

46

The lady nodded her head in understanding. 'Wow,' she said, obviously moved by what she had seen. 'It must have been *really* bad.'

She put her hand on his, and Adams was grateful for the contact. He smiled at her properly this time. 'Yes,' he said, not knowing what else to say. 'It was.'

'What?' Jacobs exploded down the telephone, his cup of tea spinning on its saucer.

'They're dead,' the voice on the other end of the line came back. 'Three out of four anyway. The other was incapacitated, in the hospital now.'

Jacobs didn't ask for details. They had underestimated Adams, plain and simple. He was known to be a recluse but they had had his file, knew his background. They should have been more careful.

'Where is he now?' Jacobs asked. It was imperative that they find him. If he made it to Evelyn Edwards, then one more person would know what had happened at the Pine Island Glacier, what had been discovered. And then more people would find out; it was inevitable, once a secret had been shared.

'He caught a Greyhound bus up to Canada, got into the depot in Winnipeg late last night.'

'Get our people at NSA checking the station's CCTV feeds, then track his movements through the city.'

Like most cities, Winnipeg had its share of CCTV cameras littering its streets. By entering certain parameters, facial recognition software could track a person's movements from camera to camera.

'Yes, sir.'

'And find out if they're having any luck tracing the movements of Dr Edwards.'

The most concrete thing they had was her location over four days ago, a cybercafé in Punta Arenas, in the south of Chile. By the time a team had arrived, she had been long gone, and who knew where. She was a resourceful woman, that much was certain.

'Yes, sir.'

'And let me know how they're doing on cross-referencing both of their files. The answer to the location of the meeting place might be right there, just waiting to be found.'

People often reverted to familiar places, and this was certainly indicated by the urgent email sent by Edwards. The question was whether the information was on file somewhere. If it was, the NSA supercomputers would find the answer sooner or later. It was just a question of crunching the data for long enough.

'Yes, sir.'

'OK,' Jacobs said in dismissal, replacing the receiver.

He picked up his tea again, but then the voice of his immediate superior, loud and clear inside his head, caused him to spill it across the desk. *Damn!*

'Problems?'

'No,' Jacobs intoned clearly. 'Nothing to worry about.'

'We cannot afford any problems. Not now, when we are so close.'

'Leave it to me.'

'Yes. There is nothing else we can do. But do not let us down.'

Jacobs swallowed hard. 'I won't,' he said finally, filled with the conviction that came from being the leader of the world's most powerful organization. 'Our dream will be realized, you can all count on that.'

'Yes,' the voice replied. 'And then you can take your rightful place among us.'

Jacobs smiled at the thought, and knew that he would do whatever it took.

Santiago held special memories for Adams, and as he stood in the middle of the Parque Metropolitano at the summit of San Cristobal, looking down over the smog-hazed city below him, the past came vividly back to him.

It was here that he had proposed to Lynn all those years ago, after riding the funicular to the top of the mountain, hand in hand. Happy. So blissfully happy.

He had stared into her eyes, gone to one knee, and asked her. And she had said yes. It had been the happiest moment of his life, and he had known that she had felt the same way.

'Hey.'

Adams' head snapped round at the voice. He had been so absorbed in his thoughts and memories that he had never noticed the lone woman detach herself from a group of tourists and approach him from the side.

Lynn.

Despite the years, she hadn't changed one bit. If anything, she looked even better now than she had done the last time he had seen her. She was obviously under a great deal of stress, but although she looked as if she hadn't slept properly in weeks, her underlying beauty shone through her exhausted features.

There was no doubt it was her, Evelyn Edwards, live,

here in the flesh. So the email was true, and she did need his help.

'Lynn,' he said finally, taking her in his arms and embracing her for the first time in fifteen long years.

4

'So HOW ARE we looking?' asked David McNulty as he drove the ball three hundred yards across the fairway. Semi-professional in his younger days, McNulty still found time for eighteen holes on a weekend, even now he was the President of the United States.

'Good,' Tony Kern replied. 'The trade delegation is due in Beijing tomorrow morning, and we think the Chinese are going to go for it. The—'

Kern was cut off by the shrill ring of his cellphone. Staring at the screen, Kern answered it instantly, despite President McNulty standing right beside him, waiting for an answer to his question.

'Yes,' he answered simply, and then hung up. Ignoring the president, who still waited expectantly next to him, he then speed-dialled a number on his phone, turning away from McNulty.

'News from the NSA,' he whispered. 'Santiago, Chile. Parque Metropolitano.' He nodded his head. 'Yes,' he finished, and hung up.

McNulty stood there, hands on his hips, staring at his assistant. 'Sorry, Tony, am I disturbing your business?'

Kern couldn't miss the acid tone in McNulty's voice, but it was of no concern. Despite being President of the United

States, McNulty was not one of the chosen. And it would not be long before their roles would be reversed, and McNulty – and all others like him – would be crushed to dirt under the feet of the world's true elite.

'It was horrific,' Lynn explained when they were back in the twin room she had booked at the Hostal Americano. A cheap, basic hotel in the downtown area of Santiago, it was nevertheless good enough for their purposes.

Adams sat on the bed opposite Lynn and listened. She had already explained how they had found a body in the ice, possibly as much as forty thousand years old but with clothing and equipment that posed a variety of extremely puzzling questions. He sipped a glass of water as she told him how the team of army engineers had descended on the glacier and extracted the body, before evacuating everyone by helicopter.

He had questions building up – too numerous to count – but didn't want to interrupt before Lynn had finished. She was clearly relieved to be getting it all out in the open, to have someone to speak to at last about her ordeal.

'I saw the blinking lights, and just started screaming for everyone to get out of there,' Lynn continued. 'And then, I don't know why, I just reacted, I yanked open the pilot side door and jumped.' Her voice choked up with emotion. 'It exploded while I was still in mid-air, the flames touching me before I hit the water.'

Her face reddened as tears ran down her cheeks. 'I couldn't save any of them!' she blurted, and Adams crossed to her bed, holding her in his arms as her body wracked with sobs. 'Oh Matt, I should've tried to get them out! But

I didn't, I just jumped, and saved myself, and all the rest are dead! They're all dead!'

Adams just held her tight as she collapsed into him. He could tell her how she did the right thing, how she would be dead too now if she had stayed to help the others, how nobody would have survived anyway, but he knew that these were just empty platitudes. Lynn was an exceptionally gifted woman, the brightest he had ever known. There was nothing he could tell her that her logical brain would not have already convinced her of. The fact was, she had done the only thing she could have done, and he knew she would come to terms with that sooner or later, no matter what he said.

And so he just held her, and let her cry.

'It was a fishing trawler that found me,' she continued later on, Adams still by her side on the bed, holding her hand. 'They'd seen the explosion. I was bobbing around in the water like a tenpin, my backpack keeping me afloat. When the crew pulled me out, I was near hypothermic, unconscious, and in shock. They took me back to shore, off the coast of southern Chile, radioed in the crash, and got me medical attention. When I finally came to, and realized where I was, I panicked. I begged the doctor to release me, and cover up the fact I'd ever been there. I told him a modified version of what had happened, told him I was scared for my life. And I was – if the crash was recorded, and it was mentioned that there was a survivor, I knew they would come for me. I was – and still am – in no doubt that the explosion on the helicopter was an execution. That body is important to someone, that's for damned sure.'

Adams considered the fact that he had further proof of that – the intercepted email, the attempt to force information from him – but decided to let her finish her own story before confirming her suspicions with a tale of his own.

'The doctor agreed, even gave me some money to help me on my way. I was on the mainland by the next day, which is where I sent the message to you. I didn't know what else to do, I didn't know who I could trust. I mean, it was the head of NASA I'd called with news of the discovery, so who else could I go to? Now maybe NASA are in on it, maybe not – maybe the message was intercepted, some other group got involved, who knows? Maybe the engineers weren't even from the army. All I know is that someone wants to kill anyone who had any knowledge of that body.'

Lynn looked into Adams' eyes and squeezed his hand tighter. 'I didn't even know if you'd believe it. I saw the news reports, how I'd been reported dead in the "accident". I prayed that it would get to you, that you'd believe it. I couldn't call, couldn't risk the fact that they could trace it. I sent the email encoded, via a few cut-off routes to lose its origin. If you hadn't turned up within the next few days, I would've tried to leave the country by myself. I still have my passport, but I don't want to use it – I'm sure they'll be looking for me at the airports.'

If four armed men hadn't just tried to beat information about Lynn's whereabouts out of him, Adams would have thought her paranoid. But it would certainly appear that there *were* people out to get her, and they had been able to intercept the email. He hoped that was as far as they had got.

54

Lynn looked up again into his eyes. 'Do you believe me?'

He stared back at her, melting in the green limpid pools of her eyes. 'I believe you.' He held her tight, kissed her cheek. 'I believe you.'

Stephen Jacobs poked at the logs burning in the vast fireplace, feeling rather than seeing when Commander Flynn Eldridge entered the living room.

Eldridge, a former commander of the US Navy's SEAL Team Six, was now in charge of an even more clandestine group. Known as the Alpha Brigade, it operated out of the Nevada desert, on the direct orders of the organization headed by Stephen Jacobs. The group consisted purely of ex-military special forces operatives, pulled in from the SEALs, the Marine Force Recon, the Green Berets, the Delta Force, and from the Air Force Special Forces. They were a private army, not operating on government orders but able to exist above the law due to the protection given to them by Jacobs' organization.

Eldridge loved every minute of it – no congressional oversight, nobody breathing down his neck, no ridiculously restrictive rules of engagement – and the only thing that mattered to Jacobs was results. Eldridge was therefore given carte blanche in his operations, as long as he got the job done, a fact that appealed immensely to his ruthless, aggressive nature. If he needed information from someone, he could torture them. If he needed to make a point for someone, he could execute the person next to them.

He was the king of his own little world, a world of hired mercenary killers, one which he dominated through sheer force of will. Sometimes he thought he was in danger of becoming like the US Army Special Forces men sent into the jungles of Laos and Cambodia to train up the guerrilla forces that 'went native' during the Vietnam War, men who were treated like gods by the tribal people, and who lost all sense of reality. But he always reigned himself back in when he felt it was getting to that stage – after all, he was a professional. Ruthless, fearsome, merciless, but a professional nevertheless.

But as he entered the large, mahogany-panelled living room of Jacobs' vast mansion house on Washington's Potomac River, Eldridge was all too aware of his recent failings. First, he had failed to make sure everyone aboard the helicopter was dead back in the Antarctic. Second, a team of his men had seriously underestimated the survivor's ex-husband, Matt Adams. Now Adams was undoubtedly going to rendezvous with Edwards, and then – who knew?

'Sir,' Eldridge announced, standing to attention behind the old man.

Jacobs continued to prod the fire, causing embers to fall, to ignite the dead areas and feed the flames. 'Good evening,' he said eventually, without turning round. He continued to stoke the fire for a few more minutes, Eldridge growing more and more uncomfortable with every passing second.

Finally, Jacobs turned round and locked eyes with the special forces commander. 'I am sure you understand how our organization responds to failure.'

Eldridge nodded, having executed several men himself who had been deemed to be unworthy of the group's standards.

'How secure are you feeling right now?' Jacobs asked directly.

Eldridge adjusted his position uncomfortably. He was not used to being on the receiving end of threats. 'I need another chance, sir,' he answered. 'I'll get them.'

Jacobs smiled, reassured by the strength of Eldridge's conviction. He wasn't sure if it was the threat of execution or the thought of the coming reward if everything went according to plan that gave the big man such convincing self-belief. Either way, Jacobs believed him.

'Good. The fact is, we need to find these two characters, and we need to find them fast.'

Eldridge nodded his head. 'Do we have any leads?'

For the first time that night, Jacobs smiled. 'As a matter of fact, we do.'

5

'IT'S SO STRANGE,' Lynn said, holding a fresh cup of coffee in her hands.

'What's that?' Adams asked, sweat starting to bead on his forehead. He had managed to sleep for a few hours on board the plane, before the nightmares woke him, but was now unable to do so again. And perversely, now his body had been rewarded with sleep, instead of being satiated, it just craved even more.

'The other helicopter,' Lynn answered straight away. 'I've been checking a few things out since I've been here, and it just seems to have vanished – no flight plans filed, no record of a take-off, no record of it ever having landed. Maybe I'm just looking in the wrong places, but it seems to have never even existed.'

'Sounds military,' Adams said, thinking about the recent visit to his house by what seemed to be government agents. 'Probably linked to the intelligence services.'

Lynn nodded her head. 'That's what I thought,' she continued. 'But why? I mean, why would they be doing it?'

'I guess the reason they'd give would be national security, but who really knows? It could be rogue elements, it could be anything. The one thing that *is* clear is that they're ruthless.' Adams pointed at the backpack. 'And that evidence you've got in there is our only potential bargaining chip.'

Adams stretched out, thinking about what was in the bag. High-definition footage of the burial site, measurements, notes, diagrams and, most importantly, DNA samples of the body itself.

'If we're going to get out of this, we have to learn more about that body – who it is, what it was doing there, and why it's so damned important.' He considered the matter further. 'We need to get back to the US and get those samples tested, get the rest of the evidence copied and spread around. Like insurance.'

Lynn nodded, knowing he was right. All of a sudden, she was extremely glad she had sent the email to Matt. He was always so sure, so strong. And despite her own strengths, she had felt so lost here, stranded and alone against the vast machine of the US government, or whoever it was that was after her.

She felt unfamiliar feelings in her gut, ones she had not felt since – well, since the last time she had been with Matt, she finally admitted to herself. Was it the stress? Or were the feelings real?

As she lay back on her bed and closed her eyes, giving in to the need for sleep, she had no answer.

Later that night, she awoke in a cold sweat, nightmares from the helicopter crash swamping her unconscious, disturbing her inner demons.

And then Matt was there with her, holding her close, whispering in her ear that she would be OK, everything would be all right.

He climbed in next to her, arms around her, and as she felt his strong embrace, she knew that he was right.

Eldridge smiled to himself as the aeroplane shot through the thin air of near-space at over four thousand miles per hour, one hundred thousand feet above the earth.

The Aurora stealth aircraft was a secret military project many thought was still years from completion, although it was in reality already mission-ready. Powered by a radical new pulse detonation wave engine, it could reach speeds once thought impossible. From the airstrip at Groom Lake in the Nevada desert to the skies above Santiago would take less than an hour.

The only unfortunate thing, Eldridge reflected as he checked the harness on his chute, was that the aircraft wouldn't be able to land – the risk of people seeing it was just too great. Instead it would take the lesser risk of slowing down and reducing altitude so that he could parachute out of it once it had reached its destination.

Eldridge was no stranger to parachute drops and was looking forward to liaising with his team. There were six members of the Alpha Brigade already on the ground in Santiago, who had been searching for Lynn Edwards in Punta Arenas since the email had been sent. More of his team would join them later; at the moment they were being recalled from other operations, and tasked to Eldridge in Santiago. They would have to travel by more conventional, slower aircraft, but they would be there by late the next morning.

And then the hunt would begin in earnest.

*   *   *

Jacobs rubbed his chin in contemplation as he relaxed in his private sauna. Sweat dripped from every square inch of his body, pooling on the Scandinavian pine-wood floor, and he breathed in deeply, then exhaled, expanding his chest.

The information had come in unexpectedly and had to be acted on fast, and he was pleased he had managed to arrange for the Aurora to get Eldridge there quickly.

Once there, Eldridge would capture Matt Adams and Lynn Edwards, and arrange for the pair to be delivered covertly to the base in Nevada for interrogation. It would be tidier if Adams and Lynn could just be taken out, executed on the spot, but it was vital that Jacobs knew what had been going on for the past week – who else Lynn had told, who *they* had told, ad infinitum until the situation was entirely contained.

And that was a definite possibility, now that the pair's location had been determined. Computer power had defined a possible area that Lynn could have reached since the crash, taking into account various factors such as data from ports, airports, train stations and bus depots, credit card use, availability of cash, use of passport, feeds from CCTV units, and basic triangulation algorithms.

This area was then cross-referenced with every available scrap of information about the past lives of Matt Adams and Evelyn Edwards, and further computer searches had finally found a seventeen-year-old credit card bill for two train tickets from Lynn's family home in Maine down to Mexico. Time-consuming manual labour had at last unearthed the circuitous route through South America taken by the young couple, and card purchases along the way provided further confirmation that it had in fact been Lynn and Adams who were the travellers.

Once the data was cross-checked, the triangulation zone matched almost perfectly with the couple's prior visit to Santiago, Chile. It made perfect sense, too – Lynn could easily have gone that far north in the time available, without having to cross any borders, and it would be easy to get lost in a city of five million people.

Once the target city had been located, it was then a matter of checking hotel bookings, travel companies, taxi services, CCTV footage, and satellite photography.

Evelyn Edwards' features had finally been caught on CCTV going into the Parque Metropolitano, and the data was immediately fed to the Alpha Brigade members who were already in Chile.

Further CCTV followed Lynn as she met a second person, whose features were subsequently confirmed as belonging to the second target, Matt Adams. The pair were then electronically followed back to the Hostal Americano, where the primary target had apparently booked a room for cash under the name of Patrice Leaky.

The five men from the Alpha Brigade were on-site within the hour, ready to roll, and as Jacobs sat in his sauna, the sweat rolling off his body in fat, thick droplets, he had to admit that it was an impressive turnaround.

With Eldridge also en route for Chile, Jacobs was confident that the pair would be in Nevada by nightfall. They would be expertly interrogated, every last drop of information forced from them.

And then they would be executed.

6

'THEY INTERCEPTED THE email?' Lynn asked over the small breakfast table, incredulous.

Adams nodded. 'They even showed me a copy. I wouldn't have known about it if they hadn't, I hadn't been home for days.'

The night before, Adams had purposely not told Lynn the details about the attack on his house, knowing how she would react. She had a terrible night as it was, and Adams knew she wouldn't have slept a wink if he had told her his own story.

But now Lynn looked as if she had been bitten by a snake, recoiling with sudden terror. 'They might know where we are!' she whispered, trying to contain her rising panic. 'If they intercepted the message, they could know anything!'

Adams shook his head. 'No. They came to me because they had no idea where you were. They needed to get the information from me.'

'And you're sure you weren't followed?'

'Pretty sure. I had a borrowed passport, used a random route, never noticed anything out of the ordinary. And I'm pretty good at that.' Adams winced even as he said it. That might once have been true, he thought, but not any more. He hadn't even seen Lynn come up to him in the park. He was out of practice, plain and simple. As it stood, Lynn seemed to be doing a better job than he was. What if he *had* been followed?

'It might not have even been *people* following you,' Lynn warned. 'Electronic surveillance – credit card purchases, closed-circuit television with facial recognition software, satellite photography, the list is endless!'

Since her escape, Lynn had been meticulously researching the techniques and methods of her potential enemies, and her razor-sharp mind had absorbed an incredible amount of information on the subject. She didn't have the practical experience but certainly now knew the theory well enough to be worried.

'Hey,' Adams said as soothingly as he could, all too aware that Lynn was right. 'I only used cash, I don't even *have* any credit cards, and I was careful to avoid cameras. I didn't use a phone either. I think we should be OK for now.'

Lynn looked at him for a moment before making her decision. 'No. We have to leave. Now.'

Adams nodded his head. He actually agreed, he just wanted Lynn to calm down, to try and relax. Mistakes were made when tensions were high, and Adams knew that better than most. 'OK,' he said, grabbing his bag from the second bed. 'I'm ready. Let's go.'

Within three minutes, Lynn was ready with him at the door. Reaching out to touch the thin wooden partition, his hand stopped, and he reflexively put out his other hand to stop Lynn, a finger going to her lips to silence her.

He pressed his head closer to the door, listening, senses tuning to the world beyond the door.

The noise was coming from the stairs. Six pairs of feet,

booted, heavy, as if each person carried something. It could be luggage of course, but it could just as easily be weaponry of some kind. There was a defined movement to the foot-steps, a rhythm, a sense of cohesion that felt vaguely military.

He felt his old senses coming back to him slowly, crawling out of the veil they had been hiding behind since that day in the desert.

He sniffed the air, and smelled no cologne, no deodorant, just a faint hint of natural soap, enough to disguise the more potent smell of body odour.

And then he picked up the breathing – regular, even, paced, but slightly elevated, and not by the exercise but by anticipation.

'Hit team,' he said to Lynn finally. 'Six men, armed, turning down the hallway now. We've got ten seconds.'

7

CERN, THE EUROPEAN Organization for Nuclear Research, is based near Geneva, Switzerland. Famous across the world for its search for the 'God Particle' at its Large Hadron Collider facility, the institution was originally founded in 1954 to unite Europe's – and later the world's – foremost nuclear physicists. Since then, its particle physics research has taken over to a large extent, and its discovery and then its creation of anti-matter is both admired and feared in equal measure.

Many members of the general public were genuinely terrified when the collider – more commonly known as the LHC – was first switched on. Consisting of billions of parti-cles being deliberately smashed together along miles of underground piping – sometimes as many as ten thousand per *second* – it was thought in some quarters that the device might create a black hole that would destroy the entire world in the blink of an eye.

Of course, no such thing ever happened, and the LHC has hummed away safely ever since, on a constant quest for the explanation of the beginnings of the universe.

Professor Philippe Messier considered the history of the LHC laboratory as he entered the elevator. He had just finished examining a damaged portion of the pipeline, which was getting the full attention of an army of engineers and machinists. Satisfied that everything that could be done was being done, he decided to check on the more important project, three hundred feet further under the surface.

Whereas the LHC was very much the public face of CERN, the project below – even though it had cost close to several *trillion* euros over the decades – was unknown by all but a handful of select people in the outside world, all part of the elite organization headed by Stephen Jacobs. The others – engineers, technicians, physicists, mathematicians, machinists, and hundreds of skilled and unskilled workers – were not part of the chosen, and would never be allowed to leave the facility. In a way, they were slaves to the machine, destined to work until they perished.

Messier smiled as he descended lower in the elevator, excited whenever he thought about the project. As the elevator came to a smooth stop, and the doors opened, the vast machine was revealed in all its glory.

Although it depended to a large extent on the power secretly generated by the LHC above, the technology that this secret device relied upon was more esoteric by far, unknown to the vast majority of the human populace. It was a gift from the gods, almost literally, Messier thought as he approached it.

Soon, he thought as he neared it. *Soon*.

A shiver of excitement ran through him as he looked through the huge observation windows. Soon it would be fully operational, and it mattered to him not one iota that the result might well be the destruction of the human race, except for the chosen few.

The chosen few who would soon be as gods themselves.

* * *

Adams ran past Lynn, who stood rooted to the spot, clutching her backpack. He looked through the window on the opposite side of the room, across the Avenue Santa Maria to the block opposite.

Within two seconds, he had spotted the sharpshooter on the roof, rifle aimed at the window, as well as the reflection in the shopfronts opposite of two men waiting by the Hostal Americano foyer below him.

'Get by the side of the window!' Adams whispered forcefully to Lynn. Then he pulled the nearest bed across the floor, using it to barricade the door. It wouldn't stop the team for more than a few extra seconds, but it would be enough.

Eldridge had met up with his men at the hotel at three in the morning. He had listened to their briefing, drawn his own equipment, and laid out the plans for the capture of the fugitives.

At seven o'clock the same morning, he had led his team down the stairs and watched as his two lead men had raced at the door, small metal battering ram held between them. The strategy was pure 'shock and awe' on the small unit tactical level – smash through the door, disorientate the targets with stun grenades, and effect a quick arrest, subduing both people with force if necessary.

But although the door had shattered, it had not caved forwards into the room as expected. *Why the hell not?*

'Murphy!' he called. 'What's the hold-up?'

As the man on the right used the ram again, he called back, 'There's a bed behind the door! They knew we were coming!'

Eldridge pressed the toggle on his tactical mic, speaking directly to the sharpshooter on the opposite roof. He would have liked to have more men outside, but their resources were necessarily limited in such a remote location.

'Williams, what do you see?'

'Nothing, movement at the window a moment ago – wait a second, they've broken through the window, the male target has something in his hand, he – arrgghh!'

Eldridge's blood went cold as the connection went dead.

Sprinting once more towards the window, Adams had grabbed Lynn by the hand, dragging her with him. In his other hand, he had snatched up a large mirror from the dressing table. At the window he pulled the curtain back and slammed his booted foot straight through it; the glass shattered, falling to the ground two storeys below.

An instant later, ignoring the cries of Lynn as he secured his grip on her wrist, Adams thrust the mirror up and out, angling its reflection straight at the sniper opposite. He saw the man recoil instinctively from the sudden, intense reflection of sunlight that hit him in the eye through the telescopic lens of his rifle, then heard the team behind him thumping against the door, breaking it down, and in that tiny window of opportunity, he pulled Lynn forward and jumped with her straight out of the window.

Adams had seen the wide, canvas awning over the entrance to the hotel's foyer when he had arrived, and then later confirmed that Lynn's room was directly above it, two floors up.

Jumping was a risk – they could easily hit a metal support strut – but the odds were more favourable than staying in the room and taking on six armed men.

Adams was pleased that Lynn didn't scream on the way down, although he didn't know if it was bravery or shock. Either way, though, silence was a good thing – he hoped that the men below hadn't already been alerted by the broken glass, as he would need every advantage he could get.

They hit the fabric straight on and, using the bounce from the awning, Adams gripped the edge rail with one hand, his other arm going round Lynn's waist, and swung round and down, letting go at the end of the swing and dropping lightly to the ground, right in front of the two men he had seen earlier.

As he landed he let go of Lynn, who staggered disorientated to the side. The men's eyes went wide as they saw him, hands on their earpieces, obviously receiving communication from the team above.

Before they could react, Adams launched himself forward, his full body weight behind a heavy straight right to the first man's jaw. Adams saw the eyes go, and as the man dropped unconscious to the ground, Adams was already twisting to the other side, throwing a left hook towards the second man. It connected but his timing was off, and the man just staggered back, hurt but still a threat.

Adams saw him instinctively go for the pistol in his belt, and then saw his head twist round from another heavy impact. He turned, and saw Lynn standing there, backpack in her hands, having swung it at the man with all her might.

Adams was impressed, but Lynn had always been a tough one. The man was still conscious but he was down. Adams suddenly remembered the sniper opposite. His vision might be impaired but he was still capable of getting off some shots.

He pulled Lynn to one side, taking shelter behind one

of the two huge terracotta plant pots stationed on either side of the main entrance even as his suspicions were confirmed and the rounds hit the sidewalk where they had just been standing. Adams noticed that the impacts left no mark, except for small black smears – rubber bullets. They could still be deadly if the target was unfortunate but it indicated that whoever was after them wanted them alive.

That was the good news.

The bad news was that they were now stuck between a sniper on one side and a team of men in the hotel behind them. The sniper might only have rubber bullets but they would still incapacitate them easily enough. If they ran into the street, they would be shot with these bullets; if they retreated back into the hotel, they would be greeted by the six men who would now doubtless be racing down the stairs to the foyer.

Adams made a quick calculation in his head – from the time he had broken the window and they had jumped, he guessed no more than fifteen seconds had passed. During that time, the team upstairs was probably only just through the door, the team leader putting it all together, deciding what to do. An armed team descending two flights of stairs would take at least thirty seconds.

Adams knew there would be a back entrance to the hotel, probably exiting into a service alley. He should have scoped out the exits as soon as he arrived. Sloppy. And sloppy could easily mean dead against these guys. He would have to raise his game if he and Lynn were going to survive.

As it was, they had thirty seconds to go back into the hotel and find their way out the other side.

It would have to be enough.

8

ELDRIDGE LED HIS men back down the stairs, cursing all the way. How had they known his team was coming? And who would have guessed they would jump out of the window? What a mess!

The latest update from Williams made him feel no better. Apparently his two men outside had been taken out, and the two fugitives had actually turned and run back *inside* the building!

Eldridge didn't know what their plan was but he knew it had been a mistake not putting people at the back door. But with such a limited amount of men, what could he do? He couldn't cover everywhere, and the back entrance had seemed a very unlikely place to need covering when he had drawn up the plans for the arrest.

Still, he considered as he neared the first landing, *plans never survive contact with the enemy*. The crusty old Master Chief who had led his SEAL training down at Virginia Beach had been right about that, at least.

As they neared the bottom of the stairs and the foyer, he realized the impression they would make, six armed men running full tilt through a cheap city hotel. The op was supposed to go down quietly, and even though they had approval from the Chilean government and the Santiago metropolitan police, Eldridge was aware that the mission was about to overstep the agreed boundaries.

The hotel foyer had been cleared of guests by the hotel staff for the duration of the op – the idea had been to bundle the arrested pair down the stairs and into the van waiting outside – but Eldridge understood what a spectacle was taking place, and how bad it might look for the US government if things continued to get worse. He stopped for a second on the last step – the van! Of course! How could he have forgotten?

'Renfrew,' he said into his mic as he took the last stair into the hotel foyer, 'get the van round to the back! Now!'

Adams and Lynn crashed together out of the metal service door into the narrow alleyway. They had found the exit through the kitchen, after sprinting at full speed through the foyer, reception and dining room.

Adams was surprised that there were no other guests around, and then realized that they must have been confined to their rooms. There were no staff members around either, and he suddenly understood how well-connected the team must be to have secured the hotel so efficiently.

As they ran down the service alley past overflowing refuse bins, towards the wider junction at the end, Adams was relieved that there had been no guard at the door. He began to believe that they might even be able to make their escape, when he saw the ominous black shape cruise across in front of them, its huge metal bulk cutting off the end of the alleyway.

It was a large, black panel van, one Adams had glimpsed only for a brief instant as they had been penned in by the sniper in front of the hotel. The race for the rear exit had obviously been anticipated, and the van had moved to cut off their escape.

The vehicle was fifteen feet away, and Adams saw the door pop open, a man leaning out towards them, submachine gun outstretched. Adams – not so sure that this gun's bullets would be made of rubber – grabbed the huge wheeled bin next to him and pushed it down the alley with an almighty heave towards the armed man.

The bin hit the van's door, knocking the man back inside the vehicle, and Adams immediately gestured to Lynn, indicating the fire escape to their left. He heaved her up on top of another bin so she could reach the first rung and she pulled herself up. Then Adams was with her, climbing up towards the roof of the building behind the hotel.

Adams looked down and saw the man below pushing the van door hard, shoving the bin back into the alleyway. The man looked up, enraged, raising his MP5 submachine gun towards them.

But it was too late. They had made it to the roof.

Eldridge was far from happy.

He had not wanted to launch the operation until the rest of his team were there, but then Jacobs had been in contact, telling him to strike now, while they were sure where the pair were. Eldridge could see the logic – strike while the iron was hot, it would be calamitous if the pair escaped again. And yet he had been reluctant to launch the takedown with just nine men. They were all experts of course, but that wasn't the point – nine men were just too few to control a building, and the area surrounding it. It was asking for trouble, and his operational experience should have caused him to tell Jacobs 'no'.

But, Eldridge reflected, you didn't ever tell Jacobs 'no'. Nobody did. And so he had followed his orders like a good soldier, and now this – a complete mission breakdown.

The two targets had escaped from the hotel, and had managed to make their way past the buildings at the back of the Hostal Americano, emerging on to the Huérfanos, the main road that ran parallel to the Compañia de Jesús. Mercifully, Jacobs had managed to get a direct satellite feed from the NSA, and his own intelligence operators in Nevada were now able to direct the Alpha Brigade team on to the targets via aerial observation.

But it was still a complete screw-up in Eldridge's eyes. A chase spilling out across the streets of Santiago was just going to involve more and more people – people whom the Alpha Brigade would end up having to silence.

It seemed that Matthew Adams and Evelyn Edwards had again been underestimated. Two teams of Eldridge's men – men of the fabled Alpha Brigade, the best of the best – had so far failed, and Jacobs had made it more than plain that anything less than outright success would simply not be tolerated.

Grimacing, Eldridge knew he would have to push on. The organization aside, he was not a man who accepted failure.

Eldridge and his men tore out of the block of buildings, hot on the tail of their two targets. He was now being provided with real-time information on the pair's movements, monitored from directly above. He knew it was from an observation satellite in low-earth orbit, and was not surprised that access to such a satellite had been granted so quickly – although relations between the various intelligence services were notoriously bad, Jacobs' organization always had a way of expediting things.

As Eldridge led his team on to Huérfanos, the electronic voice in his earpiece told him that the targets had just entered the Plaza de Brasil, less than five hundred feet directly east. Ignoring the startled look on the faces of the people in the streets as they stared at the heavily armed, masked men sprinting down the palm-lined boulevard, he quickly directed his teammates.

Two would go down each side of the square, racing round to cut off the north and south exits, while the van would drive round to secure the far west exit. Eldridge and his partner would enter the Plaza directly, and make the arrest.

He hoped.

9

THE SIGHT THAT greeted Adams and Lynn as they entered the plaza took their breath away, although they hardly paused, pressing on into the main square, and the centre of the Festival del Barrio Brasil.

Everywhere they looked, something was going on. There was street theatre, mime artists, dance troupes, art exhibitions, acrobats, music bands, surrounded by hundreds, perhaps even thousands, of captivated spectators. The big plaza was also well covered by trees, offering shade and shelter, and it looked the perfect place to get lost in the crowd.

Adams, all too aware that the armed team was probably right behind them, pulled Lynn forward further into the vast mass of people, slowing down to a fast walk so as not to draw attention.

With everything that was going on in the plaza, it seemed an impossibility that they would be seen.

Five hundred feet below the Nevada desert, the technicians monitored the live feeds coming in from the NSA satellites, as well as the Santiago metropolitan CCTV.

They observed as the targets – Charlie One and Charlie Two – entered the crowded plaza. They lost them both momentarily, but then the program software highlighted them, indicating them with a blue light, and the lead technician cross-checked the given location and patched it through to the plaza's CCTV cameras, which then turned and focused on the given targets.

Images then came up of Charlie One and Two, drifting easily through the crowd, an American Indian man and Caucasian woman, late thirties, both carrying bags, looking carefully around them.

As the technician reported the details to the field team, he felt almost guilty about how easy it all was.

Eldridge gasped as he saw the crowds, wondering how in the hell he would ever find the targets in such an environment, but then his earpiece crackled, and the information came through with crystal clarity – they were forty yards south-east into the park, directly in the middle of a group of twenty-seven spectators just to the side of the acrobat display.

He relayed the information to the rest of his team, clicked the safety off his weapon, and stalked forward, ignoring the screams of the people who saw him.

Adams didn't know which was first – the sight of the CCTV camera, all but hidden behind a large palm tree to the north of the square, turning slowly towards them, until it stopped directly facing them, or the sound of screams coming from behind them, the screams one might well imagine coming from people seeing men with guns.

But in an instant he knew they were not hidden – they were trapped. Even now, the exits to the square might be being blocked off, creating a kill zone in the plaza. He knew that whoever was behind what was going on wanted them alive, but he also realized that this might well be *preferential*, not necessarily *essential*. He certainly wasn't going to take any risks with the situation.

Frantically, he scanned the plaza, the crowds, the bands, the dancers, the exhibits, the displays, the—

He stopped dead and, despite himself, a smile broke out across his face.

There was a commotion up ahead, that much Eldridge didn't have to be told, he could see it with his own eyes, something happening in the crowd, a ripple of people, roaring, laughter, shouts.

The voice coming through his earpiece told him that the two targets had left the crowd, heading further south-east, towards what appeared to be an animal display area. They were pushing past the crowds there, approaching the animals, and then – Eldridge shut himself off, not believing what he was hearing.

Then he was there himself, pushing past people so that he could see, and he knew that the voice had been right.

He pulled back, yelling into his microphone to his team-mates. 'Get to the van! Now! They're on the back of a damn horse!'

10

Adams felt Lynn's grip tighten around his waist as he manoeuvred the horse through the rapidly parting crowd.

He knew that the two of them on the back of a horse would only draw attention, their elevated position making them momentarily more of a target, but he hoped that the extra speed they would now have would more than compensate for it. He also didn't expect shots to be fired wildly in such a packed public place, but there were no guarantees of that, and so he dug his heels into the horse's flanks and drove onwards towards the west exit.

From their higher position, they could both see more of what was going on. None of it was good. Lynn had twisted round to scope out what was going on behind, then turned and whispered in his ear, 'Two armed men right behind us.' He was amazed at the control of her voice, damping down any of the horrendous emotions that she must have been going through. At the same time, he had himself identified four policemen at work in the plaza, their attention shifting to the commotion around the animal enclosure.

Adams and Lynn had raced in quickly, Adams jumping lithely on to the back of the unsaddled horse, arm down to pull Lynn up after him. The children who had been feeding the animal hay backed away quickly, and the keeper had tried to grab Adams' leg to pull him off, but Adams had managed to kick him away, controlling the horse through the pressure of his thighs to steer her towards the far exit.

Riding bareback was a difficult skill but it was one that Adams had mastered long ago, and one which he still often demonstrated during his tours. It was made more difficult by having Lynn behind him of course, but not impossible.

He encouraged the horse – a fine chestnut mare – forwards, and she lightly skipped the barrier of the enclosure, starting to pick up pace. The crowd behind were calling for the police, and Adams knew they didn't have long to get out of the plaza.

Tim Renfrew sat watching the plaza exit in his van, submachine gun aimed out of the side window.

He was still under orders to bring them in alive if possible, so he was planning on shooting the horse instead. If the horse went down, the targets would be momentarily helpless, hopefully for as long as it took for Renfrew to get close up and taser them.

He could see the large crowd parting, pandemonium seeming to break out visibly, some people running screaming from the plaza, and then there they were. Charlie One, Charlie Two, and the horse – better make that Charlie Three, Renfrew decided as he aimed down the sight of the MP5.

But the animal was going too quickly, it was charging, galloping, and then all he could see through the sight was the fierce visage of Adams as he rode the horse hard towards the van.

And then they were all there, almost on top of him, and

he had to pull himself back into the van, out of harm's way, as the horse seemed to jump straight at him, hooves scraping the hood.

And then Renfrew looked up, and the horse and the two riders were gone, now on the far side of the van, galloping with the traffic north up the Maturana.

Eldridge was definitely not going to be happy.

Within two minutes the van was full, Eldridge's team all back inside as Renfrew piloted it into the Maturana traffic, following the fugitives north.

Eldridge was getting constant feedback on the horse's location, but it wasn't necessary; out of the windshield ahead of him he could see the animal galloping down the boulevard, Adams and Lynn tight on its back. He could also hear the sound of sirens, converging from the rear and sides.

Damn. It appeared that local law enforcement was getting involved, which might cause a whole host of problems.

'Faster,' he ordered Renfrew.

'Hey, I'm trying,' Renfrew objected as he wove the large van in and out of the constant stream of vehicles. 'There's a hell of a lot of traffic.'

Eldridge looked in the wing mirror, seeing the flashing lights behind them, closing in. 'Ram the other cars off the road if you have to,' he ordered. 'We need to catch that damn horse!'

The horse was nervous, Adams knew, and he couldn't blame her. The road was jammed up, and he had to guide her at a gallop through tons of moving steel, the sound of growling engines and blasting horns being enough to make any animal nervous – humans included, Adams thought as he struggled to control their unconventional transport.

Behind him, Lynn was keeping him posted on what was going on in the street. 'The van's getting closer, even nudging other vehicles out of the way now,' she yelled into his ear. 'Police cars too, coming up fast behind them.'

Adams nodded his head, watching the road. He then turned to Lynn quickly.

'Hold on!' he yelled as he pulled down to the left, the unbridled mare turning with his will, straight across the oncoming traffic of the Compañia de Jesús.

Adams was glad that Lynn couldn't see what was happening in front of them, as a huge Ford RV headed straight for them down the busy street. He leant in close to the mare's neck, coaxing her onwards, until she reared upwards and vaulted the massive vehicle in one smooth motion.

'Matt!' Lynn cried out as the horse landed and then immediately veered sharply around another car. As Adams turned to Lynn, he felt her grip slipping from his waist, and his eyes went wide as he saw her slide straight off the side of the horse.

'She's going!' Eldridge announced to the teammates in the rear of the van as they rounded the corner, forcing their way on to the Compañia de Jesús. 'She's going!'

In the front cabin, Eldridge and Renfrew watched as the horse miraculously vaulted the front of a huge 4x4, then snaked lithely around another car, and then – yes! – as Evelyn Edwards lost her grip on Adams and plummeted towards the hard concrete street below.

* * *

As soon as Adams felt Lynn's grip go, his body reacted instinctively, and instantaneously.

Gripping the mare's thick mane in one hand, he shifted his weight to the side, digging his knees in to tighten his grip, his other arm shooting out towards Lynn.

Just as she left the horse's back, Adams clamped down on her forearm with his powerful grip, leaning halfway down the animal's flank. The horse continued to gallop along the street, and Lynn secured her other hand over Adams' outstretched arm, screaming as she was dragged along, feet banging painfully against the rough asphalt.

Adams grimaced in pain himself as he struggled to pull Lynn back up, still trying to control the unsaddled horse. As he pulled, Lynn's hands clawing up his arm, he glanced forward, gasping as he saw the truck bearing down on them, its huge steel mass threatening to smash straight into both of them.

Lynn followed his eyes, her own going wide as she saw the truck. Adrenalin pouring into both of their bodies, Adams pulled with all his might, Lynn grabbing him tight, as he lifted her higher, higher, until finally she was up and Adams swung her on to the back of the horse once more, pulling his own body back out of the way as the truck blared its horn and passed them, just inches away.

In the van, Eldridge at least had the satisfaction of knowing that the police were no longer on his tail – Jacobs must have somehow called them off.

It was a blessing not to have to worry about the city's own police force; if it had been planned from the start to be multi-agency, that would have been different. But if additional elements started to get involved once the mission was already in motion, then things would definitely get screwed up.

More screwed up, Eldridge corrected himself, because of course things were already screwed up royally. The escaping targets had not only got through the intersection with the Ricardo Cumming unscathed, weaving their way almost magically through the oncoming vehicles, their unlikely transport had now disappeared from view entirely. Luckily, the voice through his earpiece was able to update him with an instant fix, informing him that the horse had taken a sharp right up Arz González, towards Catedral. Unfortunately, it also seemed that the distance between them was steadily increasing.

'Come on,' he urged Renfrew. 'Can't this heap of junk go any faster?'

Renfrew was ignoring Eldridge at this point, concentrating with everything he had just to keep the unwieldy van on the road. But he was determined to catch them. He'd never be able to live it down if he failed to catch a horse, driving a vehicle with a five-litre V8 under the hood. But the horse did have its advantages; it was far more manoeuvrable than a motor vehicle, for a start, able to weave in and out of traffic with ease. But surely the horse would begin to tire at some stage, and then Renfrew would have them.

As the horse pushed on towards the end of Arz González, it seemed to slow. Was it getting tired already? Renfrew gunned the engine harder.

And then something happened that caused both him and Eldridge to gasp out loud.

*　*　*

Adams saw it from a distance, and it took him only seconds to make the decision.

The entrance to the Cumming metro station was right there ahead of them, across the Catedral that transected the end of Arz González.

He slowed the mare as they reached the end, checking the traffic on the Catedral and, seeing that it was mercifully light, speeded up straight across the street, over the sidewalk, and down the steep stairs that led to Santiago's underground rail system.

11

THE METRO DE Santiago is South America's most extensive metro system. Its five lines have more than a hundred stations and over a hundred kilometres of track; servicing over two million passengers per day, it is the city's lifeblood.

As Adams led the loyal mare on to the platform, past the screaming, pointing, awed spectators, he was pretty sure that this would be the first time a horse had been on the tracks. He didn't even know if the horse would be willing to leave the platform and make the jump between the steel rails, but he knew he had to take the chance – the rest of his plan depended upon making it to the tunnels.

Lynn holding tightly to him, he pulled the horse in short on the edge of the platform, and then they jumped from the safety of the platform to the tracks beneath.

The operators in the Nevada intelligence section were having their work cut out for them.

Following a horse down city streets via CCTV and satellite imagery was fairly easy, but now the horse – and nobody in the control room had *any* idea how the rider was managing to do it – had gone down into Santiago's subway system.

The chief technician had to immediately hack into the

city's municipal transport department's mainframe, and hive off its surveillance camera footage.

By the time he had got the raw footage feeding through to his own monitors, the only image from the platform camera showed the back legs of the horse taking off at full gallop down the east tunnel towards Santa Ana.

Reluctantly, he reached for the telephone.

The reports came through to Eldridge thick and fast.

Orders were given to the transport police to immediately halt the trains on the system, and send men down the tunnels to flush the horse and riders out. Meanwhile, Eldridge was urging Renfrew faster on down Catedral towards Santa Ana station, where they planned on intercepting the pair and putting an end to their crazy race across the city once and for all.

Minutes later, Eldridge was leading his team down the stairs of Santa Ana subway station four at a time, weapons shouldered, safety catches off.

At the same time, crowds of people were surging the opposite way up the stairs towards the exit, and Eldridge didn't know if it was because the transport police were evacuating the subway or because of something else.

The team hit the bottom of the stairs at a fast run, and Eldridge could have sworn he heard the whinnying of a horse coming from round the corner.

Heading for the westbound platform, the team passed the last few stragglers as they streamed along the modern, tiled corridor and eventually turned through a grand archway on to the platform itself.

'Ready!' Eldridge called, and the team raised their

weapons in unison, 9mm submachine guns aimed straight ahead at the dark tunnel opposite them, ready to shoot the horse the moment it came through. If the two targets weren't instantly electrocuted on the track's rails as they fell from the dead animal, his men would then race forward and subdue them.

The men adjusted their positions as they heard the horse whinny again from just inside the tunnel, seeing its vague outline coming towards them, and exhaled steadily, each man holding his breath to make his shots accurate.

And then the chestnut mare burst into the light of the platform, still coming forward at full gallop, racing between the steel rail lines, a beautiful, impressive beast, its coat glistening in the fluorescent lighting, muscles rippling down her flanks.

'Hold your fire!' Eldridge yelled as the horse continued past them, racing at full speed, along the track and through into the next tunnel, until she disappeared again from sight.

The horse was an impressive sight, but there had been something missing. Something vital.

'Where the hell are Adams and Edwards?' Eldridge yelled in exasperation.

Adams had stopped the horse halfway down the tunnel, dismounted with Lynn, and then slapped the animal on the flank to send her towards the next platform. As he watched her gallop off down the tracks, he offered a prayer to the animal spirits, thanking them for delivering the magnificent animal to them, and asking for her safety.

Adams was sure that there had to be an access point somewhere along the track, a crew hatch that would lead to a service area. The tunnel was dark, though, lit only by dim red emergency lights, and his night vision was nowhere near as good as it had once been.

It was Lynn who spotted the steel door, over on the left, in the shadows.

Adams raced over and levered it open. Checking the tunnel once again for signs of pursuit, he took Lynn by the hand and pushed through into the dark service corridor beyond.

Their eyes finally adjusting to the dark, Adams decided to leave the lights off, unwilling to draw further attention to themselves. But within less than two minutes, he stopped dead.

'People up ahead,' he whispered urgently to Lynn, 'coming towards the corridor. They'll be in here soon.'

Quickly, he pulled her back down the corridor, several feet beyond where they had just come. In the dark, Adams had noticed a row of lockers and metal cupboards lining the wall, and now both he and Lynn pulled at the handles frantically, trying to find one that was open.

'They're at the door!' Adams warned, even as Lynn managed to get a door open. They pushed into the confined space, pulling the aluminium door shut behind them as quietly as they could.

The cupboard was used for cleaning products, and was full of brooms, mops and chemicals. But there was enough room for them, and they both watched through the slats in the door as the lights went on.

After a few moments of adjusting to the blinding illumination, they could make out a group of uniformed police – probably the municipal transport police Adams realized – racing down the corridor towards the tunnel.

Adams didn't know whether the horse would have been found yet – the Santa Ana platform was still some distance away from where they had dismounted, but she might have managed it if she was going at full speed – and therefore didn't know whether it was already suspected that the pair had left the tunnel via the corridor, or whether the police were just accessing the tunnel through a direct route. Either way, it would now certainly appear to the police – and whoever they reported to – that the targets were not in the service corridor, which would hopefully give him and Lynn some breathing space to make their escape.

They waited until the steel access door to the tunnel swung shut behind the men, and then opened the cupboard door, stalking carefully down the now brightly lit corridor, ready for action at any moment.

They emerged at street level less than ten minutes later, mercifully only having to hide twice more, Adams' returning senses giving them just enough time to react.

The exit took them out on to Catedral, just a hundred yards from the intersection with Brasil.

There was minimal CCTV coverage in this area, but both Adams and Lynn were now both fully aware of the danger of satellite surveillance and immediately ducked under the cover of a grocery store awning, pretending to look at the varied fruit on display.

'We need to find a car and get out of the city,' Lynn said decisively. So far, it had been her ex-husband who had been leading the way, and although she was more than grateful – it was what she had contacted him for in the first place, of course – she was not the kind of person who dealt easily with being helpless. Taking charge now would at least let her salvage something of her sense of worth.

She checked her backpack nervously, relieved – and amazed, given what they had just been through – that it was still there.

'Just what I was thinking,' Adams agreed. 'But where do we get one?'

'Right here,' Lynn answered instantly.

'What?' Adams asked in surprise, but as he saw the excited glint in the eyes of his ex-wife, he knew that her plan would be a good one.

In the control centre, deep beneath the Nevada air force base, the technicians were frantic.

They had entered the search parameters – platforms, tracks, service entrances and exits, all possible locations where the two targets could have emerged on to the streets of Santiago – and they were now monitoring each and every one of these potential areas.

The problem was that it had taken a number of minutes for the request for the satellite redirects to go through from their own organization to the NSA, and from the NSA to the National Reconnaissance Office which actually operated the satellites.

If the targets had exited the tunnels in that time and made it far enough, such a direct search would reveal nothing.

But there was still the city-wide CCTV system, the facial recognition software, and the physical eyes on the ground. If the order was given, every government agency in Santiago could be instructed to find Matthew Adams and Evelyn

Edwards. The municipal police, the national police, the paramilitary carabineros, all of these and more could be mobilized in the search.

But for now, the technicians would continue to monitor what they could, and hope for a result.

'Damn!' Eldridge exclaimed violently, punching a marble pillar in the Santa Ana foyer with a gloved hand.

Adams and Edwards were nowhere to be seen – not in the tunnels, not on the platforms, not in the service areas and, according to the information coming through his earpiece, they had yet to be picked up by any surveillance on the streets of the city.

Eldridge knew the pair could still be in the underground system – a thorough search of the labyrinth could literally take days – and started to realize that his chances of making an arrest were growing slimmer every minute.

It was an hour later when he learnt that the hunt may have already moved beyond the confines of the city.

The proprietors of the grocery store on Catedral had been found by a couple of customers – unharmed, but gagged and tied up behind the counter – and they had reported it immediately to the local police.

It seemed that the owners of the store, who lived in the apartment above, had had a car parked behind the premises, which had been stolen by the fugitives. An instant APB had been put on the vehicle, and Eldridge learnt soon after that the car had made it as far north as Mercedarios in Conchali, before being abandoned. It was unknown what had happened to the pair since – they might have stolen another car, gone back on to the subway, or even caught a surface train or bus out of the city.

The technicians back at base were running images of the escaped pair through the surveillance camera footage of all train, metro and bus stations but had so far found nothing. Information from traffic cameras, including images of the drivers as they passed speed check areas, was also being analysed, but Eldridge didn't hold out much hope.

The game was going to continue, and it was certainly going to be an interesting one.

12

Lynn checked her backpack again as she and Adams reclined in the back of the large truck. Everything was still there, mercifully intact. Evidence of the man they had found in the ice, a man forty thousand years old. A man people were willing to kill for.

As she turned to Adams, who sat next to her, it troubled her deeply that he was now a target too. He knew about the body – and even if he didn't, they would assume he did anyway – and he was therefore in as much danger as she was.

They had found the truck at a roadside stop just outside the city limits of Santiago. They had ditched the first stolen car, and then Adams had hot-wired another from a parking lot just two blocks over. They had then driven this one out of the city, careful to obscure their faces whenever they noticed traffic or speed cameras of any kind, aware that such images could be fed back and analysed. The resources of their enemy seemed truly enormous.

They had driven the stolen vehicle north to Colina, a fairly large town fifteen miles north of Santiago. There, they had parked the car in a secure underground parking lot, paying for a week's stay, sure that it wouldn't be noticed by the authorities until they were long gone from the area.

They had then hiked to a truck stop, bought lunch and

got chatting to a friendly driver, shipping computer parts up to a factory in Copiapó, four hundred miles further north. For a little *mordida*, the local term for a bit of friendly bribery which meant literally 'the bite', the driver agreed to their travelling with him. It was no skin off his nose, he explained, and he was grateful for the extra cash.

'So where are we headed?' Adams asked Lynn finally.

Thus far, it had only been clear that she wanted to travel north. 'Peru,' she said. 'A place called Nazca.'

'Nazca?' Adams asked. 'As in the Nazca lines?' When Lynn nodded in reply, he asked, 'Why there?'

The Nazca lines were mysterious etchings on the desert floor, of such incredible size that they were only clearly visible from the air. A collection of straight lines, animals, geometrical figures and birds up to three hundred metres in size, it is believed they were scratched into the desert *pampa* over two thousand years ago. Theories on the purpose of the lines included it being a vast astronomical calendar, or a collection of ritual walkways connected to a water or fertility cult, or a representation of the dreams of a drug-taking shaman; some even believed them to be extraterrestrial landing strips.

Adams had heard of them but he had no idea why they should head there. He had no problem with Peru itself – if they were trying to get back to the US, Peru was as good a transit point as any – but he knew Lynn must have a good reason for travelling to Nazca specifically.

'Fabricio Baranelli,' Lynn answered cryptically.

'Who?'

'I guess I should say *Professor* Fabricio Baranelli,' Lynn corrected herself. 'He is the top man in his field, after all.'

'And that field is?' Adams asked.

'Archaeology. He's on an expedition at the moment, mapping the area. I think he's developing some sort of new theory about the geoglyphs there.'

'Geoglyphs?'

'The lines, the marks in the earth. I don't know exactly what he's working on, but it's important.'

'And why do we want to see him?' Adams asked, still confused.

'I know him from Harvard,' Lynn explained. 'I've known him for years, and he's a dear friend. He's also the only person I know in South America who might be able to help us. The fact that he's digging around a major, protected archaeological site means he must be plugged in to the government, he must have friends in the right places. I'm hoping he might be able to use his contacts, maybe get us back into the US.'

Adams considered the matter. He had been wondering how they were going to get back to America. He was resourceful but he was having difficulty working out a plan for getting Lynn back. Her passport would certainly be compromised by now, of that he was sure. In fact, he didn't even know if he could trust his own anymore; it was feasible that the enemy might have tracked his route from Pine Ridge, discovered the passport he had been using, and flagged it up. That left crossing borders on foot, which he wasn't sure Lynn would manage, given the vast distances involved, or using other forms of transport, each of which presented their own problems. These methods were all slow as well, which gave the enemy more time to track them down.

Baranelli was an outside bet, but he might offer them something – it certainly helped to have government contacts. He might also have close media contacts, which they could perhaps use to get the evidence in Lynn's backpack out into the public domain.

'OK,' he said. 'This truck will take us as far as Copiapó, which still puts us about six hundred miles away from Nazca, with the Peruvian border in the middle. Any plans for that?' he asked, with more sarcasm than he wished.

Lynn didn't mind a bit – she realized what a position she had put him in, pulling him out of his own life and putting him in mortal danger. A bit of sarcasm was neither here not there in comparison. She smiled at him warmly, taking his hand in hers. 'Hey,' she said, looking into his dark, brown eyes, finding herself lost in them for a moment, hypnotized by his soul. She blinked out of it, and carried on. 'I'm sorry I got you into this, I really am. And I want to thank you for everything you've done for me. I owe you my life.'

Adams held her gaze for a time, then turned away, embarrassed by his own perceived failings. They had survived, but he had hardly put in a faultless performance.

He looked up into her eyes again, and Lynn could see the earnestness, the honesty, in the man she once loved. 'I'd do it again, any time you asked.'

She smiled, nodded her head, and wiped a tear from her eye. 'I know,' she whispered, holding his hand to her heart, 'I know.' She kissed his hand, looked up at him again. 'You want to know my plan for getting to Peru? *You.* I have faith in you, Matt. I need *you* to get us there.'

13

'How are things progressing?'

Jacobs heard the words loud and clear but did not have an immediate answer. What was he supposed to tell them? That he was currently pulling all the strings he could, using the full resources of the US government, just to hunt down two normal, everyday, inconsequential human beings? What would they think of him and his organization then?

But if he lied, would they know? And if they *did* know, what would their reaction be? Jacobs was not in fear for his physical safety but if they reneged on their promises as a result of the continued failure of the Alpha Brigade, it would be worse than torture and death to him.

But, he considered, their resources were necessarily diluted by distance, and as a result they needed him just as much as he needed them – perhaps even more so at this point in time.

And so Jacobs decided to give them the truth, although not a complete explanation.

'The targets are still at large,' he said finally. 'We are close to reacquiring them, however, and there is no indication that the information has gone any further thus far. And even if details of the find *are* eventually revealed, we are confident we can downplay the evidence. There shouldn't be a problem. Especially,' Jacobs continued, building in confidence, 'as the latest reports from CERN indicate that we are about to enter the testing phase for the device. Even if knowledge of your existence, and our involvement, was now made public, it would be too late to matter any more anyway.'

'You are wrong,' the voice countered immediately. 'Anomalies *always* matter. Unknown variables can disrupt things beyond comprehension. Everything needs to be *perfect*. We thought you understood this.'

'This is *life*,' Jacobs shot back, trying to rein in his frustration. 'Things *are* sometimes imperfect, you just have to deal with them the best way you can.'

'This is not how one of us would handle things,' came back the instant response. 'We do not accept imperfection.'

The connection was terminated and Jacobs sat back in his leather chair and took a sip of water from the thick glass on the desk in front of him.

So they didn't accept imperfection. Well, that was absolutely fine.

Neither did he.

'Are you OK?' Lynn asked Adams from the passenger seat of the small, twenty-year-old Fiat.

Adams was all too aware of how he must look. Sweat was rolling down his brow, he had a ghostly pallor, and he was shivering uncontrollably. The absence of sleep, combined with the adrenalin and excitement of the past few days, was becoming intolerable, and it was a lot harder than he had anticipated.

Since the incident in the desert all those years before, he

had been unwilling to talk about his problems. He had at first refused to accept he even had a problem, and even when he had finally admitted it, he had never considered asking for help. He realized now that this was unrealistic bravado and for the first time in his life he wanted help. He wanted to just crawl up into a ball and *cry* for help. But he also knew this was never going to happen.

'I think I'm coming down with a fever,' he lied.

'Do you want me to drive?'

Adams thought about it for a few moments. Concentrating on the road was hurting his head but at least it was giving him something to do. Sitting in the passenger seat, consumed by self-pity, would probably be worse.

'No thanks,' he replied, putting a bit more life into his voice. 'I'll be fine. Best I have something to do, you know?'

Lynn looked at him, as if really seeing him for the first time since their reunion the day before. 'You've changed since we were together,' she said finally.

If you only knew, Adams thought. 'How do you mean?' he asked instead.

Again, Lynn considered the matter. 'I don't know . . . Before, you seemed so full of life . . . Larger than life, really. Now you seem more . . . subdued.' She smiled apologetically at him, sorry to be so negative but curious about the change in the man she had once loved so much.

'Life does that to you eventually, I guess,' Adams replied, knowing as he said it that it was such comments that had made Lynn notice the change in the first place. 'But it's probably just the fever getting me down, you know,' he recovered quickly.

Seconds of silence passed into minutes as they continued

along Interstate Five, through the vast expanse of the Chilean desert plains.

They had reached Copiapó late the previous night, and had paid cash for the local bus to Caldera on the coast. Once in the small town, they had asked around for a car to buy, and found a willing seller just minutes away. The car was no piece of art, had no air conditioning, and was barely roadworthy, but it seemed able to go from A to B. Which was all they could ask, considering the price they paid. It was also unlikely to be traced until they were long gone. Unless their pursuers tracked them to Caldera and then went door to door until they found someone who had recently sold a car, they figured they would be relatively safe.

They'd stocked up on food, drink and jerrycans of gasoline, unsure how regular gas stations were going to be, and then started the long trek north. The road bordered the Pacific Ocean for much of its length, and both Adams and Lynn were amazed by the beauty of the route. Eventually, the coastal mountains rose up, and the road started to turn north-east, into the vast wilderness of the Atacama Desert.

They were halfway to Nazca now, and just a hundred miles away from the Peruvian border.

Adams decided to forget about the previous conversation and get on to another topic. He was also starting to feel drowsy, and needed the conversation to keep him awake. 'So tell me about the body.'

He had seen the photographs that Lynn and her colleague had secretly taken of the body when it was still half-entombed in ice, before the arrival of the military team. But he knew she must have seen more when the body had finally been extracted, and with everything that had been going on, they hadn't really had a good chance to talk about it.

'It was . . . strange, really,' Lynn began. 'From our initial discovery, it seemed that the body was a man just like modern man. He was in a depression at the bottom of a ridge, which meant that the ice hadn't crushed the body but kept it perfectly preserved, we think for about forty thousand years.'

'And he looked normal?'

'As if he'd been buried there last year. That's what makes it unique.'

'So what do we think humans looked like forty thousand years ago?'

'Well, that's something else I've been researching since getting to Santiago. Apparently, in terms of body proportions, we probably looked almost exactly the same as we do today, we've changed very little since the first *Homo sapiens* came on the scene about two hundred thousand years ago.'

'And facially?'

'Our skulls were a little different, a mix of both human and Neanderthal elements. Frontal flattening, a larger jaw, very large upper molars. So, facially, we would have looked very different.'

'And yet the body you found was the same as ours?'

'Exactly the same. But it's more what we found *with* the body than the body itself.'

'You mentioned some sort of unusual clothing back at the hotel.'

Lynn nodded her head. 'Yes, and Jeff . . .' she paused as she thought of her colleagues, remembering them. 'Well, he used to work for the National Security Agency, and he'd never seen anything like it before. And then when that military team pulled the body out, there were other things there with it.'

Adams glanced sideways at her, fascinated. 'Like what?'

'Major Daley wasn't happy having us there and he and his men made sure we didn't see too much. But the boots, for instance – they had some sort of attachment to the sides, definitely mechanical, perhaps electrical even. And then they found something else, which Tommy and I both thought looked like a motorized sled of some kind.'

Adams thought about this for some time, the desert road streaming past in one long, white blur.

'If you forget about the dating, what would you think had happened? What would the man have been doing there?'

Lynn thought for a few moments. 'Cold-weather gear, motorized sled, it would suggest he was perhaps part of some sort of Antarctic research team.' She paused. 'Maybe even just like us.'

'Could the dating be wrong?' Adams asked next.

'Possibly,' Lynn answered straight away, the thought having been constantly on her mind. 'But we were all as sure as you can be, without taking the ice samples away and analysing them in a laboratory – which is what Major Daley and his team were supposed to be doing.'

'So,' Adams said at length as he mopped cold sweat from his eyes, 'it seems most likely that the body was part of some current military or government research team, was buried there recently, and the forty-thousand-year dating is inaccurate. If they were out there testing some new cold-weather gear, it would also explain why there's been a cover-up.'

'Killing a whole team of NASA researchers just to cover up cold-weather equipment and clothing tests?' Lynn said in disbelief.

'If you'd said the dating was a hundred per cent accurate, I wouldn't consider the possibility,' Adams said. 'But it's not a hundred per cent, and even if it's as high as ninety-nine per cent, I'd still think that the one per cent chance that the body was buried more recently is the most likely.'

Lynn wanted to respond but couldn't. The fact was, he was right. In all the drama and fear of the past few days, and the excitement of the discovery, a more down-to-earth, mundane explanation had been pushed to the back of her mind. But the logical side of her understood that the more mundane explanations were, more often than not, the correct ones.

But did such an explanation make sense in light of the subsequent reaction? A team of scientists killed, the body stolen, emails intercepted, her ex-husband targeted by inter-rogators, hit squads searching South America – it all seemed too much just to cover up some new government technology. Somehow, a discovery that redefined human existence seemed more of a justification for what she had been through and the lives that had been lost.

'Well,' Adams said, 'I guess we'll have a better idea when we get the data analysed back in the States.'

Lynn nodded her head, deep in thought. 'You're right. Let's just make sure we get there in one piece.'

Eldridge met the rest of his men at Santiago's SCL Airport, where the Lear jet landed on the private runway towards the rear of the complex.

He boarded the plane alone, his nine other teammates still working with the police and government agencies back in the city, trying to come up with a movement profile for the two fugitives.

Out of the twenty-four men on board, Eldridge retained a group of four, sending the other twenty off to liaise with the existing men in Santiago. He then declared the Lear jet his new operations centre, and ordered the plane to be refuelled and ready for take-off immediately. On the orders of Stephen Jacobs, the private jet had been specially modified to accept aerial refuelling, and this was promised to be immediately available from the Chilean Air Force, enabling Eldridge to stay in the air indefinitely.

He felt that he needed to be able to react to incoming information instantly – from the air, he could get to anywhere on the continent relatively quickly. If he was stuck on the ground, it would double or even triple his response time. And with every hour that passed, every hour that Adams and Edwards were out there, the risk to the organization grew.

The surveillance footage from traffic cameras was being fed back slowly, and Jacobs was piping it straight to the supercomputers at the NSA, from where it was then sent to his own technicians in Nevada.

There was nothing so far, but Eldridge knew they couldn't have gone too far. Both of the fugitives' passports had been red-lighted, and if they were used, an arrest would be made instantly. Photo surveillance at all airports, ferry ports and transnational bus and train stations was being constantly analysed, and there had been no hits so far. This indicated two things to Eldridge. The first was that the fugitives were still in Chile, somewhere within her borders. The second was that they were using the roads, probably driving stolen vehicles or hitchhiking.

Eldridge put in requests for the national police and the Carabineros to stop suspect vehicles and check IDs, as well as to check on stories of hitchhikers. He also requested all information on recently stolen vehicles to be fed directly to him.

As he studied the maps of Chile's road system, he figured that there were again two options: they would either take their time along the slow, empty back roads, in the belief that they would be less likely to be seen; or they would take the major roads, hoping to blast along them and use speed as their ally, putting as much distance between them and their pursuers as possible.

Eldridge ordered detailed satellite analysis of the vehicles travelling along the country's back roads, the NSA's systems programmed to report any anomalous driving behaviour, and then put in another call, direct to the Chief of National Police.

'Señor Vasquez,' Eldridge began, not needing to give his own name, 'I'm afraid I have another request.' With the apparent full backing of the US government, it was more of an order than a request, but niceties had to be observed.

'What is it you want, my friend?' Vasquez replied obsequiously.

'I want roadblocks,' Eldridge replied. 'On every interstate, at hundred-kilometre intervals.'

There would be no escape, Eldridge promised himself. *No escape.*

14

Adams didn't see the roadblock until it was almost too late, so tired that his eyes closed involuntarily every so often, travelling blind for dangerous distances before his vision returned.

It was hard to judge distance against the desert backdrop but he guessed the roadblock was set up about a mile further down the long, straight highway. From this distance, he could make out what looked like three police cars straddling the interstate, waving down vehicles to check their documents.

'We've got a problem,' Adams told Lynn, nudging her awake from her own sleep.

Opening her eyes, she instantly took in the sight ahead of her. 'Oh no,' she moaned. She felt the car slow as Adams took his foot off the gas.

Adams wasn't using the brakes, not wanting to draw attention to the car by slowing suddenly, but he did want to slow the car enough to figure out a plan of action.

'What are we going to do?' Lynn asked, and Adams struggled to come up with an answer. If they stopped, it would be instantly suspicious, and the police would immediately come to them. If they got to the checkpoint, their identification would almost certainly get them instantly arrested. And Adams wasn't sure if the little Fiat was capable of smashing through the roadblock.

'I guess we're just going to have to make it up as we go along,' he said finally.

Police Sergeant Manuel Vega sat on the hood of the lead car, chatting to his men. Sitting out in the middle of the Atacama waiting for vehicles to come along was nobody's idea of fun. The temperature out in the desert could drop well below zero, and although it was the middle of the day, the men were all starting to feel the effects of the cold.

Stamping their feet to keep warm, one of the officers suddenly pointed down the road at the small car coming towards them.

Vega slid off the hood and clapped his hands together. 'Oh joy,' he said, feeling nothing of the sort. 'Another one. Still,' he joked to his men, 'at least we get overtime, eh?'

As Adams rolled the car to a stop in front of the lead police car, he rolled his window down and cold air spilled into the cabin. The sweat started to freeze on his body.

He watched with interest at the reaction of the police chief and his men. First there was total disinterest; then, as they realized the car held a Caucasian woman and an Amerindian man, there was a flutter of concern, a narrowing of the eyes, and then rapid movements as orders were given.

Adams saw the police chief check an A4 sheet of paper, presumably with their pictures on, then bark orders at his men, who then surrounded the vehicle, weapons drawn.

'Get out of the car, hands on your head!' shouted the sergeant. 'Now!'

'Just wait a minute,' Adams said reasonably from his place behind the wheel. 'Do you know who we are?'

'Terrorists, damn it!' the police sergeant screamed. 'Get out of the car, now!'

Perfect, thought Adams. Branding people as terrorists was a typical move if you wanted things to happen quickly. Tell people there's a criminal on the loose, and the wheels will turn very slowly, if at all. Tell them it's a terrorist, and the reaction couldn't be more different.

Vega watched the pair in the car with eagle eyes. He couldn't believe it was his team that had caught them! Terrorists, in his country! And *he* had caught them! He was going to be rewarded for this, that was for sure. A promotion was a certainty, possibly with a presidential citation to follow.

But why was the man so calm? And why was he asking questions?

The man's next words caused even more confusion.

'You'll know what we are carrying then,' he said, a smug smile on his face.

What did he mean? Whatever it was, it didn't matter. 'Get out of the car! This is your last warning! Get out now, or we will open fire!'

And then the woman moved, her hands raising something up to the windscreen for them to look at. What was it?

He peered forward, trying to make it out.

It was a . . . a test tube?

Lynn held one of the DNA samples of the frozen body up to the windscreen. She had been reluctant to show it, but Adams had argued that if they were arrested, the samples would be lost anyway, and so she had agreed to go along with his off-the-cuff plan.

'*Bacillus anthracis*,' she heard Adams tell the nervous police sergeant through the open window. 'Anthrax.'

Anthrax? Vega's head started to spin. He'd been told nothing about *this*! But there it was, something in a cold-storage test tube, just like you'd find in a laboratory.

Would it be anthrax? Vega just didn't know. What else could it be? Why would terrorists be carrying test tubes of anything, if it wasn't a weapon of some sort?

'Once I let go, and you gentlemen breathe in the spores,' he heard the man continue, 'you'll start to feel the effects by later this afternoon. It'll feel like flu to start with, then get rapidly worse, your body's systems collapsing until – in maybe a week's time, if you're lucky – it progresses to lethal haemorrhagic mediastinitis.' The man flashed him a smile. 'Fatal in ninety per cent of cases.'

It took less than thirty seconds for Vega to make up his mind.

'Drop your weapons,' the sergeant ordered his men, and both Adams and Lynn sighed with relief. They'd bought it, hook, line and sinker.

As the policemen lowered their weapons, Adams progressed to phase two of the plan.

'Now put your guns on the ground and step back two paces.'

The police sergeant barked a translation of the order to his men, and they all did as they were told. Passionate about their work as they might otherwise be, the threat of infection with a lethal bioweapon was more than enough to ensure their compliance.

Adams and Lynn slowly stepped out of the car, Lynn keeping the fearsome test tube held up where everyone could see it. After assessing the assembled men, Adams picked two of the most promising candidates. 'You two,' he said, gesturing at them, 'handcuff the rest of the team.'

The sergeant again translated, and the handcuffing was quickly done, the fear writ large across the faces of the officers. The handcuffed men were told to lie face down on the ground, and Adams turned back to the two policemen who had done the handcuffing.

'Now,' he said to them, 'take off all your clothes.'

Like many things in life, the discovery of the handcuffed police officers was down to sheer bad luck. Adams and Lynn were only sixty miles from the border; if the policemen had been undiscovered for only an hour, then the two of them would have made it in their stolen police car, their borrowed uniforms allowing them to cross over into Peru unquestioned. On the empty desert roads of the Atacama, it was certainly feasible. Traffic here was scarce, and it certainly wasn't unheard of for hours to pass without any vehicles whatsoever.

Adams had taken the police team fifty yards off the main road and hidden them behind a small copse of trees. He had considered taking the vehicles off the road as well but had decided against this, as he couldn't be sure if the area was being monitored by satellite. It was unlikely such units would be zoomed in, but the absence of vehicles at a requested roadblock would certainly be noticed. He had just prayed that no driver would come across the empty vehicles in the next hour or so.

But it was not to be. Not more than twenty minutes after Adams and Lynn had accelerated away in the sergeant's police car, a small livestock truck came trundling slowly up the road. The driver had slowed even further, and then stopped. After waiting in his vehicle a few moments, he had got out and wandered over to the first car. Seeing nobody, he had then checked the second police car, and then the Fiat. Still nobody. Not a soul.

The driver stood there wondering what to do when he caught motion out of the corner of his eye. His head turned, and he first of all saw the copse of trees further back from the road. And then he saw the movement again – a leg, kicking out from behind one of the trees.

Nervous, he had grabbed the shotgun from the passenger footwell of his truck and tracked slowly across the dirty scrubland towards the trees. Under a minute later he was at the copse, rounding the first tree, shotgun at the ready.

His eyes widened in disbelief as he saw the six police officers, bound back to back on the ground, screaming silently at him through their gags.

Once freed, Vega found that the police radios had been broken. Likewise, their personal cellphones had all been smashed to pieces by the crazed terrorists.

Upon quizzing the truck driver, it appeared that he had a cellphone, and Vega quickly commandeered it, finally managing to get through to headquarters.

'We have a major situation here,' he told his commander breathlessly. Terrorists were on the loose with anthrax.

* * *

Eldridge heard the conversation between Sergeant Vega and his captain in virtual real-time, and cursed his own bad luck. They were low on fuel, and were holding position as they waited for aerial refuelling. The refuelling aircraft would be with them within the next ten minutes, but the delivery of fuel would take a further hour. During this time, they would continue to head towards the fugitives from their current position due east of Santiago, but at a seriously reduced speed.

Given the current speed of the stolen police car, Eldridge knew that it was unlikely that he and his onboard team would make it to the border in time. His other men, currently scattered at various points around central Chile, would also not be able to make it in time, which meant he was going to have to trust the local authorities to pick the pair up.

But what was this about anthrax? The police sergeant had said that the pair had shown them a glass, freeze-packed test tube, which they claimed contained weaponized anthrax.

Did they? Eldridge thought it highly doubtful. Where the hell would they have got such a thing? Did they have contacts in Chile? Or did Adams use his old government contacts and get some before he came here? But if that was the case, how would he have got it past customs?

The fact that it was in a test tube was also strange, given that weaponized anthrax was designed to be used in aerosol form. But they nevertheless had a test tube, which led Eldridge to consider whether—

Damn!

What if Edwards had collected samples from the body? She always seemed to have a backpack with her, and as

Eldridge cast his mind back to the Antarctic, he realized that it was the same one she had boarded the helicopter with. Why the hell hadn't he picked up on that before?

Thinking back further, he remembered their conversation in the dining room of the Matrix base camp.

'So since talking to Atkinson last night, you didn't go back out to the body until this morning?' he had asked her, pretending at the time to be Major Daley of the US Army Engineers.

Edwards had looked at him, and then shaken her head. 'No,' she had replied. 'Samuel ordered us to return here and stay until you guys arrived.'

Eldridge tried to examine his memory of that day, extract the image of Edwards from the recesses of his mind, examine it for any evidence of lying. It was a hopeless task, he knew, and yet he tried, searching his image of her face for any waver, anything that hinted at dishonesty.

But he already knew the answer. Of course they had been back out. What scientist wouldn't? It hadn't seemed an issue at the time, as Eldridge knew he was going to kill them all anyway, but it was now apparent that he hadn't given it enough consideration at the time. Yet another mistake.

It wasn't one he would bother Jacobs with yet. If the pair was stopped at the border, he would be there within another hour, and the whole sorry incident could be wrapped up.

But they had to be caught first, and so Eldridge immediately contacted Nevada, who in turn ordered the NSA to retask the necessary satellite to provide real-time footage of the escaping police car. He next ensured that the border patrols at the checkpoint at Arica were on full alert, and reinforcements from the Chilean military were en route, just in case.

Talking to the border patrol, it transpired that they had a Lynx scout helicopter on loan from the British Army Air Corps, and Eldridge immediately gave the order for it to fly south on Interstate 5 to intercept the fugitives if possible, or at least to provide close surveillance.

Part of him was tempted to let the pair get to the border, where more forces would be ranged against them, but another part told him that they had lost them several times already, and waiting was no longer an option – the fugitives had been located, Eldridge knew where they were *right now*, and the border patrol forces had the capability of getting to them within the next ten minutes.

Yes, it was definitely a good idea to send in the helicopter, and send it in hard. Eldridge called back to make sure the men aboard the chopper were well-armed.

And then he called the authorities in Peru, to warn them what was happening over the border. And to get them mobilized.

Just in case.

15

THEY HEARD IT long before they saw it, the slow, steady *whump, whump, whump* of helicopter rotors, high in the sky above them.

Lynn turned to Adams. 'How far are we?'

Adams glanced quickly at the odometer. 'Just twenty miles,' he answered. 'Damn.'

Somebody must have discovered the roadblock cops and called it in, or else they must have escaped somehow. Either way, the border had been alerted, which meant they were going to have to come up with a new plan, and quickly.

He turned to Lynn. 'Any ideas?' he asked hopefully.

'It depends what they're up to,' she said, craning her neck up to look through the windscreen, catching just a glimpse of the Lynx scout helicopter above them. 'If they're just monitoring us, they'll follow us to the border, where the police will arrest us. We can use the anthrax ploy again, but I don't know if it'll work a second time. If the helicopter crew has been ordered to make the arrest, though, it'll have to land at some stage . . .'

Adams nodded his head, following her reasoning instantly. Given Lynn's last experience in a helicopter, he hoped she wouldn't panic. He turned to her. 'Are you sure?' he asked gently.

She nodded her head. 'It's our only chance.'

Adams returned his gaze to the road, determined. 'Then we've got to get that chopper to land.'

What was this? Captain Marco Delongis saw the police car on the highway below his helicopter brake to a screeching halt, then watched as the two fugitives leapt from the vehicle.

What was the man holding? Delongis narrowed his eyes. *Pistol!*

He fought the natural urge to command the pilot to pull up, knowing that a 9mm handgun round would do absolutely nothing to harm the helicopter. Instead he continued to watch in dread fascination as the man loosed off all fifteen rounds from the gun until it clicked empty. He then saw the man look at the gun in disgust, and fling it to the ground.

He had obviously taken the pistol from one of the policemen at the roadblock but he hadn't had the good sense to take their spare ammunition. He saw the woman screaming something at her partner, pointing up at the helicopter, and then they were running, straight off the highway and into the scrubland that bordered it.

They were obviously panicking, the sight of the helicopter causing them to flee on foot in blind fear. Delongis was always surprised when this happened, the effect his little aircraft could have on people, and always glad. It made things substantially easier.

The fact that the pair had stopped the car and fled on foot also made life easier. His orders had been to stop the vehicle and arrest the two fugitives. He would have had to manoeuvre the chopper in front of the speeding car, hovering above the highway, in order to get it to stop, and he was glad he didn't have to. Who knew how crazy this pair was? They might have driven straight at him.

As it was, he just had to land near them, deploy the four-man team from the rear, and wait for the arrest. Easy, especially as the pair was now unarmed.

But there was, Delongis reminded himself, the problem of the anthrax. The word was that the fugitives had a test tube, which indicated that it wasn't weaponized, but its presence would still be enough to make his men wary. Their orders were to bring the pair in alive, but Delongis had given his own orders: if it looked like either the man or the woman was going to use the anthrax, they should be shot immediately. There was no point taking unnecessary chances.

Adams and Lynn ran as hard as they could, legs pumping over the coarse, uneven terrain, doing their very best to give the impression of panicking, fearful fugitives.

They heard the helicopter closing in, sensed it nearing them, but they didn't turn to look, they just kept on running, eyes ahead.

Lynn's peripheral vision picked it up first, the gunmetal grey body swooping past their flank, whipping up desert sand all around them as it banked, lifted, and landed just twenty yards away.

The pair turned, exchanging glances. This was it.

Lynn held up her backpack defensively as the black-clad four-man arrest team deplaned into the swirling sands, assault rifles up and aimed.

'Down, down, down!' the lead man shouted at them as the team sprinted forward.

'Wait!' shouted Lynn, holding up the backpack higher. 'Anthrax!'

The lead man lifted one gloved fist, and the other team members stopped short. 'Put the bag down!' he announced with heavy authority. 'We are authorized to shoot you if you do not comply!'

When there was no immediate reaction from her, he pushed the muzzle of his gun threateningly towards her. 'Put it down!' he called again. 'Now!'

Lynn looked across at Adams, who reluctantly nodded his head.

Defeated, Lynn put the bag at her feet and waited helpless as the men surged forward.

16

As Delongis watched with his co-pilot from the cockpit, he was delighted to see that this was going to be even easier than he had hoped. Obviously, the sight of the black-clad SWAT team had taken the fight right out of the terrorists and they had capitulated without a struggle. There had been the threat of the anthrax, of course, but it had been dealt with swiftly.

And now his men were moving forward to make the arrest, removing handcuffs from their belts, and—

Delongis watched in horror as the man and the woman both produced handguns and grabbed one man each, arms going round their throats, guns aimed at their heads.

This was impossible. Two of his men held at gunpoint! They must have taken more than one gun from the police, and Delongis cursed his reckless stupidity. He gripped the arms of his seat, his knuckles turning white, as the other two team members threw their assault rifles to the side and then lay down on the dusty ground, forced to handcuff themselves.

And then he saw the fugitives take their hostages, the woman careful to retrieve her backpack, and begin moving steadily towards his helicopter.

Within seconds, Adams and Lynn were at either side of the helicopter, next to the cockpit doors.

'Open the doors!' Adams shouted fiercely. 'Or we're gonna blow their heads off!'

When there was no instant response, Adams pushed the muzzle of his gun further into the man's head, forcing his face into the cockpit's plexiglas window, so the pilots could see the man's fear up close.

Seconds later, the man on his side nodded his head and released the door, his partner doing the same thing on the opposite side.

'Leave the rotors turning and get out,' Adams ordered, and again both men complied. Adams glanced across at Lynn and noticed the quizzical look she gave him, but ignored it.

'Now run to your friends,' he instructed them and was gratified to see the men do as he said, running to join their compadres in the dirt.

Adams looked at Lynn and nodded his head, and the two of them simultaneously cracked their pistols across the back of their hostages' heads, knocking them both out cold.

Seconds later, they were safely ensconced in the cockpit, Adams taking the controls with swift, confident actions.

Lynn looked at him, confused. 'You know how to fly this thing?' she asked, bewildered. 'When did you learn that?'

Adams finished his checks and looked at Lynn. 'There's a lot you don't know about me,' he said, and pushed forward on the gyro.

Captain Delongis, cowering in the scrub, looked up, and with a deeply regrettable mixture of rage and humiliation saw the Lynx rise steadily from the desert and power away towards the border.

* * *

Eldridge tried hard to conceal his rage, but it was difficult.

The Lear jet was on its way to the border now, with an estimated arrival time of no more than twenty minutes. He should have been arriving at the border checkpoint to take possession of his prisoners, but now? His prey had hijacked a helicopter and was all set to just fly straight over the border and he had no way of stopping them.

Well, that wasn't quite true, Eldridge had to admit to himself; he had no *non-lethal* way of stopping them. And it had really come to that decision. Was trying to capture them alive for fear of what they knew worth the mounting costs and attention the whole debacle was creating? Eldridge was starting to think it was doubtful.

Was it likely that the pair had told anyone else, or had the ability to deliver any evidence to anyone who would even care? Surely the organization could deal with the media even if things did find their way into the public spotlight. Eldridge knew that the special programme was operating right on schedule, and soon nothing else would matter anyway.

Mind made up, he picked up the satellite telephone and dialled the number for Stephen Jacobs. He would present his case and ask for permission to blow the helicopter out of the sky, killing the fugitives and wiping them off the face of the earth once and for all.

Ten minutes later, Eldridge was being patched through to Colonel Carlos Santé, the commander of Chile's First Armoured Brigade. Jacobs had finally capitulated, and agreed to the killing of the fugitives. Although reluctant to authorize their deaths without first interrogating them,

Jacobs had seen the unfortunate reality of the situation and had surrendered to it. Rather they die now, he had said, than they escape again.

The brigade provided Chile's anti-aircraft border defence and was based in Arica, just next to the border itself. Colonel Santé was in command of a battery of Gepard 1A anti-aircraft artillery vehicles, bought only a few years before from the German contractor and recently updated to launch the deadly Mistral anti-aircraft missiles.

The conversation was brief, as Eldridge stressed the time-frame; the helicopter would be approaching the border now, if it hadn't already entered Peruvian airspace. Santé promised he would shoot the chopper down immediately.

The next call Eldridge made was to the Peruvian side, seeking permission for the helicopter to be shot down by the 1st Armoured Brigade, even if it had already crossed into Peru. The mere mention of terrorism and anthrax meant that permission was instantly granted.

As Eldridge continued his own flight towards the border, he smiled.

There was no way the fugitives would escape 20kg of high explosive hurtling towards them at 1,200 miles per hour.

No way at all.

17

THE STOLEN LYNX helicopter overflew the border just ten minutes after being hijacked, and Adams and Lynn could see the masses of vehicles congregated around the checkpoints below.

'At least we're safe up here,' Lynn said as she looked down at the desert below. As they passed into Peruvian airspace, she clutched him, holding him tight. 'We made it!' she exclaimed.

Adams just nodded, his attention occupied by – what? What was it that he'd noticed? He scanned the desert again, the masses of cars, trucks and vans around the Interstate 5 border checkpoint; but that wasn't it.

His vision drifted further, and then he saw it – about two miles out towards the west, some sort of military installation. His eyes narrowed as he tried to look at it in more detail. It was movement that had caught his eye.

'Lynn,' he said, 'check out that military base over in the west. Can you make anything out?'

Lynn looked out of the side glass, straining to see. There was movement. But what? She looked harder. Could it be . . . Surely not.

'Matt,' she said finally, 'it looks like guns. Big ones, mobile artillery pieces. And they're moving, lining up.' She looked even closer, and realization hit her. 'They're lining up on us!' she cried out. 'They're going to shoot us down!'

Colonel Santé watched as the first of his battery of artillery pieces loosed off a Mistral missile, flame shooting from the rear as it blasted into the sky, rocketing towards the escaping helicopter at over a thousand miles per hour.

The stolen chopper was now ten miles into Peru; impact would be in approximately thirty seconds.

Colonel Santé used the time to light a cigar.

Adams was coaxing everything he could out of the chopper, nearing two hundred miles per hour as they raced into the Peruvian interior.

But he was all too aware that they had no hope of outrunning an anti-aircraft missile. The radar showed that one such weapon had already been launched and was homing in on the helicopter's infrared signature.

It had been many years since Adams had been in a Lynx but instinct told him where to find what he was looking for.

He reached for the toggle switch on the interface in front of him, flipping it down hard.

'What was that?' Lynn asked, trying to control her rising panic. She had told Matt that she would be OK, but the truth was that she was scared; and not just superficially scared but scared right down to her core. Just travelling in a helicopter after what had happened in Antarctica was a struggle, but with a missile now threatening once more to destroy her, she felt her heartbeat rising, her palms turning sweaty.

Not again, the voice kept repeating in her head. *Please, not again.*

Her inner voice was interrupted by Adams' reply. 'Countermeasures,' he announced. 'Infrared, to confuse the missile's own infrared guidance system. Should make the missile fly into *it*, rather than *us*.'

'Does it work?'

Adams grimaced. 'We'll know in about ten seconds.'

Colonel Santé could no longer see either the helicopter or the missile with the naked eye, and so watched the radar with his bombardiers as he puffed away on his cigar.

The signature of the missile quickly caught up with that of the helicopter. There was a blur of light – the impact – and the men watched closely as the light dimmed.

But what was this? The image of the helicopter was still there!

Damn! The countermeasures must have been deployed. Santé puffed angrily on his cigar as he realized that the pilot must know more about the helicopter than he'd been led to believe.

'Another sortie!' he announced gruffly. 'Launch guns two through five!'

If one missile had failed to do the trick, four would surely accomplish the task. After all, the cost was immaterial – the man who had called had promised full reimbursement for any ammunition used, as well as a little sweetener for Santé himself if he succeeded in shooting the chopper down.

Countermeasures or not, four missiles were a guarantee of destruction.

* * *

Adams knew it had been a lucky escape, and that they were unlikely to be so lucky again. The artillery commander would doubtless now order a multiple strike, and if several missiles were launched, one would be bound to get through.

Another approach had to be taken, and Adams knew what it was. The only trouble would be getting Lynn to agree to it.

He waited for a moment, wanting to leave it until she really had no other choice. And soon he saw the electronic blips appear on his radar. Four of them.

He quickly calculated their speed of approach, his own current speed, and estimated the impact time at about a minute and a half. He checked the surface map once again, and reduced his airspeed. He wanted to reach the canyon at almost exactly the same time as the missiles.

'Are we slowing down?' Lynn asked incredulously.

Adams turned to her, nodding his head. And then he told her his plan.

At the headquarters of 1st Armoured Brigade, Santé watched with fascination as his four majestic birds streaked towards the unfortunate helicopter. He admired the pilot of the chopper as he carried out evasive manoeuvres – up, down, left, right – and at the same time pitied him for his futile efforts.

There wasn't long to go, and although the chopper was now almost fifty miles into Peru, he wasn't anxious about the clash of authority – he had been promised Peruvian cooperation.

He noted how the fleeing pilot deployed more

countermeasures, and how one of his missiles went for the infrared bait, exploding behind the chopper.

And then he smiled widely as the remaining three missiles struck directly, seeing the big flare on the radar screen.

He blinked, and the screen was blank.

The missiles had done their work; the helicopter – and the people in it – were no more.

18

ELDRIDGE RECEIVED THE news within a minute of the destructive impact.

So, it was over. Or was it? Eldridge was aware that he had made this mistake before, signing off on their deaths too early. Well, not this time. He would check himself. The Lear jet would be over the impact site within the next ten minutes, and there were Chilean and Peruvian military and law enforcement teams also on their way there.

He would check the site from the air – check that the helicopter was *really* destroyed, and it wasn't just another damned trick – and then he would land, and lead the crash scene investigation.

After being hit by three separate missiles, the wreckage would be an inferno, no more than a smouldering mess; but Eldridge would not be happy until he found some evidence of the bodies within.

Then he would be able to relax.

The Lear jet cruised over the crash site within the estimated ten minutes, and Eldridge was gratified to see the fiery wreckage of the chopper, buried at the bottom of a deep canyon, flames licking up the sides, almost reaching his own aircraft.

It was doubtful that anyone could have survived such an

explosion, but if his current assignment had taught Eldridge anything, it was that all things were possible.

He entered the cockpit and told the pilot to find a place to land.

It was twelve hours later, after the darkness of night had well and truly drawn in and the temperature had dropped to near freezing, that the crash scene investigators found something.

There had been low-level squabbles early on in the day about whose jurisdiction such an investigation should come under, but Eldridge and his men took control of the scene, utilizing the investigators from both countries in order to fast-track the operation.

But there really wasn't much to go on. The impact had superheated the fuselage, obliterating everything inside in an instant. By the time the Lynx crashed into the canyon's deep valley bottom, there wasn't a whole lot left to investigate.

What there was, was extracted, separated, examined and identified piece by piece. The investigators told Eldridge that the heat had been so intense that it was doubtful anything would be left of the two fugitives who had stolen the craft. The best they could hope for would be bits of charred bone, or perhaps an odd tooth or two.

Eldridge was not going to be satisfied until he knew for sure that Adams and Edwards were dead, which was why his first sense of true relief did not come until almost midnight.

'Here, sir!' the excited technician announced, carrying something in a small clear plastic wallet.

'What is it?' Eldridge demanded.

'It's a tooth,' the man replied happily. 'It's badly burnt,' he continued, holding it up for Eldridge to see with his own eyes, 'but it is the tooth of the man who was in the helicopter when it went down.'

'You're sure?' Eldridge asked, only letting his excitement rise a little at this point.

'One hundred per cent, sir,' the technician replied.

Eldridge nodded. 'Good.' He took the wallet with the tooth inside from the man. 'I'll need to get it tested immediately.'

Stephen Jacobs was excited. He had just flown to Switzerland to see the machine with his own eyes, and was delighted with the progress of the CERN team. It was really going to happen.

He was flying home now, thirty-eight thousand feet above the Atlantic in his own private jet, when the phone rang.

'Jacobs,' he said, answering the call.

'Sir,' he heard the deep rumble on the other end announce, 'it's Eldridge. The situation here has been contained.'

'Are you sure?' Jacobs asked.

'Yes, sir. The helicopter was almost totally destroyed, but we managed to find three burnt teeth. DNA testing shows two of them belonged to Matthew Adams, and the other to Evelyn Edwards. There's no way they could have survived. It's over.'

Jacobs sat down deeper into his leather club chair. It was over, yes. And yet it was also all about to begin – the deaths of the two fugitives heralded the birth of the new world order.

'Good,' Jacobs said finally. 'You can come home, and take your place among us. It is almost time.'

Jacobs could almost feel the excitement of the man radiating through the satellite phone. 'Yes, sir,' the Alpha Brigade commander said, and Jacobs put the phone down, ending the call.

Yes, Jacobs thought to himself as he stretched out in the chair, delighted at the news from Peru, *it is almost time*.

19

ADAMS SCANNED THE desert scrub for signs of life as they settled in to their temporary shelter, but found none. Satisfied that they were safe, he pulled the cover over them and put his arm around Lynn to help keep her warm.

After their helicopter had been blown out of the sky the night before, the pair had used the hours of darkness to walk across the desert. The chopper's navigation system had provided their exact location, and Adams had then worked out the direction of the nearest large town, which was Arequipa. Using the stars for navigation, by the time dawn came they had covered thirty miles and were both nearing exhaustion.

Adams would ordinarily have been able to keep on walking much further, but the recent lack of sleep was hitting hard, making him into a quivering, uncontrolled wreck. They decided that they would rest up for the day – moving at night was better for combating the freezing desert temperatures, as well as for keeping hidden from view – and Adams spent the next half an hour preparing a hide, a small natural crevasse well hidden among a scattering of sun-bleached rocks.

Adams hoped that there would be no search for them but knew they had to be cautions. A trickle of blood ran down his chin from the corner of his mouth, and he wiped it away.

'How are your gums?' he asked Lynn, the blood reminding him of what they had done to escape.

'Not bad, considering,' she replied with a smile, which showed the gap in the top row of teeth.

The night before, Adams had started to perform evasive manoeuvres, getting whoever was watching them used to the chopper's erratic movements. Then, when the missiles had been just behind them and the lip of the canyon was right in front of them, he had slowed the helicopter and taken it right down to the ground, and then they had jumped.

They fell ten feet to the hard, dusty desert floor, both of them rolling through the rough sand towards the edge. They saw the missiles hit the helicopter which exploded with a tremendous, cataclysmic roar, its destroyed body falling to the canyon floor below.

They came to a stop just an arm's length from the huge drop over the canyon, and Adams had cradled Lynn in his arms, holding her tight, protecting her from the intense heat of the explosion. As the heat started to die down, Adams had released her, his shirt smeared with blood from her mouth.

Knowing the pursuit would continue without some proof that they had been in the helicopter when it went down, Adams had used the precious seconds they had before the missiles hit to give their enemy the physical evidence that would be needed.

He had withdrawn his utility knife, snapping it round into the pliers position. He had then quickly wrenched out two of his own teeth, blood spurting from his gums across the cockpit. The pain had made his head dizzy, but he had maintained control of the aircraft, deploying one more round of chaff.

As the countermeasures took out one more missile, he had been amazed as Lynn had pulled the pliers from him and wrenched out one of her own teeth, casting it on to the cockpit floor. Blood trickled from her mouth as she looked at him, and Adams saw the determination in her eyes. He hadn't wanted Lynn to copy him, but he knew it made sense – if the pursuers just had teeth from one of them, they might well carry on their search. With definite evidence of two bodies, they likely wouldn't bother.

And then Adams had taken the helicopter down, and they had exchanged one more look of mutual reassurance before they had opened the doors and jumped.

An hour later Lynn found herself with her own arms cradling Adams, their roles now reversed. He was shivering uncontrollably, unable to stop himself, teeth chattering, his entire body convulsing violently.

They had taken extra clothing from the helicopter, as well as some emergency blankets they had found, and Lynn packed the clothing around him, covering him in the blanket; but still he shivered so hard that Lynn was scared he was going to rip himself apart.

She gave him water, and some of the rations they had found on board, forcing him to eat a couple of small chocolate bars. She then took off her clothes, stripped him naked too, and climbed underneath the same blanket as him, arms and legs entwining with his, sharing her body heat.

She held him close, and the feel of his body next to hers brought memories back to her, powerful memories from their joint past together, lying in bed for hours, making love, resting in each other's arms, and then making love once more.

They had been happy at the time, she knew that now. Why had she not known it then? It had been her work that had stopped her from ever truly living in the moment with him, stopped her ever truly being happy with him; even as they lay together in blissful harmony, she couldn't help but start thinking about her next research project. Who was she going to recruit for the project, how were they going to raise the money, what results could they expect to find? The list went on, and it eventually began to tear them apart.

Adams was a man who enjoyed life, here, in the moment, and Lynn was obsessed by her work. When her husband had mentioned having children, she had scoffed at the suggestion – had he no idea what her work entailed, how time- and energy-consuming it was? Children were definitely going to have to wait. Adams had wanted to know for how long, and Lynn hadn't been able to give him an answer. They had stayed together for a short while afterwards, but it was clear that their lives had different priorities, and eventually they had drifted apart so far that divorce had been the only option.

And now? As Lynn held Adams in her arms, the warmth of her skin flowing into his body, she recognized how mistaken she had been. Where had her work brought her? She lived alone, and people were trying to kill her, and the only person she could turn to was the man she had been with originally. She was at the top of her field, certainly, but what did that matter now?

She felt Adams stir next to her, his eyes opening, groggy and disorientated. 'Lynn?' he said weakly.

'It's OK,' she replied, holding him closer. 'It's OK. It's just a fever.'

She saw him close his eyes again, felt him breathing deeply. Then he reopened his eyes, staring directly into her own. 'No,' he said sadly, 'it's not.'

He still longed for sleep, just a few hours of *real*, honest sleep. He could have continued to pretend he had a fever but he owed it to Lynn to tell her the truth.

'I've not been sleeping,' he said plainly, registering the surprise on her face as he spoke. 'I have bad dreams.'

'But . . . You? Why?' Lynn just could not understand it. The Matt Adams she'd known had never had any problem sleeping. He had been full of life, full of optimism and hope, and when the time had come for sleep, he had drifted off with no cares in the world.

'After we broke up,' he began, glad to finally get it off his chest, to share his problems with someone, especially *this* someone, 'I was recruited by the government.'

'What?' Lynn was surprised once more. He hadn't shown any interest in working for the government when they had been together, that was sure. He had been the best tracker on the reservation, she knew that much, and he had often helped the local police with tricky cases, but government work was something else altogether.

'US Immigration and Customs Enforcement,' Adams clarified. 'They had a group set up called the Shadow Wolves, responsible for tracking smugglers through the border territories between Mexico and the US. All trackers like me, from nine different tribes. They'd heard about me, and wanted me to join.'

'And you agreed?' Lynn asked, again finding it hard to reconcile with the Matt Adams she had known.

'What else was there for me to do?' he asked in return. 'We'd just been divorced, you'd told me I needed direction in life – like you had with your own work – and the opportunity came up, so I took it.'

Lynn nodded her head, sorry she had been in part responsible for his decision. 'Go on,' she encouraged gently.

'Well, I worked with the Shadow Wolves for years, became the top man in the unit – my success record was off the chart. And then one day everything changed.'

Lynn saw the look in his eye – harrowed, guilty, tortured. She didn't say anything, knowing he would go on when he was ready.

'A call came in about a truck driven by a gang of child smugglers. We'd heard of the group before, they'd been bringing kids across the border for the past few months, but we'd never been able to get a handle on them. This time we had the make and model of the truck they were using, so we knew we had them.' His eyes wandered, lost in the past. 'We tracked the truck across sixty miles of Tohono O'odham territory, and we finally found it, just ten miles from the border.

'It was abandoned, just left out in the desert sun. We approached it carefully, ready for the smugglers to run, but when we got to the driver's cab, there wasn't anyone there. Marks in the sand indicated that the drivers had left the night before, maybe even the day before. The truck had been there twenty-four, maybe thirty-six hours.' Adams paused, taking a deep breath before continuing. 'We went round the back to open the doors and check inside, but already we could smell what it was. Dead bodies.'

He closed his eyes, trying to shut out the memories. 'We opened those doors to a nightmare. Sixty-seven children, some as young as three years old, crammed together in the back of the truck, unable to move, and then left there for dead in the middle of the desert. It was the height of summer, temperatures inside must have reached over a hundred and fifty degrees. And there was no ventilation in the truck. They never had a chance.'

Tears started to roll down Adams' cheeks as he remembered the horror of what he had seen as the truck doors opened. 'They were all dead – all of them. Died from the heat, and from asphyxiation. Can you imagine how they must have felt? Trapped in that oven, unable to get out, people dying next to you, above you, under you. There was vomit and diarrhoea everywhere, scratches on the inside of the truck as they struggled to get out.'

Adams wiped away his tears, and looked at Lynn. 'And you know why the smugglers left them there, why they ran away?' Lynn shook her head. 'It was because they'd heard that the Shadow Wolves were chasing them. They thought they didn't have a chance, so they took off, escaped on foot, leaving the truck behind. Because of us.' He looked down, too upset to continue.

Lynn held him close, their bodies warm, reassuring. 'There's nothing you could have done,' she said softly, knowing it made no difference but saying it anyway.

'I could have found that truck quicker,' Adams answered

immediately. 'I was supposed to be the best, and I failed. I failed badly, and they all died because I wasn't quick enough, wasn't good enough.

'I tried to carry on working afterwards, but pretty soon I started having nightmares about it. They began to get worse and worse, more like night terrors really, and pretty soon I was scared to go to sleep. After a while, I was completely incapable of work. I was broken. They finally let me go, and I went back to the reservation, where I've been struggling to just get by ever since.' Adams held Lynn's hands, looking into her deep, lustrous, opaline eyes. 'You might not think it, but you've given me something to live for,' he said finally. 'Thank you.'

Lynn's heart jumped in her chest. She had endangered his life, and he was *thanking* her? Tears began to stream down her own cheeks, as she realized something she had been unwilling to admit. She still loved him, even as she was sure he still loved her.

Close, their bodies still naked, intertwined, Adams wiped her tears away and then moved his head even closer, his lips brushing hers. At first the kiss was exploratory, checking for her reaction, and then she responded, pulling in tightly, kissing him back with unexpected passion.

Relieved that the desire was mutual, both Adams and Lynn let go completely, moving in perfect synchrony as the build-up of stress and adrenalin that had filled them for the past few days transformed itself into frenetic, frenzied passion, their bodies fitting into a rhythm they had thought long forgotten, until Lynn buried her face in Adams' neck and they both felt the tension escape them in a flow of sweet, wonderful relief.

20

Two days later Adams and Lynn finally made it into the small town of Nazca.

They had walked most of the way to Arequipa during the second night, then had to hole up again during the day, finally getting there the following night. It didn't take long to organize transport on to Nazca – they had simply walked around the town until they made it on to Highway 1 heading north, and then hitched a lift.

The driver of the big truck, on his way to Lima, had dropped them off in the small, dusty town just as dawn was rising. The town itself was unprepossessing, consisting of a grid-like formation of one-storey houses and shops on a section of the desert pampa that lay in the shadow of towering mountains beyond.

Although the town itself was nothing to write home about, Lynn squeezed Adams' hand tight as they watched the sun rise slowly, majestically, above the snow-capped peaks in the distance, its muted pink-red glow spreading warmth down through the valley.

They just watched it together, hand in hand, in silence for several long, wonderful minutes, all worries temporarily forgotten as they admired the imperial beauty of the natural world.

As the sun finally pushed its way above the mountaintops, Adams turned to Lynn. 'So where do we find Baranelli?' he asked her.

'I'm not a hundred per cent sure,' Lynn replied sheepishly, 'but I think I've got a good idea.'

The Nazca Lines Hotel, on Jiron Bolognesi, was just five minutes from the famed Nazca Lines, which explained its popularity among tourists, astronomers, explorers and conspiracy theorists.

The lines had originally been noticed in 1939, when an American scientist called Paul Kosok flew over the dry coastline in a small plane. The lines up until then had been thought to be part of some form of irrigation system, but Kosok, an expert in irrigation, quickly discounted such an explanation.

His flight happened to coincide with the summer solstice, and he soon discovered that the lines of the sunset ran parallel to those of a huge drawing of a bird in the desert sands, which made him dub the area 'the biggest astronomy book in the world'.

After Kosok, a young German mathematician called Maria Reiche went on to study the area for the next five decades, concluding that the colossal drawings were part of an astronomical calendar made by the people of the Nazca culture, possibly also intended to send messages to the gods.

Reiche had lived at the Nazca Lines Hotel, then known as the *Hotel Turistas* for many years, giving hour-long talks about the archaeological phenomenon every evening.

Lynn had heard Baranelli talk about Reiche back at Harvard, and felt sure that he would stay in no other place during his time in Nazca. Not that there *were* many other places anyway.

Adams and Lynn walked past trimmed lawns and baby palm trees and entered the hotel's white-painted colonial foyer. They made straight for the reception desk.

Lynn, trying not to be too self-conscious about her missing tooth and her generally dishevelled appearance, strode towards the desk, a smile on her face.

'Good morning,' she said pleasantly. 'Do you speak English?'

The young female clerk nodded her head. 'A little, yes.'

'Great,' Lynn said. 'We're fellows up from Harvard, we're supposed to be meeting Professor Baranelli here for breakfast but I think we might be a little too early. Would it be OK if we wait here for him?'

The clerk looked unsure. 'You are wanting to meet Professor for breakfast?'

Lynn nodded her head. 'That's right,' she confirmed.

'I'm very sorry, Professor Baranelli no here.'

'He's not staying here?' Lynn asked, more than a little worried.

'Oh no, he is staying here, it is that he has already left.'

'Left?' Lynn asked. 'Where's he gone?'

The clerk pointed back out across the manicured lawn. 'The airfield across the road,' she said. 'If you hurry, you might get there before he flies.'

Less than two minutes later, Adams and Lynn were back across the Jiron Bolognesi, pounding quickly through a metal archway and across the cold tarmac towards the small flight centre.

Looking up, they could see two small propeller-driven aircraft heading out across the skies. Did one of them hold Baranelli?

There were a dozen or so other planes scattered around the open hangars, three of which seemed to be getting ready for flight. For so small a place, the airstrip seemed inordinately busy.

Adams was just reaching for the door of the flight centre when Lynn tugged at his sleeve. 'Matt,' she said excitedly, pointing over to one of the three aircraft which were taxiing to the runway. 'There he is!'

Adams followed Lynn's outstretched finger, seeing a slightly overweight, balding man with a deep tan, steel-rimmed spectacles and old-fashioned khaki shirt and shorts, about to climb on board one of the little planes.

'Professor!' Lynn shouted across the runway.

The man looked her way, annoyance on his face, albeit mixed with a hint of curiosity.

When Lynn waved her hand and shouted to him again, recognition dawned and a wide smile broke his heavy features. He gestured for the pilot to stop the plane and he practically ran to Lynn across the runway.

'Lynn!' he exclaimed in an ebullient, southern Italian accent. 'What on earth are you doing here?'

'We need your help,' Lynn said directly.

After a moment's consideration, Baranelli smiled. 'Of course, whatever you need is yours. But we will have to talk on the plane,' he said, turning back to board the aircraft. 'We only have an hour where the conditions will remain perfect.'

Lynn looked at Adams and groaned. *Another aircraft?* That was all she needed.

Still, she followed Baranelli aboard the small plane, praying that for once – just *once* – she would be able to land normally.

'Most of the year, you have to be in the air mid-morning or early afternoon due to the haze at other times,' Baranelli explained as the Cessna lifted off from the airstrip, climbing high into the thin mountain air, 'but I've found recently that the early morning is best. I've been up here fifty times already, and it still fascinates me, let me tell you.'

Lynn and Adams both nodded. Lynn knew that her old friend was the most passionate of men, and no more so than when he was talking about his work. She would have to try hard to steer the conversation around to what they wanted. But just as she was about to speak, Baranelli interjected.

'Have you seen the lines from the air before?' he asked both of his guests.

Adams and Lynn shook their heads.

'No?' Baranelli said delightedly. 'Well, you're in for a treat! And who better to give you the guided tour than me? If you're lucky,' he said with a wink, 'I'll even fill you in on my own theories about the site.'

For the next thirty minutes, the aeroplane described lazy arcs across the sky as it traced the immense lines of the Nazca plain.

Baranelli was like a machine, simultaneously making notes in a dog-eared booklet, taking high-definition photographs and performing complex calculations whilst also continuously and enthusiastically narrating the history of the lines better than any professional tour guide could have done.

'Isn't it incredible?' Baranelli asked, and not for the first time. 'From here, the lines and geoglyphs look to have no purpose, meaninglessly intersected across the pampa, some expertly executed, others crudely rendered, just a big jumbled mess. But if we look closer,' he continued, nodding to the pilot who began to descend, closer to the desert plain, 'we can see the beauty of the design. We can see the wedges,' he said, indicating huge trapezoidal designs, stretching for up to two and a half thousand feet, 'and how they are intersected by the lines themselves – perfectly straight for up to *nine miles*. And then there are spirals, triangles, circles, the list goes on. These geometric shapes, do you know how many there are here?'

Lynn shook her head. 'No, I'm afraid not.'

'Somewhere in the region of *nine hundred*. Nine hundred! Can you believe it? It is truly incredible. And then there are the shapes!' Baranelli continued, in a world of his own. 'There are around *seventy* biomorphs – animal and plant figures, including some very well-known examples. The hummingbird, the heron, the condor, the dog, the hands, the spider, the pelican, the monkey,' he said, punctuating each word with a stab of his finger in the geoglyph's direction, and Adams and Lynn found themselves staring in awe at the designs, clustered together in one area of the vast plain, which Baranelli had told them was nearly two hundred square miles in area. The size of the shapes was astounding. From their vantage point, Adams estimated the pelican figure must have been almost a thousand feet in length.

'And then we have my personal favourite,' Baranelli continued, smiling. 'The astronaut.'

Peering out of the aircraft's windows, Adams and Lynn

looked down at a figure etched on to the side of a small hill. The light caught the image perfectly, and they could both see the design of a man, seemingly wearing some sort of helmet, right hand raised in greeting. But to whom? To what?

'Well?' Baranelli asked his guests, clearly excited. 'What do you think?'

'It's certainly interesting,' Lynn replied. 'What's its purpose?'

Baranelli turned away from the window and raised his eyebrows. 'Ah!' he exclaimed. 'That is the question! What is any of it for? What do you think?' he asked, a professor testing his students.

'There've been many theories over the years,' Lynn started, 'beginning with Kosok's belief that it represented some sort of astronomical calendar, but computer modelling showed that the alignments were no more common than random chance.'

'Indeed,' Baranelli agreed, nodding his head. 'And what else?'

'Well, I think the prevailing theory is that they are religious walkways, linked to water or fertility cults.'

'Yes, many people are of that opinion,' the professor concurred. 'Ethnographical and historical data seem to indicate that worship of mountains and water sources dominated Nazcan religion and culture from ancient times. The lines can therefore be seen as sacred paths, leading the faithful to areas where such deities could be worshipped.'

'Many people . . . but not you?' Lynn probed.

Baranelli laughed at the idea. 'Certainly not me!'

'And so what do you believe?' Adams asked.

'It is time we landed,' Baranelli said in reply. 'We will continue our talk over lunch perhaps?'

21

An hour later, Baranelli was ensconced with his two guests at a private table back at the Nazca Lines Hotel, a large glass of Chianti in his hand as he continued his lecture.

'Have you heard of the "ancient astronaut" theory?' he asked them.

Lynn nodded her head, sipping from a glass of water. 'Back in the nineteen sixties, Erich von Däniken proposed that the straight lines were runways for extraterrestrial spacecraft, in fact he saw the whole Nazca plain as some sort of gigantic airport.'

'That's right,' Baranelli said, 'although we're not sure if the surface would have been strong enough to take the weight of repeated landings. But he also had other interesting theories about the rest of the geoglyphs, claiming that the Nazcans drew them once these extraterrestrials had left, presumably having returned to their home planet.'

'Why would they do that?' Adams asked.

'Similar things have been documented around the world,' Baranelli explained. 'So-called "cargo cults" emerge when an indigenous people is visited by a more highly advanced culture, ascribing to them – and their advanced "cargo" – supernatural significance, seeing them as deities and gods. There was a prevalence of such cults in the south-west

Pacific Ocean in the aftermath of the Second World War, when the islands were used by the Americans and Japanese as staging posts for the war effort, bringing in huge amounts of materiel. When the bases closed after the war and these goods dried up, the island populations tried to encourage further deliveries of goods by building crude imitation landing strips, aircraft and radio equipment, and worshipping them.'

'And this is what von Däniken believed happened here?' Adams asked.

'Yes, and he didn't just stop there, he believed that religion as a whole, all over the world, was created to worship extraterrestrials who had come down to earth, amazing primitive man with their advanced technology and leaving them to come up with supernatural explanations for what they had seen.'

'You've got to be kidding me,' Adams said sceptically. 'So God was an alien?'

'One of von Däniken's chapter headings – indeed probably the one that made him famous – is "Was God an Astronaut?"' Baranelli explained, a smile on his face.

'And just what evidence did he give to support that claim?' Adams asked, still not buying it.

'You have to understand that it is not just von Däniken who has argued this over the years, but many people – astronomers, astrophysicists, historians, philosophers, you name it. There is a large body of what they would term *evidence* in support of the theory, although others would say it was a body of curious anomalies rather than outright evidence.'

'What sort of anomalies?' Lynn asked, still trying to find

a link between her own discovery and this talk of ancient aliens.

'The Nazca Lines are one such anomaly – where did they come from, who designed them, and for what purpose? Does the fact that they can only be seen from the air indicate that whoever drew them meant for them to be seen by airborne peoples? And where would this flying technology have come from so long ago? So we have an anomaly, something that doesn't seem to fit in with regular historical or archaeological knowledge.

'And what else do we have?' Baranelli asked before Adams or Lynn had the chance to reply. 'A sixteenth-century map discovered in the ruins of the Topkapi Palace in Istanbul shows Antarctica at the bottom, with the land mass shown much as it would appear if it were free from ice – something which it has not been for fifteen million years. So was this a copy from maps made millions of years ago, or did this sixteenth-century admiral have access to ground-penetrating radar and satellite analysis? And if he did, where could this technology have possibly come from?

'Then there are the various ancient artworks which show what seem to be alien visitors, or astronauts with helmets – much like the geoglyph we have just seen, in fact. These can be found from ancient cave drawings in the African Sahara to Mayan temples in Mexico, and everywhere in between – Zimbabwe, South Africa, Russia, Val Camonica in northern Italy, Uzbekistan, the list goes on and on. Always the same images – what seem to be man-like figures in strange clothes and helmets. The carving from the Temple of the Inscriptions in Palenque in Mexico, for example, clearly shows an astronaut-like figure sitting at the controls of a miniature rocket-ship. Can that be explained conventionally?'

Baranelli took a large drink of his wine before ploughing on. 'And what about such mysteries as the Mayan calendar, predicting eclipses for untold thousands of years? Where did they get the technology to calculate such things? Ancient electric batteries have been found in Iraq, nine thousand-year-old crystal lenses in Assyria, an iron post in a courtyard in Delhi that has not rusted in four thousand years, a twenty-*thousand*-ton granite block turned upside down in Peru – who can explain such things?

'And let us not forget the Great Pyramid of Khufu, and all of its surrounding temples, the Great Sphinx, and so on. Do we know, even now, how such things were built? Or why? The Great Pyramid was built from over two million stone blocks, some of which weighed as much as seventy tons. It is the most accurately aligned structure in existence, facing true north with only one-twentieth of one degree of error, and is also located precisely at the centre of the earth's land mass. The outer casing stones were highly polished and flat to an accuracy of one-hundredth of an inch, and could have been seen from Israel, and perhaps even the moon. Why? The answer is, we simply do not know. We only know these anomalies are there, crying out for an explanation.'

'And aliens can provide such an explanation?' Adams asked.

'Why not? People claim they visit us now, why should they not have come thousands of years ago?' Baranelli could see the disbelief in the eyes of both Adams and Lynn, and although he did not necessarily subscribe to the theory himself, he also knew it could not be discounted out of hand. 'Some people,' he carried on, 'see information contained in religious texts as direct evidence of alien visitation.'

'Go on,' Adams said, unsure but curious now.

'Has it never occurred to you that most religions have very similar stories in their writings? Ancient Sumer, the Egyptians, Romans, Greeks, the Old and New Testaments – all are almost identical, once you get right down to it. And where did culture – science, mathematics, agriculture, writing – originate?'

'Ancient Sumer,' Lynn answered.

Baranelli clicked his fingers. 'Exactly!' he said. 'So after millions of years of slow, painful evolution, we have a sudden spurt of development. In the blink of an eye – in evolutionary terms – we were irrigating the land, building temples, making complicated mathematical calculations, reading and writing. So what went on in ancient Sumer?

'Some people claim that it was here that alien visitors first came to us, providing us with the seeds of our modern civilization. In turn, we ascribed supernatural significance to them, and organized religion was born. Thus, "gods" coming down from heaven in fiery chariots are not dreams, visions, or metaphors, this is what really happened, aliens coming to earth in their spaceships. But how else could ancient man explain it? And so religion began in Sumer, and then spread across the region, first to Egypt, and then on to Israel, finally spanning the globe and including India, Rome and Greece in its thrall. Everywhere it went, it was modified by the indigenous people there but it was essentially the same as the factual reports of alien landings and alien technology that was experienced first-hand by the Sumerians.'

'So God *was* an astronaut?' Adams asked, still unconvinced.

'Who knows? It is a theory, yes? A story. And no more or no less convincing than any other, in my opinion.'

'Well, Fabricio,' Lynn said, 'we have a little anomly of our own.'

'Forty thousand years old?' Baranelli asked excitedly.

'Well, that's how it appeared. Obviously, most of the evidence has now been destroyed.'

'When did civilization appear in Sumer?' Adams asked Baranelli.

'About 3800BC,' the professor answered immediately. 'Nearly six thousand years ago, give or take.'

'So do you have any theories about an advanced people that may have existed *forty* thousand years ago?' Adams persisted.

'Perhaps the cycle that we saw begin in Sumer was not the first time such a thing happened,' Baranelli said, unsure.

'What do you mean?' Lynn asked.

'I mean if extraterrestrial beings could have come to the earth and provided man with civilization in 3800BC, they – maybe the same beings, maybe another group from another region of the universe entirely – could have come here forty, fifty, a hundred thousand years ago, even. We cannot rule it out. Or else mankind evolved such technology on its own during that period, without any external help.'

'And then?' Adams asked.

'And was then destroyed, like Atlantis, some global

catastrophe that completely wiped out mankind. Perhaps some pockets survived, but due to conditions on the planet had to revert to nature, as it were, becoming more primitive in order to survive.'

'Like Atlantis?' Adams asked. 'Are you saying that Atlantis existed?'

'No,' Baranelli said slowly, choosing his words carefully. 'What I am saying is that almost every modern-day culture has some form of Atlantean, pre-historic advanced-culture myth. Is it just a coincidence, or do these myths have a basis in truth? The body Lynn found would certainly seem to indicate that this is the case, no?' Baranelli asked, his eyebrows raised. 'And then you have to consider the universality of the ancient flood myths. In our Christian culture, we know predominantly about Noah and the Flood, but this, too, can be traced back to its origins in ancient Sumerian folklore. Indeed, many respected scientists believe the world did experience such catastrophic flooding, in the period between 12,000 and 10,000BC.

'But this is just an example, to show that it could well be true. Other calamities could have befallen ancient man – meteor strike, volcanic eruptions, the list goes on. The bottom line is, it is certainly possible that an advanced civilization, perhaps even more advanced than our own, once walked the earth, and was subsequently all but wiped out. You have not analysed the DNA yet?' he asked suddenly.

'No, not yet. We're hoping to do that back in the US, if we can get there.'

Baranelli nodded his head, deep in thought. 'So the body might not even be *Homo sapiens*,' he said. 'Perhaps it is some other branch of the genus *Homo*, which for some reason progressed faster than us. Maybe their reliance on technology made the catastrophe hit them much harder than it hit us, so they died out completely, allowing us to scrape our way up to the top.'

Lynn and Adams exchanged looks. Another branch of the human family? It was something they hadn't even considered, and to Adams it certainly seemed more convincing than Lynn having found an alien body or time traveller, two other possibilities that might have explained the ancient corpse.

'It appears to me that you need to get the DNA tested immediately,' Baranelli announced. 'That way we will know what we are dealing with.'

'That's why we've got to get back to the US,' Adams agreed. 'Get the evidence analysed, find out what the hell is going on.'

Baranelli nodded his head. 'It will be dangerous, my friends. It is clear that the body is important to someone, and they will stop at nothing to keep whatever secret it is that they are hiding.'

'You're right about that,' Adams said. 'I think we're dealing with some top-level government interest, with enough power to get things done well south of the border too.'

'Anybody like that who has a secret, it must be a secret worth knowing, yes?' Baranelli asked with a mischievous smile and a wink. He took another sip of his wine, and looked directly at Adams and Lynn. 'And so this is the help you need, yes? You want to know if I am able to get you back to the US undetected?'

Adams and Lynn both nodded and then watched as

Baranelli refilled his glass and polished off half of it with one long, leisurely pull.

'But only if you think you can do it without endagering yourself,' Lynn added seriously.

Baranelli waved his hand. 'Don't worry about that,' he said. 'I think I can help you, and I'm sure it won't endanger me one little bit. Besides, what's life without a little excitement?' He finished his wine. 'You will be back in the US by tomorrow, I promise. Just promise *me* you will tell me what you find out.'

'We will, Fabricio,' Lynn agreed. 'And we'll also find out who's behind all this,' she said, hands clasping Adams'. 'I'm tired of being the victim,' she continued, and Adams was shocked by the fiery determination in her eyes. 'They think we're dead, they think they've won. Well, we're going to find out who *they* are, and we're going to take this fight to *them*.'

PART THREE

PART THREE

1

DNA ANALYTICS WAS located in downtown Phoenix, one
of thousands of such laboratories scattered across the United
States. The principal work carried out by such facilities is
paternity testing, although many work in cooperation with
the FBI and other law enforcement agencies to analyse
DNA evidence for criminal cases.

Lynn chose this particular site expressly because it carried
out no governmental or law enforcement work at all, and
was thus a little more off-radar than many other such estab-
lishments. In addition, it had a sister facility in Los Angeles
that could deal with analysis of the fragments of cloth that
Lynn had collected from the burial site. This would enable
them to deal with everything in just one visit, thus mini-
mizing their exposure.

As they entered the foyer, they were surprised by just
how busy it was, from young mothers with screaming babies
to ageing college professors and white-coated laboratory
technicians, the place was a hive of bustling activity.

Adams had shaved his head and started to grow a beard,
while Lynn had dyed her hair blonde, changed her style of
make-up and clothes considerably, and put in blue contact
lenses. They had also both used powder to try and lighten
their skin tone, and both now wore glasses to adjust the

contours of their faces. Even so, they still avoided looking towards the security cameras pointing from the ceiling down into the busy foyer. They were officially dead, of course – Lynn twice now – but if the past few days had taught them anything, it was that it was impossible to be too careful.

Lynn approached the desk, backpack in hand. After a brief discussion with the receptionist, during which Lynn asked for a full DNA test for three of the samples she had brought with her, they were told that due to a backlog, results wouldn't be ready for at least a month. The handing over of five hundred dollars in cash – courtesy of Fabricio Baranelli – immediately moved that up to just over a week.

Lynn turned to Adams. 'A week,' she said, deflated even though she had been expecting as much. 'Can we wait that long?'

'Well, without access to government labs, I don't see what choice we have. I mean, the only way we'd even have access to better facilities was if we used your position, but that would mean using your name, and we definitely can't afford to do that.'

Lynn nodded, then turned back towards the receptionist. 'OK,' she agreed, and then gave her a cellphone number from a newly acquired, pay-as-you-go, untraceable handset. 'Call me on this as soon as you have anything. And there'll be an extra five hundred for you if you get those results to us in under a week.'

Walking out of the centre, Lynn turned to Adams once more. 'OK,' she said, 'now what?'

'We've done the science bit,' Adams said, 'now we need to do the real work. Let's go and meet my friends.'

* * *

Baranelli had been as good as his word. The day after their meeting, Lynn and Adams had been back in the United States.

The professor had been chartering an aeroplane for his aerial research on a long-term basis, and had simply filed a flight plan up to Mexico, citing connected research as his reason. The little bird had needed to be refuelled once in Columbia, and had then made it to Mexico, where nobody at the small airfield expressed any interest in the two passengers that deplaned and went on their way.

The pain from their hastily extracted teeth – covered by adrenalin for so long – was now becoming unbearable, and so Adams used his old contacts to make a late-night visit to a friendly dentist in a small town nearby.

An Oglala Lakota like Adams, the dentist took cash and asked no questions. He did, however, tell Adams that it was a good job that they had come; if they had left it much longer, there would have been the possibility of infection, which might have led to blood poisoning.

The old man had patched them up quickly – albeit not exactly painlessly, and then advised them to get some rest. Adams and Lynn had just smiled, sharing the same thought – *the chance would be a fine thing*.

The town was close to the border, and after their brief but necessary detour, Adams had led Lynn back along the same unmanned trails he had used to enter Mexico several days before.

As they had made their way across Arizona towards Phoenix, hitchhiking in a battered pick-up, Adams had used their new cellphone to call one of his Shadow Wolves colleagues, careful to use codes he had not used in years, aware that plain speech might well be picked up by electronic surveillance. But his friend had understood, and a meeting had been arranged for the following morning.

The Tohono O'odham Sweat Lodge was located in a part of the reservation completely out of bounds to those not associated with, or invited by, the tribe.

The sweat lodge is an ancient American Indian custom, a traditional tribal ceremony that is still carried out by many tribes across the country. It is similar to a sauna in that there is heat and moisture – people sit around a firepit filled with stones, upon which they pour water, while ensconced in a heavy, blanket-covered tent – but the sweat lodge is a more spiritual affair, the heat being used to create the atmosphere of being in the womb of the 'great earth mother'. It is intended to help purify not only the body but also the mind, emotions, and spirit.

Adams and Lynn arrived at the lodge in the early morning. Adams greeted his old colleagues with warm embraces, and was introduced to the newer members of the team. Lynn was also introduced, and she understood what an honour it was for her to be there – outsiders were seldom welcome.

Adams was pleased to see his old friends but he was disturbed not to see Mark 'Spirit From Above' Takanawee at the meeting. The fact that this was the man who had provided him with his passport and some cash for his trip to South America – as well as the troubled looks on the faces of the other men – did not bode well.

But his questions would have to wait, for tradition demanded that first they had to ritually cleanse themselves, and then light the fire for the ceremony, and only then could the talk begin.

2

ADAMS LOOKED OVER at Lynn. It wasn't the first time she had been in a sweat lodge – he had taken her to the Lakota lodge back at his home reservation when they had been married – but he saw that the extreme heat was taking its toll on her, sweat running profusely down her face and neck. As per custom, she was fully clothed. Adams wondered if she was going to pass out. It had been a long time, after all.

But she continued to hang in there, even joining in with the ritual songs and chants, in time to the steady, rhythmic beat of the drums. To Adams, she had never looked more beautiful.

'Matt,' said John 'First to Dance' Ayita, a Cherokee tribesman who was the unit leader, having moved up to the position after Adams had left, 'it is time to talk.'

And with that, the feeling within the tent immediately changed.

Adams nodded his head. 'What happened to Mark?'

Ayita looked pained, looking up to the roof of the tent, and the sky beyond. 'He was taken from us, not so very long ago. He is with the spirits now.'

'How?' Adams asked, fearing he already knew the answer.

'Heart attack.'

Adams knew the coincidence was too great. There was no way it would have been a real heart attack, and a wave of grief swept over him. It was his fault entirely. The enemy would have finally caught his image at the airport entering Chile, found out the passport he was travelling under, and then tracked down Mark Takanawee. And then they would have tortured him for information, finally staging a heart attack.

'Did you get a chance to look at the body?'

Ayita's face was grave. 'Bodaway managed to check the body out at the morgue before he was buried.'

Bodaway 'Fire-Maker' Arawan was the Shadow Wolves' chief medic, a legend among the tribes for his fusion of traditional medicine with the latest cutting-edge medical practices.

'I think it was an electron trigger,' Arawan said, voice subdued. 'Such a device is rumoured to be undergoing military trials but is not yet commercially available. A burst of static transmits from the device straight to the heart, where it interferes with the normal, regular electrical signal, producing the signs and symptoms of a myocardial infarction. I would have missed it entirely had I not been looking for something out of the ordinary. But he had two tiny burns underneath the hair on his chest, which indicate the use of some sort of electronic device.

'This also corroborates my other findings, which included several bruises and contusions on the body, symptomatic of being manhandled and bound with restraints of some type. And then there are the needle marks on the inside of his right elbow, and the unusual blood samples.'

'Unusual how?' Adams asked, the guilt eating at him painfully.

'I found traces of short-acting barbiturates, most notably thiopental, an active ingredient of the so-called truth serum, sodium pentothal. It indicates that he was kidnapped and interrogated, before being killed with an electronic device, unknown outside military circles.'

'So he was executed?' Adams asked.

'Without a shadow of a doubt,' Arawan confirmed.

John Ayita looked at Adams with steely eyes. 'And I think it's about time you told us why.'

Adams did not check with Lynn before he started the tale; he knew she would understand. Another man had laid down his life due to Lynn's discovery, and they owed it to his friends to tell them the truth.

Adams started at the beginning, with Lynn's mission to Antarctica, and described their ordeal in its entirety. It did not disturb Adams that the men he was sharing this information with worked for the same US government that was potentially behind the situation; tribal ties would always outweigh loyalty to the government.

When he reached the end of his tale, Ayita shook his big head slowly in disbelief. 'Incredible,' he said at last. 'Simply incredible. So Mark is dead now because of this discovery?'

Adams nodded his head in shame. 'Yes. He is dead because I asked for his help.'

'And now you come to us, to ask for our help?'

Adams paused. The thought that he might now be endangering his other friends had never occurred to him, and he felt the hard, hot flush of guilt wash through him once again. What had he done?

'Please forgive me,' he stammered. 'I—'

Ayita held up his hand. 'Do not worry, brother,' he said. 'Mark Takanawee was taken from us by a powerful enemy, and we will not rest until we have our revenge.'

Adams' heart glowed, hope rising within him. 'But can you all spare the time?' he asked.

Ayita nodded. 'I am afraid so,' he said. 'Since we examined Mark's body, the Department of Homeland Security has announced the dissolving of the Shadow Wolves unit. We are to return to our tribes, and disband. They have not even offered us alternative employment. The Wolves are no more.'

'You've got to be kidding me!' Adams exclaimed.

'I am afraid not,' Ayita said. 'It would be difficult to kill us all, especially while we're working for the government, so they did the next best thing, disbanding the group and sending us all back to our own tribes, scattered around the country. It wouldn't surprise me if some more of us meet unexpected "accidents" over the coming months.'

'But who are these people, that they can shut down a group like the Shadow Wolves? It's part of the damned Department of Homeland Security!' Lynn spoke for the first time and everyone in the tent looked at her.

Ayita turned to a man on the far side of the firepit, looking through the hazy, hot mist. 'Samuel?' he urged.

Samuel 'Two Horses' Stephenfield was the unit's intelligence officer. 'We have started an initial investigation already, of course,' he began, and he could see the looks of sudden interest from both Adams and Lynn. 'Have you ever heard of the Bilderberg Group?'

Lynn answered first, trying hard to ignore the suffocating

heat and humidity of the firepit. 'Isn't that just a bunch of politicians and media figures who meet up once a year to exchange ideas and phone numbers? A bit like an informal networking group for global bigwigs?' She wiped the sweat from her brow, which reappeared instants later. 'I think even Sam Atkinson went to one of their meetings a few years ago, and—'

She stopped dead as the ramification hit her. Atkinson was the head of NASA, and he was the first person she had told about the discovered body.

'Maybe you should tell us what you know,' Adams said to Stephenfield.

The intelligence officer nodded his head. 'Lynn is right to a certain extent,' he began. 'The first meeting of the group took place in May nineteen fifty-four, at the Hotel de Bilderberg in Holland – hence the group's name. It was supposedly held due to problems with cooperation between Europe and the US when it came to some of the really important issues. It was felt that a new type of meeting was necessary, something a little more off the record, without the worry of journalists or political aides reporting or commenting on what was said, especially with the looming threat of the Soviet Union.

'With the end of the Cold War, the meetings continued apace. Even without the threat of communism, western leaders still had important issues to worry about – trade, employment, monetary policy, ecological problems, invest-ment, terrorism and international security, to name but a few.

'There are usually about a hundred and twenty partici-pants, and the list changes every year. The majority are from Europe, with the rest from the US, although other nations from around the world are being increasingly represented. The list is made up of about one-third from government and politics, and two-thirds from finance, industry, labour, education and communications.

'No resolutions are prepared at such meetings, there are no votes taken, and no policy statements are issued. They are simply "talking shops" where the world's great and good can get together out of the glare of the media spotlight.'

'And how do they link in with what's going on here?' Adams asked.

'The connection arose when we started to look into who had been putting pressure on Homeland Security to close us down. After some searching, we found that it was coming directly from the White House, specifically from the office of the President's special aide, Tony Kern. We quickly found out that Kern is a member of the Bilderberg Group.'

'A member?' Lynn asked. 'I thought you just said that it's an informal network, and that a new group of people attend each year?'

Stephenfield nodded his head. 'That's true, yes. But there is also a steering committee of twelve semi-permanent members, of which Kern is one.'

'But being part of a steering committee for an international group is hardly an unusual thing for a White House aide, surely?' Lynn countered.

'Normally you would be right, of course,' Stephenfield conceded. 'But the Bilderberg Group is by no means normal. It is the subject of much international scepticism, and conspiracy theories abound regarding what these global leaders get up to at their secret meetings. Some people feel that they are deciding international policy in a very undemocratic way, unelected people discussing matters of global importance without any reporting mechanism or oversight. Some believe they are attempting to gradually impose a new world order, with big business interests behind it all.'

'But I still don't see how it ties in with the body, or the people who have been killed,' Lynn persisted.

'Perhaps it doesn't,' Stephenfield admitted. 'But Kern's membership of the group is the only anomaly we have found so far, and therefore worthy of investigation. Even more so now, as Samuel Atkinson's attendance at a Bilderberg meeting as head of NASA gives us a clear link. Your NASA group finds a body, you report it to Atkinson – who is linked to the group – and soon the body has gone missing and all your colleagues are dead. Matt goes to help you, asking an old friend for help – and then his friend is killed, and a police unit that has been operational since the nineteen seventies is suddenly shut down for no reason – again by somebody connected to the Bilderberg Group.'

'OK,' Adams said, nodding his head, 'so we have a possible connection. What else do we know about them?'

'We've simply not had the time to run a complete check on the group,' Stephenfield admitted, 'but what we have found out is interesting, to say the least.'

'What have you found?' Adams asked.

'From our initial investigations, using various government resources, which thankfully we still have unofficial access to, it seems that, far from being purely a talking shop, the annual meetings are used as a recruiting ground of sorts.'

'Recruiting for what?' Lynn asked.

'Ah,' Stephenfield replied. 'Well, that's the sixty-four-thousand dollar question, isn't it? Reports from certain attendees who have spoken about the event indicate that at some stage of the weekend conference, each delegate has to have an informal "chat" with the steering committee. This chat is held in a private room, something of an interview, it would seem. But nothing is ever mentioned about what it is they might be recruiting for. But it seems that over the years, an unusually high proportion of guests at the meetings end up having unfortunate "accidents" – car crashes, heart attacks, slipping in the shower and breaking their necks, you name it.'

'So what do you think is going on?' Lynn asked.

'I suppose one possible explanation,' Adams ventured, 'would be that occasionally one of them turns the offer down. And, now that they know what it is, the group silences them in order to ensure their true purpose never becomes public knowledge.'

Ayita nodded his head slowly. 'Our thoughts exactly, Matt,' he said. 'So the question still remains, what are they recruiting for? Something they are willing to kill for, certainly. And so I can't help but feel that it ties into your own problems somehow.'

'But how?' Adams asked, confused.

'We are still investigating, but our powers are now – thanks to Kern – necessarily limited.'

Adams and Lynn looked at each other, thinking hard. Was there anything? Anything at all that they might have missed?

'The helicopter,' Lynn said suddenly, looking up. 'I tried to find out information on the flights myself, but I couldn't get access to any of it. In Antarctica, there were two military helicopters, Chinooks I think. They had serial numbers on their tail rotor assemblies.' She thought for a moment, and then recited the numbers, glad that her scientific mind and memory of detail were still working.

Stephenfield nodded his head. 'They may have been false IDs, but given that they expected everyone on board your chopper to die, it's possible they may have been genuine. We'll look into it.'

Adams looked at Stephenfield, then at all of his comrades both new and old, until his eyes came to rest on John Ayita. 'Thank you,' he said with deep sincerity.

Ayita waved his hand. 'It is our duty to avenge the death of brother Takanawee,' he said gravely. 'And if it involves a forty-thousand-year-old body and the world's most powerful secret cabal, then that is an adventure none of us would turn down.'

3

SANTA ROSA IS a tiny township in Pima, Arizona. Less than four hundred and fifty people live there, in an area of just under six square miles, with over fifty per cent of its population existing below the poverty line. It is situated squarely in Tohono O'odham territory, and was therefore safe – outsiders were unwelcome, and very easy to spot.

The tiny flat-board house Adams and Lynn were using was one of the only unoccupied units in the township, and Ayita had organized for them to stay there for the time being. They were given a pick-up truck in case they needed to get to Phoenix to collect the lab results or if they needed to leave in a hurry for any reason, and were told that Stephenfield would visit them in twenty-four hours with news of their investigation. As telephones and other forms of electronic communication could no longer be trusted, it was decided that face-to-face meetings were the only answer.

As Adams looked out of the dirty living-room window from behind the dusty shutters, he felt the memories returning. He had spent many days in Santa Rosa – known as *Kaij Mek* to the O'odham – over the years he had worked for the Shadow Wolves, running down leads, talking to the town's inhabitants, and cutting for sign down by the area's major highway, Indian Route 29.

It was close by, just off Indian Route 15, that he had discovered the truck all those years before. And the bodies.

He turned away quickly and headed for the kitchen, and saw Lynn lying on the sofa, asleep. She had been complaining of sickness, and Adams had laid her on the couch, where she had passed out instantly.

Even asleep, he admired her beauty, the taut yet soft line of her cheek, the arched eyebrows, the way her hair fell across her forehead, arms wrapped across her body and knees up to her chest.

He crossed the room, took his jacket from an easy chair opposite and placed it over her. He bent closer, kissing her gently on the cheek.

He wondered how she felt about him. He knew that their physical reunion in Peru was probably the result of deep emotional needs requiring some sort of powerful physical release after their escape across Chile and the subsequent helicopter crash. But for him it had been more than that, something he had wanted to happen on an even more fundamental level, and he hoped that Lynn felt the same way.

They hadn't really had a chance to talk properly since then, everything had been happening so fast, but as he looked down at her, his heart skipping the proverbial beat and his stomach swimming, he knew one thing. He loved her.

He lay down next to her, cradling her in his arms, nestling his head against hers. He closed his eyes, drinking in the scent of her hair, contented for the first time in many years.

And then, mercifully, he drifted off into a deep sleep; for the first time in a long time, a *real* sleep.

* * *

Twelve hours later, Adams sensed the man about to knock on the door. He was already standing next to it. The sound of footsteps coming up the path had woken him from his sleep, and he had leapt from the couch, revitalized and filled with new life from his extended, much-needed rest.

By the tempo of the gait, he surmised it was Stephenfield – although it seemed the intelligence chief had altered the length of his stride, perhaps to test his awareness.

'Come on in, Sam,' he said, opening the door just before the knock came.

Stephenfield looked up and smiled. 'You didn't fall for it then?'

'You nearly had me,' Adams joked as he let his old friend in, 'but I guess you'll just have to try harder next time.'

'Well, you always were the best,' Stephenfield admitted as he entered the living room. He spotted Lynn sitting on the couch, rested now after her long sleep, and nodded his head in greeting. 'Hi, Lynn,' he said amiably.

'Hi, Sam,' Lynn said in return. 'I'm not sure what we have in the kitchen, but can I get you something?'

Stephenfield shook his head. 'No thanks,' he replied. 'You're probably going to want to hear this right away. We've got some news.'

Adams went to sit down on the couch next to Lynn, and they interlinked hands without even thinking. Stephenfield took his seat in the armchair opposite.

'Right, first things first,' he began. 'We checked with DNA Analytics, and they haven't got any results yet.'

Adams nodded his head. 'Yeah, it'll be at least another day or two, we figure. Hopefully the money will speed things up a bit, though.'

'And the helicopter?' Lynn asked anxiously.

'Well, it looks like we were right about the Bilderberg Group. We used the numbers you gave us and traced the helicopters through several cut-offs and back channels to the person who chartered them.' Stephenfield noted the look of anticipation on the faces of both Lynn and Adams. 'Wesley Jones,' he told them, and saw their looks turn to confusion, realizing that they would never have heard of the man. And why should they? 'Fifty-six years old, ex-Defence Intelligence Agency, rank of colonel. Now the private aide to Stephen Jacobs.'

Adams and Lynn had been given dossiers on what Stephenfield had already found out about the Bilderberg Group and knew instantly who Stephen Jacobs was.

'The chairman of the group?' Adams asked for confirmation.

'One and the same. So let me spell it out,' Stephenfield carried on. 'The aide of the chairman of the Bilderberg Group is the person who chartered the helicopters that took the team of engineers to the Antarctic, and that left with the body. We now have a clear, definite link between the group and what's been happening to you both.'

'OK,' Adams said in a measured tone. 'What else do we know?'

'John wants to talk to you about that himself,' Stephenfield said in answer, standing up from his chair. 'Come on, let's go.'

Hi Kdan Business Park is part of the San Xavier Development Authority, located in Tucson, just off the Nogales Highway. Situated within Tohono O'odham territory, it was regarded as something of a safe haven for John Ayita, who rented one of the small industrial units on a long-term lease.

The situation with Matt Adams and his ex-wife disturbed him greatly. Not only was one of their old comrades dead, but their entire unit had been shut down by an enemy that seemed enormously powerful. And what about the body that Lynn and her team – also all dead – had found in the Antarctic? What was the story behind that? What Ayita had learnt recently certainly hinted that it might be very special indeed, which was why it was attracting such very special attention. But it was where the remaining helicopter, the one that had carried the body, had ultimately landed that worried Ayita particularly. It meant the powers ranged against them, and which they would be forced to confront, were greater than they had at first thought.

They were going to have to enter the belly of the beast, and he couldn't help but wonder if Adams still had the fight for it.

4

THE SUN WAS starting to set, a huge red fireball slowly descending behind the Tucson Mountains far to the west, when Stephenfield's battered Ford sedan rolled into the industrial estate.

A large door was open in the side of Ayita's unit, and Stephenfield drove slowly through, parking his car within the building itself, safe from prying eyes. He got out of the car, followed closely by Adams and Lynn.

The inside of the building appeared to be a small warehouse, and even contained stock of some kind, although Adams had no idea what it would be. Crates on pallets ran all round the walls of the available space, and an open stairway led to a second-level catwalk and a glass-fronted office that looked out on to the rest of the warehouse. As Adams looked up, he saw Ayita in the big window, gesturing for them to come up.

'OK,' Ayita said when they were all sitting on folding metal chairs in his Spartan office. 'Sam will have already told you the connection to Jacobs, yes?' He watched for confirmation before continuing, prowling the office like a big cat. 'Right, so now I'll tell you where the helicopter with the body landed. We tracked the route to McCarran International Airport in Las Vegas. Specifically, to the Janet Terminal.'

'The Janet Terminal?' Adams asked, the ramifications hitting him like a sledgehammer.

Ayita merely nodded his head.

'OK,' Lynn said, knowing she was missing something, 'would someone like to tell me what is so special about the Janet Terminal?'

'Do you want to tell her, Matt?' Ayita asked.

Adams nodded his head slowly, turning to Lynn. 'When I used to work down here, sometimes we'd go as far as Nevada. We got talking to the local tribes around the area, they pretty much know exactly what goes on. The Janet Terminal at McCarran has always had a lot of rumours about it, but the guys we knew filled us in. We checked it out and it was all true.'

'*What* was true?' Lynn asked.

Adams and Ayita exchanged looks. 'The so-called "Janet flights" out of McCarran generally go to one place, and one place only,' Adams said at length. 'The US Air Force installation at Groom Lake. Better known to the world at large as Area 51.'

'Area 51?' Lynn asked incredulously. 'Are you sure?'

Adams nodded his head, noting that he didn't have to explain to Lynn what Area 51 was.

The base derives its name from being classified on maps of the 1950s and 1960s as 'area 51' of the Nevada Test and Training Range, a truly colossal military site of nearly four thousand seven hundred square miles – bigger than some countries.

Its very existence was denied for decades by the US government, which maintained that there was no such facility, but in actual fact, knowledge of the base's existence – if not exactly what currently goes on there – is widespread.

The base is a top-secret military test and development facility, currently operated by Detachment 3 of the US Air Force Flight Test Centre, but founded in 1955 by Lockheed and the CIA in order to test their newly developed U2 spyplane. The base has been continually expanding ever since, and has been responsible for many other 'black' projects, including the A-12 'Blackbird', the F-117 'Stealth Fighter', and the B-2 'Stealth Bomber'. It has also played a key part in developing the latest battlefield advancements, such as unmanned reconnaissance and combat aircraft.

More notoriously, Area 51 is better known as being the repository for supposed alien UFO technology, which many people believe is hidden out at the Groom Lake facility. They say it is being reverse engineered, the only way to explain the US' continued position at the forefront of military technology.

One of the primary beliefs of such conspiracy theorists is that the Air Force and CIA took possession of a UFO that was supposed to have crash-landed at Roswell in New Mexico back in 1947. They believe that it was then stored, along with its alien pilots, at Edwards Air Force Base while Area 51 was built, and was then shipped to the new facility for analysis. Many people argue that the entire purpose of the base is the analysis, reverse engineering, and use of alien technology.

With no proof, however, rumours about the base remained just that – rumours. And while Adams and Lynn both knew that this was the case, the coincidence just seemed too great, and their shared look said they were both thinking along the same lines.

'So,' Lynn said for both of them, 'the body we found is now at the one place in the world that is rumoured to be using, or have access to, alien technology?'

Stephenfield nodded his head. 'It makes you think, doesn't it?'

Adams looked at him. 'Can we get on to the base?'

'We've considered the options but it doesn't look viable. We could try and get on board one of the Janet flights and get delivered to the base directly, but the chance of being found is too great, especially when it comes to leaving the aircraft once it lands.

'The only other way would be to access the base on foot. It is not secure in the conventional manner – it is too big to fence off entirely. But there are armed patrols, called "cammo dudes" due to their camouflage uniforms. They are actually part of a private security firm, and are authorized to use deadly force on anyone crazy enough to trespass. The whole area is littered with body-heat sensors too, so it would be very hard to move through undetected.

'And even if one of us managed to penetrate the security and get on to the base, we have no idea of the internal layout of the place. Some internet sites have put up satellite photos of the overall layout, and others have taken photographs with telephoto lenses from the nearby mountains, but what is *inside* is simply not known. I mean, there's a reason it's the world's most secretive military installation. So all we have to go on are rumours. One such rumour is that there are up to ten levels to the base *below* ground. If there is even just the possibility that this is true, where would we start? Finding anything in such a huge place would be next to impossible. Another rumour is that there are seven

hangars, with concealed doors hidden in the side of a mountain at Papoose Lake ten miles to the south of Area 51. So
the chances of finding out anything of use – if we even
managed to get in there in the first place – would be next
to zero, and the chances of being caught, arrested, and probably killed would be exceedingly high.'

Adams nodded his head in agreement.

'What else do we have?' Lynn asked.

'Stephen Jacobs,' Adams answered, reading Ayita's
thoughts. 'You've looked into him?'

Ayita nodded his head. 'We have. Sam?'

'He lives in a colonial mansion near Washington,'
Stephenfield explained. 'Right on the Potomac, next door
to Mason Neck State Park near Colchester, about twenty
miles south-west of the city proper. You've read his dossier?'

Adams and Lynn both nodded their heads. In the limited
time Stephenfield and his contacts had had available, he
had not only written a briefing paper on the Bilderberg
Group itself but had also collated biographical details on
the organization's steering committee.

'So you'll know he was a DC bigwig, and obviously still
holds a lot of sway in town. Can't really find out too much
about him before the age of thirty, but since then he seems
to have literally skyrocketed through the ranks of both
military and civilian intelligence. He likes to be where the
action is, so even though he's retired, he's kept close to the
capital. Makes sense. As head of the Bilderberg Group, he'll
want to be dialled in to everything.'

'And we know something about this house?' Adams
asked.

Stephenfield smiled. 'Almost everything. We've got the

original building plans from the civic authorities, as well as internal schematics which include various security updates, and we've checked with the security firms that installed them and got further details. The place isn't military, and so we also have the latest satellite images of the place, in high definition.'

Stephenfield took out a sheaf of papers, blueprints, maps and glossy photographs, and spread them out on an old, battered card table placed in the middle of the office.

He pointed to one of the satellite photographs first, which showed Jacobs' house and grounds. 'You see the house here,' he said, gesturing at the huge, double-winged mansion. 'It's close to the edge of a cliff that descends two hundred feet to the Potomac River, set back on a lawn of about one hundred feet in length. At the other side of the house, the driveway runs almost a mile from the access road gates to the front door. And these woods that the road cuts through and that spread out for about a mile on either side? They're all his, giving him about two square miles of land, or about twelve hundred acres.'

'That's a hell of a lot so close to the capital,' Lynn observed.

'You've seen what he's worth,' Adams commented. 'What was it, two billion dollars? He can afford it.'

Stephenfield nodded. 'Yes, and that's a conservative estimate.'

Adams looked up at Stephenfield and Ayita. 'So what's the plan?'

Ayita spoke plainly. 'Our resources are limited, obviously. There are the twelve of us,' he said, referring to the unit of ex-Shadow Wolves, 'and we are also using other colleagues from the tribes. Some of our people are tracking Tony Kern already, and we've put two men in position near to Jacobs' house. They are members of the Mattaponi tribe in Virginia, brothers of Great Spirit.'

Thomas 'Great Spirit' Najana was relatively new to the team, but Adams trusted Ayita's judgement, and he had no trouble with outsourcing to the man's family – blood ties were the strongest kind of reassurance.

'We are also sending others to run surveillance on the other American on the committee, Harold Weissmuller,' Ayita continued. 'He is up in San Francisco, but we should have him by dawn.'

Weissmuller was another billionaire, a businessman who had made his fortune from oil but who had then branched out into any and every field he could, from arms sales to media ownership.

'And the others?' Adams asked.

'The other members are beyond our reach for the time being,' Stephenfield admitted. 'They are from all over the world, and hard for us to gain access to. We're trying to arrange some sort of remote electronic surveillance, though. Pretty soon, we should have a good idea of what they're up to.'

Adams looked directly at Ayita. 'I want to meet up with Thomas in DC.'

Lynn looked across at Adams, then back to Ayita. 'Me too,' she said, aware that her ex-husband would be less than happy at the suggestion.

'I'm not sure that's a good idea,' Adams interjected immediately. 'You're not used to surveillance operations, and someone really needs to stay here and wait for those lab results, and—'

Lynn held up a hand to silence him. 'Stephen Jacobs sent

the men who killed eight of my friends,' she said. 'I want to be there.'

Adams was about to protest further when Ayita raised his own hand. 'Thomas is waiting for you already,' he said, turning to Lynn and smiling. '*Both* of you.'

Adams looked up and rolled his eyes, pointedly ignoring Lynn's own triumphant smile.

5

THE LARGE MAHOGANY desk was swamped with papers, and Stephen Jacobs sat behind it with a large glass of cognac. There were twenty-three names on his list, and he had to decide on one of them soon.

Normally such selections were made at the annual Bilderberg Group meetings, and indeed up until last night they had their full complement of one hundred individuals, as agreed all those years ago. But last night one of the 'Bilderberg Hundred' had been hit by a car and killed instantly, which left a small gap that had to be filled.

He hoped when the offer was made, it would be accepted. Nine times out of ten they were; the people approached were carefully vetted, and their acceptance was virtually guaranteed. The promise of near immortality and undreamt-of power was the sort of thing that was not in the nature of such people to refuse.

But over the years, there had been some who had refused, who had demonstrated what could only be termed *horror* at the group's real plans, as if the sacrifice of human life was something abhorrent. In the main it was, of course; but for something so incredible, such sacrifice was nothing.

But the fact remained that there were the odd refuseniks, people who subsequently had to be dealt with by Eldridge and his Alpha Brigade. It was not that Jacobs regretted the killing of such people; rather, it was that if a selected candidate subsequently refused, they would have to waste time selecting another in their place. And with the device just about ready, time was something that they were quickly running out of.

Jacobs supposed it wouldn't be the end of the world if they didn't get one hundred people; after all, it would hardly affect *him*. But it was in his nature to deal and bargain and negotiate, and when he had been in the early stages of his negotiations with the group – who referred to themselves as the *Anunnaki* – he had been offered the survival of just the steering committee.

Jacobs put down the dossier he was reading and chuckled to himself. The first offer had been basic survival, and for just twelve people. By the time Jacobs had finished, he had negotiated for one hundred people and the conferring of equal status and powers as the Anunnaki themselves.

He wanted the extra people not only to make a point to the Anunnaki that they couldn't dictate terms to him, but also because the more like-minded people he had behind him, the more secure was his own position. It wasn't that he didn't trust his partners – although it was true that he didn't do so entirely – it was just that his long decades of practical experience had taught him that the more people you had in your corner, the better. If the Anunnaki were to try something, he would rather have ninety-nine capable people with him than eleven.

The whole thing was a gamble, of course; the Anunnaki might well renege on their deal, and he and his people might well end up dead, along with the rest of the world's population. But if he hadn't said yes all those years ago, somebody else would have, and he would have eventually been killed anyway. At least this way, at the forefront of the mission, there was the very real possibility of the big reward, and rewards truly came no greater than what had been finally negotiated.

Jacobs took a sip of his cognac and picked the dossier back up from the desk, when the voice came into his head, crystal clear as always.

He looked across the room to the metal box by the door, one of the machines built out at Area 51 according to the specifications of the Anunnaki.

'How are preparations?' he heard the voice say in his head, and he wondered at this 'voice' as he always did. It was not a voice in the normal sense of accent, tone and inflection; instead the words appeared directly in his brain, fully formed, almost like thoughts of his own.

'Good,' he said out loud. 'The device is almost complete.'

'When can we expect it to be operational?'

'One week from now,' Jacobs said with confidence. 'And then we will meet properly for the first time.'

The journey to DC took less time than expected. Adams had figured they would have to use roads rather than fly, due to the need to avoid airport or any other kind of security. This would have taken about two days, though, and he was relieved to find that Ayita had his own helicopter, kept round the back of the warehouse. Lynn, however, was less sanguine about boarding another helicopter. Adams had seen the fear in her eyes, but her resolve soon overcome her wariness – the time they would save would be well worth going up in the air again. At least this chopper wouldn't be stolen, or flown by remote control.

Ayita flew the helicopter himself, stopping for fuel only once at a friendly airstrip in the Choctaw Nation of Oklahoma. He finally landed just outside Fredericksville, well short of DC airspace. There, a nondescript Toyota sedan was waiting for them, and Adams and Lynn transferred quickly to the car, while Ayita refuelled once more and made his preparations to return to their home base, to monitor everyone's activities from a central point.

An hour later, the pair had arrived at Potomac Plaza Shopping Centre in Woodbridge, where one of Najana's three brothers met them. They left the sedan in the parking lot, and joined Ben Najana in his large SUV.

After introductions, Adams got straight to the point before the 4x4 had even pulled on to the main road.

'So what have you found out so far?' he asked.

'Security's good, man,' Ben said seriously. 'Better than the schematics we had. We've had a quick recon but didn't want to go in too far. The woods connect up to Mason Neck State Park and look to have some sort of body-heat sensors strung out between the trees. Cliff access looks impossible due to the breakers below – you couldn't even get close to the cliff base even if it wasn't under surveillance, which it is. The driveway is patrolled by guards and dogs, as is the lawn which backs up on to the cliffs.'

'Anything else?' Adams asked.

'The security guards are good. We estimate about a dozen of them, plus a couple of personal bodyguards. All good, professional people, the kind you're not gonna find sleeping on the job.'

'The dogs,' Adams asked next, 'what kind are they?'

'Doberman Pinschers, well-trained. There are four canine teams, one security guard with two dogs in each. They run alternate routes, swapping teams for both the driveway and the lawns.'

'OK. Where are you based now?'

'Camping up in the park. We've tried to approach the fence to his property a couple of times during the night, but it's a bitch to get over.'

Adams nodded his head. 'OK, let's get to the camp and we'll see if we can come up with a plan.'

6

By nightfall, the plan had been drawn up and rehearsed, and everyone was ready.

Lynn looked at Adams, her eyes displaying all sorts of emotions – fear, concern, belief, love – and Adams willed her to trust him. He would be going in by himself; he knew it would be safer that way. The truth was, he was the best there was at this sort of thing. It had been true before he had ever joined the Shadow Wolves, and it was true again now, his powers fully returned to him at last.

There was no need for words, just the exchanged looks of two people who had been through so much together, and realized that they still wanted to go through more. A tear rolled down Lynn's cheek, and then Adams turned on his heel and was gone, through the treeline and into the thick woods of Mason Neck Park.

The fence to Jacobs' property was an eight-foot stone wall topped by blades and razor wire, with CCTV cameras placed along its length every twenty feet. As Adams looked at it, he considered that perhaps the cliffs wouldn't have been such a bad choice.

It was a cloudy night, and at first the wood had been pitch black. Adams could have used night-vision goggles

– Ayita could certainly have found some for him – but he had never liked them, as they cut off peripheral vision and made you vulnerable from the flanks. He preferred to rely on the abilities that nature had given him, and had spent the first half-hour in the woods squatting on the cold ground, letting his eyes adjust to the dark.

The simple fact was that there was really no such thing as *pitch* black, that was just how things appeared before you let the eyes adjust. Even with clouds covering any available natural light source such as the moon and the stars, manmade sources of light were ever present, especially so close to a major city like Washington DC. Even though he was in a state park, surrounded by huge trees in an area many people would feel was in the middle of nowhere, the truth was that the nation's capital was only twenty miles away, and Mason Creek itself was separated from several major towns by only a relatively small body of water. The result was that, if you let the eyes adjust for long enough, there was enough light to see clearly with no technological apparatus whatsoever. You just had to be patient, a quality Adams had in abundance.

He also knew *how* to see things in the dark, looking at just the right angle to whatever object he needed to see, never directly at it, to maximize the effect of the available light on his retina. It was one of the skills he had learnt long ago on the plains of the Badlands.

The coating he had applied to his entire body was another. Some of the night creatures out in the Badlands, including the deadly prairie rattlesnake, relied on a type of heat-sensing vision, and he and his friends had regularly coated their bodies with cold mud when on night hunts, in order to avoid unfortunate accidents with such predators. He had done the same to himself now, every inch of his body covered with cold mud drawn up from the thick pools back at the campsite. It wouldn't necessarily fool the body-heat sensors that were supposed to be located all about the property, but it was a good back-up to his main plan, and with security like this, every little helped.

His eyes now fully adjusted to the conditions, he studied the wall, the barbed wire, the cameras, and the trees that surrounded them. It was as Najana had described: the trees from the park ran right up to the wall, while the treeline on the private side had been cut back ten feet for security reasons. He was pretty sure Jacobs would have wanted the park's side cut back too, but Adams was pleased to see that the man's influence didn't seem to extend to cutting down acres of woodland in a state park. Adams supposed the public outcry would have outweighed the beneficial effects to security. Jacobs' primary safety mechanism was probably that nobody knew where he was, and a public scene would destroy that in an instant.

The people responsible for security at Jacobs' estate would have been concerned about people simply crossing over from tree to tree, circumventing the wall by going over the top of it, which is why they had cut the trees back on their side. It wasn't going to stop Adams, though, and he examined the trees closely, walking down the line of the wall – careful to remain out of camera shot – until he came to what he thought was ideal. A big oak, whose huge, thick branches came to within ten inches of the property, four feet above the wall.

Wasting no time, Adams clambered up it, scaling the

thick trunk in seconds and hauling himself along the chosen branch until he was hanging within inches of the wall. Legs clamped tightly round the branch, lying flat on top, he looked out across the barbed wire for his first real glimpse of the estate beyond.

As he suspected, both CCTV and body-heat sensors were scattered along the open space between the wall and the treeline, ready to catch anyone foolish enough to jump from the state park side. But the sensors were designed to catch someone landing on the ground, and that wasn't Adams' intention at all.

The ten feet between the trees was too far to jump – at least in a straight line. But from a height, jumping *down*, Adams knew he would be able to cover more than ten feet.

And so he reversed back to the big trunk and kept on climbing – twenty feet, thirty feet, until he was forty feet above the ground, the branches thinner now, his position precarious as he manoeuvred out towards the end of his chosen platform.

He looked down to the trees on the other side, so far away it seemed, although they were as tall as the ones on his side. He studied the trees opposite, looking for a landing site. He knew the tree he wanted, now it was just a question of where on that tree.

The location selected, he crouched down on his branch, coiling his body like a spring, and then he released himself, launching out across the void like a jungle cat.

His extended body sailed high over the wire-topped wall, and he could feel himself plummeting to the ground with alarming speed. But the tree was also coming nearer – nearer, *nearer* . . .

Adams dropped thirty feet for the ten that he made across the clearing, and then he was at the tree on the far side, hands grasping wildly, seizing hold of branches, twigs, anything that he could, his leg catching on a thick branch, his fall broken. Then he was swinging, hands clasping other branches, until he had a secure hold, swaying upside down between two branches, still ten feet above the ground but now ten feet inside Jacobs' property.

As he lay there swinging, looking back across the monitored clearing, he allowed himself a brief smile. He had made it.

If he had been running on a track, it would have taken just a couple of minutes or so to cover the half-mile between the wall and Jacobs' house. The method of locomotion Adams had chosen, however, was going to take a lot longer.

Using the same rationale as that of entering the estate – the cameras and body-heat monitors were used at ground level, as that was where security would expect a threat to be moving – Adams decided the best way to get to the house undetected would be to use the trees. And so – slowly, carefully, often *painfully* – Adams used his superior climbing skills to stay up in the trees, working his way towards the house high up in the branches of the trees.

He was careful to keep his breathing, his heart rate and his physical movements as slow and deliberate as possible, not wanting to disturb the animals that used the trees as their home, knowing that a flock of birds escaping the treetops en masse at this time of night would be as good as a high-decible alarm call to the guards. And so what should have taken two or three minutes stretched to over three hours as he negotiated each and every tree branch by branch, sometimes able to step easily to the next tree along, other times having to jump, while on other occasions having to work his way around small clearings, which added even more time to his journey.

Twice, dog patrols passed through the woods, although never directly below him; Adams heard them a long way out, assessed their likely route, and laid up high in the treetops until they passed. The covering of mud of his body also reduced his natural scents, giving nothing to alert the dogs' acute senses.

It was a long and drawn-out process, but by the time Adams approached the edge of the treeline on the house side – the lights of the east wing shining brightly through the branches – he was sure that he had got there completely undetected.

He had considered getting the Najana brothers to create some sort of distraction, to take the security force's attention away to another part of the estate, but had eventually decided against it. Better that the security forces were not alerted at all, he had figured.

He had taken even more time to manoeuvre his way through the last few trees, knowing that the lights of the estate might now serve to illuminate him. He had a natural instinct, honed by years of practice, that enabled him to keep to the darkest areas, understanding how the trees would appear to anyone looking directly at them. He had now succeeded in attaining an excellent observation point, hidden in the treetops in direct line of sight of the east wing of the mansion house.

The brothers had offered him a collapsible, micro

parabolic mic, with which he could have listened in to voices within the house from his current position. But he had been worried about the electrical charge given off by the device, keenly aware of the security group's counter-electronic surveillance capabilities. He had therefore decided to go in 'naked', without any electrical or technological equipment. It wasn't that he didn't trust it, or thought that such equipment was useless; on the contrary, during his time in the Shadow Wolves he had used many such devices, and had at times found them invaluable. In this particular situation, however, he decided that relying on his natural resources was going to be the best option. Which meant he was going to have to get closer.

He had memorized the layout of the house – the living areas, the kitchens, dining room, study and library, the bathrooms and the bedrooms – and knew that he was looking directly at the first-floor guest bedroom, with the kitchen on the floor below. Jacobs' own bedroom was on the rear side of the east wing, facing the lawn and the bay. His private study was also to the rear, with French doors leading to the lawn's terrace. The rear façade of the house was illuminated by garden lights aimed directly at the white stucco exterior. Conversely, the eastern edge of the building that Adams was looking at was dark, unlit and shaded by the trees.

The question was, how to cross the forty feet of trimmed, open lawn between the treeline and the eastern edge of the house? There would doubtless be motion sensors in addition to body-heat detectors, not to mention the guards and their dogs. But again, it would seem that all such sensors were directed at ground level.

Still cloaked in the dark, Adams started to unravel the long, thin rope that was coiled round his body.

'Do you think he's there yet?' Lynn asked Thomas with more anxiety than she wanted to display.

'Well, he's possibly at the treeline by now, looking out over the house, probably trying to assess whether he can make it all the way with that rope of his,' Thomas responded. When he saw that this did not immediately reassure her, he added, 'But he must be doing OK, we've not heard any alarms, and there's not been any shouting or barking, so I think he must be doing all right.'

'From what I've heard about him, there shouldn't be a problem anyway,' Jacob Najana, the youngest of the brothers, interjected. 'I mean, he's a legend, right? He—' Jacob was interrupted by a bleep from the secure digital satellite radio resting between them.

'Guys,' they heard Ben's voice come through loud and clear, 'there's a problem.' Ben Najana was stationed up on Cemetery Road, observing the main access route to the house. 'Eight big SUVs just passed the main gates and are turning down the driveway. They'll be at the house in two minutes.'

Lynn went white. Matt didn't even have a radio. There was no way to warn him.

7

ADAMS HEARD THEM before they had even entered the estate, picked out the rough, V8 burble of large vehicles – eight or nine of them – travelling in convoy on the main access road to the north of his position. He heard the deceleration, the sound of tyres turning, and knew they were on the driveway, heading towards the house.

He considered his options as he hung suspended thirty feet above the side lawn from his black nylon rope. He had had to throw the rope to the far rooftop, hoping that his aim was sound. He had watched with trepidation as it had gone sailing through the night, the weighted end aimed at one of the roof's railed edges, all too aware that if it failed to hit the right spot, it would tumble uselessly to the lawn below, its forty-foot length impossible to haul back up before it hit the ground and activated every sensor and detector in the area.

But it had flown true, and anchored on the correct point, and after breathing a sigh of relief, Adams had started climbing, upside down and hand over hand, legs secured over the rope for stability.

Now he was halfway across, with around eight vehicles carrying maybe five people in each – forty extra, unknown people – about to arrive. Should he go back, or press on?

The decision had to be made instantly, as within two minutes the headlights of the oncoming vehicles would hit the house and illuminate him like the proverbial sitting duck.

Never one for retreat, there was hardly a decision to be made, and he continued doggedly on his way, one fist pumping steadily over the other.

Jacobs looked up from his paperwork as Wesley Jones entered his study.

'We've got a problem, sir,' he announced with military understatement.

Jacobs stared at Jones through his half-moon reading lenses. 'What do you mean?' he asked.

'Secret Service has just entered the estate,' Jones said uncertainly.

'What?' Jacobs nearly spilt his brandy over his papers. 'What the hell for? Where's Tony?'

'Tony is still at the White House, I just called him. He doesn't know anything about it.'

Jacobs' mind was racing. What was going on? Why had the Secret Service decided to visit him, so close to the end?

'Who are they?' Jacobs asked agian. 'How many?'

'Gate security reports eight cars, four men in each. And one of them is Lowell himself.'

Jacobs groaned inwardly. Harvey Lowell was the Director of the Secret Service. He had been a guest at a Bilderberg meeting just last year and, unknown to him, had been under consideration to become one of the chosen. He hadn't made the grade in the end, though, and the offer had never been made. His psychological profile, as well as his answers during their private, informal interview, indicated that he would have moral issues with the sacrifices that were going to be made.

But did he suspect something? Had he figured out what was going on? And why had he arrived with so many agents? Why the show of force?

Jacobs slowly took the glasses off the end of his nose and rested them on his desk, pushed his chair back and stood up.

'Well,' he said resignedly, 'I suppose I'd better go and meet him, hadn't I?'

Adams heard the vehicles getting closer and closer, could almost feel the heat of the incoming headlight beams, so heightened were his senses.

Finally, he reached the house, fingertips touching the railings, his thin-soled climbing boots resting carefully on top of the exterior brickwork of the window frame below. He would have rolled directly on to the roof, but the information gathered by Stephenson suggested that it would have its own infrared sensors strung out along the top. He therefore clung to the side of the building, melting into the dark as he disconnected the rope from the railing. He would have loved to have used the rope to get back to the treeline, but knew that a forty-foot rope spanning the space between the woods and the house would not go unnoticed for long. And so he took the weighted end and hurled it as hard as he could back at the trees he had come from, watching as it once again sailed through the air, mercifully coming to rest hidden in the uppermost branches, even as the bright headlights arrived at the turning circle at the front of the house.

He quickly pulled himself further back into the wall, flattening himself as much as he could, becoming immobile, aware that any movement now could give him away. And then the lights were brighter as the vehicles moved round the turning circle, and for a few brief seconds Adams was sure he would be spotted, certain that his dark, mud-covered silhouette would be all too visible against the white stucco of the mansion's wall.

And then, mercifully, there was dark again as the vehicles – large, black SUVs with government plates, Adams noticed – completed their turns and came to rest at the front entrance.

Adams started to edge his way down the building.

'Lowell, to what do we owe the honour?' Jacobs asked charmingly as he opened the large front door of his home.

Before him stood Harvey Lowell, tall, angular and thin, with a receding hairline and a look of fierce intelligence. He was flanked by six men, all dressed in identical dark suits.

'We need to talk,' Lowell said evenly.

'Well, why don't you come in then?' Jacobs said graciously, although he was feeling nothing of the sort. 'Where are the rest of your agents?' he asked, gesturing at the eight SUVs parked outside.

'Securing the estate,' Lowell answered simply, the implication clear: the visit was not friendly.

Jacobs smiled stiffly. 'I am sure there is no need for that,' he said. 'But you better come in anyway.'

In the study, Lowell sat down and gestured at the papers still scattered across Jacobs' desk. 'Doing a little research?' he asked, eyebrows raised.

'You know how it is,' Jacobs said non-committally.

Lowell grunted in reply.

'A drink?' Jacobs offered next, trying to keep the conversation genial.

Lowell shook his head. 'No thank you. This is hardly what you would call a social visit.'

Jacobs' eyes narrowed, and for an instant Lowell was rocked by the intensity of the man's gaze.

'Well, in that case,' Jacobs said with a hint of underlying menace, 'you'd better tell me what the hell it is you want.'

Adams entered the house through the guest-room window. As he had suspected, the house wasn't continuously alarmed; people going in and out of rooms would make such a procedure unnecessarily troublesome. And so the security measures were focused largely upon detecting threats before they ever got to the house, and less so on the entry and exit points of the house itself, especially on the upper floors.

The house dated from 1815, and although some major modifications had been made in order to improve security, it was still an old house and was relatively easy to break into if you knew how. After all, with twelve armed security guards on-site, who in their right mind was ever going to break into the house in the first place?

Adams recognized the infrared strip light running across the inside of the window frame. After disabling the lock, a simple hand-held mirror slipped between the light beam as he made his entry was sufficient to stop the alarm going off.

Once inside, he went immediately to the far wall and pulled open a cupboard. He found himself staring down the laundry chute, still in operation and exactly where Adams had expected to find it.

Perfect, Adams thought, even as he started to climb inside.

As he neared the bottom of the chute, he slowed his descent until he was moving in complete silence, ears straining for any sound. Confident that the basement laundry room was empty, Adams allowed himself to drop out of the chute and into the huge laundry bin at the bottom. He peered out over the top to confirm the absence of security guards. He didn't know what was going on upstairs but the presence of government officials meant that there were now yet more people in the house to find him, and he would have to be even more careful.

From his position in the bin, Adams confirmed the location of the CCTV cameras and planned his route to avoid them. Then he was on the move once again, moving swiftly across the room to a door on the far side. He pulled it open the instant he was there, slipped quickly through it, and closed it again behind him no more than three seconds after leaving the protection of the laundry bin.

The new room was not a room at all really but a large cupboard, filled with shelves containing various cleaning chemicals, spare sheets and other bedlinen. And according to the building's blueprints, the cupboard was located directly underneath the ground-floor study of Stephen Jacobs.

8

'I WANT TO talk about the deaths of Ryan Yordale, Frank Croaker, Yves Desault, Vitor Dzerzewski, Patek Guillaume, Stephanie Ortmeyer, Gustav Schliesser, Helen Holmes, Anthony DeSilva, Jacek Ostrawski and Nicolas St Vincent,' Lowell said, his tone grave.

Jacobs sighed inwardly. So Lowell really did have something after all; it just wasn't the most important thing he could have found, and Jacobs actually found himself relaxing slightly.

'What do you mean?' he said at length.

'What do I mean?' Lowell said, stifling a laugh. 'I mean these eleven deaths – *mysterious* deaths – all occurred to people who had recently attended a Bilderberg Group meeting.'

'And?' Jacobs asked, sure that Lowell must have more to go on than that.

'*And*, they are deaths that have all occurred on your watch as chairman of the group.'

It was Jacobs' turn to laugh. 'Eleven people die after meetings at which I presided? Harvey, I have been chairman of the group for twelve years, and with an average attendance of one hundred and twenty, that is – what? – between fourteen and fifteen hundred people. Eleven people is—'

'Zero point seven six per cent,' Lowell interrupted. 'Or

a death rate of seven point six per thousand, but as they all died within twenty-two days of the meetings, this equates to a death rate of one hundred and twenty-six point one per thousand per year, which is *twelve times* higher than the national average. How do you explain that?'

'I'm not sure I have to, do I?' Jacobs asked mildly.

Lowell's nostrils flared. 'Do you know the death rate for people attending Bilderberg meetings before you took over? It was *lower* than the national average, which is what you would expect given the wealth of the attendees and their easier access to advanced medical facilities. So what we have is a *twentyfold* increase in the death rate of attendees since you took over, a rate that has been pretty much steady for the twelve years you have been in charge.'

'I'm still waiting for the part where you tell me what you're doing here,' Jacobs said offhandedly.

Lowell slammed his fist down on the table. 'Dammit, you know exactly what I'm talking about! You're running the Bilderberg Group like a recruitment centre, we all know that. Those little private meetings, we all know you're inter-viewing for something. And maybe some people you choose, when they realize what it is you're offering, they just hold their hands up and say, "Hell, no!" And then what do you do?' Lowell slammed his fist down on the table again. 'Kill them!' He snapped his fingers. 'Just like that!'

Jacobs was silent for a time, then started chuckling to himself. 'I'm still waiting for the evidence you possess, besides some dubious statistical anomalies. Croaker died of a heart attack, Schliesser was hit by a car, Ostrawski had a brain aneurism, the list goes on, all certified by doctors, nothing untoward ever suggested or implied. Suspicious?

I'll give you that. Solid, as in court-of-law solid?' He smiled again. 'I don't think so.'

Lowell sat back in his chair and smiled his own wide, wicked smile. 'Stephen, I think you have me all wrong,' he said. 'I don't want to arrest you.'

Jacobs' eyes narrowed, suspecting what the man really wanted. 'What *do* you want, Harvey?' he asked quietly.

'I want in,' Lowell said with confidence. 'Whatever your little scheme is, I want a part of it. And if you don't let me in, I'll do my best to bring it all crashing down around you.'

What the hell? In the cupboard below the study, Adams had positioned himself on the uppermost shelf, his ear to the ceiling, senses strained to the maximum as the conversation filtered down through the old house's woodwork.

The Director of the Secret Service, Harvey Lowell, was asking to be brought into Jacobs' inner circle, become part of the project.

Was he serious? Adams couldn't believe it. Was there nothing people like this would stop at when it came to increasing their power, wealth and status? Adams sighed; of course there wasn't, he knew that about as well as he knew anything.

He listened harder; if Lowell was asking to be let in, and Jacobs capitulated, then he might just be able to learn what the hell this thing was all about.

'What makes you think I'm going to tell you anything?' Jacobs said, as he sipped thoughtfully at his brandy glass. 'Maybe you're just fishing, hoping I'm going to incriminate myself.'

'Maybe I am,' Lowell said evenly. 'But then it would just be my word against yours, wouldn't it? You can have me swept for a wire if you want.'

Jacobs looked at his glass for several moments, then pressed the intercom on his desk.

'Yes, sir?' Jones' voice came through, loud and clear.

'Wesley, get Eldridge in here,' Jacobs ordered.

Then both men rested back in their seats, looking at one another, each one trying to assess the other, weigh up their character, their willpower, their internal resources.

The spell was broken moments later by a knock on the door. 'Come in,' Jacobs said, and he looked over Lowell's shoulder as Flynn Eldridge entered the room.

'Check Mr Lowell for a wire, would you, please?' Jacobs asked him.

Eldridge nodded his head, and asked Lowell to rise from his chair. He then passed an electronic sensor over the man's body, before giving him a thorough physical check.

Halfway through the check, Jacobs managed to catch Eldridge's eye while Lowell's back was turned. He blinked twice, clearly, and then gave a coded signal with the fingers of one hand.

Eldridge recognized the order immediately, and blinked his own eyes once in confirmation.

He finished the search, thanked Lowell and turned back to Jacobs. 'He's clean,' he said, before being dismissed by Jacobs.

Once the door had closed behind Eldridge with an audible click, Lowell turned to Jacobs, all business. 'Satisfied?' he asked.

Jacobs shrugged his shoulders. 'I suppose so. What now?'

'Now,' Lowell said happily, 'tell me everything.'

'The Secret Service?' Lynn asked, wondering what it could possibly mean.

'John's confirmed the license plates,' replied Thomas. 'Looks like the director himself has gone to pay Jacobs a visit. Our guys watching Kern have also said that his phone has been going crazy for the past half-hour, so we can probably assume it's an unannounced visit, and Jacobs or his staff have been trying to contact Kern to find out what the hell is going on. And according to our guys, Kern is flapping himself, knows nothing about it.'

'Do you think the Secret Service have been working the same angles as us? Do you think they've found out what's been going on?'

'Who knows?' Thomas replied. 'But if that's the case, maybe they'll do our job for us.'

9

JACOBS FINISHED ONE glass of brandy, poured himself another and drank half of it before he leant back in his chair and smiled at Lowell.

'You want to know what's going on?' he asked.

Lowell leant forward, his glare intense. 'I *demand* to know.'

Jacobs sighed resignedly, nodded his head, and motioned to the metal cube in the corner of the room. 'We used to have to contact them through all manner of complex apparatus. Our questions took weeks to get to them, and their answers the same to return. And now we can communicate just by using that box there.'

'"They"?' Lowell asked, a look of scepticism writ plain across his aquiline features. 'And just who in the hell are "they"?'

Jacobs smiled charmingly. 'You've heard of Roswell, of course.'

'Roswell?' Lowell asked, unbelieving. 'What's that got to do with anything?'

'July the eighth, nineteen forty-seven,' Jacobs began, almost as if Lowell wasn't there. 'Roswell, New Mexico. Walter Haut, the Public Information Officer for Roswell Army Air Field, made a press release announcing that the 509th Bomb

Group had recovered a crashed "flying disc" from a nearby ranch. It was later claimed that the debris recovered from the crash site was in fact from a highly classified project known as "Mogul", a high-altitude surveillance balloon that was designed to spy on Soviet nuclear weapons tests. But the original story was in fact true. The wreckage was indeed from a flying disc, of unknown origin. Unfortunately the pilots died in the crash, but we have established contact since, aided by the technology we recovered.'

Lowell looked stunned, still not sure whether to believe a single word of what he was hearing. 'But contact with *who*?' he persisted.

Jacobs gestured at the box behind Lowell. 'Why don't you ask them yourself?'

Beneath the office, Adams tried to ignore the other sounds he was picking up from around the house, important though they were, and did his best to concentrate on the sounds above.

It looked as if Jacobs was about to open communications with whoever he was working with – or maybe even working *for* – and Adams hoped to finally learn what was going on. He pressed his ear to the thin fibreboard ceiling panel, and strained to his utmost.

'Who . . . who are you?' Adams heard Harvey Lowell, the Director of the US Secret Service, say uncertainly.

Adams waited for the answer but was rewarded with silence. He was concentrating so hard on listening he could even pick up what he took to be the men's breathing – Jacobs' deep and rhythmic, Lowell's excited and nervous. But still no answer.

'What is this?' Lowell said next, sounding shocked.

'That's the way the box works,' Jacobs answered. 'Just let it happen.'

The box? Adams wondered. *What the hell is he talking about?*

'OK,' Lowell said next, determination in his voice. 'Can you tell me what is going on?'

Again Adams tried to listen to the answer but could hear nothing, just the breathing. And Lowell's breathing was rapidly increasing. Adams wondered what it was he could be hearing.

'It . . . It can't be true!' Lowell stammered.

'Oh, but it is, my friend,' Jacobs assured him. 'And you've not even heard the best of it yet.' His tone changed, as if he was now speaking to someone else. 'Why don't you tell him what is going to happen?'

Again there was silence, and again Adams wondered not just what the two men were hearing in the room above but how they were hearing it. What was the box they had? Surely it wasn't as simple as some sort of telecommunications device – Lowell certainly wouldn't have been impressed with anything so mundane. Was it some sort of alien technology? Jacobs' talk of Roswell, and the recovered wreckage of a flying disc, would certainly hint at such a possibility, and at this point Adams was ready to believe anything.

'You're . . . You're crazy!' Lowell shouted, and the fear and horror in his voice were clear. 'You can't do this! You can't!'

'Harvey, this is why you weren't selected at the last meeting. We decided you would never approve of the plan. You're simply not strong enough.'

'Strong?' Lowell said, his voice regaining some of its earlier composure. 'This isn't strength, Stephen. It's genocide.'

'And that doesn't take strength?' Jacobs shot back. 'Something like this takes more strength than you would believe possible.'

Genocide? Adams' head was spinning.

'It doesn't matter any more anyway,' Lowell said. 'I'm gonna shut you down. I'm gonna shut it all down, and I don't care who your friends are or where they come from. I'm going straight to the president, your secret little project in Europe is *not* going to be operational next week, and those friends of yours are never going to set foot here. And you and all your Bilderberg cronies are going to jail for a *very* long time.'

There was a pause, and then Adams heard Jacobs chuckle.

'Oh, you think this is funny?' Lowell asked. 'My men are all over this place, and you're all under arrest as of right now.'

Jacobs chuckled again, and Lowell changed his tone, sounding as if he was now talking into a microphone. 'Jenkins, start rounding them up,' he said with renewed vigour. 'We're shutting this place down.' There was a pause. 'Jenkins?' he asked again, anxiously.

Still Jacobs was chuckling, and the noises Adams had tried to drown out from the other areas of the house all started to drop into place.

'Fredriks?' Lowell asked next. 'Fielding?' His voice snapped back to Jacobs. 'Damn you, what's happened to them?'

'They're dead, Harvey. Their fate was sealed the moment

ORIGIN

you brought them here. *You* had a chance, though. If you'd accepted the vision, you could have joined us. You could have been one of us.'

'Hey,' Lowell said in a placatory tone, 'let's not get ahead of ourselves, Stephen. We can negotiate, right? I mean, that was then, and this is now, right? It's not too late. I can still join you. You know I can be useful. You know that, right?'

'No, Harvey, I don't. But why don't I ask my friend?' he said reasonably. 'What do you think?' he asked, and Adams could envision him directing his question to the mysterious box.

'Well,' Jacobs said moments later, 'that seems pretty clear, doesn't it?'

'No!' Lowell yelled, and Adams heard him pushing his chair backwards, moving quickly, fearfully. 'No!'

And then Adams heard the loud, concussive blasts of three 9mm rounds fired from a semi-automatic handgun, and the heavy thud as Lowell's dead body hit the floor above him.

10

JACOBS STARED DOWN at the dead body of Lowell, lying bleeding on his study floor. It had been unfortunate but necessary.

'Why did you contact us?' The voice entered Jacobs' mind almost painfully. 'You could have dealt with this yourself. It was unnecessary to give him details.'

'On the contrary. We felt we could use him on our team before. He was a good man, we just felt he wouldn't go along with it. But then he came here, *demanding* to be a part of it. It was worth finding out.' *Especially as I still need to find one more person anyway*, Jacobs didn't say.

'Just so long as it does not interfere with our schedule.'

'It will not,' Jacobs promised. He had already decided what to do with the bodies of Lowell and his men. 'We will meet in person within the week, I promise you.'

'What the hell's going on over there?' Lynn asked, startled by the muted gunfire coming from the other side of the woods.

Thomas got straight on the secure radio to Benjamin on the main road. 'Ben, what can you see?'

'Not sure yet,' Benjamin's voice came back, crystal clear. 'But I'm pretty sure that was nine-millimetre fire, and the Secret Service carry forty cal.'

'You think Jacobs' men have opened fire on the agents?' Lynn asked incredulously.

'It's possible,' Thomas replied. 'I don't know what the hell is going on but I'd be ready to believe anything right now.'

Adams gently lowered himself from the top shelf, silently touching down on the floor.

He had outstayed his welcome and was going to have to leave. If he read the situation correctly, Lowell's Secret Service agents were all dead. It would be standard procedure for Jacobs' security team to now comb the building to make sure it was secure.

But what had he learnt? Adams began to think, but a rattle at the outside laundry door made him go instantly alert.

Damn! He chastized himself; there would be plenty of time for reflection if and when he managed to escape from this place. For now, he had to concentrate his resources on survival.

Reacting on instinct, he hauled himself back up to the topmost shelves again, lying flat just below the high ceiling. It was cramped and dark in the store cupboard, but if anyone looked directly up, they wouldn't fail to see him.

Adams concentrated on his breathing, consciously slowing it, putting himself into a state of reduced metabolism, less likely to make any unnecessary movement that would alert anyone who came into the cupboard. At the same time, he removed the blackened knife from the sheath on his belt, holding the wicked blade flat against his forearm.

Outside, he could hear two men looking around, checking

around the laundry room. He heard the laundry chute he had slid down earlier being opened, the men obviously looking up into it. He heard it swinging shut, and then the next thing he knew, the cupboard door was flung wide open and a burly, short-haired security operative armed with a short-barrelled submachine gun entered the small space.

Adams watched from above in a state of heightened anticipation as the man looked through the lower shelves, knowing that if the operative looked upwards, he would have no choice but to dive straight on to him and kill him with the knife.

But the man just moved two tubs of bleach to one side in a half-hearted gesture and then muttered to himself, turned on his heel, and left, closing the cupboard door behind him.

Adams waited a few moments more until the men had left the larger laundry room, and then exhaled slowly.

He was about to slide back down to the ground when voices from above caught his attention.

'What are we going to do with the bodies?' Adams heard, recognizing the voice as that of Eldridge, the security guard who had searched Lowell earlier.

'Round them up, put them in their own cars, and drive them out to Pahosa Point,' Jacobs said in reply. 'I've just spoken to GT, he's going to meet you up there with an oil tanker. Rig up a crash, make sure all vehicles are involved and incinerated by the tanker exploding. It'll look like they died on their way here.'

'Sir,' Adams heard Eldridge say in protest, 'those bodies are full of bullet holes. One body alone has over thirty rounds in it. It won't look like an accident for long.'

'We don't need it to look like one for long,' Jacobs replied. 'Just for a few days, and we can use our resources to slow down any investigation. After that, it won't make any difference at all.'

'Yes, sir,' Adams heard Eldridge reply, but he didn't even consider *why* it wouldn't matter in a few days' time that an entire cohort of Secret Service agents had just been massacred; instead he latched on to something else Jacobs had just said.

The cars. They were going to move the cars.

And in an instant, Adams realized he had a way out.

'OK, drag them inside,' Eldridge ordered the guards, pointing towards the government SUVs. The men nodded grimly and started to load the bodies into the large 4x4s.

The bodies of the Secret Service agents had already been recovered and arranged in front of the entranceway, a thick trail of blood and entrails leading from the house.

The agents had gone around the house, rounding up the guards by relying on their presidential authority. They had forced the guards to drop their weapons but had failed to cuff them or check them for back-up pieces, which they all carried.

When Eldridge had sent the message to retaliate, the men had simply drawn their weapons and shot the agents dead. So confident were the Secret Service men in their inviolable authority, they had been caught completely off guard, and only one agent had managed to get off a shot of his own.

Killing over thirty members of the elite presidential bodyguard would have unnerved most men, but Eldridge remained unmoved, as did the security guards; after all, they knew that the world's ultimate power was not possessed by any government.

Being one of the hundred 'chosen', Eldridge himself knew even more. He knew exactly why the deaths of all these men mattered not one bit.

They would all have been dead in the near future anyway.

Adams manoeuvred himself through the house as quickly as he could, aware that even though Jacobs' men were otherwise occupied, he could still be discovered at any time. He saw bodies being dragged through the house, blood still pumping across the tiled floors from the bullet holes that riddled them, but managed to remain undetected. And then he was at the window of the dark kitchen, staring out at the well-lit courtyard outside. The eight SUVs were parked up in a semicircular arc around the turning circle directly outside the front entrance, the bodies lined up in front of them.

Despite himself, Adams was impressed; the Secret Service agents had outnumbered Jacobs' own men by more than two to one, which meant that they would have had to shoot at least two men each before the agents could react. And although perhaps overly confident, Secret Service agents were no slouches, they were well-trained professionals.

Jacobs' men struggled to load the heavy, blood-soaked bodies into the row of cars, under the watchful eye of a large, intense man that Adams assumed had to be Eldridge. He guessed Jacobs would still be ensconced in his study, probably with Jones, trying to achieve some sort of damage control. A professional cleaning team would need to be on-site as soon as possible, for a start. All traces of the Secret Service having been here would have to be eradicated.

Adams checked the layout of the vehicles, and knew he had to make his choice quickly; although loading the bodies was a slow process, it wouldn't last forever. There was a long shadow stretching from a bush just outside the utility room all the way to the SUV on the far left side. It was possible that he would be able to slip out of the window unseen and crawl to the car within the shadow.

Adams was just about to move when he sensed them behind him. Perhaps it was the smell, perhaps the breathing, or perhaps even the feral energy, he didn't know which he picked up first; but he knew that two of the Doberman Pinschers had just entered the kitchen.

With all of the guards involved in the clean-up operation, they must have just let the dogs off the leash within the house. He wondered where the other two were, and hoped they were still outside.

He turned slowly, carefully, until he saw them, staring at him in anticipation, tails still, ears pricked, alert and ready to act. The teeth were not even bared in warning, and Adams knew that these dogs did not want to scare him but were primed to kill if necessary.

Adams stood his ground, eyes not meeting the dogs' directly but instead lowered slightly, non-confrontational. Without moving his body at all, he started to emit a low, almost inaudible hum. The dog on the left tilted his head, curious about the sound, and the dog on the right retreated a half-step.

Adams read the signal and advanced a half-step of his own, raising the pitch of his voice, looking up further, and raising his right palm slowly up in front of him.

Both dogs looked as if they were trying to resist some

unseen force, but then both capitulated at the same time, sitting down like show dogs, tails starting to move, mouths now open and tongues out as they assessed their new master.

Adams smiled as he looked at his new friends, quickly calculating how they could help him.

11

ELDRIDGE'S HEAD SNAPPED round at the sound of panting and scurrying feet, and was amazed to see the two guard dogs that had been let into the house come bounding out down the stone steps and go sprinting off into the darkness of the trees that bordered the long driveway. The guards also noticed, pulling their heads out of the cars to watch the two animals race into the woods.

'Thompson, Greer, Jenkins, Marquez,' Eldridge ordered just moments later, 'get after them, see what they're after.'

He watched as the men drew their weapons and raced off after the dogs into the treeline. The Dobermans were well-trained guard dogs, they wouldn't have gone tearing off through the estate just for the fun of it; there must be something out there.

'Ellison, Carter,' Eldridge said after further reflection. 'You too.'

The two other guards gave chase to the dogs.

Eldridge turned back to the remainder, who stood looking after their comrades. 'Back to work!' he ordered gruffly. They still had a schedule to keep to, and the oil tanker would be at Pahosa Point in fifteen minutes.

* * *

Adams was well-secured under the chassis of the big SUV when the now breathless guards returned to their vehicles. He had used the distraction of the dogs to come out of the utility room window and follow the shadow to the car. He could have tried to use the guards' preoccupation with loading the bodies to make his escape back into the treeline, but without the security of height, he was worried that the estate's sensors would pick him up. He wanted to leave the estate with no trace of his ever having been there, so he had decided that he would ride out with the guards themselves, hiding underneath one of the vehicles, knowing that they would have no reason to check there.

'And?' he heard Eldridge shout.

'Nothing, sir,' one of the men replied. 'They've just gone crazy, barking at the moon. Ain't nothing out there 'cept us and the dogs.'

There was a pause, and Adams could imagine Eldridge mulling things over. 'Probably just freaked out by the shooting,' he said finally. 'Happens sometimes, even to trained animals. OK, let's move out.'

'Yes, sir,' Adams heard the men reply, watching the booted feet marching to the other SUVs in the line and climbing aboard.

Soon, the engines started, and then the government vehicles were moving, crunching the driveway gravel as they turned towards the driveway.

Towards freedom.

'The cars are coming back up the driveway,' Lynn and the two Najana brothers heard Benjamin announce over the radio.

'Can you see who's in the cars?' Thomas asked immediately.

'Negative,' his younger brother announced. 'Headlights are on full and side glass is smoked.'

There was a pause, and then Benjamin's description continued. 'They're now at the main gate, about to turn . . . They're going right, must be headed for Pahosa Point.' Silence followed for several moments more. 'They've gone past, headed up the main road, all eight cars. Still couldn't see who was inside. I—'

Thomas' hand gripped the radio tight as the connection went dead. 'Ben?' Thomas whispered urgently down the broken line. 'Ben?' he asked again helplessly, before putting the radio down, his eyes meeting Lynn's and Jacob's.

Lynn reached out and put a hand on the arm of each brother. 'I'll stay here,' she told them. 'You go.'

'Son of a bitch!' Benjamin laughed, punching Adams in the arm.

Adams had dropped from the bottom of the SUV as soon as it had proceeded on to the main road, rolling unseen towards the grass verge on the opposite side to the estate. He had then worked his way in the dark through to Benjamin's observation point, creeping up behind him and putting a hand over his mouth.

Benjamin had immediately tensed, releasing the radio, turning round ready to strike, when he saw Adams standing there smiling at him. Benjamin was himself a highly regarded tracker and guide, and thought of himself as untouchable when it came to operating in the field, but Adams was truly something else.

'I better call my brothers back before they come down all guns blazing!' he said only half jokingly.

Adams nodded his head, looking forward to relaxing in the plush seats of Thomas Najana's vehicle.

Even more than that, he was looking forward to seeing Lynn.

12

IT WASN'T UNTIL they were all safely inside the rented warehouse in Tucson that Adams gave his full debrief of events.

Back at base camp, Lynn had embraced him with tears in her eyes, and Adams had held her tight, until their shared warmth had started to melt the mud that still covered his body. They kissed as they broke apart, and soon the whole party were packing up and moving towards their car.

There was a further change of vehicles, this time in Dale City, before Ayita picked them up in his helicopter at a friend's private airfield near Manassas. During this time, the group had mainly slept, and so by the time they arrived back in Tucson, Adams' adventures had been barely touched upon. But now, with everyone well rested, he gave a detailed, blow-by-blow account of what had happened.

'So we were right about Jacobs using the Bilderberg Group as a recruitment centre,' Stephenfield said.

'It certainly seems so,' Adams agreed. 'But we still don't know what for, exactly.'

'But we can certainly hazard a guess, from what you've told us,' Stephenfield replied.

Lynn nodded her head, the scientist in her processing the information quickly. 'It would appear,' she began, 'that there was some sort of alien contact back in the late nineteen forties, which enabled communications to be opened up between us. It is also clear that Jacobs and at least some element of the Bilderberg Group are creating a device that will enable this group to come to earth, presumably en masse. The talk of genocide is disturbing to say the least, and an agreement has probably been reached whereby Jacobs and his cohorts will be spared for assisting them. And perhaps this is what Jacobs is recruiting for – the group of people who will be allowed to survive. This could explain why some people felt it was morally abhorrent and refused to be any part of it, and why these same people then met a mysterious end soon after, before they could tell anyone else.'

Ayita nodded his head. 'It would certainly make some sort of sick sense,' he agreed.

'I'm worried about the timetable,' Stephenfield said. 'You say Lowell mentioned Jacobs' "secret little project in Europe" becoming operational next week, which presumably somehow ties in with how this unknown group are coming to earth. We also have to factor in how the Director of the Secret Service and thirty-one other agents have been slaughtered by Jacobs' men, and he didn't seem fazed in the slightest.'

'The crash with the oil tanker was reported as an accident, and the fireball that resulted probably won't give much in the way of evidence,' Ayita responded, having been monitoring the events from Tucson.

'But there will be evidence, undoubtedly; it will just take time to uncover. And Jacobs' attitude indicates his belief that such an investigation will be of no consequence by then.

Which means, by extension, that the full force of the president and the United States government will not worry him at all in about a week's time.'

Ayita nodded his head, considering the matter. 'Yes, it does look like we're running out of time,' he agreed. 'It looks like next week is crunch time.'

'But what I still don't get,' Adams interjected, 'is where the body Lynn's team discovered comes into all of this. I mean, it seems alien contact wasn't made until nineteen forty-seven and yet the body she found – and which Jacobs and the Bilderberg Group are prepared to kill for, and which might even be of alien origin itself – is forty *thousand* years old. So what's the connection?'

Lynn stared ahead, deep in thought. 'I just don't know,' she admitted. 'It still doesn't make any sense.'

'Well, I might just have some good news for you,' Ayita said, smiling for the first time since the debriefing began. 'DNA Analytics will have your results ready to pick up this afternoon.' He watched Adams' and Lynn's eyes go wide with excited anticipation. 'They said to be there after three.'

DNA Analytics was its usual bustling self when Adams and Lynn entered through the electronic double doors.

Even though they were both believed dead, they still wore dark glasses, their hair was dyed and they wore bulky clothes to disguise their physical profiles. At this late stage, there was no use in taking chances.

Adams hung back to keep an eye on things as Lynn walked up to the reception desk.

The blonde receptionist, who sported the name tag 'Angela', gave her a warm, if not exactly genuine, smile.

'Good afternoon, welcome to DNA Analytics Phoenix, how can we help you today?'

'I've come to pick up some test results,' Lynn said. 'Name of Gower, Lucy Gower.'

Angela turned to her computer, her long, false nails clacking away at the keyboard. 'Ah, yes, here you are,' she said. 'Dr Connor will take you through the results. You can find him in Room Sixteen, second floor,' she continued, pointing down a long corridor to the east of the main reception. 'Down the corridor, take a left and there are the elevators. When you get out, turn right and it's the second room on the left. OK?'

Lynn wondered just how large this place was, and how many people got lost here. 'Thanks,' she said simply, and turned round, nodding to Adams to follow her.

Five minutes later, they were outside the office of Dr Connor.

The second floor was in sharp contrast to the first. Whereas the entire first floor seemed to be a frenzied melee of people all rushing about, the second floor was almost deserted.

Adams' survival instinct was instantly aroused by the change of pace, wondering why they should have had to go to such a different area to collect their results. If going to see the doctor was standard procedure, then surely this corridor should also be swarming with people?

He felt for the Glock 17 semi-automatic pistol cinched into his waistband, feeling its reassuring weight resting there. He looked up and down the corridor, and saw two men rounding the corner at the end, deep in discussion. There were three closed-circuit television cameras, but none of them seemed to be interested in either him or Lynn.

He heard the elevator *bing* as it brought others to the second floor, and Adams let his hand rest over the butt of his pistol as he waited for the doors to open.

They opened, and another couple came out into the corridor. Adams watched them as they turned left, checked the name panel on a door further down the corridor, and then knocked. A smart young doctor opened the door and welcomed them in.

'Are you finished?' Lynn asked, frowning at him. 'I think it's all above board.'

Adams smiled sheepishly. 'I'm finished,' he said, and reached forward to knock on the door.

It opened moments later, an older yet equally smart doctor standing there with a friendly smile. 'You must be Ms Gower,' he said, extending his hand.

Lynn shook it. 'A pleasure, Dr Connor,' she said in return. 'This is my friend, James Davies.'

'Mr Davies,' the doctor said, shaking Adams' hand. 'Please, come in.'

He led them into a small but plush office, expensively furnished and clinically clean. He showed them to two leather armchairs on the other side of his designer glass desk, and then took his own seat, looking down at the papers gathered in front of him.

He looked up suddenly through his half-moon glasses. 'I'm sorry, I've not offered you a drink,' he said apologetically. 'Can I get you anything? Tea, coffee?'

'No thank you,' Lynn said for both of them. 'We're anxious to get the results of the tests.'

Connor smiled at them. 'Of course.' He tapped the papers on his desk. 'The results. Most interesting. *Most* interesting.'

Lynn and Adams looked at Connor expectantly.

'Ms Gower, Mr Davies,' Connor began, staring once again through his spectacles, 'I am the senior consultant here in Phoenix. Upon initial examination, your samples were referred to me for validation. Do you mind if I ask you where they came from?'

'We can't answer that, I'm afraid, Dr Connor.'

He nodded, and looked back down to the test results. 'OK,' he began. 'Here we go.'

13

TONY KERN LEFT the president's office and immediately dialled Jacobs' number.

When Jacobs answered after the first ring, Kern got straight into it. 'He's going crazy,' he said. 'Literally crazy. The oil tanker? He doesn't believe a bit of it. He's already ordered a full investigation and it's going to be getting priority over literally everything else.'

'But did he know anything about Lowell's visit beforehand? Did he know Lowell was coming to see me?'

Kern shook his head as he walked towards the Situation Room in the West Wing of the White House, even though he knew Jacobs couldn't see him. 'Didn't know a thing about it, which is why he's even more pissed. I mean, the Director of the Secret Service and a whole platoon of agents, all out on some unregistered operation? He wants to pull out all the stops until he knows exactly what's been going on.'

'So at the minute he doesn't know anything,' Jacobs said. 'How about anyone else at Secret Service?'

'Not that I know of,' Kern answered. 'The people with him were all loyal to the director, known to him personally. Some of them were even off-duty. So it looks like some sort of private affair, which concerns the president greatly.'

'And my involvement?' Jacobs asked.

'Well, the crash obviously occurred close to your home so it's assumed that they were on their way to see you, but there's no actual evidence for that. But I'd expect a full cohort of investigators arriving on your doorstep any minute now. Is Eldridge there?'

'He's taking care of a little business somewhere else right now,' Jacobs answered.

'Probably a good thing, he doesn't have a good reputation around here. Has the house been cleaned?'

'The whole estate,' Jacobs confirmed. 'I flew out a team from Nevada, they're used to doing deep cleans. The place is spotless, like they were never here.'

'Good,' Kern said, smiling at a pair of advisers as he passed them in the narrow basement corridor. He held the cellphone closer, whispering now. 'I know we're close, but we still can't afford to take any chances. Do we have a day yet?'

'Not yet. Philippe thinks it will be ready to go by the middle of the week.'

'OK,' Kern said, still whispering as he waited outside the closed door of the Situation Room. 'I'll try and slow things down as much as I can from here. Another week shouldn't be a problem.'

'Make sure it isn't,' Jacobs answered.

'First, let's start with the scrap of material that you asked us to pass along to our sister laboratory in Pasadena,' Dr Connor began. 'Although the exact nature of the material couldn't be determined, it is thought that it is some sort of silk derivative, much like the silk of a spider's web in terms of its strength-to-weight ratio. It exhibited remarkable thermal properties too, although the piece was too small to test as thoroughly as my colleagues would have liked.'

'Had they seen anything like it before?' Adams asked.

'No,' Connor answered immediately. 'Never. They thought it might be related to some sort of advanced military technology – we know they are looking into using synthetic materials to mimic things like spider's webs – but then they performed other tests and were forced to reconsider.'

'Radiocarbon dating?' Lynn asked.

Connor nodded his head. 'Exactly.'

'And?' Adams prompted.

Connor cleared his throat. 'The consensus – after *three* separate tests were made – is a date of 40,500BC. In other words, the bit of cloth you gave us is over forty-two thousand years old.'

Lynn and Adams exchanged looks. So Devane's off-the-hoof estimation of age from the ice layers had been pretty much dead on, and Adams' own theory that the most likely explanation was an incorrect initial dating could now be put to bed. The body, and the artefacts the scientist had found with it, were indeed truly ancient.

'And the DNA testing?' Lynn asked nervously.

'Well,' Connor began, obviously disconcerted by the radiocarbon findings, 'we carried out the usual diagnostic tests, including variable number tandem repeats, particularly short tandem repeats, and then used both polymerase chain reaction analysis and amplified fragment length polymorphism analysis.'

Lynn nodded her head, while Adams just stared blankly

ahead. The methods didn't matter to him so much as the results.

'The subject was male, approximately forty years of age, with blond hair and blue eyes. No indication of internal pathologies, seems to have been robust and healthy.'

Lynn looked at Connor, her gaze boring into him. 'Let's cut to the chase, doctor,' she said. 'Was the subject human?'

The nervous anticipation of Lynn and Adams, as they sat poised on the front edges of their seats, waiting for Connor to give his answer, was suddenly interrupted by the sound of a door crashing open behind them.

'Don't answer that, doctor!'

Everyone turned in their seats to see a large, fierce man in the doorway, flanked by three armed men on each side, who quickly fanned out through the office. Adams recognized him instantly as Eldridge, the chief of security from Jacobs' house back in DC. In his hand he held a silenced pistol, aimed directly at Connor's head.

Adams and Lynn had no time to react before each of them had three silenced submachine guns trained on them.

'You!' Lynn exclaimed as she stared at Eldridge, recognizing him as Major Daley from the Antarctic. 'You bastard, I'll—'

Before she could finish her sentence, there was a low bark and the back of Connor's head suddenly exploded across the rear wall of the office, the subsonic bullet from Eldridge's handgun leaving only a small entry wound in the man's forehead. For several moments the doctor's body held upright as if suspended like a puppet, his unbelieving eyes still covered by his half-moon glasses, and then he bent straight over from the waist, his bloody head crashing into the glass tabletop.

Lynn's eyes went wide with shock and disbelief, but Adams came to his senses. Using the sound of the doctor's head smashing on to the table as a distraction, he reacted forward to create space, going for his concealed handgun. But Eldridge's men were too switched on, and the nearest one quickly smashed the butt of his weapon into the base of Adams' skull.

He literally saw stars, his head swimming with pain from the heavy blow as he collapsed to the carpeted floor, feeling rather than seeing as another man reached forward and removed the gun from his waistband. He groaned, struggling to stay conscious.

Lynn reacted herself, moving off her chair to help Adams, but she was forced back, one man slapping her across the face with a sharp *crack*.

Adams returned to reality instantly, shooting up from the floor to defend Lynn, only to be forced back down, face pushed into the carpet as his hands were pulled violently up and behind his back, and secured with plasticuffs.

He turned his head to the side, his cheek scraping along the carpet, to see Lynn also being cuffed and hauled up off her chair.

Both Adams and Lynn were pulled to their feet and pushed up against the desk, gun barrels up and raised straight into their faces.

'Dr Edwards,' Eldridge said ingratiatingly. 'Still alive.' He clapped his hands mockingly. 'I commend you, I really do. You're quite exceptional.'

'Screw you, you murderous bastard!' she yelled back in response, only to be met with a cruel smile.

Eldridge turned to Adams next. 'And you must be

Matthew "Free Bear" Adams. Quite an exceptional man yourself, giving us the runaround the way you have.' He suddenly took two paces towards Adams and violently pistol-whipped him across the face.

Adams' legs gave out and he collapsed to the floor. Eldridge looked down at him with an emotionless expression. 'That's for my men.' He looked over at Lynn. 'I'm not the only murdering bastard in the room, Dr Edwards. You'd do well to remember that.'

'That was self-defence!' Lynn exclaimed indignantly.

Eldridge only scoffed, as Adams climbed back to his feet, a colourful bruise already starting to appear on his dark skin.

'Your mistake was sending the cloth sample,' Eldridge told them. 'If you'd just stuck to the DNA, we may never have noticed. But when we intercept emails and telephone calls about a forty-thousand-year-old piece of cloth, and discover the interest and involvement of a DNA agency, then it sets our little alarm bells ringing. You'll be pleased to hear that Dr Connor's colleagues have already been taken care of,' Eldridge continued. 'You see what you've achieved with your little games? Six other people have now been killed; maybe more if our investigations show that they told anyone else.'

'You son of a bitch,' Lynn whispered with true, unbridled hatred at Eldridge, but she was sensible enough not to try and physically engage the seven armed men lined up in front of her. 'Why don't you just kill us and get it over with?' she asked bitterly.

'Oh, I wouldn't want to spoil the fun,' Eldridge said, a genuine smile spreading across his face. 'We've got some real treats in store for you.'

He gestured to his men, and Lynn watched as one of them moved towards her, another towards Adams. Lynn opened her mouth to protest, then saw the tasers in their hands. She jerked back, trying to get out of the way, but it was too late.

She felt the sudden, fierce burst of electricity enter her body, and then everything went black.

14

Adams awoke from his deep slumber, a sharp pain shooting through his head which seemed to lance his brain.

For the first few moments, he had no recollection of anything, but then things started to filter back to him; the double pistol whipping explained the pain in his head at least.

But where was he now? And where was Lynn?

He immediately noticed that wherever he was, it was dark, almost completely so. Maybe a closed room, somewhere inside, where no light seemed to be getting through. But it was too dark, and he realized he was wearing a thick blindfold. And then he realized he was restrained too, his head, torso, hands and legs secured to a high-backed rigid chair.

He opened his mouth to speak, to try and find out if Lynn was with him in this unknown place, but he had been gagged, and his mouth moved uselessly around a heavy braided cloth, unable to make any sound other than a simple, quiet grunt.

But then he heard a similar grunt from nearby – just six feet away, maybe a little more – and he knew that Lynn was near him. She was still alive.

He tried to move his body to get closer to her, but the

chair seemed fixed to the floor, and whatever had been used to bind him was too tight to break. He might try and loosen the bonds later, maybe move his mouth around the gag and push it out, try and shrug off the blindfold. But for now, he relaxed and used his other senses to get a fix on where they were. Once he became less concerned with his restraints, he immediately picked up a low, throbbing hum that seemed to come from beneath him, or maybe to the sides; in fact, it seemed to envelop him, from all angles, as if it were being channelled down the room they were in. And then he felt a subtle vibration through his body that indicated they were moving.

Adams realized in an instant that they were in an aeroplane, in a pressurized cabin. Where the hell could they be taking them? And why?

Presumably the 'why' was to interrogate them, in order to find out exactly what had happened over the past few days, and who else they might have told. Adams baulked as he thought of Baranelli, realizing they had put him in danger.

Despite his toughness, his training, his warrior spirit, Adams was under no illusion that he would be able to resist the interrogation. It wasn't that he was scared of torture, as physical pain was something he was well used to; he was scared of what he might do if forced to witness *Lynn's* torture. And if his interrogators were to use the latest drugs instead of more brutal methods, then the matter of his power to resist would be moot anyway, as these new synthetic truth serums were virtually guaranteed to work.

But the *where* still puzzled him. He knew from Stephenfield's research that as well as Jacobs' main residence at Mason Neck, he also had homes in New York and San Francisco, and Adams wondered if they were heading for one of these. The Bilderberg Group's unofficial headquarters was at the University of Leiden in the Netherlands, from where the annual meetings were organized, and Adams knew that Jacobs also spent quite a bit of time there, as well as maintaining an apartment in the city.

As he went through the various locations, he felt that none of them was right. He didn't know why but he just couldn't see why they would be shipped to any of those places.

But there was somewhere else with which Jacobs and the Bilderberg Group had a clear connection, a place with the technological know-how to get them to talk, and where their disappearance would never be reported.

Adams knew in his gut that they were headed for Area 51.

15

An interminable time later, Adams felt a dipping sensation in his stomach and intestine as the airplane's altitude started to drop, and he knew they were finally coming in to land.

By now, he just wanted to get it over with. He was sick of being cooped up on the plane, unable to move, see or talk; he wanted to get to wherever it was they were going so he could see if they had any chance of getting out of there. With no information except for the fact that they were on an aeroplane, his options had so far been limited. He knew they could only increase upon landing.

He felt the altitude dropping quickly now, and then he heard a faint electronic grinding noise, somewhere far away, and realized it was the landing gear opening up ready for touchdown.

Three more minutes later, the aircraft was taxiing, and then it came to a complete stop.

The sound of opening doors greeted him just moments after the aircraft braked to a standstill, along with the heavy pitter-patter of several pairs of booted feet. Adams could hear the breathing, and estimated half a dozen people had boarded the plane.

There were no orders given, no words spoken, but

whoever had just boarded set to work immediately, and Adams could sense the people around him, could hear as they unlocked various catches, felt his chair loosened from its moorings, and he realized that he was in a wheelchair that had been fixed in place to the aircraft floor.

He was tilted backwards, upended but still strapped securely to his chair, and then he was being wheeled down the length of the fuselage. The chair hit a bump, was pushed forcibly over it, and then he was rolled slowly downwards.

From the length of the fuselage to the exit, and the fact that he was being pushed down a ramp at the rear end of the plane, Adams quickly grasped that he and Lynn had been flown here in a C-130 Hercules transport aircraft. A primarily military aeroplane, it lent credence to Adams' earlier guesswork as to their destination.

Still no words had been exchanged between the people who had boarded the plane, but Adams identified a slight grunt as that of Lynn, and he could hear her chair being moved too, rolled down the ramp behind him.

From the body odour, gait, and breathing pattern, Adams could tell his chair was being pushed by a man, although he didn't know about Lynn's. The people pushing them seemed to take a long, winding, circuitous route to their destination, and Adams could only assume it was part of the same disorientating process as the gags and blindfolds, designed to make them panic, and weaken their resolve. He nevertheless tried to memorize the route — if they managed to escape, he might try and reverse it in order to find their way back. Although what good that would do him, he didn't yet know. But the concentration necessary was good for avoiding the disorientation and feeling of helplessness that might otherwise ensue.

First of all, they were wheeled along an even, smooth stretch of tarmac, which Adams assumed had to be the runway. He could hear other vehicles as well: two more planes taxiing in different directions, one of which had a strange, almost electronic vacuum-like engine noise that he had never heard before; a small utility vehicle, 4x4, probably some sort of military jeep; a larger truck, further away in the distance; and then another truck, passing by just a few feet away, the deep rumble of its diesel engines covering up all other noise as it thundered past.

Then suddenly they were inside, and Adams struggled to hear anything except the dull, monotonous roll of the chair wheels, and the sharp crack of the booted feet of their escorts, echoing off what he took to be a concrete floor, and down a long, empty corridor.

And then they turned right, and were immediately assailed by a bombardment of savage noise, like that of an industrial complex at full production – electric saws eating their way through sheet metal, acetylene torches doing welding work, the grinding of heavy machinery, and voices, all with the same scientific, professional tones.

Four more turns later, they stopped dead, waited for twenty seconds, and then moved forwards again, just six feet. Adams heard some doors close behind them, and sensed they were in a very confined space. He guessed it must be an elevator, and this was confirmed just seconds later as he felt the drop in his stomach and intestines once more, but much more intensely than on the aeroplane. This elevator was terribly fast, and Adams feared that he would be sick, the gag making him choke on his own vomit.

But he kept it down, and then marvelled at how long the fast descent was taking – five seconds, ten, fifteen, twenty – and he could only wonder how far down in the bowels of the earth they now were. He knew it took forty-five seconds to get from the lobby of the Empire State Building to the eightieth floor, and almost choked again as he realized the extent of the base's secret facilities.

Before he could consider it further, they were being rolled out again, down another long, empty, concrete corridor, until he heard the opening of a metal door. They were wheeled through into a room, and the sound of the wheels indicated the floor was metal too.

Then he felt the hands on the back of his wheelchair relax, and pull away; he heard the boots retreat, back out into the concrete corridor outside.

And then the door closed, trapping him and Lynn in the mysterious metal room, hundreds of feet below the surface of the earth.

Adams could sense Lynn was in the room with him, and took comfort from the fact that she was still near, although he was at the same time terrified for her safety. But at least he knew where she was; he could only imagine how he would feel if she had been wheeled off to some other part of the complex.

They were left alone for a long time, and Adams put it down to an attempt to wear them down, to make them lose all sense of time and place. His mental tracking of their route, and his current counting of the seconds of their wait helped him retain his faculties, however, and he could only hope that Lynn was doing the same thing.

His tracking of the time took him to just under fifteen thousand seconds, or just over four hours, before the door opened again.

He heard two sets of feet enter the room, one booted, one in leather-soled shoes. The lights were turned on, and Adams could feel the intense glare even through his blindfold. He knew what was coming next.

Seconds later, a strong hand ripped the blindfold from his eyes, and Adams knew the plan was to momentarily blind them, to weaken them further. But Adams had screwed his eyes tight shut the moment he had felt the hand reach forwards for the blindfold, and although the glare of the halogen spotlights in the ceiling above them threatened to burn through his eyelids, at least the shock to his retinas was somewhat subdued.

He gradually opened his eyes, and was greeted by the unwelcome sight of Flynn Eldridge grinning at him sadistically. 'I trust you had a good journey,' Eldridge deadpanned.

Adams ignored him, instead looking over to Lynn, glad to see she had also shut her eyes when her blindfold had been removed. As she opened them, he gave a reassuring smile, trying to offer her comfort and hope with his eyes.

Turning back to Eldridge, Adams could see, over the man's muscular shoulder, a debonair, suited man of advancing years whom he immediately recognized as Stephen Jacobs. Adams was impressed. So the big man himself had come down for the interrogation.

Adams watched as Jacobs approached them, appraising

them as a biologist might examine a newly discovered life form. 'So here we are, my friends,' he said finally, his tone deep and smooth. 'You and I all know that you are not going to leave this facility alive. You are going to die, make no mistake about that.' He smiled. 'How you die, though, that might make a big difference to you.'

Jacobs gestured at Eldridge, who moved forward and removed first Adams' gag, and then Lynn's. No sooner was Lynn's off than she spat at the man, straight in his face, a look of pure hatred on her own.

'Oh, come now, Dr Edwards,' Jacobs said to Lynn as Eldridge wiped the saliva off his cheek, 'it isn't his fault. Not really. He was, after all, merely following orders.'

'Your orders?' Lynn shot back resentfully.

'As it happens, yes,' Jacobs replied, his confidence unshakeable. 'And now I have ordered our experts to interrogate you using any and every available means at their disposal, until we find out exactly what you know and who else you have told.'

'We've already found Baranelli,' Eldridge told them with a hint of pleasure. 'It didn't take much for him to squeal like a piggy. Luckily, he hadn't had time to tell anyone else. He is dead now, of course.'

Both Lynn and Adams tried to launch forward out of their chairs, to get to Eldridge; both would have dearly loved to choke him to death with their bare hands. But their bonds were too tight, and the violent movements barely caused the chairs to rock slightly.

'It probably doesn't matter any more anyway,' Jacobs said, ignoring the attempted attack by the two captives. 'Things have progressed too far to worry about what might happen if the word gets out now. But it just doesn't do to leave things hanging, so to speak. You are both loose ends, and have to be tied up. There is too much riding on this to let any mistakes occur now.'

'If we're going to die anyway, why not tell us what it's all about?' Adams said. If he was going to die, he wanted to know why, at least.

Jacobs looked at Eldridge, who shook his head, and then looked back at Adams and Lynn. 'I don't suppose there's any harm in you knowing now, is there?'

Ignoring Eldridge's disapproving look, he pulled up a plastic-topped stool and sat down, smiling at Lynn and Adams, clearly pleased with himself and what he had accomplished. If he couldn't gloat at least a little, what was the point of it all?

'Let's start at the beginning, shall we?' he said with a smile.

16

FOR JACOBS, IT was nice to be finally telling the tale in its entirety, or at least the part he had direct, first-hand knowledge of.

He had spent most of his life under a double persona, one side existing only in his mind, dealing with intimate knowledge of things most people could never even dream of. It had altered his personality somewhat, until he sometimes wondered who he really was. And now his life was set to change again, and he once more wondered about his place in all of it.

'The crash at Roswell occurred on July the eighth, nineteen forty-seven. After the initial press release, the whole incident was subsequently denied, of course. And then the National Security Act was signed, and the Central Intelligence Agency came into being in September of the same year. Coincidence?' He smiled at his two captives. 'Of course not. The Act was signed by President Franklyn D. Roosevelt when he was presented with the evidence of the Roswell crash.'

Jacobs saw the look of interest on the faces of Lynn and Adams, who seemed to have momentarily forgotten about their upcoming demise. 'Yes,' he continued, 'we found a great deal of such evidence at the crash site. There was the wreckage of a spacecraft, scattered across three square miles

250

of New Mexico desert. We boxed it up and shipped it in secret to Roswell Army Air Field for initial assessment, and from there it was later moved on to Muroc Army Air Field, now known as Edwards Air Force Base.' He paused, and held the gaze of the man and woman seated opposite him. 'We also found a body.'

'What?' Lynn asked, despite herself.

'Yes, we recovered a body from the scene. In good condition actually, although unfortunately dead. But it proved that there was *something else out there*. But what we all had to ask now was, were they friendly? What were their capabilities? And so the CIA was set up to protect the nation against all foreign threats, specifically those that were *exceptionally* foreign, even extraterrestrial.

'At Muroc, we started to reverse engineer the technology we had found, and performed an autopsy on the body. What we found was interesting, to say the least. We were able to open communication with them, which was difficult at first given our level of sophistication back then.

'It was clear that the aim of these people was to come to earth in order to take over. They had been forced into space by a planet-destroying cataclysm, and they've been up there ever since, looking for a suitable place to inhabit. They were quite open about it, and wanted our help.'

'And you agreed?' Lynn asked incredulously.

'They knew how to ask,' Jacobs answered with a smile. 'They seemed to have an uncanny understanding of human nature. They appealed to our greed and vanity, plain and simple. They told us that if we cooperated, we would be rewarded with equal status in the new world they would create, and immortality.'

'And you believed them?' Adams asked sceptically.

'We had certain guarantees and proofs,' Jacobs answered. 'But that is getting away from the story. We negotiated that one hundred people would be allowed to survive, and we set up the Bilderberg Group as a way of recruiting the best that the world had to offer. Our first meeting was in May nineteen fifty-four, and it was decided at the meeting to ratify the treaty that led to the formation of CERN, on the twenty-ninth of September that same year. CERN – or the European Organization for Nuclear Research – was established to develop the technology required for bringing our visitors to earth.'

'But the spacecraft had already been here,' Lynn interjected. 'So why did they need your help?'

Jacobs nodded. 'You're right, of course. They did have the ability to cross vast distances but only in very small, one-man craft, and it involved putting the pilot into a state of suspended animation, which was often dangerous – as seen by the crash at Roswell itself, which we believe was due to the pilot not waking up from his deep sleep. They wanted something more – their entire population to be transported here en masse, along with all of their vehicles and hardware, ready for invasion.'

Jacobs ignored the look of horror on the faces of Adams and Lynn. 'It was decided to have the location for this research based in Europe rather than the United States, in order to cover up the connection between our work there, and our reverse engineering of the technology from the crash site, which was by then being held here, at Area 51.

'Not long after we opened communication channels, it was deemed that Muroc was too public, and so the CIA sponsored the building of a new base out at Groom Lake, in the Nevada desert, a place where we were virtually guaranteed anonymity. The projects everyone knows were developed here – the U2 spy plane, the stealth bomber and stealth fighter, and all the new unmanned aerial drones – are all the result of what we discovered from that spacecraft.

'Our work at CERN is a stage further removed from that. While at Area 51 we develop technology that has ensured the West's consistent superiority over our enemies, at CERN we are concerned purely with the building of a wormhole device – the machine by which our visitors will arrive here.'

'A wormhole device?' Lynn asked, disbelieving. 'I didn't think such a thing was possible.'

'It's not, at least not with the technology that you believe currently exists. But we are working with a people who are *thousands* of years more advanced than us, and their science might as well be magic to us philistines. Even with their help, we've been struggling to get the machine working properly. Of course, ours is only one of a pair – the other is on their mother craft, millions of light years away across the galaxy. Think of it as a send/receive coupling. Their machine will bend space-time, causing it to curve; our own machine, the "receiver", will make sure that their point and our point meet, enabling them to cross over. Without both machines being perfectly aligned, they might end up anywhere in the universe.'

'And the machine is ready?' Adams asked, remembering Jacobs' conversation back at his manor house at Mason Neck.

Jacobs gave a broad smile. 'Ready within the next few days, yes. We are almost there.'

'And what will happen when they arrive?' Lynn asked.

'A global pandemic will break out, biological warfare on a colossal scale. It will decimate the world's population by an estimated ninety-eight per cent. The rest will be hunted down and enslaved for our own benefit, leaving most of the earth's vast Lebensraum purely for the visitors. And one hundred survivors, of course.'

'What makes you think they're going to let you live?' Adams asked bitterly.

'We have already received the formulas for both the bioweapons and the antidotes,' Jacobs answered. 'And the reward is worth the risk.'

'You scum,' Lynn spat vehemently. 'You're willing to kill six *billion* people for your reward? I hope you burn in hell!'

Jacobs smiled knowingly. 'Unlikely,' he answered. 'Immortality, remember?'

Adams scoffed at the idea. 'You're living in a dream world if you think they're ever going to live up to their side of the bargain.'

The confidence radiating from Jacobs' features gave Lynn pause. She thought back over the man's story, and something suddenly occurred to her. 'Why do you keep saying "we" when you talk about Roswell?' she asked. 'That was nineteen forty-seven. You must have been only a boy.'

Jacobs shook his head gently. 'Ahh, you've finally realized,' he said. 'No, I wasn't a boy. I was part of the Central Intelligence Group at the time, the immediate forerunner to the CIA. They sent me to investigate the incident at Roswell, and it was I who recommended the forming of the CIA in order to protect us from the perceived alien threat. As such, I was put in charge of this particular division – the so-called

"ET Unit" – immediately upon the agency's creation. I was the first to speak with them once contact had been made, and it was I who suggested and engineered the formation of the Bilderberg Group and of CERN. I had fought during the war as a major with the OSS, and I was forty-nine years old when the spacecraft crash-landed in the desert.'

Jacobs watched the shock in the eyes of his captives, revelling in it. 'My real name is Charles Whitworth, and I was born in Dallas, Texas, on October the third, eighteen ninety-eight. I am one hundred and fourteen years old.'

He smiled widely as he stood up from his stool, his previous bent-over posture, typical of a man in his seventies, straightening up into the rigid upright military posture of a much younger man. He removed dentures, showing a set of perfect teeth, and took the half-moon glasses from his face to display his crystal-clear blue eyes. He pulled a nap of wrinkled skin at his neck, and it stretched and broke in his hand, evidently some form of professional make-up.

'I have had the body of a thirty-year-old since nineteen sixty-nine, when I finalized the deal to bring them here,' he told them. '"Whitworth" died, and I created Stephen Jacobs as his successor, and I have lived as Jacobs ever since, having to use prosthetics and make-up when in public, in order to age according to my new birth year of nineteen forty. I wanted proof, and they gave it to me. Genetic manipulation you simply wouldn't understand.

'Look at me,' Jacobs demanded, the spark of the zealot in his eyes. '*I* am the proof of their promise to us. I am already an immortal!' He glared at them with his piercing blue eyes. 'And the earth is doomed.'

* * *

Lynn recovered from the shock of Jacobs' statement first, the scientist in her overcoming the emotional response.

'You still haven't answered the question I really want to know the answer to,' she said, holding his gaze. 'How does the body we found in Antarctica tie into all of this? Was he part of the same group that want to come here now? And if so, what were they doing here forty thousand years ago?'

Even if she was about to die, Lynn *needed* to know the answer. Not only had the discovered body started her whole involvement in this, but her colleagues had all been killed because of it. She owed it to them, if nothing else.

'The body?' Jacobs said thoughtfully, before checking his watch. 'I think I've been more than open with you already, Dr Edwards. It is now time we left. So I guess you'll just have to go to your grave still not knowing.'

He turned to Eldridge and nodded towards the door, and the big man marched up and opened it, Jacobs following. As he reached the door, he turned back to Lynn and Adams.

'You should be grateful really,' he said to them. 'Whatever is going to happen to you here is almost certainly better than what will happen to most of earth's population in the weeks and months to come. The virus that will be introduced here is not very forgiving. Nasty, even. It eats away at your flesh from the inside. Truly, you should be glad you're going to die well before then.'

'Bastard,' Adams muttered through clenched teeth.

'Maybe,' Jacobs admitted. 'Farewell.' And with that, he turned on his heel and marched with Eldridge out of the steel door, which swung shut electronically behind them.

Three other men entered the room moments later. They

seemed to be scientists of one sort or another, all middle-aged, serious-looking men dressed in white lab coats.

One of them, a small, avuncular man with a balding head and thick-rimmed spectacles, approached the two captives, appraising them. 'My name is Dr Steinberg,' he said in a friendly tone. 'I will be overseeing your treatment. My aim is to minimize your pain if at all possible. If you cooperate, I think you'll find our procedures mildly uncomfortable, nothing more.'

'And if we don't?' Lynn asked.

'Let's just say that it is better if you cooperate, and leave it at that for now,' he said diplomatically. 'But first, we're going to run some basic tests, to assess your physical and psychological states, so we can calibrate our equipment correctly.'

'You mean, so you can push us as far as you can without killing us?' Adams asked.

Steinberg smiled at him. 'Yes, Mr Adams, that is exactly the reason, I'm afraid.' He gestured to the two other doctors, who began to wheel over large trolleys with a variety of medical instruments resting on top. 'So let's begin, shall we?'

17

THE PHYSICAL TESTS involved a thorough bodily examination, with the doctors' gloved hands exploring every part of them, in addition to skin, blood, hair and urine samples, and even a muscle biopsy. The straps around their bodies had been removed but their wrists and ankles were secured to the chairs throughout.

They were put through basic psychological tests, standardized questions that both had seen before; as such, they gave answers they knew would skew the results. The doctors just smiled and nodded their heads, and then pulled out a portable MRI scanner and examined their brains directly.

After what seemed like hours, the doctors finally left the room to analyse the results, leaving Adams and Lynn on their own.

Lynn turned to Adams urgently. 'We've got to find a way out of here,' she whispered to him. 'We can't let them get that wormhole machine working.'

Adams blinked his eyes at her, gesturing with his head in the direction of a large mirror on the opposite wall. The message was clear; he was positive they were still being observed.

He had already decided that they would try and escape. They were going to be killed anyway – along with about six billion others if that damned machine at CERN became operational – so what did they have to lose? The only question in Adams' mind was how the hell they were going to do it. They were strapped down on chairs in a metal room hundreds of feet beneath the surface of the world's most secure military base. Was escape even a distant possibility?

He looked at Lynn with a reassuring nod of his head, steely determination in his eyes. The stakes were simply too great not to try. And if he believed anything in life, it was that where there was a will, there was a way.

In the observation room, the three scientists sat at their computer monitors, analysing the test results.

Steinberg looked through the two-way glass at the captives, who were looking into one another's eyes, remarkably unafraid and seemingly filled with an unquenchable fire that threats of death and torture would not easily extinguish.

'Tough sons of bitches,' he murmured, mostly to himself. As Chief of Section 8, Area 51's medical interrogation division, Steinberg had seen dozens of people pass through here over the years – and knew that hundreds more had preceded them, before his own time – but never had he witnessed the relaxed confidence of the two people sitting in the room now.

'Interesting,' one of his men said quietly, breaking Steinberg's reverie.

He turned away from the window and looked at the man. 'What is it?' he asked.

'*Very* interesting,' the man said again, as he looked closely at a very specific set of results displayed across the computer screen in front of him.

* * *

Four more hours passed before the scientists re-entered the room, flanked by two security guards, two hospital gurneys between them.

'Hello again,' Steinberg said, still friendly. 'I'm sorry for keeping you, but we had to make sure we checked all of the results.'

'I bet you did,' Lynn muttered. 'Can't have us dying too soon, can you?'

Steinberg chuckled. 'How forthright you are,' he said almost admiringly. 'And you are right, of course.'

He gestured to the security guards, and they went to the side of the captives, one guard with one gurney to each. The doctors removed hypodermic needles, and started to fill them from two separate vials.

'We need to move you now,' he said apologetically. 'You will both receive individual treatment, in individual rooms. I am afraid you will never see each other again.'

He watched Lynn and Adams stare at each other, desperation creeping unbidden across their faces for the first time.

His features softened. 'Did you know of your condition, Dr Edwards?' he asked.

Lynn frowned. 'What condition?' she asked uneasily.

Steinberg looked at her with pity. 'I'm sorry you have to hear this from me, and in this place of all places, but . . . you are pregnant, Dr Edwards.'

18

THE SHOCK WAS writ large across Lynn's face. She looked at Adams, who looked just as shocked. 'Wh-what?' she stammered, even as the doctors moved towards them, liquid dripping from the ends of their needles.

'You are pregnant,' he said matter-of-factly. 'Eight days.'

Lynn didn't have to do the calculation; she knew it must have been when they had made love in the desert after their escape from Chile.

'I am afraid that we cannot alter the eventual outcome of our procedures,' Steinberg said apologetically. 'But we will try and make the process as comfortable as possible. And for what it is worth, I am sorry.'

Lynn just looked ahead blankly, her brain frozen. She was pregnant. She was going to be a mother. And Matt was the father, which was exactly what he had wanted all those years ago, the big issue that had eventually led to them splitting up.

And now here they were, reunited and with a child at last, with only the promise of death to look forward to.

Adams stared at Lynn, not believing what he had just heard, still trying to process it. Lynn was pregnant?

And to be told that she was still to be interrogated and killed, along with his unborn child?

He knew the doctors were going to inject them with some sort of anaesthetic so they could be transferred peacefully and without struggle to the gurneys positioned adjacent to them. They would then be wheeled off to other rooms, where the 'fun' would really start.

The leather straps that secured his arms and legs to the chair were tight; he had already tried to struggle free of them on the aeroplane on the flight over. But he knew this in his conscious mind only, and as he watched the doctor approach Lynn and their unborn baby, hypodermic needle reaching for her bare arm as the guard moved into position next to her, this conscious part of his mind collapsed entirely, leaving only his raw, animal self, a visceral beast that operated on pure, unbridled instinct.

He roared, his body convulsing against the straps, muscles bulging as they contracted against the straining leather, his back arching off the chair. His eyes were popping out of his head, a feral look on his face, and it appeared that his entire body was going to break in half.

'Secure him!' Steinberg yelled to the guard next to him, who had been surprised into inaction by Adams' sudden, violent convulsion. 'Get that needle into him!' he shouted at the doctor, even as Adams' body contracted again, and again, and again, the straps straining more and more each time.

The other guard ran across to him from Lynn's side, and both men tried to force Adams back into his chair, pushing his arms down as his body continued its violent, unpredictable convulsions.

The doctor tried to aim his syringe at the right point, but Adams' thrashing body meant that he couldn't see his target well enough to get a clear shot. One of the guards reached for the taser on his belt, pulling it clear of its holster and pressing it towards Adams.

But then Adams convulsed again, even stronger this time, and screamed at the top of his lungs – a piercing, animalistic howl that penetrated deep into the people around him, causing them to recoil for just a split second.

In that brief fraction of time, the leather strap that had been securing his right wrist finally gave way. In the next instant, Adams' free hand snaked out and gripped the wrist of the guard holding the taser, violently jerking it towards the doctor.

The contacts jammed into the doctor's body, sending 50,000 volts of electricity into the man, shutting down his system completely. He dropped to the ground, the hypodermic needle spilling across the metallic floor.

In the same movement, Adams continued to twist the guard's arm, even as his entire body continued to convulse in violent anger. And then the second strap gave way and his left hand was free, grasping the second guard's belt and pulling him close, straight on to the taser.

The guard fell to the floor unconscious, and Adams – straps still securing his ankles – rose slightly out of the chair, catching the guard in front of him with a punch to the jaw. Disorientated, the guard was powerless to stop Adams bending his arm back on itself, the taser electrocuting its owner.

With three men unconscious on the floor, Adams immediately switched to the other two – the man with the hypodermic still dangerously close to Lynn, and Steinberg who seemed to be stuck to the spot, mouth open in disbelief.

Then the man with the needle leaped towards Lynn, and Adams threw the taser straight at him. Not waiting to see if it struck the target, he bent down, quickly unfastening the straps round his legs. As he did so, he heard the impact of the small metal unit and a grunt from the doctor.

He looked up, and launched himself at the man with the needle, who was heading back to Lynn after the momentary distraction of the thrown taser. Adams crashed into him, driving him forcefully backwards into the wall, knocking the breath from him. He collapsed to the floor, and Adams sent a knee straight into his face, slamming his head back violently into the metal wall.

Adams turned and saw Steinberg still staring, still not reacting. And then, as Steinberg saw the murderous intent in Adams' eyes, he finally moved, reaching for the wall-mounted electronic intercom.

Adams snatched the taser from the floor and raced towards him, punching it hard into Steinberg's neck just as his hand touched the button. His body went stiff, and he collapsed to the floor.

Adams kicked him violently in the gut – once, twice, three times, violence emanating from his body. He picked his foot up high, ready to deliver the *coup de grâce*.

'No!' Lynn shouted, and the spell was broken. Adams put down his foot and looked round.

'We're going to need him if we're ever going to get out of this place alive,' she said.

It took less than five minutes to fully secure the two guards and scientists, who were starting to come round. Adams bound their hands and feet and gagged them, before hitting them with another 50,000 volts for good measure. He had no desire to kill them but he didn't want to take any chances, and he figured that the longer he could keep them unconscious, the better.

With Lynn, he placed Dr Steinberg in one of the wheelchairs, securing him just as they had been only minutes before. They pocketed the Sig Sauer pistols carried by the guards, along with their radios, and moved towards the laboratory door.

Adams had noticed that, other than the two-way mirror, there were no cameras in the room. Presumably, given the location, it was thought unnecessary to monitor things too closely down here; security would normally take care of itself. But he was also very conscious that there would now be two missing guards.

'Where's the guard post?' he asked Steinberg, who looked up at him through drowsy eyes.

'One floor up,' the doctor murmured, still struggling to recover fully.

'How many?'

'On that floor?' Steinberg asked. 'About thirty, but they cover three floors.' As a professional interrogator, he realized that resistance was futile, and he might just as well tell the truth right from the start. They would probably kill him anyway, but he would at least spare himself a lot of pain.

Adams tried some quick mental arithmetic, but failed. 'How many on the base in total?'

'Close to three hundred.'

Adams and Lynn exchanged looks, then Adams turned back to Steinberg. 'When are these two,' he gestured to the unconscious guards, 'expected back?'

'They were to be attached for the duration of the interrogation, to be relieved at the end of their normal shifts, replaced by two more men.'

Adams examined Steinberg's face for any sign of dishonesty, but found none. 'How long to the end of their shift?'

'They've just started, so about eight hours, give or take.'

Lynn leant down to the man who had been about to oversee their torture and death. 'Is there a way out of here?' she asked. 'Can you get us out?'

'And just why would I do that?' Steinberg scoffed.

Adams looked at Lynn, and then back to Steinberg. 'What exactly do you know about Jacobs' plans?'

It took no more than a few minutes to outline what Jacobs had told them, and the effect on Steinberg was electric.

'The bastard!' he muttered. 'How can he hope to get away with it?'

'He already *is* getting away with it,' Adams reminded him. 'He'll be halfway to Geneva by now.' In a way, Adams was surprised by Steinberg's reaction. After all, the man had made a living out of torturing innocent people. But global genocide was a different thing altogether, especially if you just found out that you were going to be one of the unfortunate victims.

Steinberg just sat there, shaking his head in disbelief. 'I knew about the alien research of course but I had no idea we had opened up any sort of contact with them. I just can't believe it, I—'

'Doctor,' Adams interjected forcefully, trying to get Steinberg's attention back on track. 'We need to get out of here, and to CERN. Can you help us?'

Eventually, Steinberg looked up and met Adams' gaze. 'There might be a way,' he said earnestly.

Ten minutes later, Steinberg was out of the wheelchair, and they were walking with the doctor down another concrete corridor, the sound of their footsteps echoing in the concrete space.

'Why is it so deserted down here?' Lynn asked.

'This floor is classified A1 Ultra,' Steinberg told her. 'Not that many people are authorized to be here, and a lot of those who are have recently been shipped off somewhere – I guess to CERN, from what you've just told me. There's only a skeleton staff remaining here now.'

'What goes on down here?' Adams asked next.

'What you would probably classify as "alien" research,' Steinberg admitted. 'It is here that we develop related projects directly connected with the technology discovered at the Roswell crash site. This entire floor is unknown to the majority of the people working here at Area 51. I don't know many details myself, I just run the interrogations. We have our base here because this is the most secure level. The elevators normally stop on the floor above unless you have a special access key.'

Lynn nodded, and they walked on in silence for a few more moments, following Steinberg's directions. He had a final destination in mind but was withholding it for fear of being executed if he revealed it too early, as his captors would then have no further need of him.

'Careful here,' Steinberg told them as they turned into another long, concrete corridor. 'There's a laboratory down here. Should be empty now but you never know.'

They were silent until they reached the laboratory door, but Lynn's curiosity was piqued. 'What do they do in there?'

Steinberg smiled at her. 'That is where they keep the bodies,' he whispered.

'The bodies?' Lynn asked for both of them. 'Which bodies?'

'The original pilot of the craft that crashed in nineteen forty-seven,' he told them proudly. 'Perfectly preserved, despite full autopsies having taken place several times over the years.'

'And who else?' Adams asked.

'Oh, various other bodies of questionable origin that have been found over the years.'

'Like the one my team found in Antarctica?' Lynn asked, and Steinberg nodded his head. 'You mean there have been others?'

Steinberg smiled. 'Of course there have,' he said as if to a small child. 'Would you like to see?'

Adams knew it was not a wise move. Things were happening too quickly in Geneva, the machine at CERN too near becoming operational to waste time on what amounted to no more than scientific curiosity. And yet he knew that to Lynn it was more than that – the body her team had discovered in the ice had led to their execution, and she felt it was her duty to them to follow the discovery to the end of the line. She owed them that much.

And Adams himself had to admit that he was more than a little interested to take a look in the room himself. And anything that they learnt there could be useful when it came time to confront Jacobs and his men in Geneva.

But it was a risk. Who knew if it even contained what Steinberg said it did? Maybe the doctor had tricked them and led them straight to the main guard post. Adams couldn't be sure if Steinberg had really believed the story about Jacobs, or if he had just pretended in order to lead them into a trap.

But Adams had examined Steinberg's physical signs as he spoke – his pallor, his heart rate, his respiration, his perspiration – and, save for the expected display of nervousness that would naturally come from being escorted at gunpoint, it seemed that he was telling the truth, as far as Adams could tell. He had confidence in his ability to read such things, and so finally agreed for the small party to enter the room.

'Now I don't know if there will be anybody inside,' Steinberg told them honestly. 'So we need to be careful.'

Adams nodded, withdrawing his pistol as he moved into position to the side of the door. Steinberg leant forward, pressing his palm against a security panel, which then flashed on to his retina. The door unlocked, and swung open.

Adams nodded to Lynn, who entered the room one step behind Steinberg.

'Andrew!' Adams heard Steinberg say in a friendly tone. 'I thought you'd have gone with the rest of them.'

'Willie!' Adams heard an older man exclaim. 'What are you doing over here?'

In a flash, Adams rounded the door frame and entered the room, gun levelled at the scientist before him, no more than twenty paces away.

The look on the man's face indicated that he wasn't going to shout or move, as he was more or less rooted to the spot in shock.

Adams ran towards him, forced him to the floor and

cuffed him with plasticuffs he had taken from the guards back in the interrogation area. At the same time, he scanned the rest of the room for more people but found none. What he did see was more than interesting, though, and as he hauled Andrew back to his feet, he continued his inspection of the laboratory.

But it was more of a morgue than a laboratory, he soon saw. The room was a large metallic cylinder, with dozens of mortuary drawers cut into the walls. At the head of the room, in pride of place, was a tank filled with fluid, a body suspended within.

Adams and Lynn both saw it at the same time and their jaws dropped.

Steinberg saw their expressions and smiled. 'Mr Adams, Dr Edwards,' he said formally, 'please let me introduce you to Exhibit 1A, the pilot of the Roswell spacecraft.'

Lynn walked with Steinberg towards the tank, while Adams pushed the other man – whose name tag read 'Professor A. Travers' – alongside them.

They stopped at the perspex unit, eyes wide. Lynn was surprised to see that the body bore no resemblance at all to the one they had found in the ice, save for having the normal complement of arms and legs.

The 40,000-year-old body in the Antarctic could have been buried there only last week, such was its similarity to modern-day humans, but the dead body she was looking at now literally screamed 'alien'.

The body was small, its limbs short and slim, its stomach slightly distended so that it looked not unlike a child suffering from famine. But the skull was large, much larger than a modern human's, and the eyes were also oversized, set into deep pits below the enlarged cranium. The face itself was small like the body, the mouth even smaller, almost as though evolution was in the process of eradicating it altogether. But the circumference of the brain case must have been twice that of a man's, indicating great intelligence.

Adams was struck by how similar the body appeared to popular images of such creatures – large head and eyes, small child-like body. The skin had a strange, grey pallor, as if the species had not seen the sun in millennia, which perhaps explained why 'eye witness' evidence had resulted in such beings being labelled 'Greys' by the UFO press.

'Which planet does it come from?' Lynn asked with unbridled excitement, turning first to Steinberg, and then to Travers. 'Is it from the same place as the body we found?'

Steinberg and Travers exchanged looks, and then Travers turned to Lynn, nodding his head. 'Of course it is,' he said, slightly confused.

'Why "of course"?' she asked immediately.

'Because both this body and the body you discovered in the Antarctic are from the same species – *Homo sapiens*.'

He saw the look of utter shock on her face, and decided to confirm his statement.

'They are both human.'

19

'HUMAN?' ADAMS ASKED, breaking the silence that had hung in the air for several seconds. 'How in the hell is that thing human?'

'Oh, it's human all right,' Travers said. 'It's just undergone a very specific form of evolution for the past fourteen thousand years or so.'

Adams knew they were pressed for time but he felt the need to know more, and knew Lynn would too.

'I think you'd better explain that,' he said.

Travers thought for a second or two, then looked at the pistol in Adams' hand still aimed at him, and nodded curtly. 'Very well,' he said. 'Follow me.'

They followed the professor to one of the mortuary drawers, which he pulled open. Lynn gasped as she saw the body on the metal slab, the one Tommy Devane had stumbled upon in Antarctica.

'I'll try and make this as simple as I can,' Travers said. He pointed at the body. 'This body that you found was part of the group of *Homo sapiens* that inhabited the earth from as early as two hundred thousand years ago, a highly advanced people who were expert in science and mathematics.'

'Two hundred thousand years ago?' Lynn asked. 'Highly advanced?'

Travers nodded his head again. 'Yes, and don't ask me how they evolved, as they don't even know themselves. One moment the earth had other *Homo* species, including *ergastor, heidelbergensis, rudolfensis, habilis, neanderthalensis*, among others, and the next, we had *Homo sapiens sapiens*, fully formed not only physically but also mentally. We've known for some time that anatomically modern humans existed as long ago as two hundred thousand years. But we had no idea that mentally advanced human beings inhabited the earth so long ago. There seems to have been an entire era of high human advancement, stretching far into pre-history.'

'So if we accept this,' Lynn said, 'then what happened to this ancient civilization?'

'Destroyed,' Travers said simply. 'Or at least, almost destroyed. People, buildings, vehicles, entire cities, lost forever.'

'But how?' Adams asked.

Travers held up a hand. 'Before we get into that, we need to look at how human society was before the destruction. This will help you understand what happened.'

Both Adams and Lynn, along with a seemingly fascinated Steinberg, looked at him expectantly, urging him to continue.

'As technology moved on and humans became more and more advanced, the world was much the same as it is today – various nation states looking after their own citizens while vying for power with each other. War followed war, followed war, until democracy started to spread, and federal blocks of like-minded nations joined forces. After several false starts – remember that this process took *thousands* of years – a true world government emerged, bringing peace to the earth.

'But what occurred then was that society started to split down the middle, the rich became richer and the poor became poorer, until there were essentially two tiers. The "upper" tier, if you will, were known as the "Anunnaki", which translates as "those who from heaven came to earth", while the lower, much larger tier, was known as the "Arkashians", or the "Others", and they essentially became slaves to the Anunnaki. The Arkashians spread to the far corners of the world, living mostly unsophisticated lives, while the Anunnaki created one supreme city-state, located off the coast of what is now the Atlantic Ocean.'

'Atlantis?' Adams asked with disbelief.

'Yes, Mr Adams,' Travers confirmed. 'There was indeed such a place, and it was the single, most highly advanced centre of civilization ever seen on the planet, before or since.'

'So if these events were recounted for future generations, then presumably there were survivors of whatever disaster befell them?' Lynn asked.

Travers grunted. 'There are *always* survivors,' he said. 'And in this case, there were two sets, which brings us nicely on to the next part of our story. Fourteen thousand years ago, the world saw the flood that has found its way into tales of every single civilization and religion ever since. But it really happened, and wiped out an estimated ninety-five per cent of the world's life forms current at that time.'

Lynn gasped. 'A meteor?' She knew NASA had looked into various ways such a flood could occur and she had read the research. One of the most likely explanations was that if a large meteor hit the earth in an oceanic area, the impact would create a mega-tsunami that would completely change the face of the planet.

Travers shook his head. 'No, although the effect was much the same. At the time, there was a huge rocky island, just off the African coast – a little like the Canaries, only much larger. It had a cliff on one side, five hundred metres high, essentially a waterside mountain, that eventually just collapsed. Possibly seismic activity was the cause, but a huge chunk of this cliff just basically sloughed off and crashed into the sea. We're talking about *millions* of tons of rock slipping straight down towards the ocean floor, the resulting force of which created a tidal wave two miles high that sped across the Atlantic and completely destroyed the eastern seaboard of what is now the United States of America.'

'And Atlantis,' Adams added.

'In a way,' Travers offered non-commitally. 'But it didn't end there, as the incredible force of the impact threw up billions of tons of debris into the atmosphere, which then inflamed and landed all over the planet, causing vast devastation by forest fires, which in turn caused carbon dioxide gases to clog up the atmosphere, until there was a nuclear winter that helped stamp out much of what life remained.'

'How do you know all this?' Lynn asked.

'I'm the foremost expert on the Anunnaki,' Travers answered. 'I've been working with them for years, I'm an expert on their history.'

'Working with them?' Steinberg asked suspiciously.

Travers smiled. 'I'm in communication with them,' he answered. 'There is a device I use, one that enables me to link telepathically to the Anunnaki, and I've been piecing together their entire history – as it's related by them, at any rate.'

Adams nodded his head, not surprised that there was more than one communications box. He was sure it would be a device identical to the one that Jacobs must have been using back at his house in Mason Neck.

A sudden thought entered his head. 'Where is it?' he asked. 'The box?' If it was in the room, could the Anunnaki be reading their thoughts right now?

'Relax,' Travers said calmly. 'It's in another room entirely. We have a research library dedicated to learning and preserving their history and culture, and it's based there. We use it regularly, and they are only too happy to provide answers to our questions. A remarkable people, really,' he said with considerable respect.

'Going back to the flood,' Lynn said to Travers, directing the conversation back to the matter at hand. 'Who survived?'

'The Anunnaki, of course,' Travers informed her. 'They were aware of the possibility of the mountain caving into the sea long before it happened, but despite their technical expertise they could find no way of averting the catastrophe. Instead, they put their resources into developing their city-state of Atlantis into a spacecraft.'

'They what?' Adams asked, surprised. 'They made a city into a spaceship?'

'They were already very advanced in terms of space travel,' Travers explained. 'They had explored every planet in the solar system, and were in the middle of developing technologies that would allow intergalactic travel. And think about Plato's description of the city of Atlantis – the central island surrounded by concentric rings, joined by bridges. It's a spacecraft, plain and simple. The central island was the actual craft, and the rings – spinning once the craft was airborne – helped to create artificial gravity for their long voyage. And then the whole thing simply lifted up and blasted away into space.'

Lynn considered the matter. 'At least that explains why Atlantis was never found,' she said. 'Because it's no longer on earth at all.'

Travers smiled. 'Exactly right,' he confirmed. 'The Anunnaki escaped the devastating flood by venturing up into space in Atlantis itself.'

Adams looked at a digital clock embedded into the laboratory wall and turned to the others. 'Talking about making an escape, I think it's time we started moving.'

Steinberg looked up at the clock and nodded his head in agreement. 'Yes, I think you're right.' He turned to Travers and gave him a brief rundown of what was going on, and Jacobs' plan for the earth's population. 'I'm taking them down to the Roosevelt Exit,' he explained. 'You should come with us.'

Travers stared at the tank containing the Anunnaki's body for several long moments before turning back. 'Yes. Of course I'll come. There are still some things I need to explain.'

Steinberg smiled and turned to Adams and Lynn. 'OK,' he said, 'let's go. We're still about a mile away from the exit.'

Moments later they were once more walking the deserted corridors of Level 36, footsteps again echoing off the concrete as they passed cavernous storerooms and hi-tech laboratories.

'So what happened after the flood?' Adams asked, still curious about the story Travers had so far told them.

'Well, most of the Arkashians were wiped out,' Travers

continued, seemingly glad to be back in the role of educator; Adams supposed it kept his mind off their precarious situation. 'But small pockets survived around the world, and we are their direct descendants. The most successful survivors were those that converged in a narrow area of the Middle East, the conditions there allowing them to develop into the agrarian cultures of Sumer, Babylon and Egypt.'

'But what happened to all the evidence that must have remained from the earlier civilization?' Lynn asked.

'Most of it is underwater,' Travers answered, 'as you would expect after such a flood. But most of the high technology was centred on Atlantis, which was no longer on the planet. The Anunnaki's previous technology across the globe had already been destroyed by the Arkashians long ago. Some artefacts are still discovered here and there, along with bodies like the one you found, but almost all of them end up here.' He gestured back the way they had come. 'That room back there alone contains several hundred examples of bodies of these ancient humans, including several well-preserved specimens like the one you found. There are other storerooms down here containing thousands of other examples of their ancient technology.'

'And what happened to the people who made these discoveries?' Lynn asked bitterly.

'Most were debriefed here, before memory erasure or death,' Steinberg admitted. 'Others, who for whatever reasons we couldn't get here, either met with unfortunate "accidents" or were just subjected to ridicule in the press, their "evidence" being systematically discredited and then openly mocked. That's why you sometimes see such discoveries in the popular media, and why they are always denied by the scientific establishment.'

Lynn snorted. 'You guys really do control everything, don't you?'

'We certainly try to,' Travers said.

'So what happened to the Anunnaki?' Adams asked.

'Well, they spent the next few thousand years travelling through space – much of it in suspended animation due to the vast distances involved – trying to find a new planet to colonize. Eventually, they discovered that there *were* no other truly habitable planets within the reach of their starship and so they decided to make the spacecraft itself their permanent home. As such, without the physical pressures of a planet-based existence, the evolution that you saw in the Roswell pilot occurred. They had no use for powerful bodies or limb strength and so on, which is why their physical shape shrank to that of a modern child's. But their brains – and their intelligence – continued to grow, leading to the abnormally large craniums you see. Their other physical senses – touch, sight, smell and hearing – also became greatly diminished over time, and once they developed telepathic communication abilities, their mouths started to become smaller and more useless with each generation.'

'That's great,' Adams said. 'So if they're so perfect in their own little spaceship world, why do they want to come back and take over?'

'Simple mathematics,' Travers explained. 'At the moment, they are all but immortal. Due to advances in medicine, they really have no upper age limit, as their cells are kept from dying artificially. But they understand that to keep evolving, they need to keep on reproducing – but where do they have room for the new people? Not on their little spaceship. They want to keep evolving, and to do so they need more space, it's as simple as that.'

'But why now?' Lynn asked. 'Why did they return now?'

'World War Two,' Travers said. 'The atomic bomb. Even in the depths of space, their sensors picked up the detonations, and it was clear that they were manmade. This told them that not only was planet earth still habitable, but we had the technology to make their return here a real possibility, although we would of course need their guidance to create the means.'

'I'm surprised they didn't leave sensors here in the first place, some way of monitoring what happened after the tidal wave hit,' Lynn said.

'They did. They left a "stay back" team, orbiting the earth in a smaller craft, to report back on what happened.'

'Really? And what happened to them?' Lynn asked.

'You've read the Bible?' Travers asked with a smile. 'It's all in there.'

20

'WHAT DO YOU mean?' Adams asked as they rounded yet another corner in the underground labyrinth.

'Pretty much everything in the Torah, the original books of law from the earliest Bible, relates to the crew of the ship that stayed behind,' Travers explained. 'And because the Bible was built on earlier myths and tales, you can also read the history of this people in the writings of the ancient Sumerians, Babylonians and Egyptians. And because the same stories were told again by the Indians, Greeks, Romans and even the Vikings, you can read them all again in their own various religions and mythologies.'

'It sounds like what Baranelli was telling us,' Adams said to Lynn.

Lynn nodded. 'Yes, we studied comparative religion at Harvard,' she said. 'And it's true that there are some remarkable similarities in otherwise disparate religions all over the world. The Great Flood, for example.'

'Exactly,' Travers agreed. 'And it is clear that almost all faiths describe "gods" or "angels" descending from the heavens, often in rather complex machines.'

'And you're saying that these "gods" were in fact men left behind after the flood, who were now based in an orbiting spacecraft?'

'Yes. They monitored from a distance, unsure whether the Arkashians would survive, or whether the atmosphere of the earth was too compromised. And so they observed as generations came and went, until communities became established in the "cradle of civilization" as we know it, and started to farm the land.'

'Did they send their reports back to the mother ship? To Atlantis?' Adams asked.

'That was the aim, but it soon transpired that their communications were for some reason not making it back to their comrades who were now in deep space, and so these people were there on their own.'

'What became of them?' Adams asked.

'Aware that they had lost all contact with the rest of the Anunnaki population, and now sure that the earth was truly safe to re-inhabit, they started to visit us. They came down in small spacecraft, and were instantly perceived as gods by the ancient Sumerians. Indeed, the name "Anunnaki" for these gods is clearly preserved in Sumerian literature.

'Of course, having been alone for so many generations, the visitors revelled in the glory and attention that they received here. In order to further their status, they began to teach those early civilizations the rudiments of reading, writing, and mathematics – not at an advanced level, but enough to whet the appetite, so to speak, in order to ensure the people's continued worship, which they now craved.

'Despite their advancement, they were still human, and were subject to the same human emotions as us. They therefore ended up interbreeding with us – which *proves* that these visitors were human, as members of different species can't interbreed successfully – and were finally subsumed into our own populations, although with their offspring they created "royal" dynasties that lasted for hundreds, if not thousands of years. The royal line of David, for instance, can be traced back to these early visitors.

'Their relationships were like some sort of modern-day soap opera, as you can see from the tales of the Greek gods, most of which are based on much earlier stories, originally true for the most part. Some of the stories really do have to be read to be believed. And then there are all the reports of advanced technology and weaponry. Zeus' lightning bolt? A laser weapon brought down from the spacecraft.

'Similar stories are found elsewhere. The spacecraft themselves are to be found described in the Indian Vedas as "vimyana", and they came from a "star" in the sky that could be readily identified. It was of course the orbiting space station, which could indeed be seen by the naked eye in much the same way as our own international space station can.

'In the Bible, the destruction of Sodom and Gomorrah was based on an actual event that occurred long before the book was written, when an entire city was razed by a nuclear weapon. And there's a lot more, throughout religious literature.' Travers cleared his throat. '"When mankind had spread all over the world and girls were being born, some of the heavenly beings saw that these girls looked beautiful, so they took the ones they liked . . . In those days, and even later, the Nephilim were upon the earth, who were descendants of human women and the heavenly beings. They were the great heroes and famous men of long ago." Sound like a virtual history of extraterrestrial visitation and interbreeding? It is. Genesis, chapter six, verses one through four.'

'You're joking,' Adams said.

'He's not,' Lynn broke in, her mind racing. 'The Nephilim were sometimes referred to as "the giants" in other translations, but the exact meaning was never known.' She turned to Travers. 'So you're saying that the Nephilim were the surviving Anunnaki?'

'Absolutely. "Nephilim" is, in fact, a direct transliteration of "Anunnaki" into ancient Hebrew from their own language. It's all there,' he continued, 'written plainly in black and white, in front of all of us. The entire history of our world. Everyone's read it but nobody truly understands it. Some believe that the gods described are actually supernatural beings, while others believe that they are the result of drug-induced hallucinations or visions, or are merely symbolic. Nobody really takes the stories as the *literal* truth. The closest are those who tout the ancient astronaut theory, who say that these ancient gods were in fact aliens.

'But the truth is even more amazing. These ancient gods, the whole basis of all religions and all faiths, were men and women. We were, and still are, worshipping humans.'

21

'WE'RE HERE,' STEINBERG said as they rounded another corner, suddenly confronted by what looked like an elevator door. 'This is the Roosevelt Exit,' he explained, 'built some time after the original construction, on presidential orders. Roosevelt – who visited us here from time to time – was a claustrophobic, and something of a paranoiac. He hated the idea of one single elevator being the sole means of escape should anything happen down here, and so ordered a secret tunnel to be built.' Steinberg leant forward and pressed a button to the side of the elevator door. It opened smoothly, showing a standard elevator interior. 'It was disguised as a normal lift, which has always been out of order, eventually being decommissioned as unsafe. But,' he continued, tapping a code into the control panel on the inside wall, 'it was never intended as an elevator at all. At least not in the normal sense.'

As he finished speaking, the rear wall of the elevator slid to one side, showing an inordinately long tunnel stretching at a slight incline as far into the distance as they could see.

Adams peered into it. 'If we're thirty-six storeys below ground,' he said, 'then at that angle, the tunnel would have to stretch—'

'Five miles,' Steinberg finished for him. 'It comes out just near the "Extraterrestrial Highway", Route 375, that runs up to the base perimeter. The tunnel exit is just outside the fence line. It's still on US Air Force property – the whole area for hundreds of klicks around is Air Force property – but it might just be far enough for you to make it out of here.'

Adams gestured to a metal cart on the right of the tunnel, resting on what looked like a rail track. 'What's that?'

Steinberg smiled. 'I would ignore that if I were you. It was intended for a quick escape but it's sat there unattended for the last forty-plus years, and even if it did work, the G-forces probably wouldn't do you any good at all.'

Adams nodded. 'Let's go then,' he said, stepping into the tunnel, Lynn next to him.

He turned back round when he realized the two scientists were not following them.

And then Lynn gave a startled yell and Adams' eyes went wide as they saw Professor Travers standing there with a pistol aimed directly at Steinberg's head.

22

'DID YOU REALLY think I was just going to let you walk out of here?' Travers asked. 'Did you think I was unaware of the plans?' He laughed at them. 'I was a guest at the Bilderberg Group meeting of two thousand and two, picked for the Hundred immediately.' He gestured back down the corridor. 'You hear that sound?'

Adams could hear it, and cursed himself for not picking up on it sooner. It was the sound of boots, lots of them, running towards them. He had allowed Travers to distract him with his stories. From the sound of the echoes, Adams estimated they would be upon them within the next sixty seconds.

'Twenty members of security,' Travers said, a wicked smile painted across his features. 'And they are not known for their tolerance of escapees.'

Adams saw the look of indignant rage on the face of Steinberg long before Travers did, and was gripping Lynn's hand and moving for the tunnel even as Steinberg let out an angry yell and launched himself at his colleague.

Steinberg clasped both hands round Travers' pistol and yanked the arm upwards. A loud blast rang out, and a single supersonic round ricocheted down the corridor as both men struggled for control of the weapon.

Adams could hear the footsteps just about to turn the

final corner, and pushed Lynn into the metal cart, looking in vain for the controls.

Steinberg saw what they were trying to do and yelled to them, 'The left-hand side! The red button!'

Adams turned and saw the armed guards storming into the corridor, submachine guns raised at shoulder level.

He flinched as they pulled their triggers, heard Lynn cry an exultant, 'Yes!' saw Steinberg ripped to bloody pieces by hundreds of nine-millimetre hollow-point rounds, and then felt his own body surge back into the metal cart with tremendous force as it tore free from its moorings and accelerated at terrifying speed up the tunnel, leaving Travers and the twenty guards as tiny, insignificant specks in the far, far distance.

Steinberg hadn't been joking about the G-forces, Lynn realized.

At first, the shock of the cart's speed made her brain all but malfunction, the incredible force pinning her against the back of the cart, her face rippling under the intense pressure. But her faculties started to return, and she estimated the G-force to be in the range of 4 or 5.

During her time with NASA, she had experienced forces of up to 12 G in inverted dives when she had been invited to observe pilot training, but that had been wearing a special G-suit which mitigated much of the shock. And although 4 to 5 G was about the same as a high-G rollercoaster ride, those figures only applied to short spells on the fastest parts of the ride. Here, there were no protective suits, and the acceleration was constant, for a prolonged period of time.

She soon started to feel the effects. The first thing she noticed, after only thirty seconds of hard acceleration, was a progressive blurring and greying of her vision, the long tunnel ahead of her losing all colour and clarity. She closed her eyes to try and gather herself, but soon started to feel nauseated.

Opening her eyes once more, she experienced an intense tunnel vision. The fact that she was in a tunnel anyway didn't help, but her range of vision was becoming progressively – and rapidly – diminished. She had no idea how fast they were going but she knew that the tunnel was five miles long. Even at two hundred miles per hour, the journey would take longer than one and a half minutes, and she was unsure how much time had already elapsed. How much longer could she hold out? She felt her vision start to fail completely, blackout coming on fast now, and knew that unconsciousness would follow soon after, with death being a significant possibility.

Blackness started to creep into the corners of her vision, and she knew all would soon be lost, but then she felt the cart slowing; it was gradual but she could sense the deceleration, and as the cart slowed, her senses started to come back to her. First the blackness ebbed away, then the tunnel widened out ahead of her, and then finally colours returned and her perception cleared totally as the cart continued to slow until it came to a complete stop.

Her hand went to the side of the cart for support as she was hit by another wave of nausea, her head swimming, but then she felt a hand on her arm, and turned to see Adams looking at her through bleary eyes.

'Come on,' he said weakly, pulling her by the arm. 'Let's go.'

* * *

Colonel Briscoe Caines stood at the main bank of monitors in the Main Security Building, a large brick structure located next to the new base headquarters, in the dead centre of the plethora of other buildings that littered Area 51.

Caines was in overall command of physical security at the base, a task he carried out with ruthless dedication. He had been a major in the US Special Forces before transferring to the Defence Intelligence Agency, where he had risen to the rank of full colonel before moving to Area 51.

Although his appointment had been made by the US military, in cooperation with the CIA, he had really been co-opted by his old friend Stephen Jacobs and was under no illusions about who really led security at the base: Commander Eldridge and the men of Alpha Brigade. Eldridge and his cronies had, however, recently decamped to Geneva, leaving Caines alone to clean up this mess.

He had been woken up when the emergency call had come through ten minutes before, the watch officer in something of a blind panic. He swung his feet out of the bed in his private room in the dormitories to the rear of the MSB and started to get dressed even as he listened to the report.

An emergency distress signal had been sent to the guard room on Level 34 from Laboratory 8 two levels below, from Professor Travers. It seemed that the two captives who had recently been brought to the base had overpowered the two guards assigned to them, along with two of the interrogators, and had managed to convince Dr Steinberg to try and get them out. Caines had scoffed when he heard that – what possible chance did they have?

But then it became apparent that they were headed to the Roosevelt Exit, and all of a sudden the possiblity became somewhat more real. Ordering a section of men to hunt the escapees down through the vast corridors of Level 36, and all other base security personnel to be on immediate standby, he left the officers' dormitory at a full run, getting to the MSB in record time.

By the time he got there, however, things had gone even more wrong. Although Steinberg had been killed, Adams and Edwards had made it into the escape tunnel and had vanished towards the exit in the magneto-electric cart.

'Converge on Groom Lake Road!' he yelled into his radio mouthpiece, panic creeping now into his own voice. 'All units!'

23

ADAMS HOISTED LYNN out of the cart and pointed upwards. The rail track stopped several feet from the end of the tunnel, which turned sharply upwards into a short vertical shaft. A ladder was bolted to the wall, which snaked its way up through the dark cylinder to what looked like some sort of submarine hatch.

Adams started climbing the ladder and Lynn followed him immediately, turning to look back down the long tunnel for only a second to make sure that they were still alone.

Her head had recovered from the shock of the cart's acceleration, and the nausea had now left her completely, although her stomach still felt more than a little nervous, given that they still had to make good their escape from the most secure military base in the world; and not only was there a team of trained killers hot on their heels behind them, they had no idea whatsoever what would be on the other side of the hatch above them. Still, she stayed close behind Adams, watching as he reached the top and entwined his feet in the rungs so that he could brace himself to open the metal hatch.

He tried to twist the circular spin lock but it was too tight.

He looked down at her. 'Damn thing's rusted shut,' he

said sourly. 'Probably hasn't been opened in the last fifty years.'

Despite the seeming pointlessness of it, he turned back and twisted again, until he was red in the face and the skin on his hands started to blister. But still it wouldn't move, the inoperable hatch teasing them cruelly with the possibility of escape just beyond.

Caines checked the monitors. Although the corridors of Level 36 were conspicuously absent of security cameras, being almost completely off the grid, the team headed up by Captain Aldo Barnes was feeding images back to him from their own helmet-mounted imagers.

He was happy to see that Barnes had had the foresight to bring some L-84 'Ramcarts' down from the upper guard-room. The vehicle was basically a modified golf buggy, and although not anywhere near as fast as the device that had whisked the escapees away at such high speed, it was considerably faster than making the pursuit down the tunnels on foot.

Caines watched as half of the men managed to squeeze into the two small vehicles and then took off up the tunnel at a rapid thirty miles an hour, while the rest of the men started to jog along behind them. Then he turned away to check on the progress of his other units, who were headed for the tunnel's surface exit.

Barnes took point in the lead buggy, the noise of the diesel engines deafening in the confines of the narrow tunnel, a savage grin on his face as he checked the magazine on his Steyr AUG assault rifle. The couple just a few miles up ahead had left two of his men unconscious on the floor back in the interrogation rooms, a professional insult to Barnes, and one that would soon be avenged.

Adams heard the noise of the engines first, even with his ears pulsing with blood from the pressure inside his head as he continued to struggle against the spinlock.

The damn guards must have brought some sort of vehicles into the tunnel and would be upon them a lot sooner than Adams had hoped. A team of armed men on foot would probably have taken close to an hour to reach them. But in motorized transport? It depended on the exact speed, of course, but it would certainly be a lot less than an hour, that was for sure. It could even be as little as a few minutes.

Adams looked down at Lynn, saw that she, too, had heard the roar of engines; could see the look of worry in her eyes, not only for themselves but also for the unborn child she now knew was growing in her belly.

Adams turned back to the cursed, rusted hatch and attacked it with renewed ferocity. The damn thing was going to open one way or another; he could not let it be otherwise.

Moments later, he felt Lynn move up beside him, feet entwined with his, her back braced against the tunnel wall opposite.

She smiled reassuringly at him, reaching up to take hold of the opposite side of the lock. She looked at him, more than simple love transmitted by her gaze; it was understanding, belief, mutual recognition of their deepest feelings for one another.

'Let's do it together, OK?' she said to him, and Adams

knew that she wasn't just talking about opening the hatch.

He returned her look with one of his own, one that he hoped transmitted just as much to her, and nodded his head.

'On the count of three, we both twist together,' he said, as the noise of the diesel engines grew louder and louder.

'One,' he said, as they both tightened their hands around the stainless steel hatch seal. 'Two,' he continued, taking a deep breath. 'Three!' he shouted, and they both hauled on the ring as hard as they could, muscles contracting with such force that the veins started to pulse blue in their foreheads, threatening to burst from their skin.

At first there was nothing, not even a hint of movement, but as both of them continued to exert an almost inhuman level of force, there came the very first slip of metal on metal, a grinding sound and slight judder that they both felt through their hands.

Adams looked at Lynn, unable to talk with the effort; but his eyes said it all. *We're almost there! Harder!*

24

THE RAMCART BUGGIES built up to their maximum speed of fifty miles per hour just one mile into the long tunnel, and Barnes calculated that they would reach the end within seven minutes of setting off from the disguised elevator entrance.

He checked his watch as six minutes came around, gesturing for his men to get ready. They would make the assault as soon as they arrived, hit the two escapees hard and fast.

And then he saw the end of the tunnel coming up, the cart abandoned. The man and woman were not readily apparent, which meant that they were probably stuck up the access tunnel, struggling to open the metal hatch.

Barnes smiled to himself; the hatch was as good as welded shut from years of neglect. It was on the 'to do' list but always seemed to be one of the things that never got done.

The buggies cruised to a stop and Barnes and his men spilled out into the tunnel, guns raised, sprinting towards the vertical shaft. It was going to be like shooting fish in a barrel.

Two of his men got there before him, assault rifles

pointing vertically up the short exit tunnel. Barnes was momentarily confused when no shots were fired, but then he was there, looking up towards the hatch himself, and understood in an instant.

For there was nothing there to shoot at; the shaft was empty, the steel hatch open to the night sky above.

Adams and Lynn had finally managed to turn the steel rim enough to break the rusty seal, the sound of tortured metal giving way to a freer, easier movement, until the hatch had opened fully.

Dirt and soil had collapsed on their heads as Adams pushed the hatch gingerly open, and he held it open a few inches as he and Lynn moved to the side and waited for the soil to work its way down to the tunnel floor.

Adams pushed again, and although he met with resistance, he continued the effort until it was halfway open. For reasons of safety, he hadn't wanted to open it all the way anyway, as he didn't want to attract too much attention if there were any guards in the vicinity. He presumed that the guards from Level 36 would have issued a general alert, and that they may therefore have already reached the tunnel exit, if they could find it.

Holding it open just enough for someone to crawl through, he gestured for Lynn to come across to him. She transferred to the ladder side, bracing herself as she took the weight of the hatch. Adams pulled out his handgun, kissed Lynn quickly on the lips, and edged his way slowly out into the moonlit night.

He kept his profile low to the ground, slipping out of the

semi-open hatch slowly and silently. Once his upper torso was out, he stopped and monitored the immediate area, keeping his head still while his eyes roved.

There was no movement, of that he could be pretty sure. He was an expert in tracking animals at night and was used to searching for movement even on the darkest nights; but here there were no telltale signs whatsoever. But that wasn't to say that there wasn't anybody further out, monitoring them electronically, or behind the hatch cover where he couldn't see.

And so he slowly extricated himself from the hatch completely, allowing his body to turn in order to check the rear area as well. He swept the entire horizon for three hundred and sixty degrees, until he was happy that nobody was there.

But, now clear of the engine noise in the tunnels below, he began to pick up the noise of other engines, on the land, converging on them, and he knew security must know where they were and already be on their way.

He pulled up on to his haunches, reached for the hatch and ripped it open completely, the earth that had been resting on top now flung to the side. He reached further in and grasped Lynn by her arms, pulling her up and out of the tunnel in one smooth motion until her feet hit solid ground next to him.

He gestured to the noise of engines to their right, and Lynn followed his gaze. There was a high chain-link fence just twenty feet from them, and they could see the brightly lit runways just beyond the fence line. The noise was coming from the runway, and they quickly realized that armoured vehicles were approaching at speed, using the runway as a fast road. To their left, a narrow empty road ran far into the distance. Other than that, the area resembled the barren scrub of the Chilean and Peruvian deserts from which they had so recently escaped.

'They're on their way,' Adams said to her. 'We need to leave. Now!'

25

Barnes emerged from the hatch as the headlights of four large off-road vehicles headed across the bumpy terrain towards him, body-mounted .50 calibre machine guns trained directly at him.

'Stand down!' he shouted into his tactical mic, tuned to the wavelength used by all the different elements of Area 51 security. He raised his arms as the lead vehicle's searchlight hit him straight on, illuminating him perfectly.

The rest of his men poured up and out of the tunnel behind him as the four 4x4s steered to a stop around them.

'They're out here somewhere,' Barnes announced, 'and they've only got a few minutes' head start.'

'Do we have monitors out here?' came a question from the interior of the second vehicle.

'Affirmative,' Colonel Caines announced from his station inside the MSB. 'We have sensors all the way out to the main gate.'

Because it was so large, the actual perimeter of the Groom Lake base was not fenced in; rather, the sole approach road – Groom Lake Road, just fourteen miles from Highway 375, known affectionately by locals as the Extraterrestrial Highway – was marked with a variety of vivid signs warning people not to go any further. Anyone who did was instantly caught by the private security guards – the 'camo dudes' – who then handed them over to the County Sheriff's Department. The land between the outer perimeter and the base itself was monitored by an array of heat sensors and motion cameras, as well as by the men who kept a visual lookout from the high hills that surrounded the approach road.

'Barnes, you and your men will continue the search on foot,' the colonel continued, 'and I want the jeeps to extend the search area, right up to the main perimeter. We've got two hundred more men coming into the search zone within the next ten minutes, along with dogs and thermal imagers. Helicopters are being made ready and will be airborne soon, extending the zone further. Now let's get going!'

'Yes, sir!' Barnes responded. 'You heard the man!' he said, turning to his team. 'Let's move out!'

Four long, terrible, migraine-inducing hours later, Colonel Briscoe Caines sat rooted to the monitors. The entire security apparatus of the world's most secure military facility had been mobilized to find just two lightly armed escapees, in an open desert, without success. Three hundred men, two dozen off-road vehicles and fourteen helicopters had searched five hundred square miles of desert and had still found nothing.

So what in the hell was going on? Even though a lot of base staff had recently transferred to Europe on the orders of Stephen Jacobs, Caines was hardly without resources. But no trace was found anywhere, save for a pair of tracks that led from the tunnel exit across the desert sand on to Groom Lake Road.

Where could they have gone once on the road? There had been no sign of any vehicle. Perhaps someone had turned up in a car and whisked them away. Or maybe a couple of motorbikes had been left by the tunnel for them. But how on earth would that have been arranged? And the helicopters would certainly have found them anyway, if the sensors had not.

Caines was at a loss to explain it.

Lynn shifted her weight, struggling to get comfortable, but it was impossible.

After leaving the tunnel, Adams had dragged her to the left, out towards the paved road, where he had rolled himself along the tarmac, encouraging Lynn to do the same. 'To confuse the dogs,' he had told her, before taking her hand and pulling her back, retracing their steps to the tunnel exit. Adams had made sure they stepped into their previous footprints, covering up the fact that they had returned.

He had then gone to work, digging earth from next to the hatch until, with Lynn's help, a small hollow had been cleared. Then he had pulled her down into the small pit and started to cover their bodies with the loose soil.

'How are we going to breathe?' she whispered breathlessly shortly before they were completely covered.

Adams pulled out his pistol, ejected the magazine and slipped it into his pocket before racking the slide to eject the round in the chamber. He gathered it up and put this in his pocket also, as Lynn started to do the same with her own gun.

Putting the butts of the guns in their mouths, they continued to cover themselves until they were completely buried, the barrels of their pistols sticking out of the dirt very slightly, allowing the cold night air to filter down to them.

And they had been like that ever since, lying immobile, hardly daring to breathe when the team had come up from the tunnel and the 4x4s had arrived on the scene, terrified that their pistol barrels would be found or their body heat would register on the guards' hi-tech monitors.

But the barrels had been missed in the excitement – with two escapees on the loose, a mound of earth disturbed by the hatch being opened wasn't of prime consideration; and their body heat wasn't picked up by the sensors, thanks to the cold earth covering them.

They were still in place when the dogs had come and the sound of dozens – perhaps hundreds – of more feet had descended on the area; but again, the sounds came and went, and the mound of earth remained undisturbed.

But they had been in the same position now for far too long, and Lynn was starting to suffer from an intense claustrophobia that she had never before experienced. Even though there were only a few inches of topsoil separating her from the outside world, there might as well have been a thousand. She felt as if she had been truly buried alive, like one of those people who were declared dead a little too prematurely and then woke up buried in a coffin under tons of earth. Some of them had clawed their way out, Lynn knew, and now she felt that same desire, the intense need to just start digging.

She felt movement next to her, and realized Adams was doing exactly that; he was escaping from their earthy prison. Had it been too much for him?

303

Lynn started to dig her own way out instantly, and she was almost there when Adams reached in and helped pull her out, the heavy soil tumbling down her hair and off her skin as she removed the jaw-achingly wide gun butt from her mouth, eager to breathe in a full lungful of *real* air. As she took those first few precious, wonderful mouthfuls of clean air, Adams scanned the immediate area.

'They're not here, for now at least,' he said with some satisfaction. 'They're probably scouring every inch of land around the base.'

'So what do we do now?' she asked him, her composure returning slowly.

'Now we escape,' he replied with confidence.

'Which way?'

Adams smiled at her and pointed over her shoulder at the chain-link fence surrounding Area 51.

Lynn turned and looked, then groaned in disbelief. 'Oh no,' she said forlornly. 'You've *got* to be kidding me.'

26

THE FENCE WAS not in fact the formidable obstacle it at first seemed. It was really a demarcation line more than anything, a way of letting base personnel know where they could and could not go. In terms of security, it was assumed that it was impossible to get past the body-heat and motion detectors placed all over the surrounding desert, and the roving patrols of guards.

Getting closer, though, Adams could see that although the fence wasn't physically impressive – just one row of chain-link, ten feet high – its entire length was linked to both motion and body-heat sensors. Perhaps it wouldn't be so easy.

Adams crouched in the shadows, his night vision picking out what looked like a gate some distance away, and after a moment's observation, he could see that this was where the security vehicles must have passed through.

'Come on,' he whispered to Lynn, motioning towards the gate.

'The main gate?' she asked in disbelief.'

'It's not the main gate,' he whispered back, 'it's a minor side gate. And I think it's still open.'

He took her by the hand, keeping low as they moved along the fence line towards the gate. Fifty metres out, they both crouched down again, straining to make out the details of the gate. Around them, far out in the desert, they heard the sound of off-road vehicles struggling over the rough terrain, helicopters circling the skies above, and voices shouting orders. Here, though, there seemed to be a complete absence of activity; Adams could only presume that the gate had been left temporarily open to aid the vehicles that would doubtlessly be streaming in and out all night.

Suddenly, engine noise from the rear caused him to grab Lynn by the arm and pull her down close to the sandy ground. Looking over their shoulders, they saw two 4x4s heading back to base. They watched closely as the off-roaders crashed along the bumpy terrain before passing through the gate, their headlights illuminating what Adams could now see was a small, deserted sentry box.

They continued to watch for several moments, until Adams turned to Lynn. 'Other vehicles are at least a mile away,' he said, able to pick up the sounds quite easily across the barren desert. He gestured for the gate. 'It's time to go.'

'So where are we?' Caines asked over the secure comms link, hoping for something – *anything* – that would help resolve this terrible situation.

'Nothing so far,' he heard Barnes report back immediately. 'There's nothing out here but the damn sand!'

Caines could hear the man's frustration, and it was reflected in the answers that followed from the drivers of the 4x4 recon vehicles and the pilots of the helicopters. Nobody had found anything.

He turned back to the monitors, the bustling team that swarmed around the office all but invisible to him.

Where the hell were they?

At the same moment that Caines was asking himself that question, his prey were within less than a hundred metres of the Main Security Building, both parties unaware of the other's presence.

Adams knew what the large brick building across the runway tarmac was, however, having been briefed on Area 51's major structural layout by Stephenfield, and he knew to avoid it. It was to the south-west of a similar building, which he knew to be some sort of laboratory for something called Precision Measuring Equipment. To the north of that, and now directly opposite him, was the very large building that housed the base headquarters. But he still couldn't tell where the underground building in which they had been held was. But, he supposed, he didn't have to know; what he wanted was now within reach anyway.

Both Adams and Lynn were amazed by how big the base was, how sprawling, almost like a small township, albeit one that consumed the same amount of electricity as a large city. Dozens of buildings, from small barracks to large warehouses and vehicle hangars, were spread over a vast area, and then there were the seven brightly lit runways, each with their own command towers and support vehicles.

The inner base, however, seemed to be almost deserted, the search for them outside the base mercifully consuming almost all of the security force's resources. They had crossed one runway after another, moving low across the terrain between them and fast across the smooth tarmac, always keeping to whatever shadows they could, until they reached the runway nearest the headquarters building.

As they crouched there, Adams pointed to the row of six Boeing 737 passenger jets, their fuselages painted white with a red stripe down each side. 'The Janet planes,' Adams whispered to Lynn, before pointing to one on the far side, which a crew was busy fuelling.

Adams looked up at the moon and stars in the sky. The base's high-powered floodlights made them more difficult to read but not altogether impossible. 'It's just after five,' he told Lynn, dawn still a long way off on the winter morning. 'First flight out is at six o'clock, when the non-resident workers are flown back home after the nightshift.'

'And what does that have to do with us?' Lynn asked, although she suspected she already knew the answer.

'We're going to catch it with them,' he whispered back.

The plane doors were closed and locked, Adams knew that even from their position across the runway, but they couldn't afford to wait. Before long, the non-resident workers would be streaming out of headquarters and arriving in minibuses from other parts of the base, all ready for home, and the plane would be surrounded with people.

And so he and Lynn edged as close as they could, waited until all support personnel had left the area, and then ran across the tarmac to the landing gear at a near sprint, careful to keep low and within whatever shadow they could. Then Adams pushed Lynn up the massive tyre of the lead wheel, before pulling himself up behind her, continuing on up into the wheel housing, into the deep, dark bowels of the aircraft. They squeezed up past the tightly packed machinery, now out of sight of anyone outside, until they made it up to the top of the housing.

Clutching the top of the landing gear strut, Adams reached around in the dark until his hand found a lever. Pulling it, a small square access port opened into the aircraft proper, and he crawled through first, his body only just fitting. He thought at first that his shoulders wouldn't fit but finally managed to collapse them sufficiently to edge through. He pulled Lynn in quickly after him, her lithe body proving a much easier fit.

Adams left the hatch open, the reflected light from the runway beneath providing their only source of illumination. His eyes adjusted quickly, and he saw that they were inside the cargo hold, which was half-filled with metallic containers.

The crates were secured to the floor, and Adams picked out one that nestled close up against the rear bulkhead. He closed the hatch, the darkness immediately enveloping them like a thick blanket, and took Lynn's hand, leading her to his chosen hiding place behind the crate. They wouldn't remain hidden if the cargo hold was checked but Adams figured that with attention focused out in the desert, the chances of a search weren't likely.

Then they waited, and waited, for six o'clock, hoping against hope that the schedule would be adhered to.

At six o'clock the aircraft started taxiing, and within ten more minutes they felt the small Boeing accelerate off down the runway and lift into the air.

Relief flooded them both.

27

THE FLIGHT FROM Groom Lake to Las Vegas was only a short haul.

Adams held Lynn as the aircraft touched down on what he knew would be the north-west runway of McCarran International Airport, adjacent to the Janet Terminal.

They stayed hidden behind the crate as the Boeing taxied along the runway, gradually slowing as it circled and then came to a halt at its final resting place.

'Come on,' Adams said, leaving the confines of their hiding place and heading straight for the wheel housing, Lynn right behind him.

He opened the small hatch and slipped through more easily this time. He stopped at the top of the wheel strut to help Lynn through. Once out, she turned and closed the hatch. Still hidden within the wheel housing, they were out of sight of anyone on the runway, and also gone without a trace from the cargo area in case anyone should check it now the plane had landed.

Adams' mind calculated what to do next. The night crew would be deplaning any minute, and then the airport's service crew would be at the plane, refuelling it and preparing it for flying again. Timing would be everything.

He slowly turned himself upside down, his legs clenched

around the landing strut to support his weight, keeping his hands by his side, so that only the top of his head would be visible if anyone was watching as he lowered himself to see what was going on around the aeroplane.

A set of stairs had already been brought to one side of the aircraft, nearest to the large white terminal building. On the far side of the terminal was a huge parking lot; and beyond that, the super-hotels and casinos of the Strip, the colossal black glass pyramid of the Luxor just opposite.

He heard an electric engine from the other side, and turned to see a service wagon coming across the runway towards them. Adams didn't move a muscle, realizing that with the light as it was, only movement would give away his position, unless someone came right up to the wheel housing and looked straight at him.

He continued to watch as the first sets of feet started to descend the steps, and then as a service crew got out of the wagon, extended a ladder from the top of the vehicle, and entered the plane through the rear service hatch.

Realizing that everyone's attention would now be on their own particular job, he spun his body back round, nodded to Lynn, and descended the strut, sliding straight down on to the tyre. Looking up to check that Lynn was with him, he then dropped from the top of the tyre to the runway tarmac.

Lynn joined him moments later, and he grabbed her hand and ran with her to the far side of the service wagon, using it to block the view of anyone in the Janet Terminal. They edged round the vehicle to the far side until they were at the rear.

Adams took another visual sweep of the area, gesturing

with his head towards the parking lot just thirty metres away across the runway. Lynn looked across and nodded.

Adams turned to her and mouthed silently, 'Three . . . two . . . one . . . go!'

Together they sprinted as fast as they could across the dark paving, running in the direction of the thick shadow of the plane's fuselage cast by the powerful terminal flood-lights. They covered the distance in five seconds, arriving at the fence line breathless, adrenalin coursing through their systems. Adams was sure they had remained undetected but every second that passed made them more of a target.

'Up and over,' he said to Lynn, and she turned to the fence, bending one leg and placing her foot into Adams' cupped palms, which he then pushed upwards, boosting her up to the top of the fence. She grabbed at the top, pulled her body across and over, and dropped gracefully to the other side.

Adams backed up a couple of feet and then launched himself at the fence, swinging up and over in one smooth motion. He landed in a crouch and turned back to look through the fence, to see if their escape had been seen by anyone. But nobody had turned towards them. The Area 51 workers were making their way into the terminal building like sheep into a pen, the service crew continued to buzz around the plane doing the jobs they were paid to do. The busy main terminal buildings were far over to the south-east; the north-west corner was deathly quiet by comparison, almost like a private airfield all on its own.

It was clear that their presence had not been noticed, and so Adams and Lynn backed away from the fence, straight-ened up and turned to face the parking lot, just another couple returning to their car. And then, arm in arm, they headed towards the unmanned exit.

Ten minutes later, they had crossed Haven Street and Giles Street, made their way through the parking lot of Motel 8 Las Vegas until they had emerged on to South Las Vegas Boulevard, the fabled 'Strip'. They crossed the wide, busy thoroughfare, and headed north until they reached the Luxor's gigantic pyramid, the world-famous hotel and casino that Adams had spotted from the wheel strut of the Boeing.

Anywhere else on earth, a couple entering a casino just after seven in the morning might have caused a few raised eyebrows; in Vegas, however, such a sight was as natural as night following day. It was a true twenty-four-hour culture here, and some of the regulars literally spent every hour of every day of their stay behind the slot machines or at the roulette tables, betting their life savings on a roll of the dice.

As they entered the one hundred and twenty thousand-foot casino floor, they were amazed by the hustle and bustle around them, hundreds, maybe thousands, of people swarming from gaming tables to slot machines and back again. It was chaos, pure and simple.

Adams turned to Lynn and smiled. 'It's perfect.'

John Ayita was a man with a number of concerns, none of them minor.

Ten of his Shadow Wolves were dead, including his team in San Francisco and the Najana brothers. In fact, as far as he was aware, there was now only him and Stephenfield left.

He hadn't heard from Adams since he and Lynn had
gone to pick up the test results from DNA Analytics. He
could only assume that the Bilderberg Group had somehow
found and captured them, and forced them to talk. What
else could have happened?

And yet he couldn't believe Matt would have talked, not
the great 'Free Bear'. Maybe Lynn then? Or maybe they'd
just used drugs on them; Ayita knew it was impossible to
resist certain types of truth serum. Either way, his men had
been wiped out by Jacobs' Alpha Brigade, and he was on
the run for his life.

He had had to abandon his warehouse headquarters and
go deep into hiding, and he knew that Stephenfield would
be doing the same.

He was in a bar in downtown Salt Lake City, downing
a beer and considering his next move, when his cellphone
rang. It was a clean phone, as he had rid himself of his other
units for fear that he could be tracked, but he had rerouted
those numbers to his new phone.

After a moment's consideration, he pressed the answer
button, although he didn't say anything.

'John?' He heard Matt Adams' voice coming through the
line, speaking in the Lakota language, but he still did not
answer. He was glad Adams was still alive at least, but didn't
know whether he could trust him. Maybe he was making the
call under duress. Or maybe his voice had been sampled and
was now being simulated by a computer. He had no idea.

'Look,' the voice continued in Lakota, 'I can't talk over
an open line, we need to meet.' Ayita considered the use of
the tribal language. If Adams was being forced to make the
call, why use the language? It made more sense that he was

aware that calls could be monitored and was using Lakota as it was so hard to translate.

'When and where?' Ayita asked finally.

By the afternoon, Ayita was in a motel room with Adams and Lynn, just off Highway 80 outside Carson City. Stephenfield was with them too, Adams having also managed to make contact with the only other surviving Shadow Wolf.

Security arrangements had been made carefully, none of the parties entirely trusting the other, but eventually the meeting had been made, and each person explained their part in what had happened.

Adams was distraught over the loss of his friends, but as he explained what had happened to Lynn and himself, what they had found out, and what was about to happen, such a private tragedy began to pale in comparison.

'So we need to get to Geneva as quickly as possible,' Adams finished. 'The stakes really don't get any higher than this.'

Ayita bowed his head as he considered the matter. Adams was right, of course. Their own lives were as nothing compared to the fate of the whole of humanity; there was no use in hiding now. He turned to Stephenfield. 'Can you still get passports?' he asked.

Stephenfield considered the matter before nodding his head. 'Given the alternative of not getting to Geneva, you bet I can.'

Three hours later, Stephenfield returned to the motel room. It never ceased to amaze him what could be accomplished if you had enough cash, and he hadn't been shy with his money. If they couldn't get to Geneva to stop Jacobs, what would be the use of money anyway?

He reached into his bag and pulled out not only passports, but also driving licences and social security cards, as well as a variety of cloned credit cards. He put them all on the table between them, and Adams was surprised when he noticed that there were four passports.

Stephenfield smiled at him. 'You didn't think you and Lynn would be going alone, did you?' he asked.

'Look,' Adams argued, 'I don't want you risking your lives as well, it—'

'You need us,' Ayita said, steel in his voice. 'And what do we have to stay here for anyway? If what you say is true, if you fail then we'll all be dead anyway.'

Adams realized he was right. 'OK,' he said. 'We'd better book some tickets out of here then. What are our new names?'

'I'll give you the lowdown on the way,' Stephenfield said. 'Flights are already booked, we leave from Reno-Tahoe International in two hours.'

Adams smiled. 'Excellent,' he said, happy to be leaving immediately. 'We'll get to Geneva, and then we're going to make those bastards wish that "contact" had never been made.'

PART FOUR

PART FOUR

1

FOR THE FIRST time in as long as he could remember, Jacobs was excited.

He had lived as Jacobs for several decades now, and no longer thought of himself as Charles Whitworth. But Whitworth he had been, firstborn son of Benjamin and Mary Whitworth, and he had cut his teeth at the back end of the First World War. He had done and seen it all. But this would outdo everything.

He couldn't wait to meet the Anunnaki, and he had none of the doubts that Adams and Edwards had tried to instil in him. They would keep their end of the bargain; of course they would, he was already an immortal. But the real reason that Jacobs trusted them – at least for now, anyway – was that the Anunnaki needed him and his chosen colleagues.

For all their hi-tech advancement, the fact remained that the Anunnaki had not lived on a real planet for several thousand years; their minds were strong but their bodies were weak, and they needed assistance if they were to truly enslave the rest of humanity. The deadly virus would only do so much; the survivors would need hunting down, which was why the entire Alpha Brigade were also to be spared. The Bilderbergers' mission was to use their various talents to lure out the other survivors, so that the Alpha Brigade could capture them. This physical task was something that the Anunnaki could simply no longer manage. They had the technology to build all sorts of robotic or cybernetic answers, of course; but they didn't have the space – which was why they were coming back to earth in the first place.

And so Jacobs was more than happy to trust the Anunnaki upon their return. He had no doubt they would look for a way to get rid of him and his allies at the first available opportunity, but he planned to make himself indispensable to them in the short time he had, which he was more than confident he could do. He also harboured another, altogether more ambitious plan but was wary of thinking about it too much due to the Anunnaki's telepathic abilities. Over the years he had developed a technique for getting around this to some extent. He had learnt that the thoughts or words had to be fully formed before the Anunnaki could interpret them, and therefore when he was thinking about anything he didn't want them to know about, he never let anything become fully realized in his mind. It was almost like trying to see something in the dark; you didn't look at it directly but glanced to the side so that peripheral vision picked it up instead.

And so it was that Jacobs' ultimate plan lay just out of reach of the Anunnaki, and although he had no guarantees that it would work, it was certainly something that was worth pursuing when the time was right.

For now, though, he was just enjoying the anticipation, as he was whisked through the dark, snow-filled streets of Geneva. He and his colleagues – they were the Hundred once more, after his invitation to Saul Rubino, a billionaire diamond merchant, had been accepted – had arrived at the airport late the previous evening and had decided to spend the night at the Palais Grande, overlooking the wonderful lake that had made the city so famous.

Wesley Jones had stayed behind to manage affairs back in Washington, aiming to stall the investigation into the crash site near Jacobs' house, but he was due to get to Geneva in time for the arrival of the Anunnaki. Jacobs had come to rely on Jones over the years and found himself hoping that he would make it.

The rest of the Bilderberg Hundred were now in convoy, travelling out of the city and taking the autoroute through the glorious foothills of the far mountains, heading for the Large Hadron Collider facility of CERN, the organization he himself had helped to establish for the express purpose of bringing the Anunnaki back to earth.

Philippe Messier had come to join them for dinner at the hotel the night before and, over lobster and Dom Perignon, he had informed the assembled group that the device would be operational by the following afternoon. There had been cheers and celebration, and Messier had been toasted time and again, until he could barely stand.

As the first rays of dawn started to appear over the mountains, Jacobs rested back in the deep leather seat of the huge Rolls-Royce limousine, and took a sip of early morning cognac.

His telephone rang as he put the glass to his lips, and he quickly retrieved it from his pocket. He saw who it was and answered the call immediately, the blood draining from his face.

* * *

It wasn't a call Colonel Caines had wanted to make but better it came from him directly than that Jacobs heard it from another source, which would surely happen before the morning was out.

'Mr Jacobs,' he started uneasily. 'I'm afraid I have some bad news.'

Jacobs listened intently as Caines gave him a rundown of what had occurred over the past few hours.

'Do you have any leads whatsoever?' Jacobs asked.

'No, sir,' Caines admitted, glad Jacobs was not in the room with him. 'We have no idea where they might have gone as of this time. But we're doing everything in our power to relocate them.'

For a brief moment, Jacobs considered shouting at Caines, screaming down the phone at him for his ineptitude and threatening him with torture and death for failing in his mission; and then he would have liked to smash the phone to pieces.

Instead, he merely closed the phone slowly, cutting off the call without a word, succeeding in his efforts to control himself. It was no use shouting at Caines. What purpose would that serve now?

Adams and Edwards were clever, and now they were even more dangerous than ever. Why had he told them everything, back in the laboratory? His pride had got the better of him, that was why. He was certainly old enough to know better, but just as there was no use in shouting at Caines, there was also no point in beating himself up either. Instead, as his limousine glided along the smooth Swiss roads, he considered how they might have performed their vanishing act.

Moments later, he snapped upright and grabbed his phone to call Caines back.

Caines saw that it was Jacobs calling and reluctantly answered. 'Yes, sir?' he said gingerly.

'Caines, have you checked the inner base?' He could hear Jacobs' excited tone.

'I'm sorry, what do you mean, sir?'

Jacobs sighed audibly in exasperation. 'I mean have you searched inside the damn base?' he almost screamed down the line.

'Er . . . no, sir,' Caines answered, never having considered that the fugitives might have broken back *into* the base.

'Well, get checking now!' Jacobs ordered. 'If you can't find them outside the fence line, they must have gone back in!'

Adams looked out of the small window next to him, watching the thick clouds obscuring the view of the Atlantic Ocean far below, and allowed himself to relax ever so slightly. The flight from Reno-Tahoe to Zurich took sixteen hours, giving him the opportunity to do nothing *but* relax.

A flight to Geneva would have been ideal, but the international flights went to Zurich, and they would have to arrange onward transportation from there. Once Jacobs had learnt of their escape he would doubtless have arrivals at Geneva monitored anyway, so it was probably just as well that Zurich was the destination. A fast train from there to Geneva wouldn't take long, and the train stations would be easier to arrive at unannounced.

To avoid any undue attention, the four of them were

sitting in seats well away from each other, so Adams didn't even have anyone to talk to. The in-flight magazine didn't keep him occupied for more than a few minutes, and he had no interest in the mediocre selection of films that were on offer. And so he was left alone with just his thoughts for company. Still, that was no bad thing, he considered. He had known no other way for many years.

As he sat there, he tried to concentrate on what they would do once in Zurich. It had been decided that Ayita and Stephenfield would deplane first, try and spot any surveillance and draw the attention of anyone who may be there waiting for them. He and Lynn would follow, if the coast was clear. They would then go separately through passport control, and each get taxis to the main city square. They would meet up and make their way on foot to the train station, using cash to purchase four tickets to Geneva.

Once in Geneva, things would get a little more problematic, Adams knew; and yet try as he might to think things through logically, his mind kept returning instead to Lynn.

Evelyn Edwards, his ex-wife and now the mother of his as yet unborn child. So beautiful, so intelligent, so resourceful, even all these years after they had first met. To some extent he couldn't believe that she had ever fallen for him in the first place.

He still loved her, he knew that for certain. That had been a part of his problem for so many years, the fact that he was still in love with her. It had stalled the rest of his life, making him incapable of carrying on fully. And now she was pregnant, and they were going to have a child of their own. Adams just didn't know how to feel about that. The larger part of him was almost indescribably happy – he was to have the child he had always wanted, with the woman he wanted. But there was a deep conflict too. Given all that was going on, what would happen with the baby? Would he or she ever be born, or would humanity be wiped out before that glorious day?

The weight of the responsibility came crushing down on him. It was up to him to make sure that never happened, just like it had been up to him to get to that damn truck in the desert.

But unlike then, he promised himself now that he would not fail, no matter what it took.

2

JACOBS WAS IN the foothills just ten kilometres from the fabled CERN Large Hadron Collider when the call came through from Caines, the man's tone now more optimistic.

'You were right, sir,' he said with some excitement.

'You've found them?' Jacobs asked immediately.

'Not exactly, sir,' Caines answered, the nervousness back in his voice. 'What I mean to say is that they *did* come back on to the base but they left several hours ago.'

'And just how in the hell did they manage that?' Jacobs almost exploded.

'We checked all CCTV footage of the base grounds, and although the film is a little dark and hazy, it looks as if they managed to sneak on board the six o'clock Janet flight to McCarran.'

'You've got to be kidding me. So where are they now?'

'We're still investigating, sir. Terminal CCTV has them leaving the plane and escaping into the parking lot. Using traffic cameras, we've traced them to the Luxor Hotel and Casino. It looks like they made a call from a payphone next to the slot machines, and we're following up on that. But we're confident we can reacquire them in short order, now we're on their trail.'

'Good,' Jacobs said. 'Keep me informed.'

Adams took the bumps slowly along the desert road in his Toyota Landcruiser, taking the twists and turns at under five miles per hour, the vehicle seemingly unable to go any faster.

He could barely see, and didn't want to crash off the road. What good would he be to anybody then?

He looked through the windscreen up at the burning sun, and looked away, his head aching, in agony.

He pulled over to the side of the road. It was no use. He'd been on the truck's trail for three days now and was no closer to catching it. He needed a rest, just half an hour to shut his eyes. He'd been here before so many times, knew what the consequences would be if he fell asleep, and yet he was powerless to resist. He had to carry on, had to try and get there in time, at least once, at least this time. But he was so tired . . .

He was in the desert, on foot now and tracking the tyre marks that had gone off the road just half a kilometre from where he had been resting. The sun was lower in the sky, several hours having passed. He cursed himself, knowing what that would mean. He would find the truck like he had a thousand times in the past, open the doors, hoping that this time it would be different.

But it wouldn't be different; there would still be the same rotting bodies lying dead in the rear of the scorching hot truck, dead because he couldn't keep himself awake.

Still he soldiered on, trapped in the dreamland version of the event that had destroyed his life. He tracked the tyre marks for another mile over the dusty terrain, until he found the truck lying there deserted in the dying rays of the afternoon sun. He moved close, and immediately knew that there was something different this time.

What was it? He tried to think, to clear the fuzz from his head.

The smell! It wasn't there! Were they still alive? Quickly, he rushed to the rear doors, pulling them open in excitement.

And there they were – dozens of children, dazed and starving, but still alive! They looked at him in wonder, and then there seemed to be more, and instead of dozens there were hundreds, and then thousands, until there were as many as there were grains of sand on a beach, until his vision could take in nothing else.

He heard a ticking sound, and his head turned to it. There was a small clock on the truck wall, counting down the seconds, and Adams instinctively knew that this was the amount of time the children had left until they died. He moved forward immediately but was halted by a voice to his rear.

'Matt!' Lynn's voice called out, and his head snapped round at the sound.

He could see Lynn with a newborn baby – *his* baby – cradled in her arms, mother and child both teetering on the edge of a cliff, about to fall.

He looked at the clock on the truck's wall. Ten seconds.

He turned back to Lynn and the child. Her foot slipped, rock and shale falling into the chasm below, her balance lost.

Adams froze, unable to move, caught in indecision. In the truck were thousands, millions of people to be rescued.

On the cliff was the woman he loved, and his own child, a part of himself given life through that love.

What should he do? How could he save both sets of people in the time he had available? He had to do something but he couldn't move; he just didn't know which way to turn.

An alarm sounded, and he turned to the truck; and then Lynn screamed, and he turned to the cliff.

His mouth went wide as he saw Lynn and their baby fall over the cliff edge, and he started towards them, but was halted by the screams behind him, the cries of millions of souls in torment.

The sun above him seemed to grow larger, increasing in size as it came towards him, bigger and bigger, hotter and hotter, until it was all he could see, all he could *feel*.

And then Adams did the only thing he could do; he collapsed to his knees and screamed.

'Are you all right, sir?' the portly Texan next to Adams said with concern, shaking him awake.

Adams snapped out of it immediately, doing his best not to look around the cabin and bring even more attention to himself. 'Yes, I'm OK,' he said to the kindly man. 'Thank you. Just a bad dream.'

The Texan nodded his head in understanding. 'I know what that's like, son,' he said. 'Ain't nothing you can do about your dreams.'

Adams nodded his head. 'I guess not,' he said, giving the man a reassuring smile, making clear that he was now OK.

The dream was new, but it was most definitely bad. Was there truly nothing that he could do about it?

Adams felt a drop in altitude, heard the change in engine speed, and then saw the seat-belt lights come on. They were coming in to land, and he rested back into his seat, understanding that he was probably about to find out.

3

THE SIGHT WAS glorious as always, the myriad buildings that made up the ground-level complex of the LHC facility. They were not at all beautiful in and of themselves; rather it was what they represented that was glorious.

The wormhole device was so secret that it didn't even have a code name; only those few selected knew of its existence, apart from the specialist technicians who worked on it, and who would never see the light of day again after it became operational.

Jacobs' limousine passed through the main gateposts, and he wondered how long it would take to gather everyone together. Most of the Bilderberg Hundred had been at the dinner the night before, but some members had still to make it to Switzerland. He hoped they would be here before the device went operational; they wouldn't want to be caught outside after the Anunnaki had returned.

The car continued on through the outlying buildings, winding through the snow-covered inner roads until it came to a stop outside the main administrative building.

Jacobs' driver went round to open his door, and as he stepped out, he was pleased to see Philippe Messier striding out to meet him, hand extended.

'Philippe,' Jacobs said in greeting as he shook the proffered hand. 'How are we looking?'

Messier smiled in answer and escorted Jacobs towards the entrance. 'Let's just say I hope the others get here soon.'

Eighteen hours after boarding the flight at Reno-Tahoe, Adams found himself in Das Central, the main square in the old historic area of Zurich.

He stood at the barrier overlooking the Limmat, a chillingly cold body of water that nevertheless sparkled under the rays of the winter sun. He took up a position where he could monitor both banks of the river, checking on the comings and goings of the streams of people, ever vigilant against the threat of surveillance.

He hadn't been stopped at the airport, and as far as he could tell nor had Lynn or the others, which indicated that they were not under observation but he knew he couldn't be sure.

His counter-surveillance picked up both Lynn and Ayita long before they arrived at his position by the bridge. He was careful not to show too much emotion as Lynn approached, although he was overjoyed to see her; they were just a group of friends taking a tour of the city. Stephenfield arrived last, and although he was the least observable, Adams was pleased that he was still able to pick him up before he was upon them; if he could spot an intelligence operative as good as Stephenfield, then his skills were probably sufficient to spot anyone else that might be observing them.

'Was anyone followed?' Ayita asked when they were all together. When they all replied in the negative, he turned to the north. 'Come on then. The train to Geneva leaves in twenty minutes.'

As they set out along the Neumühlequai, Ayita continued, 'We'll board the train and get our tickets from the inspector once we're travelling. We don't have time to get them in the office, and anyway, the purchase doesn't get reported this way.'

They turned north-west along Museumstrasse, all of them keyed up, constantly checking about them. But as they neared the Hauptbahnhof, the city's main train station, they realized that no one was watching them, and they might yet reach Geneva unopposed.

Philippe Messier was proud; indeed, this week was surely to prove the proudest of his incredible career.

As Director General of CERN, Messier was directly responsible for the success of the Large Hadron Collider project. The LHC, like the invention of the internet before it, had given CERN its current status as the world's primary scientific research centre. The main work of CERN was now particle physics research, and the LHC – as well as the other experimental particle accelerators and the single decelerator that were also to be found on the site – was rightfully famous around the world for both its scale and its cost.

Particle physics centres on the study of subatomic particles, and how they create matter. The trouble is, to thoroughly understand such a subject, the particles themselves have to be broken down into smaller parts, and the only way to achieve this is to have them crash into one another at incredible speed.

Thus particle accelerators came into being, designed to

fire particles up to the required speeds for such a collision. The LHC is the world's largest such 'collider', and consists of a circular tunnel 27 kilometres in circumference, buried a hundred metres underground. The extreme length is to give the particle beams the distance necessary to accelerate to the required speed. The beams are fired in opposite directions, in the hope that they will collide upon meeting. However this is, in the words of the LHC's chief engineer, 'like firing two needles across the Atlantic and getting them to hit each other'.

Messier smiled when he thought of this quote, knowing that it was in fact easier than the public at large was led to believe. The technology that the Anunnaki had gifted the Bilderbergers essentially ensured that each time the machine was fired up, there was a hit. But even within CERN, only a handful of trusted staff knew that this was the case, because the purpose of getting the beams to collide was to carry out research, not to harvest the energy that resulted from such super-collisions. But harvesting the energy was exactly what Messier had been doing, and transmitting it to the secret experiment further underground.

The wormhole device required power, and lots of it. Controlling the bending of space-time as it did, a normal power source was simply not enough. The experiments going on above with the LHC, however, created a constant stream of antimatter, the most powerful energy source in the known universe. It was the need for antimatter as an energy source that had led Charles Whitworth to lead the drive for CERN's creation in the first place, back in 1954, and it had taken since then – even *with* external help – to perfect the technology.

Messier looked across the chic, ultra-modern bar at Stephen Jacobs, as Whitworth had been known since the sixties. The man was living proof of the abilities of the Anunnaki, and verification of their promises.

Messier raised his champagne flute in salute, and saw Jacobs smile and raise his own.

Soon they would meet the Anunnaki face to face; and both men felt ready.

Jacobs felt his phone vibrating in his pocket. He pulled it out, and saw it was Eldridge.

After the disaster at Area 51, Jacobs had made a grudging Eldridge take control of the situation, which meant that the commander of Alpha Brigade would have to delay his journey to CERN. This had displeased him greatly, Jacobs knew, but at the end of the day, if Eldridge had done his job right in the first place, they wouldn't be in such a situation now.

Jacobs answered the phone. The call was coming from his private jet, which was once again being used as their mobile headquarters, as it had been in South America.

'What's the status?' he asked without preamble.

'I think we've got them, sir,' he heard Eldridge announce with confidence. 'I'll wrap this up once and for all, and then meet you for the big finale.'

'Not the finale, my friend,' Jacobs corrected. 'Remember, this is just the beginning.'

4

LYNN SAT BY the window, watching as the large Geneva-Cornavin train station appeared out of the freezing fog ahead of her.

The fog had descended just an hour into their two and a half-hour journey, and had obscured what had up until then been beautiful views of the Swiss countryside.

At any rate, now they were here, and she had to concentrate on what was going to happen next. As before, Ayita and Stephenfield would get off first, checking the platforms for any sign of the enemy. If the coast was clear, she and Adams would leave the train and the four of them would move independently to the taxi rank outside the station.

Their taxis would take them to four random places, from where they would all move on foot to Moilebeau Park. They would meet up there, and then pair up in two more taxis, Stephenfield and Ayita in the lead, with Lynn and Adams following, and ask to be taken to Maisonnex Dessus, the suburb to the north-west of the city just before the foothills of the Jura Mountains. The CERN facility was located very close to this small town, and the four of them would meet up once more and confirm their final plans for entering the base itself.

Lynn was all too aware that the plan for her was to remain

in the town of Maisonnex Dessus, monitoring communications and acting as the central point of contact. She understood the rationale behind this, as the fact was that out of the four of them, she was the only one untrained and without direct operational experience. If that had been the only consideration, she would still have insisted that she accompany them into CERN. But as the others had all pointed out – Matt with *extreme* conviction, understandably – she was pregnant, and couldn't take the risk of getting involved in the action directly.

It was sensible to have someone keeping an eye on things from a distance, and when all things were considered, it could really only be her. Stephenfield had shown her how to operate the array of electronic machinery he had somehow managed to carry with him from America, and so it wasn't as if she would be doing nothing; but a part of her still wished she would be taking a more active part.

Another side of her – a more powerful side? – demanded that she follow their recommendations and stay out of harm's way. She didn't know if it was mother's instinct already making itself felt, or if she was just afraid. But maybe the two things were linked – perhaps she was afraid not for herself but for her unborn baby.

And, she decided, she could live with that.

Eldridge and his men landed at a private runway at Geneva International, and immediately transferred to a squad of Audi 4x4 vehicles, tearing away from the airport on a direct run for Geneva's Cornavin rail station.

The big break had come through electronic monitoring of local CCTV surveillance. It had been Caines' team back at Area 51 that had made the match, picking up an image of Lynn Edwards at Reno-Tahoe airport.

As it was a minor transport hub, the team were not quick to find the match, and by the time the facial recognition software had found and analysed the image, the flight had already landed in Zurich.

Once Edwards had been identified, they discovered that Adams had been on the same flight, and a quick investigation into the passenger list revealed their new passport details. Where they could have got such identification in so short a time, Eldridge could only wonder.

Caines, to his credit, had then ordered a satellite to be rerouted to cover Zurich, as well as real-time monitoring of ticket information systems; the passport details Edwards and Adams had flown under were red-flagged, and the fugitives' latest images were uploaded into the surveillance systems of the Swiss capital.

They had then lost them for a short while, before a partial match – again of Edwards – was made at Zurich's Hauptbahnhof. It seemed that Adams – as expected, given his background – was rather more adept at hiding from the surveillance cameras.

There had been no ticket purchases made in the names of the passport holders, but when Caines had made his report, Eldridge had known there was only one place the two of them could have been headed – Geneva, on their way to try and stop the return of the Anunnaki.

If only Jacobs had kept his mouth shut. Why did he have to tell them everything? What possible good could it have served? But tell them he had, and now they were on their way.

Eldridge had accessed the train timetable and identified the most likely routes, then ordered Caines and his men to analyse satellite images of the platforms as the trains boarded.

The matches had not been one hundred per cent but they were good enough for a partial ID, this time of both Edwards and Adams. And so now Eldridge and his men were racing through the streets of Geneva for a deadly rendezvous with their targets.

Adams watched through his window as Ayita descended from the now stationary train on to the platform. Although it wasn't obvious, Adams could tell that he was doing a thorough counter-surveillance run.

Less than a minute later, Stephenfield also got out, subtly checking out the platform from the other side. After another minute, both men extended their right forefingers, indicating that it was safe for himself and Lynn to leave the train.

Having Ayita and Stephenfield along was proving invaluable, Adams acknowledged. He knew the search would be primarily for himself and Lynn, and so it was immensely useful to have two such seasoned professionals able to check out their route beforehand. It also made him feel much better that they would be accompanying him to the CERN laboratory instead of Lynn. He was uneasy about Lynn having come this far but he knew she would never have stayed in America. At least this way she could be of help and still stay relatively safe.

Adams rose from his seat, about to turn into the gangway, but suddenly went rigid, his eyes picking up movement from Ayita's right hand. All four fingers went straight, the signal that somebody was there; the coast was *not* clear.

Adams stayed where he was as the other passengers continued to filter out. Pretty soon he would be the only person left in this compartment, and if Lynn had also seen the signal, which he hoped she had, she would also be left alone in hers, which would make them both stand out.

Ayita must have had his reasons, and Adams knew it couldn't be anything good. He began to move, walking as calmly as he could for Lynn's compartment just through the next door. If something was about to happen, he wanted to be with her.

He saw Lynn through the little porthole window and put his hand to the door handle, pushing down.

And then all hell broke loose.

5

ELDRIDGE WAS TIRED of playing nicely. Too many times now he had tried to capture Adams and Edwards, or lie in wait for them, or try and catch them out in some sort of sophisticated trap. But no more. This time they were going down.

He and his dozen men, all top commandos in the Alpha Brigade, had left their cars running outside the train station and went through the doors at a sprint, cocking their assault rifles as they went. Eldridge had cleared their presence with the municipal transport police, but if they tried to stop him anyway, he would have no problem adding a few of them to his tally of corpses.

He led the surge on to Platform 5, an internal line with a train just in from Zurich, and ordered his men to spread out down the length of the stationary train, guns trained on the doors. He and his men ignored the screams of the throngs of passengers as they left the train, concentrating instead on their faces. Adams and Edwards were not among them. And then Eldridge scanned the windows, and a smile spread across his face as he saw both of his targets, in two separate carriages. Perfect.

The smile was wiped off his face instants later. The shock of the bullet hitting him in the shoulder spun his upper torso round while his feet remained rooted to the spot. Pain ripped through his hips and chest.

He hit the ground, gasping for breath, and saw his men turn and open fire at a man standing on the platform, a pistol in his hands. The man dived for cover behind a metal bench.

As Eldridge checked that his armoured vest had successfully stopped the round that hit him, two of his men were hit, by rounds coming from the opposite direction. Eldridge turned to look and saw a second man aiming a pistol and firing at his team, loosing off an entire magazine before dropping to the railway tracks, using the concrete platform itself for cover.

From inside the train, Adams and Lynn, now in the same carriage, watched in horror as the thirteen armed men stormed the platform, and then as Ayita and Stephenfield opened fire and were in turn fired upon.

Adams had seen enough. He took his own pistol out and shot through the glass of the opposite window. Then he turned to grab Lynn and pulled her to the other side of the train.

'But the others!' she cried. 'We can't leave them!'

'We have to,' he snapped, disgusted with having to make the decision. 'If we stay, we're dead. And then what happens if the wormhole opens?'

Lynn paused for a moment, then nodded her head and followed Adams to the shattered window, her thoughts still on Stephenfield and Ayita as she went.

John Ayita watched from behind the bench as Matt and Lynn escaped out of the other side of the train.

He saw Stephenfield was holding his own, hiding down behind the platform's edge. His friend pulled up, fired three shots – two of which hit their targets – and then dropped low again. Ayita fired his own gun twice more, then stopped to change magazines. As he did so, Stephenfield popped up again, raised his gun, and then – and then . . .

Ayita couldn't believe his eyes as he saw the top of his friend's head explode, a 9mm round taking the skullcap straight off, the reddish grey mass of the brain quivering as Stephenfield staggered backwards, before he took twenty more shots to his centre mass, his entire body quivering under the massive shock of the bullets' impact.

And then Ayita felt pain of his own, his ankle exploding in agony. He looked down and, saw the huge wound in his lower leg, blood staining the ground around him.

Ayita spat on the platform. He was wounded, his friend was dead, but he wasn't going to go down without a fight.

Eldridge watched with satisfaction as his men took the first man down, and realized that the man behind the metal bench would probably be distracted.

From his position on the ground, Eldridge could just about see the man's feet and ankles underneath the bench, and so aimed his submachine gun and loosed a single round. It hit the man's ankle but didn't make him drop to the ground as he had hoped it would. The man was tough, whoever he was.

And then the man appeared from behind the metal bench, a crazed look on his face, seemingly ignoring the gunshot wound to his leg. It was then that Eldridge realized it was John Ayita, the head of the Shadow Wolves whom he had failed to find when recently ordered to execute them. Which meant that the other man was probably Samuel 'Two Horses' Stephenfield, the unit's intelligence chief and the only other member to have successfully evaded Eldridge's death squad. Until now.

Ayita shot his pistol with unerring accuracy, taking one man down after another, but the result was inevitable; like Stephenfield before him, Ayita, too, was eventually shot by Eldridge's expert team. The first rounds entered Ayita's gut, doubling him over, making him drop the gun; the next four tore into his chest, ripping into his internal organs. But still he kept coming, the warrior in him not dead yet, and Eldridge was amazed as Ayita reached into his belt and pulled out a hunting knife, raising it above his head and charging the rest of the men on the platform, letting out a ferocious war cry as he did so.

But the cry was caught in his throat as another forty bullets entered his body almost simultaneously, hurling him backwards ten feet on the platform, his torso all but destroyed, his lifeless eyes staring up at the steel-girdered platform roof.

Eldridge got to one knee, and then to his feet. He looked through the train window.

Damn! Adams and Edwards had gone.

6

TRYING TO IGNORE the sounds of gunfire behind them, Adams sprinted across the tracks on the far side of the train, away from the platform. Ahead of them was another train, making ready to leave the platform. The doors on this side were closed, but Adams knew they had to make it if they were to stand any chance of getting out of there alive.

The gunfire was still continuing as they reached the train, and Adams grabbed Lynn and hauled her up into a locked doorway, pulling himself up after her just as the train pulled out from the platform.

Holding on to the exterior as they were, they were sitting ducks if one of the armed men on the far side decided to take a shot at them, and so he helped Lynn round to the small handholds to the side of the door, which acted as a ladder, and gestured for her to climb.

And climb she did, reaching the top and then helping him up.

He rolled on to the top of the train as it passed the end of the platform, mercifully leaving the station.

And then the sound of gunfire stopped.

Eldridge saw what Adams and Edwards were doing and immediately ordered some of his men back to the cars, to give chase if need be, and others to race around to the other platform.

Meanwhile, as his targets climbed the ladder to the top of the train, Eldridge went down on one knee to stabilize his position, put the stock of his assault rifle tight into his shoulder, took aim and squeezed the trigger, firing off one shot.

The round only narrowly missed, passing between their bodies, but it was enough to unbalance Lynn. She turned on the unstable top of the moving train and slipped, falling over the side.

Adams reacted in an instant, his hand grasping her arm as she went over the side, holding her weight as she dangled in front of a carriage window.

Digging his feet into the metal roof and gripping a side rail with his free hand, he started to pull her back up.

Eldridge cursed and licked his lips, taking aim once more.

He squeezed the trigger again, and was gratified when the round went through Adams' upper arm with a spray of blood.

Adams felt the round enter his arm and his grip loosened instantly.

He watched as Lynn fell to the tracks, and moved to follow her; but instead, his head filled with pain, his vision turned cloudly, and he passed out, unconscious on top of the moving train.

Eldridge watched as his men jumped from the opposite

platform, picked up the unconscious Evelyn Edwards and carried her off the tracks.

He took another aim at Adams, his body slumped over the edge of the train's roof, but the train rounded a bend, taking his target away.

He turned to look at his men across the train station and keyed his mic. 'Do not kill the woman yet,' he ordered. 'Stop that train, and make sure the male suspect is dead first. For now, bring her back over here. We may still need to use her.'

It was the searing pain in his left biceps that woke Adams eventually, his head first lolling groggily to one side, and then snapping up when he realized where he was, and what had happened.

Ignoring the pain in his arm for the moment, he pulled himself up to a crouch, looking back down the length of the train and the track behind it. The Geneva-Cornavin station was now just a small spot in the distance, and Adams could only assume that he'd been out for a full minute or two. Easily time enough for Eldridge and his men to have got to Lynn.

His whole body convulsed in anger, and only with the recurrence of the pain did he look down to check the damage to his arm. It seemed like a clean wound, the 9mm round having passed through the meat of the biceps like a hot knife through butter. The bone was undamaged but the wound was bleeding badly, and he knew if he didn't stop it soon, he would pass out again from a drop in blood pressure.

Even though instinct told him to instantly leave the train

347

and race back to the station, years of training and experience dictated that he first of all tend to the damage to his arm. If he did not treat that as a priority, he might not make it off the train at all.

He took off his jacket and tore the sleeve from his shirt to expose the wound fully, then tore off his other sleeve and wrapped it round the bullet wound in a tight compress. He then tore off the bottom of one trouser leg and cinched it round the makeshift dressing, tying it off in a tight knot. He put his jacket back on to conceal the damage. Not perfect, but it would do.

The train was picking up speed but was not yet travelling too fast to dismount. He would climb carefully down the side ladder, get as close as he could to the tracks in order to minimize the impact of the fall, and then he would jump. He just hoped his arm would hold up.

And then he heard the scream of tyres and the gunning of loud, powerful engines, and turned to look. Just twenty metres away, racing down the city streets parallel to the tracks, were two Audi 4x4s, keeping pace with the train.

He recoiled instinctively when he saw rifles coming out of the side windows of each car. He pushed back and rolled, just as the top of the train carriage lit up with sparks, high-velocity rounds ricocheting off the metalwork. The rounds chased him over the roof, eating up the metal so close to him he could smell the cordite, and then he was off the roof entirely and falling through the air on the far side of the train.

It wasn't the exit he had hoped for, and although he tried to roll as he hit the tracks, the impact knocked the wind out of him, dazing him momentarily. He broke the fall with his damaged arm, fighting against the desire to use the good one. The bad arm was already useless, he figured, so why risk hurting the one that still worked? It took great presence of mind to wantonly endanger the damaged limb, but the jarring pain just caused his mind to sharpen even more, driving him up and off the tracks, racing for the far side, away from Eldridge's men.

He managed to get to the far side, diving over the side of a huge metal barrier before the length of the train passed by and betrayed his position to his pursuers. Stuck as they were on the road, unable to close in on the tracks, the soldiers would have to abandon their vehicles and give chase on foot.

Behind him was another barrier, and when he went to look over the side, he saw a shopping concourse down below. Without pausing, he leapt over the side, clinging to the metal girders that supported the track, and edged down to the shopping level using his legs and one good arm. He knew he would be being tracked by satellite, and realized that he could use the underpass to lose the surveillance. He had to be aware of CCTV, but he was used to that.

He joined the throngs of shoppers making their way through the underpass, trying to act as normally as he could, while still keeping an eye out for both his armed pursuers and for the inevitable CCTV. He noticed a sign for an underground parking garage for the shopping concourse. It was just what he needed.

He knew it was useless to return to the station now, even though he wanted to with all his heart. Ayita and Stephenfield would both be dead, and Lynn . . . But he didn't want to think about that now; if he was to be of any further use, he couldn't. He had to put aside what had happened at the station, box it up in a far corner of his mind, to be dealt with at some point in the future.

If he ever survived to see the future, he thought grimly.

'We've lost him,' Eldridge heard one of his men report in. 'He fell off the roof on to the tracks but by the time we left the vehicles, he was long gone. We've searched the area but there's no sign of him.'

Eldridge double-clicked the radio in acknowledgement. *Damn it.* He had already received notification from the team at Area 51 that satellite surveillance had tracked him as far as the underpass and had not reacquired him. Either Adams was still somewhere in the underpass area – unlikely, if his men hadn't found him – or he had managed to escape the area somehow.

Still, Eldridge now had Evelyn Edwards as his hostage and he was certain he would be able to use her as leverage if Adams came at them again.

He keyed the radio. 'OK,' he ordered, 'that's it then. Start making your way to base. It's almost time.'

'Yes, sir,' he heard the confirmation come back to him, eagerness in the man's voice.

Eldridge turned to look at Lynn Edwards, unconscious and handcuffed in the Audi's leather bucket seat next to him.

One out of two wasn't bad, he figured. At any rate, it was going to have to do for now, at least.

Just a few miles behind Eldridge, unbeknown to both men, Adams drove his recently stolen car. He had hot-wired it in the parking garage and was now on the road to CERN. There was to be no more subtlety, no more attempts to second-guess. There was no time. He was just going to go straight up to the main gate of CERN and demand to be let in.

He had remembered something that Professor Travers had said during their impromptu 'hidden history' lecture in the bowels of Area 51, and it had given him something that at least resembled a plan.

He just needed to make a quick stop first.

By the time the big Audi reached the main Mysen entrance to the CERN facility, Lynn was awake, although she chose to hide this fact from her captors.

Her immediate thoughts were for the baby. Would it still be OK after such a fall? But there was nothing she could do about that now; only time would tell.

But what about Matt? What had happened to him?

As she looked about the car with hooded eyes, she recognized the large bulk of Eldridge next to her and realized she had been handcuffed to him. But Matt was nowhere to be seen, and she wondered what that meant.

Had he escaped? She hoped with all her heart that this was the case. But what if he had been captured, and was in another car? What if he was dead? But the fact that she was still alive lent credence to the possibility that Matt was alive too. It made sense to hold her as a hostage if he hadn't been killed yet.

The thought gave her hope, despite her current situation. If Matt was alive, then maybe they still had a chance.

7

Eldridge looked down at Lynn. 'You might as well cut the pretence and open your eyes, Dr Edwards,' he said bluntly. 'I know you've been awake since the city.'

Lynn opened her eyes and stared at him. 'Well, clever old you,' she said sarcastically.

Eldridge smiled. 'I don't think you're in any position to poke fun,' he chided. 'We are allowing you to live, for now. You would do well to remember that.'

She ignored him, and they proceeded in silence. The car drove through the gate to the CERN laboratories, a rather unassuming barrier that looked as if it was guarding nothing more than a regular, run-of-the-mill industrial estate. As they passed nondescript office blocks, temporary accommodation and the occasional larger concrete laboratory, Lynn wasn't surprised to find that the rest of the complex, like the gate before it, was also not dissimilar to a standard industrial estate.

During her time in NASA, she had come to understand that many of the world's most famous and highly regarded scientific facilities – the kind of places that the public imagined would be all spotless, gleaming stainless steel and high-end electronics – were in actual fact very often depressingly mundane, and it seemed that CERN was no different.

After a few minutes, they halted in front of what appeared to be the administrative headquarters. The front seat passenger got out and opened Eldridge's door, and the big man got out, pulling Lynn along behind with him.

They pushed through the heavy front doors, and Lynn was surprised to see that the foyer was rather more plush than the exterior would suggest. But then, she figured, the research carried out here depended to a large extent on donations and external funding, and in her experience the people signing the cheques liked to be wined and dined in fine style.

There were a few people wandering around, and Eldridge was careful not to make a show of the fact he had a woman handcuffed to him. The desk security guard noticed but merely nodded his head at Eldridge.

They remained silent as they passed through the foyer, and Lynn noticed the first signs for the Large Hadron Collider, labelled in several different languages. They turned down a long corridor and followed it to the end, and despite circumstances, Lynn found herself excited to be here. The LHC was the world's scientific Mecca, and she had always wanted to see it.

Eldridge noticed her interest and smiled. 'Want to see the collider, eh?' he asked. When Lynn just ignored him, he continued anyway. 'Not on the agenda for today I'm afraid, Dr Edwards. But what you're about to see is a lot more special, believe me.'

And although she hated the man next to her, Lynn suspected that in this case he might just be right.

They found the elevator at the end of the left-hand corridor and went straight in. Eldridge pushed the button for the LHC level, one hundred metres below the surface. Once the elevator had stopped, Eldridge removed a key card and entered it into a concealed slot, and the elevator started moving again, further into the bowels of the earth, and Lynn was instantly reminded of her similar subterranean trip back at Area 51.

Another minute later, surely another hundred metres below the tunnels of the LHC, the elevator eventually came to its final stop.

The door slid open to reveal an enormous, luxurious conference room. It was filled with people, well over a hundred, and as Lynn examined the faces, she was sure she recognized many of them.

There was Scott Keating, the famous Hollywood movie star; Roman Parlotti, the notorious Italian media magnate; Kristina Nyetts, the director of the world's largest pharmaceutical company; Tony Kern, the special aide to the US President himself; and many more besides. So here they were, the Bilderberg Hundred, in addition to the men of the Alpha Brigade. The most powerful people in the world, all joined together in the hope of becoming more powerful still, no matter what it took.

And then her eyes wandered to the corner, and she saw Samuel Atkinson, the Director General of NASA, sipping casually from a champagne flute and chatting animatedly to Stephen Jacobs, the architect of this entire insane project.

Seeing her old boss, someone she had trusted and who had betrayed both her and her entire team, chatting to Jacobs as if he had not a care in the world, destroyed what little composure she had left.

'Son of a bitch!' she screamed at the top of her voice,

and the room went deathly quiet as she launched herself across the room at the two men.

She was yanked backwards painfully by Eldridge who gave a sharp tug on the handcuff that still joined them. She tried to go again but Eldridge moved in and grabbed her in a bear hug, lifting her off her feet.

Atkinson looked at her, then down at the floor as recognition dawned. Jacobs felt no such guilt, though, and smiled across the room at her.

'Ah, Dr Edwards,' he said charmingly, 'how good of you to join us. And as luck would have it, you're just in time.'

8

Since the room was already quiet, Jacobs went on to address the assembled visitors.

'Ladies and gentlemen, our mission here is an extraordinary one,' he intoned, two lifetimes of public speaking ensuring he commanded everyone's attention, 'and we are extraordinary people. The road has been long and hard, consisting of twelve years of selection for our little group, and nearly seventy since contact was first made. Since then, we have used our influence around the globe to bring the whole world under our control. For we all know that it is not politicians who wield the power.

'How long can a president stay in power, after all? In the United States, a maximum of eight years. You can stay in control of a company for *eighty* years, and the money wielded by congressional advocates on behalf of those companies ensures more political clout than any ten presidents combined. Actors, singers, writers, they change and influence the culture around us to a much greater extent than politicians can, or ever could, and yet they are not accountable to anyone.

'What we have, gathered here today, are the one hundred most influential people in the world, people who have made the world what it is today. We have achieved this by all manner of manipulation, by corruption and, yes, sometimes through violence, but achieve it we have. As such, we are indispensable to the coming Anunnaki. We control the world as it is, so who else would they allow to survive? They *need* us, let us never forget that.

'And we will soon have our reward. We will rule the world openly, and live in unimaginable luxury and comfort for the next thousand years. The world as we know it will be at an end, of course, but is this so regrettable? Humanity needs purging, we have grown too weak and need a re-injection of suffering in order to propel us to new achievements. And so I welcome our visitors, the Anunnaki, who, let us not forget, are our own ancestors, the original human race.

'So without further ado,' Jacobs concluded, gesturing to a set of gilded double doors behind him, 'let us see for the first time what our efforts over the years have helped to fund and create.'

The crowd surged towards the oversized doors, which were ceremonially opened by two uniformed guards.

'Ladies and gentlemen, I give to you the world's first controllable cosmic wormhole.'

Lynn felt Eldridge pull her through the doors into the chamber beyond, but pulling her was no longer necessary; she *wanted* to see it.

Lynn gasped as she passed through the doors.

This was the kind of hi-tech facility that people would probably have expected to find upstairs. The room was large, dozens of immaculately presented white-suited technicians scurrying from one bank of monitors to another. The room was a hive of activity, and yet it was so perfectly clinical, Lynn couldn't help but be impressed.

And what was even more impressive – although more ominous, given its purpose – was the fact that CERN employed several thousand scientists and support staff, and yet almost nobody knew this place even existed.

The other half of the room was some sort of observation gallery which stretched for two hundred feet to either side of the doors. Ahead of them was a huge perspex window, with luxurious leather-upholstered benches lining the gallery from one end to the other.

Lynn tried to see through the long window, but whatever was on the other side was shrouded in darkness.

Despite the situation, and despite what the device was intended for, she was still curious about it. A real, operational wormhole? What on earth would such a thing look like? Even with her own high level of scientific knowledge, she could not imagine.

As the gathered members of the Bilderberg Group took their seats, Professor Messier strolled to the front, smiling broadly.

'My friends,' he said, clapping his hands together in delight, 'first of all let me say thank you. Thank you for helping to fund this project. Since CERN's first days in nineteen fifty-four, the creation of what you are about to see has consumed the modern equivalent of six *trillion* US dollars, most of which has come from Bilderberg Group members like yourselves. Stephen has spoken of the importance of the project already, and I do not wish to labour the point. I will just show you instead.'

Messier nodded his head to one side, and all of a sudden the chamber beyond the huge viewing window was cast into bright illumination.

He was pleased with the looks of amazement on the faces in front of him.

Lynn, too, was astonished by what she saw. She had imagined something like the Large Hadron Collider itself, a gigantic piece of machinery, something that shouted 'high-tech, super-advanced physics'. But here there was only a massive, colossal underground canyon; a truly gigantic pit dug deep into the earth, walls of bedrock stretching up and around as far as the eye could see.

'What is this?' she heard one member of the Hundred exclaim, confused.

Messier held up a hand. 'I know, I know,' he said. 'It's not what you were expecting, eh? Well, don't worry, there are plenty of exciting metallic bits and pieces dotted around that cavern, all designed to focus energy to the centre. But think about it logically. We are bringing back an entire people, approximately twelve *thousand* of them. In deep space, the wormhole device they have created is outside their own starship, and their entire starship will be going through it and returning here. And remember, if you will, that their spacecraft is Atlantis itself, regarded as an entire city-state when last it was on earth, which should give you some indication of its size.

'In fact, the craft is so big that it will literally fill that vast cavern completely. It will be an incredible sight to behold,' Messier said, his eyes shining. 'We will witness the return of Atlantis, the return of an ancient pre-historic civilization, the return of humanity's *gods*, and the return of our direct biological ancestors, all at once.' He looked down at his watch. 'And it will all happen within the next hour.'

9

ADAMS DROVE HIS car down the streets of Maisonnex Dessus until he eventually reached the main gate of CERN.

The guardhouse wasn't much, but the sentry got on the phone as soon as he saw the car, doubtless calling Eldridge or another of his Alpha Brigade goons. But Adams didn't care; getting picked up by the brigade was part of his plan.

As he halted at the gate, the sentry got out of the shack and approached him warily. 'If you wait there, sir,' he said nervously, 'someone will be right with you.'

Adams just nodded his head and waited.

Sure enough, within minutes his vehicle was surrounded by a dozen armed men, all screaming at him to get out of the car with his hands where they could see them.

Adams complied, got out of the car and rested both hands on the car roof, even though it caused tremendous pain in his arm.

Two of the men searched him thoroughly, then spun him back round, pushing him against the car. Backing away, they raised their rifles, ready to execute him on the spot.

And then Commander Eldridge was there, Sig Sauer pistol in one beefy hand.

'Mr Adams,' he said graciously. 'We meet again. Although

I'm afraid this time I'll have to make it quick, we've got to get back in time for the show.' He smiled and raised the handgun.

Adams stared down the end of the large barrel. 'Wait!' he shouted, and the urgency in his voice caused Eldridge to hesitate for a moment. 'I have information about the Anunnaki.'

Eldridge scoffed. 'What could you possibly know about them that we don't?'

'Something Travers told me back at Area 51, something that might be useful to Jacobs. All I want to know is if Lynn is alive. If she is, then release her and I'll tell Jacobs everything. If she's not, then you might as well shoot me now.'

Adams watched Eldridge's face, and knew the man was weighing his options. Suddenly, he flipped open a phone and dialled a number. He quickly relayed what Adams had told him, listened, and then turned back to Adams. 'He's not interested.'

'Tell him it's about where they come from. Originally, I mean. I don't think Jacobs knows, does he?'

Adams remembered Travers' history lesson, and clearly recalled him saying that advanced humans arose on the earth many thousands of years ago, but nobody – apparently not even the Anunnaki themselves – knew how this had happened.

Eldridge scowled but relayed the message to Jacobs. He then waited – for what seemed to Adams an inordinately long time – for a reply. Eventually, he gave a confirmatory 'Yes, sir,' and ended the call. He turned to his men. 'Did you search him?' Two of his men told him that they had performed a thorough search, and Eldridge turned back to Adams, looking him up and down with suspicion. 'Well,' he said, 'search him again. He's going inside.'

Jacobs had no idea what information Adams might have, if any. He realized that it was probably just a ruse to get inside, but there was an outside chance that Travers had told him something; the professor had spent more time in contact with the Anunnaki than even he himself had.

He also knew that, despite his confidence with his guests, their position wasn't as secure as he made out; the Anunnaki were far more powerful than they were, and there were no guarantees that things would be as promised. As such, any scrap of information that might be of use to him in his dealings with these ancient humans would be worth having. Knowledge of their origins, for instance, might be of great value.

And so he left the viewing gallery and went back inside the conference room, where he took a seat and waited for the arrival of Matthew Adams.

10

ADAMS WAS PUSHED into the room minutes later, forced to sit in a chair directly opposite Jacobs.

Jacobs smiled warmly at him. 'We really must stop meeting like this,' he said. 'But I'm afraid there's no time for pleasantries, so we'll get straight to it. What is the information you have?'

'Is Lynn still alive?'

'Yes,' Jacobs answered simply. 'We thought it best to keep her alive as collateral in case you decided to come here. Now what is the information? Where did the Anunnaki come from?'

'Not until I see her,' Adams responded.

Jacobs nodded to Eldridge, who grabbed Adams' head and slammed it into the glass conference table, before pushing him back in his seat, blood leaking from his nose.

Adams just held Jacobs' gaze, silent.

Jacobs watched Adams for several moments, searching for any sign of weakness, but found none.

Finally he tutted to himself and gestured to Eldridge. 'Go and get Dr Edwards, please,' he said in resignation.

Philippe Messier had retired to the control room to oversee the operation of the wormhole, but his voice could still be heard on the speakers dotted throughout the viewing gallery.

'The energy that will be generated in the chamber will be enormous,' he explained over the PA system. 'The viewing glass in front of you is ten inches thick. Without it, and without the protective bedrock surrounding the cavern, this whole level would be destroyed when the wormhole becomes active. But don't worry.' He chuckled. 'You'll be fine right where you are. It has all been modelled and tested a thousand times before.'

In her seat, Lynn laughed to herself. Tested before? Maybe by a computer, but for real? It was hard to make predictions about a technology that had never been used before.

'We are now about to start our lead-up procedure,' Messier explained. 'You will now see some of the power that we are able to generate by harnessing the antimatter produced by the LHC above us.'

There was a short lull, when everyone went quiet and the lights flickered off and on; and then a sound like an electrical generator, only much louder started up. It was a loud, deep, throbbing *hum* that passed through her body like a physical blow to her gut. And then the viewing gallery lights dimmed again, but stayed dim this time, revealing the chamber beyond in even greater clarity.

Seconds later, the lights went out in the chamber itself, and Lynn could hear the groans of disappointment around her.

'Just wait,' she heard Messier say. 'One moment.'

And then lights appeared far into the recesses of the chamber's cavernous roof. They were just sparks at first, but then they blossomed larger, each one bright enough to illuminate the entire chamber. Before long, the whole cavern was sporadically lit up by these energy sources, like trapped lightning, flickering with vast energy.

Lynn was transfixed, and then felt a hand on her shoulder.

'Come with me,' she heard Eldridge whisper in her ear.

Adams' heart fluttered in his chest when he saw Lynn enter the room. She *was* alive!

He saw the excitement in her face too, which turned to a wince when she was unceremoniously dumped into the chair next to him.

'Now, Mr Adams,' Jacobs said, 'tell me what you know.'

'Not until Lynn is safe,' Adams said. 'She leaves CERN *now*, escorted off the premises.'

Jacobs nodded to Eldridge, who grabbed Lynn back out of her chair, a blade appearing in his right hand, held close to her right eyeball.

'Or you could just tell me now, and Eldridge here won't cut out the bitch's eyes,' Jacobs shouted angrily, aware that the device was already starting to become operational in the next room.

Adams looked around the room. The door to the gallery ahead of him was guarded by two men of the Alpha Brigade, as was the door to the elevator behind them. Then there was Eldridge, holding Lynn in his strong grip just a few feet away, and Jacobs directly opposite him, across the table.

A light started to flash above the double doors to the gallery, and an electronic voice came over a PA system. 'Three minutes to wormhole opening,' it said without emotion. 'Everyone to their stations.'

Jacobs turned to Eldridge. 'Cut her!' he ordered, tired of playing games.

Adams saw the glint in Eldridge's eye and reacted an instant before he did.

The darts were in the roof of Adams' mouth, and had thus been missed during the two body searches. Adams had picked up the wood at a hardware store in Geneva, along with a knife, and had worked them himself before setting off for CERN. They were small yet heavy, and very sharp. Dropping one from the roof of his mouth to his tongue, he curled his tongue up and round it, and blew it out of his mouth as hard as he could.

He had learnt the technique as a boy, and had spent hundreds of hours training to hit a one-inch target from twenty feet, until it had become second nature. It was possible to hold up to half a dozen poisoned darts in the mouth without risk, although he had been unable to source any poison in the short time he had had to prepare. But he had coated the tips of the darts with chilli powder, and when the first dart entered Eldridge's right eye, it made the man recoil in agony, screaming at the top of his lungs.

He let Lynn go instantly, dropping his knife to the floor, his hands going to his ruined eye, legs going weak with the shock of the excruciating pain.

Adams turned to Jacobs, knowing he had only one shot at the man before he would have to deal with the guards. He fired out another dart, but Jacobs was quicker to react than Adams had expected, diving for cover behind the table, and the dart whistled away harmlessly over his head.

Adams swooped down to pick up Eldridge's knife and

hurled it across the room at the guards by the double doors. Then he swivelled to the two men by the elevator. Their weapons were already up and aimed, but Adams loosed two darts in quick succession, both of which struck the men in the face. They weren't disabling but were sufficient to take the guards' attention off shooting him for a few vital moments.

He heard a muffled cry behind him and turned to see the knife he had thrown sticking out of the chest of one of the other guards. The man fell to his knees, eyes wide with surprise, while his partner opened fire on full automatic.

As Adams and Lynn took cover behind the metal struts of the glass table, Jacobs scurried for the double doors.

Glass shattered and bullets ricocheted off the metal legs. Adams pulled the near-blind Eldridge towards him with his bad hand and punched him on the jaw with the other, knocking him out cold. Adams reached to get his gun, but Lynn was one step ahead of him, the pistol already in her hand, aimed at the men by the elevator.

The two guards were now recovering from the darts in their faces and were raising their guns again, but they were rocked backwards into the metal door of the elevator as Lynn loosed off four rounds, two bullets hitting each man directly in the chest. Plumes of blood exploded across the polished wooden floor.

Adams looked at Lynn with momentary surprise, then turned back to the double doors.

'Damn!' Lynn said as she saw Jacobs disappearing through the doorway into the safety of the gallery beyond. The remaining guard opened fire at them again, and then Lynn drew his fire by rolling one way, returning fire of her own, while Adams rolled to the opposite side, loosing off his two remaining darts.

The last guard was punched to the side as one of Lynn's bullets struck his hip, and then he keeled over backwards as both of Adams' darts entered his throat.

'Two minutes to wormhole opening,' the electronic voice announced.

'Come on,' Adams said, getting to his feet. 'Let's get in there, now!'

11

THE ATTENTION OF the Bilderbergers was concentrated entirely on the viewing windows, and they watched with fascination as the antimatter-powered machinery throughout the vast cavern started to activate fully. Beams of intense light were cast from seemingly every nook and cranny of the distant roof, and it looked like some sort of incredible thunder and lightning storm inside the chamber. The vast power being harnessed was clear for all to see, and nobody was in any doubt as to what they were witnessing.

But then the double doors to the conference room burst open and Jacobs came tumbling in, falling to his knees as he crashed through the doors.

'Block the doors!' he screamed, although his cries went unheard over the thunderous roar of the wormhole machinery.

And then the double doors burst open again, and Adams and Lynn came storming in, submachine guns aimed into the room, sweeping along the rows of leather benches. The Bilderbergers dropped to the floor as one, screams starting to ring out, and then the two intruders raised their guns and fired up at the ceiling, and everyone hugged the floor harder, heads down.

Four men – men of the Alpha Brigade, unarmed in this

supposedly sacrosanct area – started to run towards Adams and Lynn but were cut down instantly, their bullet-riddled bodies hitting the ground hard.

'Turn the machine off!' Lynn screamed at the top of her voice. When nobody moved, she let off another burst from her rifle, the rounds passing just inches over the Bilderbergers' heads. 'Turn it off!' she screamed again.

Still there was no response, and Adams leapt across the benches, having seen Jacobs cowering below. He reached down and hauled him up, placing the barrel of his gun underneath the man's chin.

'Turn it off,' he whispered with truly menacing intent. 'Turn it off or I'll blow your brains out right here, and you'll never get to see the Anunnaki anyway.'

'One minute to wormhole opening,' the electronic voice advised again.

'Do it,' Adams said again, even more forcefully.

'You can't stop it now,' Jacobs said through gritted teeth. 'It's over.'

Adams was about to pull the trigger when the double doors opened once more and Eldridge burst through with a submachine gun in each hand.

Half-blind, face bloodied, and incensed with rage, the big man opened fire immediately, raking the viewing gallery with high-powered .40 calibre rounds.

Adams and Lynn dived for cover and the bullets smashed into the viewing glass, ricocheting off the armoured material.

'No, you fool!' Jacobs called from the ground. 'You'll kill us all!'

But Eldridge wasn't listening and opened fire again, the

bullets tracing a line across the room, shattering and destroying an entire panel in the nearby control centre.

'No!' Messier cried out, running to the panel to try and save it. But it had been destroyed beyond repair. He turned to Eldridge with all hope drained from his features. 'What have you done?' he asked. The scientists around him were scurrying about the laboratory in blind panic.

Suddenly, the armoured viewing panel hissed from its frame, lifting and tilting, opening like some sort of huge vent, and Adams realized that Eldridge must have hit the operating mechanism.

The lightning in the chamber beyond grew even brighter, and the one hundred Bilderbergers screamed in earnest now, remembering the words of Messier. Without the protective glass, they would be doomed.

'Thirty seconds and counting,' the voice continued to report, without emotion.

12

'CLOSE THE WINDOW!' came the same cry from dozens of mouths. The whole viewing gallery erupted into chaos.

But the window couldn't be closed, it was too large, too heavy, and the control panel had been completely destroyed by Eldridge's bullets.

And then Eldridge's guns clicked empty. Adams surged forward and tackled him off his feet, smashing him back against the double doors and through into the conference room. Eldridge used his superior size to turn Adams and run him through the room until he slammed into the hard metal of the elevator doors.

Adams gagged from the pain shooting through his shoulder, and then Eldridge shoved a huge, meaty forearm across his throat, leaning in with all his weight, crushing his windpipe and choking him slowly unconscious.

Adams saw the maniacal look in Eldridge's eye and knew the man would not stop until he was dead. He started to feel his eyes going dark, the air being cut off to his brain, and his fingers reflexively reached out, searching along the wall beside him.

'Twenty seconds and counting,' the voice announced, and then Adams' fingers found the button he was looking for. He pressed it and the elevator doors opened. As the men fell through on to the metal floor, the pressure on Adams' throat eased.

Adams used the momentum of the fall to place his foot in Eldridge's stomach and flip him over his head. The man's huge body crashed into the elevator's far wall. Adams felt the elevator rock with the impact, and then the doors closed, and the elevator began to ascend. Eldridge's body had hit the controls.

Adams heard the electronic voice one last time.

'Ten seconds and counting.'

13

BACK IN THE viewing gallery, the excitement of the Anunnaki's arrival had given way to abject fear and horror at what was about to happen.

In the chamber beyond, the lightning flashes became more concentrated, more permanent, as the beams began to centralize in the middle of the cavern and a ball of light formed on the rocky floor before their very eyes.

As Lynn watched, she knew what she had to do. She didn't know why or how she knew, but know she did, with every fibre of her being.

While everyone else tried to flee from the giant window, she started to move towards it, until she was running towards the light-filled cavern.

Suddenly, a hand on her shoulder arrested her progress, and she turned to see Jacobs' horrified face staring at her. 'Stop!' he shouted. 'Don't go in there! You'll ruin everything!' He reached for her throat, his crazed hands trying to strangle her, face only inches from her own, and she could finally see the insanity in his eyes.

She didn't even have time to feel satisfaction as she pulled the trigger of her submachine gun and a burst of .40 calibre rounds ripped through Jacobs' guts. He dropped to the floor with a groan, fingers slipping from her throat and going to his belly, intestines spilling out over his hands as he looked at them in disbelief. His eyes went up to meet Lynn's, but she had already turned away, towards the open window.

And then she threw the rifle to one side and mounted the wide window frame, legs bent, breathing deeply.

'Five,' the voice announced, 'four . . . three . . . two . . . one. Wormhole opening.'

And then, saying a prayer for the first time in many years, she jumped.

14

THE ELEVATOR WAS rising rapidly, unbalancing both men, but Adams realized Eldridge was still stunned from his impact with the elevator wall.

He took advantage of this, pushing him backwards and then thrusting the web of skin between his forefinger and thumb into the man's unprotected throat.

Eldridge gurgled, his larynx shattered, but he surged forward, clasping Adams in a bear hug, squeezing the air out of him with his powerful arms. Blood started to seep through the makeshift bandage on his upper arm, and he felt his vision going hazy.

But he wasn't beaten yet, and he was damned if he was going to give in. His knee came up sharply into Eldridge's groin, his forehead slamming into the man's face, breaking the nose, but still Eldridge held on to him, crushing even tighter.

And then the elevator started to wobble, to shake, to seemingly rip itself apart at the seams, and Eldridge finally gave up his grip. Adams hit the floor, which was searingly hot, seemingly superheated from underneath.

He recoiled reflexively, and as he did so, the whole elevator floor gave way.

He instinctively gripped the elevator's handrails, watching

as the floor, and Commander Flynn Eldridge along with it, tumbled down through the elevator shaft, which was filled with a strange green flame.

Eldridge's face went white with shock as he plummeted down the burning shaft, fear finally entering his eyes just moments before his body hit the flames.

15

LYNN ENTERED THE chamber in a flying leap, just as the lightning strikes solidified into one solid mass, enveloping the whole chamber in a ball of pure energy.

As the only living thing in the chamber, the energy converged on her falling body, pulsating around her like another living entity. And she found herself suspended in the air, the ball of intense lightning energy coagulating around her with the feeling of warm liquid. The light became even more intense, and she lost all sense of who and where she was, all sense of existence.

And then everything went black, and she felt nothing at all.

16

THE STRANGE GREEN fire died away almost as soon as it had appeared, leaving Adams clinging to the handrail of the elevator, staring down at the charred, burned elevator shaft and the lumpen mass of Eldridge's ravaged body below.

He gingerly touched the wall exposed below the elevator, and was surprised to find it cool. He felt around, and found everything was cool, as if it had never been burnt.

He slowly lowered himself through the elevator floor, using handholds on the shaft to climb down it.

At the bottom, he stared at Eldridge's body. The flesh looked as if it had been steamed clean off the bones. He almost gagged at the smell.

With energy like that having burst through the entire level, what would have happened to Lynn? He almost didn't want to go back but knew he had to.

Would the Anunnaki be there?

Adams swallowed hard, and pressed on. There was only one way to find out.

He reached the conference room to find the wall separating it from the control room and viewing gallery now just a shattered shell, and no sign of any activity in the chamber beyond. There were bodies everywhere, and most of the flesh had been seared from the bones. He pressed on to the huge windows. He stood at the ledge and peered into the cavern beyond, and it was immediately obvious that there was no 'mother ship', no Atlantis spacecraft carrying the genocidal Anunnaki.

But where was Lynn? He turned away from the cavern and looked at the dozens of ruined bodies.

He gritted his teeth and began to search.

17

An hour later, he finished examining the bodies, convinced that Lynn was not among them. Where was she? Had she managed to escape somehow? He hoped so, with all his heart.

But what had happened here? The energy had obviously centred on the cavern – the walls bore the same burn markings as the rest of the ravaged underground level – and yet the wormhole had not opened.

Or had it?

He considered Lynn's disappearance again, and looked back at the cavern with new eyes.

Lynn was alive, he knew it. He didn't know where, but somewhere in the universe, she was alive.

And he would never rest until he found her.

PART FIVE

1

LYNN AWOKE, HER hands instantly going to her belly. She had no way of knowing but it felt OK, and that would have to do for now.

But where was she? It was dark, and the ground was rough beneath her.

Was she still in the cavern? She looked up, and was greeted by the sight of stars. No, she was outside somewhere.

So what had happened? Her presence in the chamber had obviously altered the mechanics of the wormhole in some way, causing it to act in an unplanned manner.

She suddenly had the unpleasant thought that she might be anywhere in the universe, anywhere at all.

Her head snapped up to look at the stars again, and she was instantly reassured. She was still on earth, no question about it. In the northern hemisphere in fact, and she could make out the familiar sights of the Big Dipper, Orion's Belt, and Venus, all in their familiar places in the sky. And behind her, when she turned, she saw the moon in all its glory, casting its light down upon her. Besides which, she realized that if she was indeed on another planet, it would be highly unlikely that she would be able to breathe the atmosphere.

She still didn't know where she was, though, and so she started to walk, examining the landscape around her.

But soon she was tired, so very, very tired, and she felt the need to lie down. She found what she considered a safe place, in the lee of a large rock, put her jacket down as a makeshift pillow, and within seconds was asleep.

She awoke the next morning with the rays of the sun upon her.

She shook the cobwebs from her head, and then the sound hit her. It was strange, like nothing she had ever heard before; a curious rasping sound, like a lizard growling.

She looked around, and her eyes went wide as she saw the animals over the crest of the small hill in front of her. They were enormous furred creatures, and as she watched them stalk across the barren landscape, she was sure she had never seen anything like it. Or had she?

Lynn looked up at the sun, as if to reassure herself that she was still on earth.

She got to her feet and started to walk again. She walked and walked, and it seemed she was in a desert wilderness. She walked for hours, until she was exhausted, and still she had found no sign of life except for those first strange creatures. There was also no sign of human habitation.

She sat down and examined the desert landscape. The shrubs she could see looked like the familiar varieties but what did she know about desert shrubs? Not a lot. But those creatures bothered her, reminding her of something she had seen once before, in a textbook at school, or perhaps university. But a textbook on what?

When the answer finally hit her, it was with the force of a sledgehammer.

2

SHE CONTINUED TO move across the landscape over the next few days and eventually came to a river, flowing powerfully through the otherwise arid terrain. It was a true life-saver, and she decided to stay close to it, scavenging what she could from the desert around her to eat, and drinking the wonderful, clean water from the river.

And then one day she saw them, at first in the distance – a group of half a dozen, making their way to the water. She hid behind a rock pile as she watched them, creatures of a type she recognized with horrifying certainty.

They walked erect on two legs, were about five and a half feet tall, with hair covering much of their muscular bodies. Their features were not dissimilar to her own and the people she knew but they were not *Homo sapiens*.

She watched them as they drank water and bathed for a leisurely hour, communicating in a mixture of grunts and whistles. And then, finally, they left the river and lumbered off back to wherever they had come from.

The recognition she experienced upon seeing them made her start to understand what had happened. To test her hypothesis, she spent the next few nights staring up at the stars, measuring the movements as best she could.

After several nights, she was sure; horrified, but sure.

* * *

The creatures she had seen by the river were featured heavily in many books she had read at Harvard on human evolution, and several that she had studied during her recent research.

They were members of the extinct hominid subspecies *Homo neanderthalensis*.

This realization confirmed her recognition of the massive furred creatures she had seen that first day as ground sloths, animals that were also long since extinct.

Her astronomy was better than her paleontology, and yet it had only served to confirm her fears.

The night sky was very similar through time, but over very large timeframes, there were subtle differences that could be observed, even with the naked eye. She knew that Neanderthal man had died out tens of thousands of years ago but this did not help to prepare her for the conclusions she drew from her astral observations, for the position of the stars in the sky were as they would have been about two *hundred* thousand years ago.

She had indeed been caught in the wormhole, but instead of bending the fabric of the cosmos in order to send the Anunnaki through space, it had instead sent her through time.

And as she considered what had happened, she couldn't help but remember the words of Professor Travers.

'Yes,' he had said when asked about the Anunnaki, 'and don't ask me how they evolved, as they don't even know themselves. One moment the earth had other *Homo* species, including *ergastor, heidelbergensis, rudolfensis, habilis, neanderthalensis*, among others, and the next we had *Homo sapiens sapiens*, fully formed not only physically but also mentally.'

And as she sat by the banks of the river, and once more touched Matthew Adams' baby that grew inside her, Evelyn Edwards finally understood everything.